TERRIBLE SWIFT SWORD: LONG ROAD TO THE SULTANA

a novel

Dr. Nancy Hendricks

ISBN: 1507764685
ISBN 13: 9781507764688
Library of Congress Control Number: 2015901731
CreateSpace Independent Publishing Platform
North Charleston, South Carolina

AUTHOR'S NOTE: FOREWORD

This is a work of fiction. Any similarity to persons living or dead is purely coincidental.

Having said that, the characters in this book represent real people, the kind of average people whose stories are rarely told. They have been fleshed out from bits and pieces of research into what little we do know of Civil War-era lives.

Like most survivors of war, they might simply say they did what they had to do. For those survivors – men, women and children – the war did not end when a piece of paper was signed. Most carried the mental and physical scars with them to the end of their days.

After the Civil War, it was common to see an entire generation horribly maimed, arms and legs gone, faces scarred. Malnutrition and exposure led to diseases that lasted a lifetime. It is hard for many in today's world to fathom the sacrifice of both soldiers and civilians.

It is also difficult to fathom some of the events that led average people on their long road to the *Sultana.* Sometimes, the coincidences seem staggering. But the events depicted were all too real:

the "Greek Fire" plot to burn New York City, the one and only performance by the three Booth brothers, General Order 11, flooded prison camp, train wreck on the way to the boat, and of course the "coal bombs" that were small enough to fit in one hand but caused so much pain and destruction. Today, we might call them "improvised explosive devices."

The long road to the *Sultana* was also traveled by women. About forty were aboard the doomed vessel. Almost all perished. And yes, a Civil War soldier was indeed decorated for bravery in battle – and gave birth to a baby one month later.

It is the author's hope that readers may find something uplifting in the characters depicted here. The story of the *Sultana* is a tragic one, but the people in this book might provide inspiration to others who suffer.

For those who seek more information about the events depicted here, there are excellent nonfiction sources listed in the Afterword. The facts are all there.

A murderous despot once said, "*The death of one man is a tragedy; the death of millions is a statistic.*"

This book is an attempt to put human faces on those statistics. It is dedicated to all people who have suffered through wartime, and who carried it with them to the end of their days.

PROLOGUE

APRIL, 1912

The world is crashing into the sun! Blinding fire – scalding heat – smoke – terror – screams – the screams – dear God, the screams!

Bodies hurtling into black water – some are on fire! They're *on fire*! All around, the shriek of crashing metal and the groan of collapsing timbers. And always the screams! *Help, please help! Please, HELP!*

Another scream, different somehow. Then he knew. The last scream was his own. And now suddenly, silence. As if from a great distance, a clock in the darkness chimed twice. Wiping sweat from his forehead with a shaking hand, he tries to slow his frantic breathing. The room is cool. The air is fresh. It's all right, he can breathe. It's his own little room, in his own little house.

Still shaking, he feels a soft hand, a woman's soft hand on his face. Now he spoke in gentle words, comforting words, telling her it was only a dream.

Only a dream. He almost laughs.

"No," he says after a moment. "I was there again. Guess I'll keep going back there until it's done. Reckon it's time."

Now more resolutely, "It's time."

CHAPTER 1
NOVEMBER, 1864

Damn – they're gaining! His mind was racing along with the hoof beats that were closing in. *Steady now, stay calm. They'll never catch up, not with both of them riding one horse and me going full out on the other.*

At least, that's what he kept telling himself. He wished he was a bird, just fly away from the thunder of hooves, the cursing, the angry shouts, the gunshots. But of course a bird had no use for what was in the saddlebag with CITIZENS BANK on it.

He should have known. It was too easy, and nothing had ever come easy for him. Well, it was their own damn fault. They should never have turned their backs on the horses when they stopped to eat. They should have kept hold of the bank's saddlebag for dear life. But they were lazy, and now the horse and saddlebag were his!

He smiled at his own notion of a bird flying away with the money bag full of gold – take a mighty big bird to lift it. *Stop! Think about right now, right this minute! Ain't no game!* If they caught him, they'd shoot him dead without a moment's thought. And here in some miserable stretch of backwoods Ohio, no one would find his body but the crows – unknown, unmourned, unwanted. Just like it'd always been in life.

Concentrate, dammit! He was a good rider most of the time – when he could steal a horse, that is. But now he was ducking bullets and tree limbs, either one of which would bring a sudden end to this enterprise. He liked that word, "enterprise." Made him sound like a businessman. And this was his business, a damn serious one. It was survival.

He knew those bank riders would never give up, never just let him take the money and be gone. That'd be the best thing for them to do, he thought – just let him go. No one had got hurt, he figured, just their pride maybe, and anyway the bank had more money where this'd come from.

But he knew they'd keep coming. Prob'ly their jobs depended on it. Prob'ly they're embarrassed to have been surprised. Prob'ly madder than all hellfire to double up on one horse like no man should have to do.

In retrospect, he knew he should have grabbed the other horse by the reins and pulled it along with him. At least, he did have the sense to unhitch it and give the animal a swat on the rump, thinking it'd run. But the beast just stood there, blinking. So with the precious bank bag on the first horse, he simply took off as fast as he could, with the plan already going astray.

And the funny part was he had only intended to come up on them, friendly-like, to ask for a bite of their food. He was that hungry, starved enough to beg from strangers. It was only when he saw the bank bag still on one of the two horses that … well, before he really thought about it, there he was, in the saddle and off at a gallop. It was what you might call a Golden Opportunity. Sure, he'd stolen before, maybe a cash drawer or two, but he just knew this would be the one that would set him up fine for a few years. Maybe start a business of his own … *what kind of business? … what do I like doin'? … where do you go to change gold into cash? … is it marked by the bank …?*

And then he was almost down, his own fault, smacked by a tree limb when his brain was off at some bank teller's window cashing in the gold. *Pay attention, dammit!*

Stream-bed up ahead – *isn't that supposed to be good for escaping a posse and the like?* He pulled the horse up short to take a sharp turn into the water, and that was his fatal mistake. The horse lost its footing and went down in the mud, dumping him face-first into the muck before it scrambling to its feet, galloping away from the ever-closer gunfire. The money! It was still in the saddlebag on the horse! He ran like his life depended on it, which it did. He had to catch the horse with the money bag, which he didn't. The horse was gone, headed downstream, and his only hope to survive what was about to happen lay in the thick woods. Up the bank and into the bramble. *Run like hell*!

His pursuers made it across the stream easily and started after him in the tangle. His lungs were bursting, but then there was hope – he heard them pull their horse up short.

The bank riders were yelling at each other. "Get the money! Go after the money!"

"He's gettin' away!"

"Get the horse – now! We'll catch him later, he can't get far. Get the money!"

"He's runnin' into the woods! He'll get away!"

"Go after the horse! That's where the money bag is! Soon's we get my horse and the money, we'll catch up with that sumbitch! He won't get far on foot! Go after the horse – now!"

The debate apparently over, he heard the splash of their horse going downstream. No doubt they'd catch up to the other horse and the bank bag. Part of his heart just broke to lose it that way, it had been so close. But he could mourn for it later. More pressing problems now. Keep from being shot down like a dog.

Wet, cold, boots full of water, heart pounding, gasping for breath, still weak from hunger, he scrambled through the thick woods. He knew they'd be back for their vengeance. He'd shamed them, and he'd pay.

Legs torn by brambles right through his pants, face slashed by twigs, fallen tree limbs trying their best to trip him up. It was all a big blur now, survival the only goal. Crashing into branches, zigzagging his course, gasping for breath, looking behind him, staggering, falling, getting up again, staggering, down again – *maybe curl up under a dead tree trunk and hope they'd miss seeing him?*

That voice in his brain kept saying to just stop a minute and rest, *just for one minute, just one little minute* ... But he knew despite the pain in his chest that it would mean an eternal rest. *Keep going!*

Now he was losing his mind. He thought he heard music. *Out here?* Band music, marching music. *Did they call out the Army on me?* Well, the Army had to follow the law, didn't they? He'd surrender to the Army, not those other two trigger-happy thugs who hated him, who he'd robbed, who he'd shamed, whose horse he stole.

He could actually see it now – a clearing, the town square of a small village, the kind of friendly little spot that never had a place for him. Military drums, simple army drills in front of what must be the courthouse, a few dozen men—boys really—awkwardly learning to march. *Sure, there was a war on, but who in his right mind would go marching into Confederate rifles?* Or Union guns, for that matter? He'd have stopped to watch for fun, thinking what idiots they were, but he had more pressing matters.

Pay attention. No time for deep thoughts. You're not clear yet. Find a spot, go to ground.

Stumbling cautiously around the edge of the town, he saw smoke – and then a smokehouse. Oh, yes, that was the goal! It was attached to some kind of tavern with a window near the back door. Men coming and going, some in blue uniforms, some in rough town clothes. Lots of loud male voices, hearty with bravado, shouting, laughter.

Pay attention! Someone at the window. Did they see him? Naw, it was a woman more interested in the two meat pies she was setting on the sill to cool. If he'd been a praying man, this would be the answer to his prayers. He moved toward the window with what he hoped was the stealth of a cat. Arm's length now, almost there. After grabbing his prize, he'd find a place to hide and enjoy the bounty. *Almost there …*

Then the back door flew open and he was down! A man was on top of him, flailing helplessly – well dressed, slick-looking. Maybe about twenty-five or so, just like him, but looked a whole lot younger, like the man had lived a soft life.

Just be friendly and turn on the charm. He knew that's what he needed to do now with this slick-looking fellow on top of him and the Army all around.

"Sorry, mister!"

The other man was not friendly at all. "Why don't you watch where you're going!"

"I'm sorry, mister, honest I am! I didn't see you comin' through that door. No offense meant – right, mister?"

The slick-looking man was on his feet now, stood a minute, smiled a little, then even offered a hand to help him up.

"It's all right, friend. No offense taken. Guess it was partly my fault too. Didn't look where I was going when I came out the door. You going inside? Here to enlist? The Union needs good men! They're going in the front door, that's where you go to sign up."

"Enlist, I don't know, sir. I guess. Maybe. Guess I'm a little turned around. Listen, I'm sorry about tripping you up."

"No, it's all right." The Slick Man was becoming all neighborly now, just when a person was hoping to ease away. The meat pie would have to wait.

"Still making up your mind, that it? You want to do what's right, serve your country, fight them Rebels," Slick was saying. "You know, I may be able to help."

There was the sound of good-natured laughter from inside the tavern, and God, those meat pies smelled so good. Slick Man eyed him now, took his measure, but no real sign he'd call the sheriff. Not yet, anyway. Was there an opportunity here? *Rich-looking man, maybe with a gold watch? Roll of bills? Sure, this slick man looked like he would have both.*

No! He stopped that train of thought dead in its tracks. *Think of something else.* Like just being a nice calm citizen in town for whatever's goin' on. Just nod to whatever his slick new friend was saying. Keep an ear out for something that required a response. Like right now.

"I'm sorry, didn't quite catch that, sir."

"None of that 'sir' business, not now," said Slick. "We're buddies! We've rolled around on the ground together, guess we know each other pretty well. I just wondered if you'd like to join me inside for a drink. We can talk for a while, friendly-like. Train won't leave for a while and the tavern's nice, they know me there. Food's good. We can talk in private."

He almost laughed. "I imagine privacy would suit," he said to Slick's offer. "You know, those meat pies sure smell good. Your invitation sounds mighty kind indeed, but I have no money, sir."

"I do. Plenty of it. And maybe even a business proposal for a fine fellow like you."

Well, that settled it. He'd made it to Heaven. He'd been shot out of the saddle at the stream-bed and he was dead. But no, couldn't be Heaven, though. Not for the likes of him. And yet, he was too tired and hungry and miserable to argue. If the Devil wears slick duds like his new friend here, and comes offering attractive invitations involving food and drink, then maybe his stay Down Below won't be too bad.

They walked through the back door into the tavern where his slick, well-dressed friend motioned him to a corner table in the back. Fine with him, he thought, grabbing the seat facing the front door.

A barmaid, small-town pretty, wandered over and said nothing. She just eyed Slick, who dropped some coins on the table.

"Anything you want, my friend, just ask Maynette here."

"Yes, ma'am," he said, keeping his head down as best he could so maybe she wouldn't recall the face. His pursuers were bound to find this town, start askin' questions. Maybe later, he should shave off the beard, cut his shaggy hair ... but all that would have to wait.

His slick new friend was quick to make the decisions. "Tell you what, Maynette, bring us a couple of beers and one of those meat pies."

She kept on giving Slick the eye, smiling in an insolent way. "Didn't hear the part about 'Please.'"

Slick curled his hand around her rump, like it was a spot he was familiar with. "I'll be paying you, Maynette. That should do."

She giggled and was gone. Slick leaned over, just two men-of-the-world here, whispering, "Won't be the first time."

"Yes, sir." What else could he say?

"Well, as I said, let's drop that 'sir' business."

Just then the front door burst open, and he almost dove under the table. But it was just some of the locals, back-slapping and shouting to their buddies. The drumbeat from outside drifted in.

Time to get down to business with Slick.

"Sounds like big doin's here today. May I ask who are you, mister?" All charm when he had to be. If this was the law, he had to know it now.

"Well, if you're from around these parts, you know who I am," said Slick, kind of smug. "If you do business here."

"No sir, ain't from around here."

"Oh? Where you from?"

"Ain't what some would call important." Remember the charm. And the meat pie. Smile. "With respect, sir."

Hearty laugh from ol' Slick. "No, as a matter of fact, it sure is not important. Might work even better if you don't have kinfolk hereabouts."

"None anywhere. You said something about a business proposal?"

"What did you say your name was?"

Stay sweet, but this has got to stop. "I thought we already had that part of the conversation, about some things not being important." *Smile, all good-natured like.*

"Well, what do you think of the name 'Nicholas Morgan'? That's mine."

Thank the Lord, here comes the girl with the food and drinks. Two large beers and a meat pie. *Please don't let me be dreaming.* He practically dived into the meat pie and washed it down with just about the whole glass of beer before he remembered Slick had said something. A name. Nicholas something. *Be sociable and don't forget the host hasn't paid up yet.* Still, Slick was smiling, so maybe he didn't take offense at the momentary inattention.

"Sorry sir, you were saying?"

"My name. I am Nicholas Morgan, Nicholas Morgan the Third – two illustrious forebears who hoped I'd follow in their footsteps."

"Yesshur." Hard to talk with his mouth full. He supposed he couldn't exactly tell Slick to hush whilst he could eat.

But Slick kept on. "Shall we get right to business? After all, that train will be here soon enough and it won't wait."

What train? What business? And what might be in it for me?

"Sir? I mean, Mr. Morgan?"

"I assume since you were entering the tavern today, that you were planning to enlist anyway."

Noncommittal grunt with a mouth full might do the trick.

"Mmm ...?"

"That's why the town is full of people. Mustering the regiment. You were planning to enlist, weren't you?"

Now Slick was looking suspicious. Meat pie almost gone. *Play along.*

"Yes sir, of course."

"Well, I believe I can make it worth your while. After all, the Enrollment Act makes it perfectly legal. And I can pay you now, no need to wait on your bonus. You can sign up as my substitute. There is just one thing. One small thing"

So here it comes. He squinted warily toward the door, ready to bolt.

"You the law, mister?"

"No, no – hardly. I am not with the law or the government. Nothing like that. Hardly, as I said." *Did Slick just wink?* "I am simply looking to make a private transaction. All perfectly legal."

"Well, like you said, sir, paying a substitute to fight for you ain't against the law. Don't want to go play soldier, huh?" *Careful, smile now – that was a dumb remark – might cut too close to the bone.* Just in case things were coming to a close here, he added, "You want the rest of that meat pie, mister?"

Slick pushed it toward him. Along with the other beer, untouched. He drank greedily on his second beer, feeling fine and listening with as much feigned interest as he could muster.

Ol' Slick kept going. "Now, along with this excellent meal, I can offer you, oh ... say ... forty dollars in gold for your service. That's gold, not paper, and I can give you half right now."

Half of forty dollars gold sounds good, but it pays to negotiate.

"Half?" he said between bites.

"Be realistic, my friend. How would a person know ... not to imply ... not you necessarily, but there's some who might take the money and desert first chance they got. No offense meant, of course."

This might be a good time to start making an exit. Those two bank riders aren't going to miss spotting this town forever. He started pushing away from the table.

"No sir, no offense taken. Look, maybe I'd best be movin' on. But all the same, thanks for the meal. Been a pure pleasure."

Slick put a hand out in a friendly way, not quite touching, not quite blocking the way, well, not quite ...

"Listen, my friend, no need to leave just yet. Maynette, a couple more beers, *please!*" That last Slick added for her benefit, kind of a private joke between the men, old buddies now.

"Now, friend, I never meant to imply that you would desert, not you personally. I can tell you are a man of honor. I can sense these things. I pride myself on being a good judge of character."

The girl called Maynette brought two more beers, smiling at Slick in what she probably thought was a flirtatious way. *Good, less time for her to take a look at me.* Those bank riders were coming, he just knew it, he could feel them getting closer, closer …

On this third beer now, his head was getting cloudy but he had to keep his mind on whatever business was going on here. Getting half the gold right now, that was it. *Well, I'm not a pushover.*

"What if I'm not alive to collect the other half of the gold?"

Slick looked all studious. "I can see you are a man of the world, my friend, and you do drive a hard bargain." Now, as if his back was to the wall, ol' Slick sighed. "All right, the whole forty dollars gold, right now, with your solemn word that the transaction, per our agreement, will remain private. Very, very private!"

It was really getting hard to follow all this. "So if'n I understand, you'll give me …" *Concentrate*! "You'll give me forty dollars gold, right now, in my hand, to enlist in the Army as a substitute for you?"

"More or less, that is correct. Let's say Yes. And to save time, you'll simply need to present my identity disc when you board the troop train. They'll muster you in once you're on board. Let me show you. See, it's already made out in the name Nicholas Morgan."

There it was, in his hand, all official-looking. He didn't know how it went in the Army, but he had an idea old Slick, this Nicholas Morgan, was about to skip. *Careful now.*

"So I'd pretty much just *be* you? With respect, sir, that don't sound like the way they mostly do it."

"Please, my friend, have another beer, and I'll explain," Slick said, sliding over number four. Slick's voice was so smooth, it was a pleasure just to eat and drink and listen.

"You see, it's nothing to you, my friend, and everything to me. I'm paying you to join the Army as Nicholas Morgan. To serve as Nicholas

Morgan. I'm paying you so my father can proudly say his son is a soldier of our glorious Union."

Best be cautious. Those bank riders won't give up. "Where will this servin' take place, sir? Around here?"

Slick had a laugh over that. "Hardly! Nicholas Morgan – *you* – will get on the train and go wherever it goes, wherever they need good men. It's 1864, this war can't last much longer. When it's over, you've got the gold – and your Army pay, that's thirteen dollars a month – you can go wherever you please. No need at all to ever come back here. Ever! Understand?"

"Not coming back to these parts would suit me fine, sir."

"Should be lots of opportunity for a man like you after the war, friend. And as I said, it shouldn't last much longer."

"Where will you be, Mr., um, Morgan? You'll stay here?"

"Why don't we begin calling *you* Mr. Morgan as of now, my friend. No, I rather like the idea of being one of those nameless adventurers who go West. Perhaps make my own fortune there. Or perhaps come back here after the war like the Prodigal Son to claim my inheritance, a hero who bravely served his country. My father will be so proud."

"What if I get my ass shot off?" *Oh, now, that was the beer talking.* Need to handle this just right. "Sorry."

Slick had an answer, though. "Well, of course, neither of us wants that. But should the name Nicholas Morgan III appear on the casualty list, I simply reappear after the war, claiming it was a terrible mistake. After all, things do get muddled during wartime. I imagine even my father would value me at that point."

Somewhere in the distance was the sound of a train whistle. Things were probably coming to a close here. Time to get what he could from Nicholas Morgan, the real one, and be on his way.

"Any chance of getting a meat pie to take with me, sir? Maybe another beer? By the way, sir, with respect, I ain't seen that gold yet."

Sure enough, Slick took a small pouch from his pocket and placed it in center of table. "It's yours. Assuming you've agreed to our arrangement. And you can take a sandwich to eat on the train. We'll ask Maynette on our way out. She can put it on my tab."

Slick slid the pouch closer. "Under the table, please," said Slick.

Well, all right. That's reasonable under the circumstances. Especially since any minute now those bank riders could come busting through the door. No need to be flashing money around. Counting the gold pieces as best he could under the table, it seemed to be in order.

"Yes, sir. Forty dollars gold, far as I can tell."

"So, as you see, I have kept up my end of the bargain." Slick was standing up now. "As I now have faith you will keep yours."

The train whistle was getting closer now. Good time to make his exit. He could get nice and lost on the way to the train station, which he had no intention of ever seeing. Pocketing the gold, smiling, he stood and said, "Looks like I've got me a train to catch."

Slick was getting up too. "They'll muster you in on the train, give you a uniform and all. They want as many men as they can get. They'll be very grateful for your service to the country in this time of need. Whoever thought this damnable war would drag on for so long?"

Maybe if I just move toward the back door, Slick won't follow. He wiped his mouth on the cloth napkin, then decided to hang onto it. You just never knew when something might come in handy. "Well, maybe the war'll be over with soon. Sir, about that sandwich…?"

Slick seemed just as happy as he was to head out through the back door. After all, he was previously acquainted with it from when he was skipping out earlier. That part was for sure. The slick man was used to giving orders, too.

"Maynette, a sandwich for this gentleman. And be quick about it. He's got a train to catch."

The girl called Maynette did her part, and ol' Slick settled up. That's when she got real cozy, it looked like not for the first time. "Will I see you tonight, Nick?"

Slick looked her in the eye with a touch of mockery. "We'll see, Maynette. We'll see."

They left the tavern through the back door, and Slick guided him toward the center of town. *Have to make this quick, there'd be too many people around if we get to the station. Have to find a back way out of town.* "Sir, would you mind if I answered Nature's call? All those beers ..."

Surely Slick wouldn't follow him. He'd head for the woods. Somehow he could make a break.

"Oh, don't worry, my friend. They have facilities on the train. And we don't want you to be late. Do we?"

He heard the train's approach as the station came into sight. All right, he'd have to try this some other way. Slick didn't bother shaking his hand, just pushed him toward the platform and onto the train.

The rail car was packed, men in uniforms and other men in their own clothes, waiting to get done up in Union blue. He was determined not to be one of them. Laughing, shouting, slapping each other on the back, it was confusion everywhere, which could only help his plan. Some hung out the open windows of the train, sharing last good-byes with loved ones. Some big man in uniform was shouting orders for everyone to shut up and sit down.

No matter, there were still plenty of men jostling around in the train car. All that movement really did not help his head which he would admit was muddled after four beers. Still, he'd keep his wits about him, he was sure he could. Outsmarting a city boy like ol' Slick couldn't be all that hard. He turned unsteadily toward the exit at the back to the train car, looking for all the world like he'd forgot something important. As he got there, he took a quick look out the train window and there was ol' Slick, right outside, smiling. Their eyes met, and Slick nodded, still friendly-like, casually raising his arm as if to wave goodbye, but showing the gun beneath his jacket. If he ran now,

Slick could still gun him down and claim robbery. The gold in the pouch would be evidence.

This might prove worrisome. He looked out the other side of the train, but there was no platform, just a very steep drop-off where a man could get mighty hurt trying to jump off. Besides, that would be the way the bank riders would come. No, he'd head for the exit in the front of the car, even though that man in uniform blocked the way. But he had to get out and make a run for it.

Looking out the train window, he saw Slick following his every step, dodging the loved ones on the platform, hand on gun now, with a deadly look that counseled against a double-cross. Somewhere in his beer-sodden brain, he got the feeling the Old Nicholas Morgan was inside his head, reading the mind of the New Nicholas Morgan, the Morgan that was on the train, the Morgan that had bought the name for forty dollars in gold, the Morgan that was trying to keep the gold and get out of the deal.

The train lurched and almost threw him to his knees. It was moving. Where in hell would he end up?

CHAPTER 2
NOVEMBER, 1864

As the train carrying the New Nicholas Morgan headed their way from about forty miles up the track, two men stood outside a nondescript storefront. The town looked like dozens of others the railroad passed through in Ohio, except that this town boasted its own newspaper, a point of civic pride that was becoming more tenuous by the minute.

The little building sported a sign proclaiming proudly: "Newspaper Office, *The Phoenix*. John Deacon, Editor and Publisher." Below that, a smaller one, handwritten, much more humble: "FOR SALE."

John Deacon was indeed proud to be a newspaper publisher, though he bore no resemblance to his hero, Horace Greeley of the *New York Tribune*. Only years later would Deacon discover that he bore a much stronger similarity to a Hungarian immigrant arriving in America around the same time as he stood talking. The impoverished Pulitzer József was paid two hundred dollars to enlist in the First New York Lincoln Cavalry. John Deacon would have jumped at that kind of money.

An outsider observing the scene would have assumed the well-dressed older man counting out money was the newspaper publisher and the young man in the shabby suit was an office boy waiting hat-in-hand for his meager salary. But it was the younger man who spoke first.

"Mr. Lowery, are you sure you can't give me just a little bit more? The presses alone are worth ..."

The older man ignored him as he continued counting. "Eighty … ninety … hunnerd … hunnerd twenty … and … five. That'll do it."

Deacon, the younger man, took a long time looking at the bills. Then he closed his eyes as if in pain. "Mr. Lowery, I just don't know if I can – I just don't know …"

The older man held on to the money. "John, you see anyone else willin' to pony up good Union greenbacks for a rickety building – a shack, really – and some broke-down presses that nobody got any use for? This is Ohio, boy, not New York City. Thought we had us a deal. Well, if you're not interested…"

Lowery started to put the money back in his pocket, which he knew would put an end to Deacon's bellyaching. Lowery hated doing business with amateurs. Except for the financial rewards, that is.

"No, sir! I didn't mean anything by it, Mr. Lowery. Well, it's just that those presses alone – I toted those presses all the way from back East myself ..."

"Yes, John, we've all heard the story of your struggles. Very commendable."

"... by oxcart and flat boat and wagon...

"And we all appreciate you starting a newspaper here where t'weren't one before."

"... and every last cent I had in the world went into them and fixing up that building, you're right, maybe it was a really more of shack when I found it, but look at it now. Why, now it's worth ..."

"And now, John, it's time to take your reward for all your hard work."

"But Mr. Lowery, a hundred and twenty five! It's all worth at least ten times that ... the presses alone are worth more ..."

Lowery was starting to tire of this. A deal was a deal. "Don't let's go into that again, John. You agreed. Best offer you had, ain't it?"

Deacon, in a soft, sorrowful voice, looked down and had to agree. "Yes."

"Sorry, son, didn't quite hear that." Friendly as pie, but the older man knew how to make his point.

"Yes, Mr. Lowery. You're right."

Lowery wasn't the town's richest businessman for nothing. He knew when he'd won and Lord, he enjoyed it. Time to show this little upstart kid with his edu-*cation* what life in the real world was all about. A good lesson for him, really, if he expected to survive. And Lowery was happy to be the teacher.

"*Only* offer you had, ain't it, John?"

"Yes," Deacon mumbled.

Now, Lowery thought, *this lack of respect has got to stop.* "Pardon? Didn't quite catch that, John. Older you get, the hearing starts to go."

"Yes ... sir. Only offer."

Deacon's long face was a clear indication he'd learned the lesson that Lowery wanted to teach. All right, the older man thought, we're burning daylight. Time to close this deal and be off. Supper always tasted so much better in the crisp cool air this time of year. When he left home this morning, he'd spied a pot roast waiting to be cooked. Should be just about ready by now. Sure, Mrs. Lowery had to nag him at first that they absolutely had to find some townswoman to handle the chores, but now he had to admit that hiring the cook was a good investment.

"Alrighty, son," Lowery said, "we got us a deal. Truth is, you won't find much call for buying a newspaper office at any price these days, not in these parts. Ain't that right? Happy to help you out from under it, son, happy to help. Just sign the bill of sale, right here."

As he slowly signed, Deacon couldn't help himself. He blurted out, "You'd think, with a war on, folks would want to know what's going on. Especially with so many Ohio boys serving. It'd be a help to them to know what's going on with the war, and in Washington and ..."

Not this again, thought Lowery. "John, maybe you're meant to serve your fellow citizens by doin' just what you're doin.' Joinin' up, gettin' in the action! Land, that's where I'd be if it weren't for my gout and rheumatis'! I'd be out there in the thick of it!"

"Mr. Lowery, if you could just keep the newspaper open, I could send dispatches ..."

Not again! "We've done gone all through that, John. I just need the building, not to work myself to death runnin' some damn newspaper that don't make money in a town where most people can't even read!"

"But in time, they'll learn! People need to know what's going on in the world, in this country, all around them, what this war is all about!"

"John, son, I am trying to be patient. I am doing you a favor. How old are you anyway? Twenty-five? Twenty-six? You've still got a lot to learn. More important, you still have the time to make a success of yourself. You're young yet. When this war is over …"

"But Mr. Lowery …!"

Pocketing the bill of sale, Lowery was frustrated, eager to be off. He handed the money to Deacon, and tried to speak kindly, he really did.

"John, let it go! Now, you best put that cash somewheres safe. You don't want to take it with you into the Army, no tellin' what kind of thievery goes on."

A new thought! Reaching casually to get the money back, Lowery said, "Perhaps I should hold it for you? Til after the war. No extra charge."

Replying a little too quickly, or so Lowery thought, Deacon said, "No! Thanks anyway Mr. Lowery. I'm taking it over to Odom's store. Already made an agreement, he said he'd hold it for me.

"Trust him, do you?"

"Much as anyone. Anyway, most of it's going on account over there. To pay a friend's debt."

"None of my business, John, but if you knew what was good for you ... and for *her* ... Well, you wouldn't, that's all. Payin' her debts ... looks a certain way. Fact is, folks do talk…"

"Yes, I'm sure they do. Guess they got nothing else to talk about. After church, say, even with the Union breaking up. Suppose Mr. Lincoln and ol' Jeff Davis just not interesting enough."

"It's not me, you understand. You're a fine young man, John. I'm quite sure there is nothing improper between the two of you, not anymore at least."

Deacon felt his face getting red in a display of anger that was unusual for him. If Lowery went any further …

"Well, thank you, sir. Our business is completed, I believe." Deacon started to move off across the square.

But Lowery kept up the pace, walking beside him, wouldn't let it go. "I mean, what with her husband gone off to war and all, it just looks a certain way. To some folks."

"Well, I got lots to do before I muster. Goodbye, Mr. Lowery." Deacon slowed only to take a long look at his building – his former building – and the newspaper sign. He felt his eyes well up. "Take good care of ..."

Lowery finally stopped walking with him.

"We'll think of you, John. You and all our brave boys goin' off to war! Preservin' the Union! The town's right proud. Right proud! War'll be over in no time, can't last much longer now, not with brave boys like you at the front! Wish I's goin' with you! Goodbye now! Best of luck to you, son!"

Out of habit, Lowery started to tip his hat to Deacon as he usually did at the close of business, or even as he did when passing townsfolk in the street. Made them think you were one of them, that as rich as he was, he was still so … well, so *nice.* But this young upstart Deacon already had his back turned, and the boy would probably never make it back home anyway. No one was looking. Why bother making the gesture? Lowery pulled his hat tighter on his head against the wind, and let visions of pot roast carry him home.

Deacon kept his head down as he walked. He didn't want to glad-hand any well-wishers sending him on his way, along with their thanks for bringing the newspaper to town. Didn't want to hear how *proud they was* of him, how he'd *win that dad-blamed war all by hisself,* how they *wished they's going* right along with him, *show them Rebs a thang or two, by jingo*! He felt bad mocking their speech, even silently in his own mind. But none of them had come forward to help so the newspaper could stay in business.

Well, maybe nobody really could. Most didn't have much more money than him. How many times had he accepted chickens or a bag of corn meal or a jug of brew in exchange for their payment.

Mostly he was angry – angry at himself. He had come close to begging back there with Lowery, groveling in the dust of the main square for all to see. The trick was, he believed, to pretend all was well – wonderful, really, couldn't be better – and Heaven knows, things would only be getting better from here on out. It was called "optimism." Which was something he wished he actually had.

As he turned the corner toward Odom's General Store, he stopped short. This was exactly what he'd hoped would *not* happen. And, at the same time, exactly what he'd wanted *to* happen. Old Man Odom was coming out of the store, carrying packages to put in a wagon.

He was followed by a fine-boned, blond woman who Deacon thought was the most beautiful girl in the world. Her back was straight, which made Deacon feel bad for the way he'd skulked across the square like he'd been beat. Even in simple traveling clothes, she had the elegance of a queen, maybe like that Queen Victoria over in England. That's how Deacon had always thought a queen would look, or maybe a princess. Just like his Ella Rose.

Deacon was close enough to hear Odom, and wondered if he could back away before they saw him. Still, he had to hear her voice one last time. Odom was saying, "Imagine this'll do ya, Miz Ardent. I'll load them in the wagon myself, just right. I believe if we just tie 'em down, they'll stay put. Now, mind yourself crossin' creeks, even if they look shallow. You lose these supplies, you'll be without. They say t'ain't much of anything left to eat down South, not in Mississippi, not where you're going. You're a mighty brave little lady."

Then she spoke, his Ella, his own. How he loved the sound of her voice. "I'm not brave, Mr. Odom. I'm scared to death. Just doing what I have to do. Have to bring my husband home, don't I?"

"Still, a lone woman goin' South in the middle of this war ..."

"Mr. Odom, thank you for your help. Is this everything? I want to get as far as I can before nightfall."

"And that's another thing, Miz Ardent. Where you think you're going to be bedding down for the night? Ain't like you can stay in one of them fancy ho-tels like they got back East.

Woman alone, no tellin' what all ... Army deserters from both sides ... bushwhackers, outlaws ... and what if you end up in the middle of some battle? What if …"

"Mr. Odom, I don't wish to appear rude, really I don't, but there is simply nothing else for me to do. There's no one else to do it. I just have to face whatever comes. I have no choice. In any case, I do thank you for extending our credit. I know how far behind we are ..."

Just then, Odom spied Deacon. "Well, howdy there, John. Just seein' Miz Ardent off. She's a mighty brave little lady."

Deacon came closer and shook Odom's extended hand.

"Well, good luck to you, ma'am," the shopkeeper said to Ella as he walked back into the store, adding to himself, "Good luck. Sure gonna need it."

Deacon turned to the young woman with more bravado than he felt. He'd already been beaten badly once today. Now he was about to lose everything. His Ella.

"Afternoon, Ella Rose. Miz Ardent, I mean. Didn't wish to bother you, just on my way into the store." Looking ruefully at the bills in his hand, he added, "Hoping Odom will hold this for me. It's what I got for the newspaper. Not much to show for ..."

"I'm sorry, John. Everyone's heard how you had to sell the paper. I'm just so sorry. So very sorry."

"Naught else to do. No one in this town is crazy enough to take it on. This war has gotten pretty bad if the Army wants a lowly newspaperman!"

"Will you be coming back here after you get out?"

"This town, you mean?" Deacon laughed bitterly. "Nothing for me here anymore. Had only three things in the world, three things I loved. Those big old printing presses, big dumb machines that were always breaking down and more trouble than they're worth, but I loved them. Now they're gone. Brought 'em all the way from New York. No telling what Lowery will do with 'em now."

Ella started to speak, but lowered her head instead.

Deacon continued, though he knew he was talking gibberish. "Well, still got my boots, my second thing to love. You'll think I'm mighty foolish, but they were made for me special on that trip to New York City. Nicest things I ever had in my whole life. Thought they'd bring me luck. You'll laugh, but I thought my New York Boots would help me to climb what some call the Ladder of Success."

Why on earth am I babbling, especially about boots, *especially at this moment?*

She smiled. "They're fine boots, John."

"Don't you want to know what the third thing was, Ella Rose, the last of the only three things I had in the world?"

She said nothing, just put a few more things into the wagon, and looked ready to be off. Well, the time had come and he wasn't ready for it, wasn't near ready.

"Ella, can't you spare me even a minute?"

"The recruits are already mustering in the Square, you'd best get going too."

"Not until we speak, Ella. This at least you owe me. Don't you want to know? I'll bet you already do. The only other thing I had in the world was you. But of course you knew that." He gently took her arm. Oh, the feel of her!

"John, please! Everyone will be talking!" Even as she spoke, she was looking around to see if anyone was watching. She spoke more quietly, privately. "Talking even more than they already do."

"More than now?" he laughed "How could that be? This town got nothing better to do! I know, it's my fault, I should have packed up and left, started the newspaper someplace else..."

"Johnny, this isn't the time."

"Ell, there may *never* be a time after right now, this minute! I respected your choice. I know marrying him was what you had to do. I don't begrudge you that. We've known each other since we was kids, no one knows you better than me. But when I went away to New York, it was for *us*, to get those presses, to start a life for us that wasn't all backbreaking work on a farm. So's you could live in town, like a lady, the way you deserve. Something better – for *us* together! I told you that when I went East!"

"You also told me you'd write, Johnny! I never heard a word! Didn't know if you were alive or dead or found yourself that better life back East or found some*one* else ..."

He could see her struggle to take control. He did the same. This was the critical moment when at last, at long last, he thought he understood.

"Ell, I wrote. Just about every day. You were the only one I could talk to, the only one in this town I could ever talk to. Writing letters, it was like standing here talking like we are now. I wanted to share every day of the trip with you."

"I never once heard from you, Johnny, not once."

So that was how it happened. Deacon almost smiled at the pity of it. Well, he sure wished they'd been able to talk this way before now, any time before now. Intently, he asked, "Ell, could your folks have kept my letters from you? Did they hate me that much?"

Ella looked like she'd either laugh or cry. "Well, they always did believe you were a bad 'un, filling my head with outlandish ideas"

"Like the idea that life is more than killing yourself on some dirt-poor farm where it's always too hot or cold or wet or dry? Ell, please tell me. We may never have another time. They forced you to marry him, didn't they?"

"It was just ... Pa was dying. There was nothing Mama and I could do to feed ourselves. How were we to live?"

"Maybe a hired hand, someone to work the place 'til I got back and we could figure something out ..."

"Johnny, I didn't know if you *were* coming back! And anyway, do you see many hired hands around here? Most of the men and boys are gone to war. Mr. Ardent – William – was ... well, he was *here*. What was I to do? There aren't many choices for a woman alone."

Deacon tried to keep his voice calm. "I been hearin' he doesn't treat you well."

"Please, let's just please stop."

"All right, Ell, what's done is done. But why do you have to go after him? Don't you know how dangerous it's going to be, for anyone, much less a lone woman?"

She tried to smile. "Even one as mean as me?" He bet she was scared to death.

"Well, Ella Rose, I wouldn't want to be in the shoes of no bushwhacker that crosses paths with you, no sir!"

"And I wouldn't want to be the Rebel who gets in your gun sights. I know what a fine marksman you are!"

This was good, he thought. The private joke between them, that time she beat him shooting. Things were lighter now, almost as they'd always been. "I told you the sun was in my eyes, Ella Rose!"

She smiled. "No one else ever calls me that."

"I think it's the most beautiful name in the world. My Ella Rose." Could a person really feel it when his heart was breaking? Because he felt it now, thought his heart would burst. All right, now or never. "Ell, don't go. Don't go! We can plan something together, figure something out."

"I have to go after him. He's in some hospital down South. He's my husband, better or worse. They wrote he wants me to come get him. And I need him. How else can I live?"

Deacon started to speak but she kept on. "... and I better get going before I lose the sun." She tried to joke. "Wouldn't want it to be in *my* eyes, now would I?"

He came close, too close he knew, but he had to, had to feel her next to him one last time before he lost her forever. "Ella, you need to know. I have always loved you and I love you now and if I don't make it back from this war, my last thought on earth will be of you. And then I'll look for you in Heaven."

"Johnny, please stop. Don't do this!"

"What do you think you're doing to me? I'll worry myself sick over you, going South all alone just to bring home a man who treats you like ..."

"Worry about yourself, John. You'll be the one in battle."

"I'll be with a bunch of soldiers, all armed to the teeth. You'll be a woman alone. Why, there's thieves and deserters out there, and ..."

"If you're trying to scare me, John Deacon, you're doing a darn fine job."

"Ell, you're so brave. And strong. And smart. That's why to me you've always been the best girl in the world. Only one for me, now and ever."

He wanted so badly to kiss her. But she knew what to say, to make the moment less heartbreaking than it truly was.

"Flattery, that's what I always liked about you, Johnny. Best get going now."

"At least ride with us on the train! You'd be safe there."

"Need this wagon to carry him. Anyways, got no money for a train."

Deacon started to hand her the money he was still holding. "Look, this is for you. You'll need it. How else you going to survive?"

"Put it away! I will not take your money!" She looked around frantically to see who was looking. "What will people think?!"

"I'd hope they'd think that a man going into battle took this one last chance to help someone he loves more than anything else in this world. Now and always. You're all I've got. No family, no nothing, Ell, just you. I don't care what people think. Let's do it! Now! Don't think, just do it! We'll climb in this wagon, go away together, somewhere out West where no one knows us. Make a new start!"

But then they both heard the whistle of the approaching train. "That'll be your train, John. You'd best be going. You're a soldier now. God be with you."

She started climbing into the wagon. As he helped her up, he was able to slip the roll of money into her bag, unseen. Odom could do without being paid for now. "God be with *you*, Ella Rose."

As he watched her ride away, he added to himself, "Only wish it was *me* with you."

CHAPTER 3

NOVEMBER, 1864

The train was slowing, like it might be pulling into the next town. There was still time to jump off with Mr. Slick's identity disc and money. Especially the money. Forty dollars gold! If he could just keep this sergeant in the blue uniform away from him.

The sergeant was asking a bunch of questions and giving orders when all he wanted to do was find a quick escape route when the train stopped. Night was falling fast. It was hard to think with that sergeant bellowing in his ear.

"You! I'm talking to you, soldier! What's your name?!"

He didn't want to cause trouble. He just wanted off the train. Maybe if he cooperated, they'd forget about him. He dug into his pocket for Slick's identity disc and handed it to the sergeant.

"Yes, sir, it's right here, on my identity disc."

The sergeant took the disc, looked it over, then rustled through a sheaf of papers. "Sign this muster roll."

This was an unexpected development, but he could do it. Just needed to get the identity disc back to help him along with the correct letters and all.

"Yessir, sergeant, if I could just have that disc back." Try to keep it friendly, what with the sergeant looking at him like a mean dog. Perhaps a little humor. "I mean, if we was to be in a train crash in the next few minutes, that way they'd know who I was."

Problem was, he'd never been much for reading and writing. Not growing up like he did. If his mama had stayed alive, maybe she'd have taught him to read the Bible. He'd have liked that. But as it was …

The sergeant intruded in his thoughts. "I said, sign the list! You're a soldier now. You do what I say the minute I say it, and no sass about train crashes! You can sign your own name, can't you?"

He looked as quickly as he could at identity disc, but knew his limitations. Still, he gave it his best. He tried to copy each letter on the identity disc but the sergeant kept watching. It made him nervous.

"All right, Shakespeare, hurry up!" the sergeant said. He wasn't sure who that Shake Spear fella was, maybe some Injun. Well, the sergeant would just have to wait, he was doing his best.

He thought he'd gotten to the end of the name when the sergeant snatched the paper from his hand. "Let me see! Can't hardly read this. M-O-R-A-N. All right Moran, move on!"

Now, that didn't sound right. "Sir, I may have left something out."

He showed the identity disc to the sergeant, the disc with the name 'Nicholas Morgan.' "Ain't that a 'G,' sir? I think I left it out."

The train was slowing and some of the gear that was stowed above the seats started falling on the men who jumped up from their seats to dodge the avalanche, yelling and cursing. The sergeant now had other matters to attend to. "Out of my way, Moran."

"But sir, I don't think I signed my name right."

"I said, move it along. Or are you a troublemaker, Moran?"

"No, no trouble. You're right, sir – 'Moran' it is."

As the sergeant shoved his way past, he said, "I got my eye on you, Moran."

To that, the newly-minted Private Moran could only reply under his breath, "Not fer long."

The train was stopped now, taking on more recruits. It was already crowded. Well, he'd be happy to leave and make room for one more. Moran made his way through the jostling throng of men toward the rear exit. So close now. He allowed a smile to cross his face. As he got close enough to feel the cool air from outside, some other man in a blue uniform stopped him. This one had two stripes and was standing in front of the door. No, not now! He had to make his escape now! There was no time. The new men were just about all on board.

Two-Stripes blocked the way. "Get back, soldier!"

"But sir, I just have to step outside for a minute." Not his best story, but there was no time to think of something better.

"I said, sit down, soldier! Find a place to stand if you ain't got a seat!"

The train lurched forward. Now Moran knew how a trapped animal felt. And he knew what they did to get un-trapped. There was just nothing for it. He tried to muscle Two-Stripe out of the way. He had to. The train was moving now and the sun was setting. It had to be now!

"Get back!" said Two-Stripe.

"But sir, I got to …"

"You heard me! Get back! What's your name, soldier?"

Things took a turn for the worse when the sergeant appeared. "Problem here, Corporal?"

"This man ain't much for obeying orders yet, Sarge."

"I know him. His name's Moran."

"Well, he's a troublemaker, Sarge."

"Not in my outfit. We'll break him of that!"

The sergeant had a way of saying things that lacked any attempt at the pleasantries. Maybe if Moran politely spoke in his own defense. "No, sir, Sergeant sir, honest, I just ..."

Two-Stripe just had to add his piece: "Shut up and get back, Moran! Sit down or find a place to stand. It's going to be a long ride!"

Now there was really nothing for it. The train was moving at a pretty good clip. Moran decided to wait for the next town. Maybe the rapidly-falling darkness would actually help. As for now, he'd do what he was told, thinking, "Yep, a long ride. A very long ride."

He tried to move down the aisle of the swaying rail car, but could not help himself from lurching into another soldier who responded by raising his fist angrily. When Moran raised his own arm defensively, the sandwich tucked in his belt became visible. It was the sandwich Slick had bought him back at the tavern. The sandwich he had hoped would be his breakfast on the road.

"What you got here? Hey, Stoner, give me a hand," said the soldier, grabbing the sandwich while his buddy held Moran's arms. "Lookee what I got!"

"Hey, wait!" It was all Moran could think of to say, nothing else to do, not with the sergeant and corporal around. It was two against one. The two soldiers split the sandwich, their looks daring Moran to do something about it. He chose not to.

The sergeant and the corporal were giving out uniform jackets now. They threw one Moran's way and moved on. Well, at least it gave them something to do instead of giving him a hard time. He shrugged his shoulders into the jacket before they could yell at him for not doing it fast enough. He was downcast. His only thought had been of getting off this train, and now that prospect was looking like it could get bleak.

At first he'd been glad of the train. It would carry him far away from the bank riders. Now Moran wasn't so sure. If this was Army life, it didn't appear to suit. And he had the flicker of a thought that leaving now might mean he was a deserter. If they caught you, the penalty for that was worse than what they doled out to the Rebels. And where was this train rolling to, anyway? From what he could see of the setting sun in the west, his bearings told him they were headed south.

With no seats, he stood, swaying with the motion of the train, which did nothing to help his beer-sodden head. Exhaustion caught up with him, slammed him hard, shrouded him like a thick, poisonous fog. His whole body ached. He was just spent, about to give out. And to think – it was a day that had started out with such promise. If he'd'a just asked those bank riders for a bite of their food, just left it at that …

He felt the train pick up speed and watched the last rays of sunset surrender to the blackness of the November night. Didn't someone say something about it being a long ride? "I believe that's so," he thought. "Yes, I do believe that's so."

Halfway across the continent, another man impatiently rode a train, though this man's journey would soon come to a happy and expected end. Unlike Moran, he knew exactly where he was going on this late November night in 1864. And he knew why.

This man was known only as Alpha, and he hoped to keep it that way until the war ended with a Confederate victory. None of his colleagues knew him by any name other than Alpha, and he'd even started thinking of himself that way. At times, he almost forgot his given name, though he hoped that the history of the new Confederate States of America would list him by his real name in its pantheon of heroes.

Alpha had been sent by the Confederate government in Richmond to Toronto, Canada. There, it would be his job to plan what he called "private militia operations" against the Union.

When the war had begun in 1861, he felt the same way as everyone he knew. He assumed the brave cavaliers of the South would sweep to an easy victory over the fat, hypocritical, complacent North.

And at first, things had indeed gone well from Alpha's point of view. The Confederate Army's General Lee inspired miracles from his men, winning battle after battle. But by 1864, things were looking somewhat discouraging for the South. The North simply had more men, more guns, more resources, more everything. A supplemental strategy was needed, and Alpha was the man to do it.

Alpha had no particular misgivings against vanity. He knew he looked every inch the war hero. Ladies adored him; men admired him. And everyone – *everyone* – respected him, especially when he fixed his steely eyes on them. He had a well-earned reputation as a sharpshooter and an expert duelist with a violent temper. Few had the temerity to test him.

His one weakness, if modesty forced him to name one, was his passionate love for the South. It filled his entire being, his complete sense of self. After all, his bloodline, his kin, were some of those who tamed the terrible, exotic land. The South was in his blood, and he'd be the one to save the South in its time of need. He'd kill anyone who got in his way, and do it without a moment's regret.

His land, his beloved South, was being ravaged. Those twin devils of the North, Sherman and Sheridan, were sweeping through his beautiful country with their obscene "scorched earth" policy. And they bragged of it. He'd read the cheerful reports in a New York newspaper. The words, so glib, burned in his brain. How Sheridan, advancing through Virginia, torched over two thousand barns filled with wheat, hay, and farm implements along with mills filled with flour.

It was all his people had left, all they had to sustain them, especially the dear, brave ladies of the South. That was the one bad thing about the crop that yielded the bounty of the South: you can't eat cotton.

Sheridan was pressing on to Richmond, and Sherman was slashing his way through Georgia on his relentless march to the sea.

That was not warfare fit for gentlemen, not a noble meeting on the field of battle in worthy combat. It was … well, Alpha was a man of the world with a fine education; even so, he could not think of a word vile enough to describe the Union tactic. But he agreed with his superiors in Richmond as to what must be done: repay in kind.

There were *two* sides to this war, he thought. Northerners must be made to understand they cannot relax in comfort and wealth while the South bore the agony. Alpha had been thrilled the previous year when General Lee brought the war to Pennsylvania, in the town of Gettysburg. Let them see what it's like to have your home turned into a battlefield!

But that campaign had not gone well. Gettysburg in 1863 had preceded crushing losses in 1864. Now, with 1864 drawing to a close, Alpha knew he would have to be the one to reverse the trend.

When his fellow operatives had arrived in Toronto, he called them together to make their plans. With his classical education, Alpha appreciated the fact that they would call on an ancient weapon, "Greek Fire." It was a mysterious mixture of sulfur, naphtha, quicklime, sometimes phosphorus, sometimes other chemicals. A jar of the stuff ignited easily when it came into contact with air. Best of all, it was hard to extinguish. Fire that wouldn't die! Imagine the terror!

Alpha was taught that the lethal mixture had been invented by the ancient Greeks. He'd heard that the Byzantines of the Eastern Roman Empire had used it to destroy a Saracen fleet in holy wars of the seventh century. To Alpha, this new incarnation, the one he was fighting over a thousand years later, was another holy war.

Alpha would bring the war to the North, exacting revenge for the desecration of his beloved South. When the enemy saw the stakes had risen, the war would be brought a quick, honorable close. Alpha would be one of the founding fathers of the new Confederate States of America.

Reading newspapers, talking with businessmen, and simply observing from afar during the pleasant Canadian summer of 1864,

Alpha knew the re-election of the Union's president Abraham Lincoln that November was in doubt. He knew many Northerners were sick of war, eager for peace, and ready to resume reaping serious, uninterrupted profits.

Alpha's plan was for his group to enter the United States at Buffalo and travel to New York City just prior to Election Day, November 8, 1864. In quick succession, they would set off Greek Fire attacks in crowded locations all over the city, instill panic, and disrupt the election while the city was in flames. They would garner widespread support to end the war, and they'd plant the Confederate flag over New York's City Hall.

He and his men had crossed the border and made it to New York City just before Election Day. The plan would have gone perfectly if it hadn't been for one of his own people. There was a double agent in the group – that cur! – who revealed the threat. Thousands of federal soldiers were sent to New York under the command General Benjamin Butler. Alpha knew of him. Butler was called "The Beast" for his brutal military occupation of New Orleans.

Alpha and his group could barely move about New York City without tripping over well-armed Union soldiers. He could only watch, seething with anger, as Lincoln was elected to a second term.

Still, even this thwarted exercise was informative. Abraham Lincoln did *not* carry New York. Alpha felt there was enough opposition there for him to rally supporters to the Confederate Cause. The Stars and Bars could still fly proudly over New York City Hall!

With only a few men on whom he'd bet his life, Alpha re-gathered the group in Toronto later that same month. They crossed the U. S. border again and took separate trains from Buffalo into New York City.

On November 25, 1864, as the man now known as Moran rode another train across the country gloomily pondering his fate as a brand-new Union soldier, Alpha emerged from his rail car exultant with hope for the Confederacy.

As soon as Alpha walked casually out of the rail station in New York, he saw what men like him were meant to see: the continued presence of Union troops around government buildings. No matter, thought Alpha, smiling to himself. Government buildings were not the targets.

Alpha made his way to his contact's shop in a basement off Washington Place. The deal had been arranged on his trip to the city earlier that month. His contact had insisted on being paid with U. S. dollars, not Confederate money. This almost drove Alpha to distraction. He considered killing the man for his impudence, but decided he might need the chemist again in future.

So, after a substantial payment, the wizened old chemist handed over a heavy satchel which, he said, required great caution. It contained twelve dozen bottles of the highly flammable Greek Fire mixture.

With infinite care, Alpha had no choice but to ride among the jostling crowd on a streetcar to meet the others at the rendezvous point.

When he arrived, he was pleased to see them all again and to note they had followed his instruction. Each carried a cheap black case. None of them seemed to be attracting undue attention. They moved calmly to a secluded spot. Alpha divided up the jars of Greek Fire and wished them all Godspeed.

Separately, each of Alpha's men traveled along Broadway. One by one, they registered under assumed names at various hotels along the busy street. They felt quite at home, thanks to a spread in *Harper's Weekly* which had brought Broadway to a national audience in February of 1860. Alpha vividly recalled the double-page picture which captured lower Broadway's pulsating energy. The magazine called Broadway the most striking place in the United States, conveying the bustle of America's great center of commerce.

No building within Alpha's gaze remained free of signs. "Knox Classical Hatters: Hats, Caps and Furs" – "W. A. Hayward Manufacturing & Jeweler" – "Bassford's Billiard Table Factory" – and conveniently around the corner, "Wallace & Reeve's Billiard Rooms."

Festooned with Union flags, the buildings were an insult to Alpha's sense of morality. Atlanta had boasted a busy commercial district too, but now it was in ashes. He hated everything and everyone he saw in New York, so arrogant, so comfortable. He hated them all.

Towering above them was the nationally-known "American Museum," five stories tall. Its owner, P. T. Barnum, had incurred Alpha's wrath early in the war by prominently placing a newspaper ad. From his comfortable perch in New York, Barnum had used the country's turmoil to promote his business. Under the glaring headline "THE CRISIS AND SECESSION," the ad had read: *"Nobody would think there was trouble in the 'American Camp' if they would look in at Barnum's Museum, either afternoon or evening, and see the smiling, happy faces, and hear the merry laughter of old and young, over the great showman's novelties and amusements."*

It seemed to gleefully proclaim that a bit of carefree amusement at Barnum's museum and theatre was the perfect remedy for the annoyances of the conflict. Barnum, safe from harm, grew richer and richer on the profits. Alpha hated the man and all Northerners, hated their smug attitude toward the suffering of his people. Alpha would make them pay.

The crowded hotels and theatres of the city presented themselves up to Alpha as a gift. They were ideal spots to whip up panic. If a few – or a few hundred – casualties resulted, so much the better. It was exactly the fate of civilians from Virginia to Georgia.

Alpha's men were assigned four hotels each, while Alpha would carry out his own attacks on piers, theatres, and any targets of opportunity. The Greek Fire assaults were to begin at precisely 8 p.m.

Barnum's museum and theater were packed that night. This would be a pleasure. Women and children starving in the South, and these beasts were out having great fun. Alpha paid for a ticket and entered the museum. He launched the fire in a stairwell, then watched delightedly from the street as patrons panicked, stampeding outside. But remarkably, no one appeared to be dead or even seriously injured. Alpha was not pleased.

He hurried to his next objective which he hoped would prove more satisfactory. The Lafarge House was not only a sizeable hotel, but it also adjoined the Winter Garden Theatre. On any night, the Winter Garden would have been an alluring target. But this was Friday, November 25, 1864, and the auditorium was packed to its rafters.

The Winter Garden was managed by the great actor Edwin Booth. This evening's performance would be a one-night-only gala to raise money for a statue of William Shakespeare to be placed in New York's new Central Park. Here they were, raising money for a *statue* when the people of the South had no food! Let them raise money for that! Alpha hated every person in the jam-packed theatre.

The event was so crowded because it was the very first time all three of the famous Booth brothers were acting together. World-renowned tragedians Edwin Booth, Junius Booth Jr., and John Wilkes Booth were appearing this night only in Shakespeare's play about the assassination of Julius Caesar. Part of Alpha almost wished he could watch the performance. He recalled what the assassin Brutus was said to have shouted when he attacked Caesar: "Sic semper tyrannis!" – "Thus always to tyrants!" Alpha would have loved to shout it at every person in the packed theatre as he set off the Greek Fire.

Instead, he went quickly to the adjoining Lafarge House. It was almost 8:30 and he still had work to do. He emptied the Greek Fire mixture on the third floor and also on the furniture in the front parlor before dashing outside. Finally he heard the jarring sounds of fire bells! He could imagine the panic in the Winter Garden when the fat New Yorkers smelled the smoke!

The horse-drawn fire engines clattered to a halt on the busy street opposite Alpha's vantage point. Still, nothing happened. No one ran screaming into the street. Only later would Alpha learn that Edwin Booth, still in the toga of Brutus, had stepped out of character to calm the audience. From the footlights, he reassured them that they were in no danger if they remained quietly in their seats. Headlines proclaimed that such was the power of the actor Edwin Booth – no panic ensued.

And only later would Alpha recall that event at the Winter Garden when one of the actors there that night, John Wilkes Booth, went on to make headlines of his own. Almost all the newspaper stories four months later would include the fact the John Wilkes Booth was heard to shout "Sic semper tyrannis!" as he ran from the stage of Ford's Theatre in Washington.

All that was in the future. For the moment, Alpha was now counting on his colleagues.

At final count, Alpha's group set off nineteen fires, including rooms in thirteen hotels along Broadway. Some people did indeed rush into the streets, but soon the fires were quickly extinguished. None of the hotel fires spread beyond the rooms where they had been set. They were easily put out by hotel staff. Most of the "Greek Fire" had simply sat and smoldered. Alpha blamed the chemist.

Afterward, there was very little question about the methodology. Several of Alpha's co-conspirators had attracted attention when they checked in at the hotels wearing obviously fake wigs and moustaches, and they were nowhere to be found after the incidents. One had even left behind an empty bottle of Greek Fire with his black satchel.

And they all made a major mistake: They kept the windows closed in their rooms. Without air circulation, the fires lacked the oxygen they needed to flare up.

As the conspirators joined the crowds of New Yorkers in the streets, they did not hear the public outcry they had hoped for. People were already speculating about it being a Confederate plot, which federal authorities quickly confirmed. The mood of the crowds did not reveal any sudden pro-Southern leanings. Quite the opposite. No one rushed to raise a Confederate flag over City Hall. Rather, it steeled New Yorkers more strongly against a common enemy.

Alpha and his group boarded a single train, no attempt now at covert action. They crossed back into Canada. They stayed apart, careful not to arouse suspicion. Some of them also feared Alpha's wrath. After a short time, Alpha's colleagues quietly left Canada to return to the Confederacy. Alpha did not.

He would no longer depend on others. He thought of his colleagues from the ill-fated New York venture as incompetents who didn't have the sense to open a window or to avoid leaving evidence behind. From now on, he would depend only on himself. No well-meaning but bungling comrades. And no suppliers like that sharp-dealing New York chemist.

From now on, Alpha would act alone. He'd make the weapons by himself. The devices would be simple, innocent-looking, and so easy to carry that they'd fit in the palm of his hand.

He quietly entered the United States near Detroit, though he did not linger. Alpha was on the move, headed due south.

CHAPTER 4

NOVEMBER, 1864

After he watched Ella ride away, John Deacon ran home for what would be the last time. This was the beginning of his new life. He'd change into uniform and become a soldier!

It was really rather exciting. Even though he knew vanity was some kind of sin, he was proud of what he was doing.

He knew most of the other fellows in his unit from around town, and he liked them. He'd been interviewing local volunteers since the war started in 1861, writing little stories about them in the paper as they left with their units. At first, most of them were in a hurry to have their stories written. They were afraid the war would only last a few months, and this would be their only chance at glory! And, my, wouldn't the womenfolk love it!

They'd almost all been farmers, and they believed strongly in the *United* States, in keeping the Union together. They didn't hate southerners, not at first anyway, but they sure thought the secession of the southern states was a rebellion, pure and simple. The South simply had to be brought back into the union of the states, whether they liked it or not.

Some of the men from his town wondered if it wasn't the politicians, North and South, who'd gotten them all into this mess. It seemed to Deacon's neighbors that it was easy for rich old men to declare a war when it was the young ones who'd have to go fight it.

Still, the men from his town didn't mind all that much, not at first, not back in 1861. It would be an adventure! So much more exciting than farm work! Just about anything was, after all. The womenfolk could take care of the farm for the few months they'd be gone, maybe even appreciate their men a little more when the unit got back home. The fellas who'd mentioned that last part quickly asked Deacon not to print it.

Something else they had asked Deacon not to print was their thoughts on slavery, if they brought it up at all. When the war began, most of the men from his town had never seen a person with skin darker than their own. But they knew about that *Uncle Tom's Cabin* book which had been published just a few years ago in 1852. In ten years, it was selling more copies than anything other than the Bible. People passed *Uncle Tom's Cabin* around, talked about it after church, about what it would mean to be a slave or to own other people. The book seemed to be tying it all to Christianity, that true Christians believed in doing unto others as you'd have others do unto you. And who would want to be a slave?

The men of his town, the ones who tried talking about it at all, had a hard time expressing their conflicted feelings. They'd never seen slavery up close, and believed in minding their own business. Some even went so far as to joke about how nice it would be to have a slave of their own to help work the farm, sort of a hired hand who didn't have to be paid. But then they'd laugh nervously and quickly add, "Only joking about that, Mr. Deacon, didn't really mean it." If they could put their feelings about slavery into words at all, most of them said something like, "Just doesn't seem right."

But there was something deeper that they couldn't quite explain. People in Deacon's part of the country were living west of the

Appalachians, still considered the frontier. They were far removed, mentally as well as physically, from the great entrenched society of the east.

Though they never used an expression like "middle class," Deacon's friends were proud of their place in the fabric of America. Neither rich nor poor, they worked for everything they had, putting in an honest day's work to feed their families. Some had parents who'd sailed from Europe to escape the whip hand of overlords. Some locals had emigrated themselves, starting over in America with nothing to their name. They knew about the fine lords and ladies back in their homeland, so-called "nobles" who felt no shame for their cruelties and who grew richer on the backs of others.

At first, that was how they saw the South from a distance – wealthy aristocrats living off the toil of the poor. But that was 1861 and now it was 1864. The "few months" of the Civil War had stretched into a bloodbath lasting years. More boys from northern farms were now seeing the South first-hand. And they didn't like what they saw.

Deacon read every newspaper he could get his hands on, including the small camp papers written on the front lines by soldiers themselves. Most Southerners were not wealthy landowners, but it was the massive estates and plantation homes that made the biggest impression. That was what the camp papers focused on.

The northern farm boys saw the misery of enslaved people – men, women, children. *People.* They saw the trappings of wealth enjoyed by the white aristocrats. And they began to think of themselves as combating something more than rebellion. Though the words and music would not be written for a few years, men like Deacon's friends began to think of themselves as Christian Soldiers.

The people of Ohio were proud that more Union volunteers came from than their state than almost any other. New York and Pennsylvania might be sending more men total, but Ohio sent sixty percent, the highest percentage of population. Deacon knew there were men in more than two hundred Ohio regiments – infantry, cavalry, artillery, sharpshooters. And now Deacon was one of them.

Probably he should have gone before now. The Army was taking men as young as eighteen and as old as forty-five, though many, too young or too old, lied about their ages to get into service. Deacon had truly felt he had a duty to print the news so that people would know what they were fighting for, to honor the dead, and to raise up the cause. But by 1864, he knew he had to go. That was why he made the painful decision to sell what little he had and join up. And that was why he was proud to be getting into uniform.

Deacon took off his town clothes and began changing into the light blue wool federal-issue trousers they'd given him when he signed up. Just then he heard a tiny knock at his door. Ella? Shirtless, he ran to open it.

Not Ella. He tried to replace his disappointment with a smile. It was Andy Andrews, a boy from town who'd helped out around the newspaper office. In his twelve-year-old way, he'd been Deacon's friend. Now the boy looked as though he was trying hard not to cry.

"Leaving so soon, Mr. Deacon? Heard the train whistle from up the line but thought maybe there'd be more time."

"Have to change into uniform and muster up on the Square with the other men," Deacon said. He hoped the boy wouldn't bring up the matter of selling the newspaper, and where he now might find a new job. The boy, to his credit, did not.

"Goin' to go like that?" Andy said with a smile. Deacon realized he was still shirtless. "Looks like you need someone to help you get dressed, Mr. Deacon."

The boy's real name was Allie Eldon Andrews, but everyone called him Andy. He was smart and he was a hard worker. Deacon liked him, and guessed the feeling was mutual because sometimes Andy confided in him. "Goin' to be a doctor one day, Mr. Deacon," he'd once said. Deacon always believed the boy would do just that. Now he just hoped the war wouldn't drag on to the point where they'd be taking twelve-year-olds.

"What's this?" the boy asked, holding up the wool flannel army shirt the quartermaster had provided. The boy felt it, then scrunched up his nose. "Can't be a shirt. It's too scratchy."

"That's what I've been hearing from soldiers," Deacon said. "According to them, Army-issue is so itchy, most just wear cotton shirts from home," he said, shrugging into one of his own white shirts. "Same for drawers," Deacon said conspiratorially.

"Well, no one can see them anyway," said the boy. Then he blushed.

Deacon smiled. He was actually glad Andy'd come around. The boy would be here for the best part. The blue wool jacket of the Union Army. It had four shiny brass buttons on the front. He'd heard soldiers say it was remarkably comfortable to wear. Most kept it on all the time.

Andy reached for the jacket and helped Deacon into it, holding the garment with a reverence almost like the robing ceremony for a bishop or a king. The boy buttoned the brass, snapped the jacket sharply into place, and couldn't help admiring his handiwork. "You look right handsome, Mr. Deacon. You're a fine soldier."

Deacon couldn't keep from smiling. "Hang on, Andy, before you start handing out medals. You haven't even seen the finishing touches." Deacon added the wool forage cap with its leather visor in front and rounded flat top. On the train, he'd sew on the corps badge and attach the brass numbers of his regiment.

Next came the thick black leather belt with "US" on the buckle. His leather cartridge box hung off the belt. Andy filled the canteen with water while Deacon checked the items in his canvas knapsack. Between the knapsack itself and the leather straps on top, it could hold a lot. There was room for a few rations like three days' worth of coffee, salt pork, and hardtack. The Army issued a tin cup, metal plate, knife, fork, and spoon. Deacon packed an extra shirt, underclothes, a toothbrush, tooth powder, comb, and soap. Some of the fellas grew beards, which cut down on shaving supplies and looked pretty good.

"Well, Andy, I guess that's about it."

"No sir, you forgot the most important thing. It's … well, it's something from me." Andy handed him a small crudely-wrapped package. The boy was right. It really was important. In fact, it was the best gift Deacon had ever received: writing paper, pen, and a small container of ink. If the boy saw Deacon's eyes welling up, it'd just embarrass both of them. Deacon busied himself tying his rolled-up blanket into the leather straps of his knapsack.

Andy kept the conversation going. "I know they've got those merchants that follow the troops, you could prob'ly have bought some from them. Settlers? Is that what they're called?"

"They're called sutlers," said Deacon, "and you've saved me a lot of time and trouble. I appreciate the gift." Deacon realized, with no family of his own, it was the only one he'd gotten. To change the subject, he said, "You hurry up and learn to be a doctor, Andy. If I get shot, I might need your services."

The minute the words left his mouth, Deacon knew it was the wrong thing to say. "Please don't," said the boy. "Don't get shot. Please come back."

"Well, of course I'll be back, Andy," Deacon lied, knowing he hadn't given one minute's thought to ever coming back here. "I will if I have to walk all the way. Luckily, I've got good boots."

"These army shoes?" asked Andy, picking up the thick black brogans Deacon had been issued. He made a face of disapproval. "These are the heaviest, awful-est shoes I ever saw. How can you walk in them?"

They *were* heavy, and they were too small. Deacon couldn't imagine trudging across town in them, much less marching thirty or forty miles a day, hard miles under a full pack. They were thick black leather with heavy soles and heels tacked together with wooden pegs.

"You know, Andy, I see in the newspapers from back East that shoes are starting to be made special, one for the left foot and one for the right."

Like most footwear of the day, these army-issued shoes were identical, neither left nor right. The prevailing theory was that your feet would stretch them however they needed to be. But the number of agonizing blisters argued against it. And then there was the blood poisoning after the blisters got infected. And then amputations because of the infection, and even death – horrible to think about. He sure wouldn't bother Andy with all that.

"Not going to wear those army shoes, Andy. I'll bring them on the train and give them back, maybe someone else can use them. I'm wearing *these*." Deacon pointed proudly to what he thought of as his New York Boots.

It was the only extravagance Deacon had ever allowed himself in his life. When he was in Manhattan with his life savings, tracking down used printing presses, he saw a cobbler's shop window advertising boots made to order. Through the open door, he could smell the splendid rich leather and wondered if he would ever have the courage – and the money – to walk in.

After he'd bought the presses and paid for the oxcart he would use to carry them home, there had been a little money left over. Deacon knew he'd have been smart to save it for food or emergencies on the trip back. But that shop seemed to be calling him. He went back to the cobbler, paid the money, and never had a moment's regret.

"Andy, these boots came all the way from New York City. Made special for me. Feel like walking on a cloud."

"Maybe they'll put you in the cavalry, Mr. Deacon. All cavalrymen have tall, shiny boots."

"Need a horse for the cavalry. I'll go wherever they put me, just a plain foot soldier. I'll do fine with these to carry me."

They both heard the train whistle coming closer. Deacon had never noticed before what a mournful sound it was. He saw Andy's sad face and thought, "Please don't let the boy hug me." Instead, Andy surprised him by thrusting out his hand. He shook Deacon's with a strong grip, like the man he was going to have to be, much sooner than he ought.

"Take care of your mama and sisters, Andy. You're the only man they got now." And then it was Deacon who surprised himself. He hugged the boy, held him close.

"Please come back, Mr. Deacon."

"I'll try, Andy. Sure will try." He ran for the train, quite certain he'd never see the boy again.

There were no seats on the train. Deacon and his unit were told to stand until things could be sorted out. An angry-looking sergeant and corporal were trying to impose some sort of order as the train lurched out of the station. Some of the new volunteers were still being issued uniforms. Deacon thought he could help.

Assuming the sergeant would be glad of the fresh new volunteers in the shared fight, Deacon approached him like a comrade, smiling. "Sergeant, I have my own footwear, and have no need of these. They may be useful to one of the other men." He held out the army brogans.

In a la-di-da voice, the sergeant said, "Well, aren't you a sterling chap? Who told you what you'd wear and not wear, and more to the point, who are you to tell me?" Judging by the sergeant's tone and angry glare, this was not going the way Deacon had hoped.

"You'll comply with Army regulations if you're going to be in my outfit, which you are," added the sergeant. "Now get into those brogans, give your civilian boots to the corporal, and stop bothering me. I've had enough of troublemakers for one day."

Deacon believed further discussion might still be in order, but the sergeant clearly showed no intention to pause for a chat. Being branded as a troublemaker on his very first day was not what Deacon had hoped. So he did what he was told.

He found a place to stand after squeezing into the too-small brogans. There was nothing to do but think. The swaying of the train induced an almost dreamlike state. Maybe later he could resume negotiations, after he had proven to the sergeant he was a good soldier. It seemed like a small thing, but his New York Boots were a talisman to him. From the first moment he'd slipped them on, he felt like nothing could go wrong for a man who was wearing those magnificent pieces of leather. And they tied him to the Magical City.

Four years earlier, back in 1860, it had been like journeying to a mythical place beyond human grasp, other-worldly, the moon, Mars maybe. New York City. Deacon had never seen anything larger than his own small town. He knew that the last census had awarded his town around a thousand people. That estimate seemed high to him.

But that same census showed New York City at about a million people, almost twice the size of runner-up Philadelphia. And that didn't even include more than a quarter-million in the neighboring town of Brooklyn, New York, listed in the census as America's third-largest city.

Twelve years prior, Deacon's parents had died, leaving left him alone and penniless. All he'd known to do then, at age fourteen, was go work on neighboring farms. But he made himself useful. He'd taught himself to read and write, and then made small amounts of money teaching the same skills to others. He was also paid to read and write letters for people who could not do so themselves.

He'd saved every cent he earned until he had enough to buy the small shed of a building that would become his newspaper office with a room in back to call his home. Loyal friends who wanted a newspaper in their town donated small amounts of money, and by spring of 1860, he had enough to make the journey East where he heard there were used presses for sale. New York City papers had the wherewithal to buy the newest, biggest, fastest, most up-to-date equipment. They had no need for old junk.

With little money for travel, the trip had taken Deacon a while. He'd begged rides on the wagons of fellow travelers, hired out as a crewman on canal boats, and sometimes just walked day after day toward his destination. Whenever he stopped, he wrote Ella back home, usually every day, describing all he saw. He asked her to save the letters – maybe when he got back, he'd use them to write a real book. Country boy in the city!

Then one day, he rounded a bend to see the tall buildings from miles away. He sat down immediately to record his thoughts in a letter to Ella, how that was the moment their life together was really going to begin.

He even mentioned his great embarrassment. He had no need of secrets from her, and it might make an interesting chapter in the book he was already writing in his head. As he had approached the city, he was stopped short by an obstacle he had not considered, a massive river.

He was glad at least no one from back home, especially Ella, could see his dilemma. Certainly in his reading he'd seen the term "Manhattan Island" but he never quite equated it with New York City being surrounded by water. At least he had money for a ferry. It made him feel he was riding in style, floating toward the glorious city that was drawing ever closer.

After disembarking, Deacon settled in the cheapest room he could find. It was an area they called Lower Manhattan, far from the city's northernmost boundary of Forty-Second Street. Then, to the business at hand.

What a thrill to visit New York's newspaper offices in search of old presses, just one newspaperman talking to another. It was dizzying merely to walk in those buildings with the names on the door! *New York Evening Post, New York Herald, New York Tribune,* and of course *The New York Times,* less than ten years old and already a legend.

He finally found presses he could afford at a small paper that was going out of business. They seemed glad of a buyer, even helped him arrange for an oxcart and team to make the trip home when he was ready to leave.

But he couldn't leave just yet. He wanted to see as much as he could in walking distance of his room. There seemed to be something wonderful around every corner. He didn't begrudge those staying farther "uptown" at the Fifth Avenue Hotel on Madison Square, or at the Astor.

But he'd made a point at least to gaze inside at the lobby of the Astor. It was the hotel where Mr. Abraham Lincoln had stayed a few months before. In February of 1860, Mr. Lincoln made a now-famous speech at New York's Cooper Union for the Advancement of Science and Art. Most people just called the place "Cooper Union" and most people agreed the Cooper Union speech had made Lincoln, a small-town Illinois lawyer, into a national figure. And now, right there in New York City, in the early summer of 1860, Deacon heard the news that Lincoln had been nominated for President of the United States! Deacon couldn't help but see *himself* as a presidential candidate someday. Wouldn't Ella make a splendid First Lady of the land? He just knew it would all somehow begin here in New York. Anything was possible in a city like this.

Deacon wondered if Mr. Lincoln had walked the streets of New York as he was doing now. Storefront signs written in indecipherable languages, lettering that bore no earthly relation to English. And the languages themselves – people hollering in some tongues that sounded like they were made up of all vowels, and some that sounded like they didn't have any vowels at all. Was this what the Bible story of the Tower of Babel was all about? Strangely-dressed people babbling – Babel-ing – hawking their wares.

Many of the items being sold were food. Deacon did not have a lot of money for meals, and hated to admit that even if he'd had the funds, he couldn't recognize a lot of what was on display. He was sorry if that marked him as provincial, but he would not have experimented. However, he could not resist purchasing one of the big, soft, warm pretzels that street vendors carried on long poles – heavenly!

Deacon marveled at the tallest building in New York, Trinity Church, which had stood on the same spot near Wall Street since the late 1600s. He even stopped in for a moment to say a prayer.

But he also he happily went without meals to indulge in other, non-spiritual experiences. New York City had ten full-time resident minstrel companies, and Mr. P.T. Barnum's American Museum had a huge auditorium where they showed plays like *The Drunkard.*

He was most impressed with Miss Laura Keene's theatre. It was simply remarkable that a woman could be both an actress and a manager, all by herself. Deacon was disappointed not to see her in the comedy he'd heard so much about. It had been called *Our American Cousin* and she'd presented it at her theatre two years before, in 1858. However, it was said that she'd present it again one day, maybe even take it on tour to big cities around the country. So perhaps one day he'd still get to see it.

Instead he saw Keene in *Seven Sisters* which was called a "musical burletta" and was the hit show of 1860. Laura Keene starred as one of seven female demons who come up from Hell to go sightseeing in New York. Its finale featured a rousing rendition of the minstrel classic, "Dixie." Deacon had loved the show, but decided that when he got back home, he'd mostly tell people about Trinity Church.

Then with what little money he had left, he returned to the cobbler's shop to buy his New York Boots. Someday, he thought, he'd wear them back to Manhattan again. By then, a success. Boots like those could carry a man anywhere.

That had been back in the warm summer of 1860. Now, in late November of 1864, the presses were gone, the boots were gone, and his life as he'd imagined it – life with Ella – well, that was gone too.

In his new blue uniform, he stood swaying to the motion of the train. He allowed his thoughts to grow somber. He hoped the gathering darkness outside was not some sort of symbol of things to come. He wondered if he'd ever see New York again.

He would never know that across the country, right at that moment, desperate men were trying their best to burn his beloved city to the ground.

CHAPTER 5
DECEMBER, 1864

Even in winter, New Orleans had a lush, luscious indolence in the air. Charity Boudry stood on a small iron balcony overlooking the city's Gallatin Street. The balcony was not as pleasantly filigreed as some, but it allowed her a little air and a view of her very restricted world. She knew there was another New Orleans, another world out there. But from her room on Gallatin Street, that part of the city might as well be on the dark side of the moon.

All she could see along Gallatin were the saloons, dance halls, and "houses" like hers here at Madame's. It was a filthy dark street that always smelled of rotting garbage and human waste. Even during the daytime, it was home to thieves and murderers who boldly walked the street knowing that few policemen dared to approach.

For the sailors and immigrants who were disgorged at the nearby docks, it was the first place they could find when they set foot on dry land. For poor immigrant girls, or abandoned women of all sorts, it was a place where they thought they would only stop a while, until their situation improved. But for the vast majority of them, their situation only worsened and they were never able to leave. Battered signs swayed in dark doorways, proclaiming 'rooms' for rent. It didn't take long for the women to discover how high the rent would be when paid with their bodies.

Though treacherous activities never ceased, it was after dark when Gallatin Street took on an atmosphere which was at once both horribly menacing and yet somehow festive. Even now, Charity could hear the upbeat piano music drifting up from downstairs in her own "house." It was a mockery, an obscenity really. It was meant to boost a party atmosphere in the bars and parlors below, as if going upstairs with a girl was just a natural extension of the fun.

There was nothing natural about it, nor fun. She heard the usual drunken laughter, glass breaking, thuds of violence. Sometimes there would be a scream. Sometimes she expected it to be hers.

She pulled the loose red dressing gown more tightly around her. She thought it might be about time for Christmas to come, though the day meant nothing to her. She had lost all track of days and weeks, of months and years. There was only this room and what she could see from the small iron balcony.

But each time she stood here, she thought about how everything she saw might somehow prove useful. She stared into the night for a long time. It would happen soon. It had to.

She caught a glimpse of herself as she walked past the broken mirror. One side of her head looked just fine. Men had always told her she was beautiful, with her thick dark hair, exotic eyes, and a mouth they called "sensuous."

Most of them were not interested in her face for long after they got down to business. Afterwards, some of them left a reminder on that face, as if marking their territory. She turned toward the other side of her face and saw this newest set of bruises already rising. She felt her eye swelling, and still tasted blood in her mouth.

And there he was. Sprawled on the bed, snoring, whiskey bottle on the floor.

She knew the house rules, that she should be getting him up, moving him out, making room for the next unless this one paid for another round. Instead, she stood and stared at this lout, wondering how God could have made such beasts who claimed to be in His image.

For warmth, she reached for the black shawl hidden under the bed. There were no closets in these rooms, no need for them, as Madame had snorted. If Charity kept the shawl in plain sight, one of the other girls would snatch it and fight her to keep it. It was the finest thing Charity Boudry had, but she could not remember where it came from. A girl who died maybe. But no name came to mind. Which was far better. You could never keep track of all the girls who'd come along and inevitably disappeared. This was no place for friendship.

It would only make you sad to think about all who had come and gone, and sadness got you nowhere. It was also a whole lot better not to think about the daily facts of life – the drink and drugs, the stabbings, beatings, and killings, and always that most intimate of brutalities.

Charity was just about the only girl she knew, among all those who had come and gone, who didn't drink. And she especially dodged the drugs that most thought would make their hideous lives more bearable.

She didn't begrudge it to those who did. Whatever got you through one more day and one more night. But for herself, she didn't see the profit in it. For one thing, it cost in more ways than one. The girls had to buy their whisky or absinthe or laudanum from Madame, who kept it conveniently handy for impulse sales.

Cocaine, laudanum, marihuana, hashish, morphine or opium were easy to get. In fact, most of the house owners encouraged their girls to indulge. The girls' near-constant stupor made them easier to control, and their dependence on the drugs made them loyal. There were financial benefits to the house as well. The girls would have to really hustle for clients and work hour after hour to feed their habit, while the house raked in the customers' cash.

Charity had already seen the ravages of drink, even back before her drunkard of a father sold her as a child, sold her into the depths of hell. She and her two older sisters, ironically called Faith and Hope, found early in life that their names belied their grim existence. They cowered wherever they could find shelter after Pa had beaten their mother into unconsciousness, and then came after them.

One day their mother never woke up at all. Their father dumped *Maman*'s body unceremoniously into a pirogue and set off across the swamp. One of her sisters had courageously asked where he was taking her. He said it was to the doctor, before slapping the girl for not minding her own business. *Maman* had never come back. Though Charity was the youngest, she had no illusions as to whether her mother had ever reached the other side of the swamp.

With no mother to soften the blows, life around the Boudry shack became unspeakable. Her older sisters were always bruised, always bandaged, always limping or clutching an arm in a makeshift sling. They were all malnourished, though there always seemed to be enough money for drink. To make sure they would "stay put," their father would sometimes tie them to chairs while he went to the nearest town, to indulge in whatever the town could offer.

Charity sometimes allowed herself to think that he loved her best. That was why he rarely beat her, she thought. Well, at least not in ways that were too obvious. And he did not come after her in the dark, as he did to her sisters. He said he had to keep the goods intact, whatever that meant. He always told her how beautiful she was, how men would always want her. As a child, she was not quite sure what that was all about, but if it had to do with being liked and somehow getting away from that shack, it was fine with her.

One day, when he was out fishing, her older sisters gave her some berries covered with sugar. "It's your birthday, *chérie*," they'd said.

"Nothing here to make a cake with, but it's your twelfth birthday and it needs to be marked."

Soon after that, Pa took her into town. He gave her to a man in exchange for some money. The man brought the terrified girl here to Madame's. She never saw her sisters again.

And so this was where she'd been until this moment. They'd taught her the trade that would become her life. It was probably four years now, maybe almost five. Her father had been right, men always did want her, wanted to use her. To her mind, all of them looked just like him. And she wanted to kill them all.

That was why she'd avoided drink and drugs. It was the one part of herself that she felt was her own. It was the one thing she could control. But she knew things were about to change. This meant she could no longer allow herself the luxury of planning. She had to act, and act quickly.

Most girls in her situation lived only about four years after getting into the life. For some, the end came from being eaten up by disease. Some died in childbirth or bled out after a miscarriage or ghastly medical procedure. For some, it was an overdose that everyone called accidental.

Charity knew there were no accidents in this life. Those girls either took their own life to end the misery, or their lives were taken from them. Customers wanted girls who were young and fresh. The ones who reached Charity's age were put out on the street to fend for themselves, a futile effort that didn't last very long before they were dead. Or they were taken to The Cellar.

The cellar in this house had a side door. That was where the garbage was hauled out to the alley, and where the lowest forms of human life slithered in. Girls who had grown too old or used-up were locked down there to be finished off by the men who were too poor, too diseased, too depraved to be allowed upstairs but who would still pay for their "recreation."

Charity had never known a girl to come back up from The Cellar. The threat of being sent down there was used to keep the girls in line. While they lived in Hell, they were never allowed to forget that there was an even lower depth.

That was why Charity made sure she did what she was told, caused no trouble, and tried to be polite and cheerful around Madame. But she sensed it was all about to change.

"You're a good girl, Charity," Madame had said a week or so ago. "You've kept your looks and you've kept clean. The clients like you. You've been good for business."

"*Merci, Madame,*" Charity had replied while her mind raced. She had an idea of what was coming.

"Soon you will be old enough to strike out on your own."

"Perhaps I could stay here a while longer, Madame. I could be a helper to you." Time, time – Charity needed more time.

"*Tu es trés gentille,* child," said the old woman. "That is kind, but the owners of the house would not permit."

"*Oui, Madame.*" Charity loved speaking French, even Cajun French, with the old hag. She felt it set her apart, especially from the immigrant girls who could barely speak English. Right now she would need every bit of Madame's good will.

"Do you know when I might be leaving, Madame?"

"Soon, *ma chérie.*"

"May I beg a favor, Madame?"

Silence. The old witch didn't like being asked for anything.

"It is only ... you see, Madame, sometimes I have trouble sleeping. I wondered if you knew of something ... *je ne sais pas.*" Don't be too direct, let Madame rise to the occasion, let it be her idea.

Now, at last, Madame chose to respond. "So, a sleeping draft might be helpful, *ma chérie*?"

Laudanum, you old witch, thought Charity. You know what I mean. Laudanum, and plenty of it. But what Charity said was, "*S'il vous plait, Madame.* It would be a great help."

"How much will you want? If, of course, it could be arranged."

"I do not wish to trouble you, Madame. Perhaps enough to keep from having to be a bother too often." Charity wanted a lot of it, all at one time. This was crucial.

"You know, *ma chérie*, it is expensive to come by. You'd have to work harder to pay for it."

No, it wasn't expensive. Not for the owners to buy. Just for the girls to pay for. "*Je comprends, Madame.* I understand and will do what is necessary to repay your kindness. *Merci, Madame.*"

"Now, back to work."

"*Oui, Madame.*"

A day later, Madame gave her six vials of laudanum. Charity was suddenly terrified that Madame would want to watch her take it. "Madame, if I could also trouble you to buy a bottle of brandy, I will take it in my room and keep it safe." Of course, no place was safe in this house.

Suspicion in Madame's eyes? "This has been a costly purchase for you, Charity." No more '*ma chérie*' now. "You must work very, very hard to repay me. No sleeping when you should be working!"

"*Bien sûr, Madame. Merci beaucoup.*"

Of course Madame sold her the brandy. The old woman saw it as one more addiction, costly to the buyer. Charity took it to her room, placing the bottle on a small table. After putting one vial of the laudanum aside, Charity kept the remaining vials in her black shawl under the bed. Someone would eventually steal them, *bien s r*, so the time had to be soon. She had no idea exactly when, but she knew she had to be ready.

Charity was determined they'd not send her to The Cellar to drain the last bit of life from her. They'd not put her dead body out with the trash to be dumped in the big river. She would go up! She would soar! Even if she crashed, for those brief moments she'd be close to Heaven.

Like everyone else in the city, Charity knew there was a war going on, and that New Orleans was a glittering prize. After all, the side that controlled New Orleans controlled the Mississippi River.

She had heard the men talking in the parlor. Those arm-chair warriors ridiculed Southern strategists for assuming a Union attack would come down the Mississippi, not up from the Gulf of Mexico. The Confederates had concentrated their forces far north of New Orleans to stop federal gunboats coming down from Memphis. They left a small militia, two warships that had yet to be completed, and a few steamboats to defend the treasure that was New Orleans.

In late April of 1862, the Union attack had indeed come from the Gulf and easily vanquished the ragtag defenders of the city. To avoid the bombardment of the civilian population, Confederate troops were pulled out of New Orleans and the Yankees moved in. On April 29, 1862, Confederate flags in New Orleans were lowered, replaced by the stars and stripes of the Union.

Like New Yorkers, the merchants of New Orleans were practical people. The Union offered safe passage behind Confederate lines for those who wished to leave their occupied city. Many did. Those remaining were compelled to take an oath of loyalty to the Union. By early 1863, two-thirds of the city's population had done so.

The Confederacy had lost the city many called its crown jewel. The Mississippi River belonged to the Union all the way up past Vicksburg.

That night on Gallatin Street, it was business as usual. But that same night, Vicksburg was very much on one man's mind.

Alpha was on the move.

Between the artistry of Confederate forgers and Alpha's own skill at allaying suspicions, he had made it out of Detroit and on down the Mississippi River. He knew federal authorities had mounted a manhunt for the perpetrators of the attacks on New York, but that had been a few weeks ago. He assumed at some point they'd find other things to occupy their time.

Now that he was on a riverboat headed south, he allowed himself to relax just a bit. Though the river was in Union hands, just being in the South again would calm his soul. He felt it as soon as they passed Cape Girardeau.

Missouri was a bloody mess. Trying to remain neutral had only resulted in the state becoming a killing field for both sides. Just around the next bend, Alpha would be back in the Confederacy, with the great river bounded by Arkansas on one side and Tennessee on the other.

At Cape Girardeau, he went out on deck so he could watch as the South unfold before him. He almost smiled at the possibility of his being picked off by a sniper from the Missouri riverbank. That was an interesting idea – Confederate snipers firing at riverboats. They could create quite a turmoil on the Union-controlled river. He'd have to remember to bring it up with his superiors in Richmond.

Alpha stood on deck as they passed through the waters of Arkansas and Tennessee, and on into the state of Mississippi. Won't be long now, he thought. His destination was Vicksburg.

Poor, proud, brave little Vicksburg. The town had held out longer than New Orleans had done. Under siege by the Union, constantly bombarded, no food or water or medicines. His heart swelled with pride at the city's courage, especially its gallant ladies.

Alpha knew Abraham Lincoln himself had called Vicksburg the key to control of the Mississippi River. Lincoln had looked at a map and saw the hairpin turn at Vicksburg. With the town sitting high on bluffs above the river, shipping in both directions was exposed to artillery fire from the shore.

It took that monster Grant a while to do it, thought Alpha. But on July 4, 1863, to be exact, the victorious Union army marched into Vicksburg – after warring for months on women and children.

Yet, during the Union siege and bombardment of their town, the citizens of Vicksburg had hit upon a clever plan to survive. Men, women, and children took up shovels and dug caves into the hillsides.

They stayed there every night and most of the day. Alpha's favorite story about the "siege caves" was that some were furnished with items dragged from home.

And even with artillery shells bursting around them, the ladies of Vicksburg emerged to brave the streets so they could assist at hospitals. Even though they themselves were malnourished and dehydrated. Ah, he thought, our magnificent Southern women – those glorious ladies!

Alpha would be their champion. He would avenge their suffering and honor their sacrifice. Northern women would have to bear *their* share of the burden.

After he disembarked at Vicksburg, he went immediately to one of the siege caves where a pre-arranged meeting would take place. A remarkable new weapon had been devised by a former Vicksburg resident. Alpha was pleased that his new assignment would start here.

It was called a "coal torpedo" or simply "coal bomb." The small hollow casing was made to look like a simple lump of coal. Mix gunpowder inside, seal it, and toss it in with a coal shipment being loaded aboard Union boats. When the coal bomb was shoveled into the ship's firebox, it would explode. At the very least, it would disable the boat by bursting the boiler. At best, from Alpha's point of view, it would ignite the wooden vessel and kill as many Union men as possible in a blazing inferno.

Alpha wanted to take the war home to the North, planting the bombs on as many boats as he could, either military or commercial boats serving the military. The Confederate Congress had insisted that civilian ships would be off-limits.

That, Alpha felt, showed the humanity of the Confederacy. It was more than the Union deserved. But that restriction had come *before* Sherman's relentless advance through Georgia, *before* Sheridan's scorched-earth policy in Virginia, *before* the butchery of the North upon Southern civilians.

The well-educated Alpha knew the expression from the Latin: "*Extremis malis extrema remedia*" – or roughly, "Desperate times require desperate measures." The South was being bled dry by the superior manpower, matériel, and weaponry of the North. The South needed whatever weapons it could find. A new kind of warfare was called for. Surely the Confederate Congress could not fault him for seeing that.

Alpha met with his contact, a mild-looking older man, who took him deep into one of the siege caves. There, the man revealed the well-concealed hiding place of the hollow castings which looked like lumps of coal. The gunpowder was in a cave nearby. Alpha had specifically ordered that the castings remain empty and the gunpowder stored separately.

He alone would load the gunpowder and seal each coal bomb. Alpha trusted no one but himself. Recalling the double agent on the New York foray, he was not even pleased at involving this unknown contact who had been arranged by a third party. But Alpha needed the supplies, and the two men knew nothing of each other's identity. As soon as the old man was out of his sight, Alpha would begin moving the casings and gunpowder to other caves. If the contact was indeed a double agent, at least the authorities would have to work at finding his cache.

Vicksburg was a major port town, the perfect spot for his activities. And so very fitting after what the Yankees had done to it. It was Alpha's war now, and the fate of the Confederacy could well be in his hands.

CHAPTER 6
DECEMBER, 1864

This was the hour Moran liked best. Eating rations around the campfire, friendly conversation, everyone getting good and drowsy. Best of all, just enough light after sunset to figure out an escape route. When the time was right, he'd be gone. He'd had enough of Army life. They could brand him as a deserter, but they'd have to catch him first.

He was sick of being awakened at dawn. It was not like they'd be doing anything that required an early start. Drills in the morning, drills in the afternoon, day after day after day. They said it was practice for battle. Moran figured the key to battle was simply to shoot someone else before they shot you.

But the officers in charge kept saying each man had to know his place so's the troop could fight as a unit. Fighting collectively, forming a moving wall of men, advancing toward enemy rifles, and obeying commands without thinking – that was the officers' idea of victory.

As a little diversion between drills, there were chores. They had to clean up the camp and take turns cooking. They had to fix their uniforms and clean their equipment. At night, they'd have guard duty.

For some people's idea of real fun, lots of the fellas enjoyed singing songs around the campfire and writing letters home. All this, Moran felt, made for a long day.

And it was tiring. In his unit, each man on the march had to carry eight days' worth of rations, an extra shirt and drawers, some socks, and an overcoat. Then there was sixty rounds of ammunition, a rifle, wool blanket, rubber blanket mat, and shelter tent. Moran figured it weighed upwards of fifty pounds, probably more. On the march, hour after exhausting hour, it all had to be carried fifteen to twenty miles a day in every kind of weather. It became tiresome.

Well, all right, Army life had a few benefits, he had to admit. Supposed to be regular pay one of these days, whenever they got around to it. He'd never earned thirteen dollars a month in his whole life, so that suited him fine.

Regular meals was another. At first, they too had suited just fine.

It was almost a bounteous feast compared to what he was used to. So far, supplies had been right on time. There was a routine for divvying things up, coffee for example, and so far, Moran felt that the system was pretty fair.

After the supply wagons had been unloaded, the sergeant and corporal stood beside two army blankets laid out on the ground. On one there were several dozen carefully divided mounds of ground coffee. The other blanket held an equal number, this time piles of sugar.

Most soldiers agreed the most important part of their ration consisted of coffee and sweetener. Since there were no scales while they were on the march, the measurements couldn't be done precisely. Some might be a little bigger and some a little smaller, but as long as the piles looked reasonably the same, no one minded.

After creating the piles, one for each member of the unit, the corporal and the sergeant would turn away from the company. The sergeant held the muster roll, and with eyes closed, pointed at random to the men's names. The corporal would see who it was, call their name, and wait for each man to stake his claim until all the piles were gone. Moran's name had been called along with all the rest, so he had no dispute with the process.

The coffee was not only a way to stay warm and increase energy, it also made the rest of the rations edible. On the march, which it seemed to Moran was all the time, the men received salt pork and hardtack in addition to the coffee and sugar.

Moran had gone hungry many a time in his life, and if given the choice between hunger and hardtack, he might have a tough time making a choice. Hardtack was a kind of hard bread in three-inch squares. Government-contracted bakeries made millions at a time, using just flour, water, and salt. Moran had no idea what the stuff might have been like in its original form, maybe a kind of cracker which wouldn't have been bad. But by the time it reached the troops in the field, it was so hard that some of the men took their rifle butts to it just to break it into bite-size pieces. If a river was nearby, they tried mixing it with water to make a kind of mush. That wasn't the worst of it.

Sometimes, it arrived covered with mold or riddled with worms. On a long march, it could be the only available food. Its nickname of "worm castles" didn't add to the appeal. The best way of dealing with the wildlife was to drop it into hot coffee and skim off the worms when they floated to the surface. Some laughed and said it was their only source of fresh meat.

When the hardtack was edible, it could be used to make a sandwich with the salt pork, or if one of the fellas didn't mind coking it, made into a stew.

Things would be grim if it wasn't for the sutlers. Army rules allowed unit commanders to appoint a sutler to follow along as an authorized vendor. Moran thought that was the only reason soldiers didn't drop from scurvy before they ever came near a Rebel bullet. He hated the sutlers' high prices, but, oh the array of delights! Canned fruits and vegetables, pies and cakes, butter and tobacco!

The men could supplement their Army-issue with extra blankets or other items.

Moran still had his source of funding from Mr. Slick to finance his purchases from the sutler, but that was running low. Especially since he didn't have the luxury of the other soldiers' very favorite source of provisions: packages from home.

A guy named Deacon and him were the only ones in his outfit that didn't seem to have families or sweethearts who would send things from home. If the unit stopped a while, wagons would bring the marvelous gifts of food and provisions that made him think of pictures he'd seen of Christmas. At first the other fellas had laughed at him and Deacon, the two who never got anything. But soon the laugher died, probably turning into pity.

Moran didn't ask for pity. He didn't ask anything at all from the world, just to be let alone and maybe survive another day. Most of his life, he'd ranged the backwoods of Kentucky, Ohio, Indiana – he never quite knew where he was. He'd heard rivers marked state lines, but a river just meant one more problem, trying to find a way to cross. Other than that, state lines meant nothing to him.

He had the idea in his head that he'd been born in Kentucky. Well, that makes three of us, he sometimes thought. A man of action, as he saw himself, did not spend much time looking at newspapers, even if he could read. But honestly – you simply could not escape it! Everyone kept going on and on about how both Abraham Lincoln and Jefferson Davis were natives of Kentucky, one now the president of the U. S., and one the leader of the Confederacy.

For several years now, Moran held to a very logical theory that back in 1861, both of those men, representing the North and the South, should have been lowered into a pit. Each would be allowed the knife of his choice. The one who came out alive won the conflict.

Moran didn't much enjoy fighting. After his Mama died, there'd been enough of that in a one-room cabin with a Pa who'd start swinging when he got likkered up. Moran had tried to protect his sisters – they reminded him so much of Ma – but they had the good sense to run off and get married first chance they got. Moran struck out on his own after that.

He didn't mind having this new name of "Moran." In fact, he'd used several over the past few years, especially when he'd tried his hand at being a confidence man. Selling shares in a nonexistent gold mine out yonder in California appeared to be the easiest way a man could make a living. But somehow, there had been no takers.

He had embarked on that career after finding that being a farm laborer didn't pan out. He'd do the backbreaking work for weeks or months at a time, and then end up not being paid a dime. The landowner would just say his wages were being withheld for "room and board," though that might be a stall in the barn and whatever root vegetables he could find to choke down.

So a life of petty crime seemed the only way for someone with no particular skills. He was tired of being cheated, so maybe he'd see what it felt like to actually *be* the cheater for a change. But his life of crime never quite seemed to pay off. He'd rob a cash drawer right after the store owner had taken the money to the bank that afternoon. He'd steal a payroll strong box only to find that Payday had been the day before, leaving it empty. Becoming a professional gambler had left him high and dry. His luck would run hot, and then inexplicably would change. Trying his hand at being a pickpocket had almost got him shot.

Sometimes he started to suspect that when it came to a life of crime, he just wasn't very good at it. But it wasn't his fault! Even the dad-blamed horse, back during the bank bag robbery that had got him into this mess, had just stood there after being swatted. Moran had known some horses who'd bolt if you even looked at them funny. But no, not this one. Just stood there. That was an excellent example of just the kind of thing he meant. And that horse had directly been the cause of him now wearing a blue uniform under the name of Moran.

Army life wasn't as bad as he'd feared, but he'd just about had his fill. No one knew exactly where they were, Tennessee maybe. He'd bet there'd be a way to profit if he acted quick. It was almost 1865. The war couldn't last forever. If he ran out of his gold pieces from Slick, he'd have nothing left to start out with. If they were in Tennessee, he could follow the sunset west to the Mississippi. Surely, on the great river, there would be something for him.

Moran moved quietly to the bushes as if to answer Nature's call. That was one good thing. Modesty prevailed, and men were allowed to go singly to a private spot for relief. He'd even heard there was a kind of unwritten rule that both sides observed, North and South, even whilst they were slaughtering each other on every other occasion. He'd heard it said that no enemy soldier would shoot a man with his pants down. There was some dignity to that. Moran approved.

He also approved of the privacy it allowed. He crouched down, waiting for the sentry to pass, to see what kind of time and distance might be involved in an escape plan. He must not get caught. The penalty for desertion was death, though he did not fear that very much. It was said if they shot every deserter in both armies, North and South, they'd have no one left to fight the war. That'd show 'em, thought Moran. Let the politicians fight their own war.

Probably to avoid having the war fought by politicians, the firing squad was rarely used. Instead, they branded captured deserters with the letter "D." The poor man, or rather a scared young boy in all actuality, would carry it with him all his life. Moran would just have to be careful.

Just when that thought had formed itself in his mind, Moran was startled by the sergeant. Could the man read his mind?

"What you doin' out in these woods, Moran?"

"Just what a man usually does in the woods, Sarge."

"Do your business and get back to camp. Rumor is there's Rebels in this area. In fact, I want to double up the guard. For once, you're in the right place at the right time."

Moran had carried his rifle with him in anticipation of an escape, so at least the sergeant couldn't fault him for negligence on that score. But he doubted he'd be doing guard duty for long. The sergeant was walking behind him. Once the man turned back to camp ...

That was when Moran saw one of the men slumped against a tree, appearing to be asleep. Their sentry? At first Moran was indignant, thinking they could be overrun by the enemy. But the penalty for sleeping on guard duty was horrible. That was what he didn't like about the Army, treating its own soldiers so bad. He stopped so short the sergeant ran into him. Stumbling, pointing with his rifle in the opposite direction, back toward camp, he hollered, "Sarge! Over there! What's that?"

The sergeant looked in the opposite direction, just as he was supposed to. "Shut up, Moran! What do you see?"

"Well, if I was to shut up, Sarge, how am I supposed to tell you what I saw?"

As intended, the ruckus aroused the sleeping guard. "Halt! Who goes there?"

"You see anything out here, Deacon? Moran thinks something could be out here."

"No, Sergeant. Nothing."

"Well, keep your eyes open, Deacon. Private Moran here is going you help you walk the perimeter."

As soon as the sergeant started back toward camp, Moran was startled when the other man shook his hand like it was a well pump.

"Thank you, my friend. Moran, isn't it? I'm John Deacon. Thank you for rousing me. I swear I just closed my eyes for a minute, couldn't've been more than a minute. I swear!"

"Well, my advice would be to make sure you don't do it again. Army's kind of strict about that."

"I know. Believe me, I know. And I understand the reason. But marching all day, and no sleep at night ... Well, I'm just sorry." He started back walking the guard. Moran joined in.

"So, Brother Deacon, got any tobacco on you?"

"We allowed to smoke on guard duty?"

"You see anyone here to stop us?"

"Mightn't the enemy see the flare? Well, anyway, I don't have any tobacco on me."

They resumed their march in silence.

"You limpin,' Brother Deacon?"

"It's these army boots. When we started marching, after about thirty miles or so, they cut into my feet, got all blistered real bad. Can't hardly walk now."

"Blisters get infected, you'll have a problem."

Deacon laughed, "I think I'm scared of that more than being in battle."

"Scared, whyever for?" Moran asked sarcastically. "You'd get the best medical care the United States Army can provide. In other words, you'll be lucky if they pour a shot of whiskey down your throat before they start cutting off your leg."

"Thanks Moran, you're a morale-booster. Anyway, the sergeant has my boots, I saw them on his feet. Keep hopin' to somehow get them back."

"Well, there's always the possibility he'll get in the way of a Rebel bullet."

Deacon started to laugh, then felt bad about it. He'd never wished another man dead before, and didn't intend to start now. Even Ella's husband, though he wouldn't be sorry if it happened. Not in the least.

The two men walked a while.

"So, Moran, where you from?"

"This an Ohio unit, ain't it?"

"Well, I mean where in Ohio?"

"You do ask a lot of questions."

"Didn't mean to pry. Used to be a newspaperman. That's what we do – ask questions."

"Well, listen Deacon. I might need a favor from you."

"Sure, what do you need?"

"Need you to keep others from askin' questions. Might need you to forget we ever spoke. Might need you to be real convincing pointing folks in some other direction. Fact is, friend, if I turn up missing here in a little bit, I'd mightily appreciate your forgettin' we ever met."

"You mean – deserting?!" Deacon struggled to keep his voice down, but in truth he was appalled.

"I'd prefer not to use that particular word. I'm thinking more of an unscheduled furlough. Ain't meant to be here anyway. Wasn't supposed to get this far. Besides, I don't like the idea of fightin' our own people, Americans-like."

Deacon was shocked. "You a see-cesh?" He couldn't believe his new friend could be a secessionist, a supporter of the Confederacy.

"Not hardly. Don't care if the South stays or goes. I just want to be let alone."

Moran marched off to walk his post farther away, signaling that the conversation was over. It didn't pay to get too close to folks. He didn't really think this Deacon fella would turn him in, but you just never knew about people.

"Hey, Moran?"

Was this guy Deacon going to keep bothering him? Moran needed time to think out his plan. None too enthusiastically, he said "Yeah?"

"Thanks for what you did before."

Moran stopped, sighing. In his pocket he still carried the cloth napkin he'd taken with him from the tavern, that day with Mr. Slick.

Ever since, he'd kind of felt bad, hoping the girl called Maynette wouldn't get in trouble when it turned up missing. He bit into it with his teeth and tore off about a third which he put in his pocket. He threw the remaining two-thirds to Deacon. "Listen," he said, "tear this up and use it to bind up the blisters."

"Moran?"

"Yeah?"

"Thanks."

Deacon didn't want to risk the sergeant catching him sitting down while on his post, so he waited until someone came to relieve him from duty near dawn. Back in camp, he fell exhausted on his blanket. He removed the bloody army boots and tore the linen into strips, wrapping them like bandages. He thought they helped.

That fella Moran was thoughtful to do that. Deacon got along well with the other men in his outfit, but no one he was really close to. The other men all had families or sweethearts, insisting on talking about them, showing the daguerreotypes they carried close to their heart. Deacon smiled through it and said all the right words, but sometimes thought he'd scream if he had to look at one more picture of a sweetheart, a wife, a baby.

Might be nice to have a fella to talk to, someone who seemed to be just like himself, someone who never got provisions from home. But what Moran had said troubled him. Deserting! No, Deacon couldn't hold with that. Might be some distance would be the best thing.

He pulled his blanket tighter and hoped for an hour or two of sleep. Meanwhile, in these blessedly quiet moments, he'd think of Ella.

CHAPTER 7
DECEMBER, 1864

At that very moment, as he thought of her, Ella Ardent was thinking of John Deacon. She was wrapped up in her mother's quilt, resting in the back of the wagon. It would be dawn in a little while, and she'd need to be on her way as soon as the sun rose so she could see where she was going. She'd have to keep her wits about her then, alert every minute, and not let other thoughts intrude.

But for these last few moments, she allowed herself to think of him. Whenever she did, her thoughts became scattered. The pleasure of the past, of their childhood friendship that grew into something so much deeper. The way she had felt in his arms, their secret summer world atop a blanket at sunset, thinking – no, *believing* – life would always be just as fine as long as they were together. He made her believe the world held such promise for those willing to work at it.

Those stolen summer moments were rare. Johnny was always working, clawing for every penny he could earn, any way he could do it. Her father, Owen McAdams, had worked him hard, but Johnny never shirked. When chores were over, John had hired himself out to neighboring farms if there were any daylight hours left. Then, he walked to town at night. There, he would compose letters for people who couldn't write, and they happily paid him.

Sometimes he was quietly hired to teach reading and writing. His students were usually grown men who were too ashamed to venture near the children's schoolhouse. At first he declined to be paid for his services, thinking that he was doing God's work in bringing those noble souls the gift of reading. The men were usually embarrassed at not being able to 'cipher. Most had been put to work on the family farm as soon as they could walk, with no time for frills like education. Most of them said they were only giving it a try to please their wives. But they themselves saw no need for it, they claimed. Already knew all they needed to know for farm work.

But soon random scrawl revealed itself as letters, letters became words, words became sentences. When the moment came that they could read a Bible passage to their wives, their simple pride almost brought Deacon to the same joyous tears the womenfolk openly shed.

When work was done on the McAdams farm and they could escape her father's watchful eye, Deacon sometimes took Ella with him on what he called "the circuit." On horseback, he would travel the countryside, knocking at doors both in town and on the farms, homes of people he knew and those he didn't, asking if the householder had any books he could borrow.

Everything John Deacon knew, he'd mostly taught himself. When his parents had died, he no longer had the luxury of going to school. That was when he hired out to the McAdams farm.

At night, Ella could see dim lamplight in the barn loft where Johnny slept. The light had to be faint lest her father spot the illicit glow. She knew her father was terrified of the lamp setting the barn on fire. But she also understood Johnny's unquenchable thirst for the knowledge he'd need to better himself.

Even more than the forbidden lamp, that quest for knowledge had enraged her father.

Owen McAdams was not a cruel man. Far from it. In fact, Owen McAdams and John Deacon had a lot in common. In another time or place, they might have been great friends or loving family. Like Deacon, Owen McAdams had been orphaned at a young age. Between famine, disease, and religious warfare, almost all families in the north of Ireland had lost someone they mourned.

With the help of a few cousins and friends, Owen McAdams found passage in the hold of a ship bound for America. All he took with him were the effects of malnutrition and cholera that would ravage his body until the end of his days. But he bore up, joining others of his kind bound for the frontier of Ohio. There, he worked like a banshee, determined that someday he would be the owner of his own land and be dependent on no man.

He took a good Irish Colleen as his wife, and when their child was born, they named her Ella after his dead mother and Rose after hers. When he was finally able to buy a piece of land, he built his farm and provided for his family. He feared neither landlord nor any other man. When it became clear Ella would be their only child, he saw the arrival of the orphaned Johnny Deacon as a gift from God. That boy, he felt sure, would be a good husband for Ella and the salvation of the McAdams farm.

That was at first. The Deacon boy worked, no doubt about that. But then, after a time, when the boy spoke, it was like a slap in the face of Owen McAdams.

"Farmers are the world's biggest gamblers," the boy had declared. "All year, every year, it's always too hot or too cold or too wet or too dry. Even in a perfect growing year, even without some kind of blight or plague of insects, a farmer is always bound to the marketplace. That's what sets the price of their crops, the farmer has no control. Why, some years, a farmer might not even make back the cost of putting seed in the ground."

All it was good for, Deacon had proclaimed, was the bare subsistence of your family. A farmer was a slave to the soil.

Owen McAdams had to restrain himself from striking the boy. Deacon's words were the vilest insult to everything Ella's father had worked for. Why, Owen McAdams was considered quite a success back home in Ireland. A man from their very village who owned his own land! The Deacon boy cut down everything Owen McAdams held dear.

And McAdams was no fool. He saw the way the boy looked at his daughter Ella, and how Ella looked back. If the boy had kept a civil tongue in his head, had kept his insulting ideas to himself, Owen McAdams would have been proud to welcome John Deacon as a son. That way, they'd keep the farmland in the family. Because Owen McAdams had a secret. He kept it to himself, but he knew his body was failing.

The years of backbreaking work on a body that had been ravaged while young had taken its toll. Owen McAdams knew he didn't have long to put his affairs in order, to provide for his soon-to-be-widow and only child.

Enter William Ardent.

Ardent's property adjoined McAdams'own. In some ways, Ardent reminded McAdams of the English landlords back home – arrogant, haughty, overbearing. But he presented those traits to Ella quite differently.

"Sturdy, a man of distinction, my girl," McAdams had told his daughter. "Good qualities in a future provider. You're of an age to be thinking of it now. Think of it, Ella dear. Combining his lands with ours, why you'd be mistress of a fine big estate."

Ella's mother agreed. She was fearful of her husband's health, though she kept it to herself. She knew William Ardent was keen to take her daughter, but was of two minds. The man was closer to her husband's age than her daughter's. And though Ardent was unfailingly polite, she sensed something beneath the surface.

There was talk at church that he drank. There was gossip that he visited girls in the next town, girls of loose morals. There were whispers that a previous wife had simply vanished. Some put forward the theory that he had worked the woman too hard and she ran away. Others had a darker interpretation that involved the woman displeasing him once too often, and what just might be buried beneath a desolate patch on his land.

Ella's mother shared none of that with her husband and simply prayed things would work out for the best. To Owen McAdams, that day came in 1860 when Deacon opened his little newspaper, moved to town, and collected enough money to go East for printing presses. Before he left, Deacon had stopped by the McAdams farm. Ella's father knew what was coming.

Sure enough, the boy took Owen McAdams aside and announced his intention of asking for Ella's hand when he returned.

"I have nothing to offer her now, sir. But when the newspaper gets up and running, Ella can be a proper town lady. The newspaper will be a success, sir, I know it will. Everyone needs to know what's going on in our country. Every day, something new – something important! New territories, referendums on extending slavery, the compromises in Congress – why, there's history being made every day!"

Owen McAdams continued his policy of saying nothing, as if thinking deeply about the boy's high-flung ideas.

"Everyone says there's a war coming, sir. I can protect her in town. Not out on some isolated farm."

Keep talking, boy, thought McAdams. *This so-called isolated farm you think so little of is her legacy. This land belongs to her family, she's a part of it. She'll never turn her back on this land or her people. You'll never take her.*

But what he said was, "Well, Johnny, sounds like you've got some big plans. We'll be thinkin' of you on your journey."

"I'll write as often as I can, sir! Every day!"

Do that, boy, the older man thought. *You just do that.*

Owen McAdams destroyed every one of Deacon's letters when they arrived, and did it without a moment's regret. He loved his beautiful daughter, he wanted the best for her, and this was best. William Ardent came around more often, especially after McAdams took to his bed, never to rise from it again.

McAdams spoke quietly with Ella in the evenings when she came to sit by his bedside. He never pushed, just spoke quietly of his wretched life back in Ireland, the cruelties of the landlords, how families could be put out at any moment, what it meant to him to own his own land here in America. He took her hand, said how much he loved her and how he wanted her future to be a happy one with a man she could depend on. It came from his heart.

With no word arriving from Deacon, he knew she feared the boy had abandoned her, though she never mentioned it. When William Ardent came to his room to "ask his blessing," McAdams almost laughed out loud. He knew Ardent would do what he wanted and that the man had already told Ella that he, William Ardent, was the anointed one.

A week later, in the back room where her father struggled sit up in bed, Ella McAdams married William Ardent. A week after that, her father died.

She never knew how Deacon heard about the marriage when he finally returned to Ohio. Someone in town, no doubt. Whether he was angry, hurt, or some combination of the two, he never spoke to her, just nodded politely after church.

Ardent seemed to sense something between them, the way a reptile senses an intruder into its territory. The beatings became more pronounced when they got home after those encounters. She stopped going to church or anywhere else her path might cross Deacon's.

Those were also the times when Ardent made a special point of claiming her as his own. Most of the time she could beg off from his touch with excuses like an aching head, excuses that even she knew were stretching thin. But on those occasions when they'd come across Deacon, no excuse would suffice.

She had so hoped Ardent would allow her mother to come live with them, but he would have none of it. After her father's passing, Ella could see the woman growing more and more frail before her eyes. Ardent brought in a crew of hired hands to work the McAdams farm, now part of his land, but they never checked on the old woman.

One day when Ella begged to visit, she found the body.

When the war came in 1861, Ella did not try to talk her husband out of enlisting. She had to admit he looked dashing in the officer's uniform she had sewn for him. She had the uncomfortable image of a piece of fruit, shiny on the outside but rotten within.

After he left, Ardent wrote letters to her demanding that she send food and other items, which she did. She wrote back dutifully, chatty letters that didn't say much.

One thing she never mentioned was that old man Odom had revealed how far in debt they were to his store. IOU's signed by her husband went back to before the war. She knew Odom sold whiskey from the back room, which she heard also housed a regular card game. She wondered if that had anything to do with the "political meetings" which had suddenly taken up so much of her husband's time.

Then William's letters stopped coming. She went to church one night and by candlelight, prayed God to forgive her for the wicked thought that had crossed her mind.

Then one day, a message came in a strange hand. It was sent from a military hospital in Vicksburg, Mississippi. It said simply that Captain Ardent required her to bring a wagon to take him home. So that was what she would do. Disobeying William's wishes carried serious consequences.

The first part of Ella's journey went as planned. Early in the war, John Deacon had printed stories of the brave wives, daughters, and sisters who brought the bodies of soldiers home for proper burial. It was unconscionable that their loved one should lie beneath unmarked earth far from home.

Perhaps that was it – perhaps the doctors knew Ardent was dying and alerted her to start out on her trip. She knew that military hospitals, especially after several years of the brutal war, were bursting at the seams. Perhaps they were happy to let family members come and take patients home to care for them, or to bury them if they were beyond care.

Ella studied whatever maps she could find to determine her route. She knew if she headed south and west, sooner or later she'd come to the Mississippi River, and that led to Vicksburg. She had only a horse and wagon which would have to go where roads were blocked or nonexistent. And of course there was the matter of the war. At a moment's notice, any pleasant meadow might turn into a battlefield.

The shortest route looked to be dropping down from Ohio into Kentucky and heading west toward the river. Kentucky was one of the Border States, remarkable for being a slave state but remaining in the Union. Deacon had written an editorial pointing out that both Abraham Lincoln and Jefferson Davis were natives of Kentucky, which underscored its dual nature.

When the secession vote came, the Kentucky legislature voted to remain neutral. Kentuckians who supported the South were furious. Many joined the Confederate army. Ella wasn't worried about them. It was the bushwhackers that were a constant threat.

In border states like Kentucky and Missouri, roving bands of outlaws saw the states' neutrality as open season for villainy. With no particular loyalty to either side, they looted supply depots, stores, farms and homes. They burned bridges to aid their escape, created road hazards, and killed with abandon.

Another problem was that a traveler like Ella would never know where she could safely spend the night. In isolated areas, travelers might knock on the door of a farmhouse to be questioned about which side they were on. The wrong answer at that particular house would mean a slamming door.

Ella hoped that being a woman might keep doors from slamming in her face, but her gender could also be a severe drawback. She was a target.

Her trip was taking even longer than she'd feared. Deacon's newspaper had printed a story about Eliza Johnson, the sickly wife of Andrew Johnson, military governor of Tennessee. That state was in turmoil. Though a Confederate state, some parts of Tennessee were in Union hands, which was why Johnson had been appointed governor by Abraham Lincoln, not Jefferson Davis.

From the Union-held state capital of Nashville, Andrew Johnson made speeches that were, in Ella's opinion, unwise. Johnson's family was still in Confederate-held East Tennessee, and Johnson publicly denounced threats against them by Southern forces. The response came in 1862, when the bedridden Eliza Johnson and her family in East Tennessee were given thirty-six hours to leave the region.

The journey to Nashville was arduous at best. They had to acquire travel permits to cross both Union and Confederate lines, encountering menace from both sides. They often had to take long detours over dangerous dirt roads to avoid hostile situations. They had to seek shelter nightly at unfriendly homesteads. In Murfreesboro, they were detained by authorities and forbidden to leave. The family had to go door-to-door in foul weather begging shelter from hostile strangers. No one would take them in from the rain.

Deacon's story told how they spent the night in an abandoned shed with no food. When they were finally allowed to leave town, their carriage was attacked by a violent mob that threatened to kill them. When Eliza Johnson and her family finally made it to the middle of the state and arrived in Nashville, it had taken more than a month to get there from East Tennessee.

Ella was going a much farther distance than poor Mrs. Johnson, and it was taking much longer. Most of the time, she wasn't sure where she was. Sometimes she heard gunfire in the distance, and would detour over to find another route. She had evaded roadblocks so far, but her luck couldn't last much longer. Her food was running low, and her horse was wearing out.

This night, she saw a farmhouse but didn't dare knock at the door. Anyone could attack her, or at least commandeer the horse and wagon. Weak from hunger and freezing from the cold, she decided to take her chances by slipping into the barn unseen.

She quietly opened the barn door. Empty. No dog to sound the alarm. On the side of the barn unseen from the farmhouse, she unhitched the horse from the wagon and led him inside.

She stroked his mane. "You're a good old fella, aren't you? I'm sorry to drive you so hard. But we've got to get where we're going. Won't be too many chances like this. Get some rest."

She filled a bucket with water from the trough and brought over some hay which the animal devoured. Wrapped in her shawl and her mother's quilt, she made a bed for herself in the straw, covering up as best she could in the sweet-smelling hay. For a pillow, she used her small bag. Hugging it, she smiled.

She'd never forget the moment she found the money which Deacon had concealed there. She knew it was him, the exact amount he'd gotten for selling the newspaper office. And she'd certainly needed it along the way, for food and a new shoe for the horse and the luxury of staying inside one night at an inn when the temperatures at night dropped well below freezing.

She clutched the bag and thought of John Deacon. That was when the heard the riders.

She prayed the horse would keep quiet. Whoever it was would want the animal. She peered through a broken slat on the side of the barn. About a half-dozen men in civilian clothes thundered to a halt in front of the farmhouse.

She watched in horror as they burst in to the cabin, then came out again dragging an old man out of the house.

"Your money! Give us your money!"

Bushwhackers.

Even from where she watched, she could hear the terror in the old man's voice.

"Ain't got none. Don't have nothin.' All I had is what I grew to survive, then the Army took all that. First one, then the other. They took it all!"

"I bet you got money, old man. Where you got it hid?!"

"Ain't got no money!"

"String him up, boys. We'll loosen his tongue."

"No! I swear!"

The outlaws held the old man, took a rope and fashioned a noose. They threw one end over a tree limb, tying the other to a saddle horn. To Ella's horror, she watched as they put the noose around the old man's neck and led the horse backward, hoisting the man off the ground. The old man thrashed as the outlaws continued their demand for money. Suddenly the old man stopped moving.

The leader of the outlaws shouted, "Let him down! Bring him to!"

They brought the horse forward, laid the old man on the ground, and slapped him until he regained consciousness, gasping for air. Their leader stood over him.

"You want more?"

The old man choked out the words. "No! Please!"

"Where's your money? Where you got it hid?"

"Ain't got none! I swear!"

To the gang members, the leader shouted, "Again!"

Ella had no weapon other than a small knife in her bag. Could she hold them off with that? She tried desperately to think of something to do. She watched horrified as the gang repeated the horrendous process of hanging him, reviving him, and demanding money. After the third time, the old man's body hung from the rope lifeless.

One of the gang members chuckled. "Guess he really didn't have nothin'."

The leader yelled, "Check the house! You two, look in the barn!"

As the bandits approached the barn, Ella desperately sought an escape. Grabbing her quilt and bag, she had just enough time to kick through two slats from the back of the barn before she heard the wooden barn door thud open. She crouched down, slithered through the narrow opening, and ran for her life into the nearby woods.

She heard whooping and hollering, knew their eyes would be on the prize – a horse! Her horse. Her only friend since she started this journey. But she knew they'd treat him well. Horses nowadays were to be treasured.

"Look in the side yard – maybe there's another nag," she heard one of them yell. This was followed soon by louder whoops and shouts. They'd found the wagon with the last of her food.

When their leader ran over to see what the ruckus was about, he spotted their prize. "Knew that old man was lyin'! Leave him hanging. He's an example now for anyone else who tries to hold out. Hitch up the horse. We'll take the wagon. Fill it with as much hay as it'll hold. Then put a torch to this barn! And burn the house!"

Running back to the house, the outlaws unwound the rope from the saddle horn and tied it to the tree, leaving the old man hanging. The ancient dry wood of the barn burst into flames. Then they set fire to the small cabin. Ella prayed they wouldn't stay a while to revel in their vicious handiwork and find her crouching in the woods.

Soon, they mounted up and rode away, hollering in triumph. When she was sure they were gone, Ella emerged from the woods and ran to the tree. She used the small knife from her bag to cut the old man down. She tried everything she could think of to revive him, slapping his face as she'd seen those monsters do. But his life was gone.

She tried desperately not to think about the part she might have played in his death. Surely they'd have killed him even if he'd known she was there with the horse, even if he'd revealed it. At least he never had to make the choice, his life or hers. She believed those devils would have killed him anyway.

"Our Father which art in Heaven ..." Were those the words to say over the dead? She couldn't remember what they'd mumbled at her father's grave. So she improvised.

"Mister, I'm sorry I don't even know your name. I'm sorry if I played any part in your death. The shelter you gave me for a little while, even without you knowing I was there, meant more to me than I can say. I'm sorry there is evil in the world. If you believe in Heaven, maybe you're on the way there now, to be with those you loved and lost. I'm sorry you died alone. Maybe your spirit can see that I'm here with you now, someone who cares about you. And don't worry, I won't let your body just lay here for the animals to find."

The December soil was too hard to dig a grave, even if she'd had a shovel. The barn was completely engulfed in flames, so there'd be no help there. She remembered the stories Johnny had shared, about the ancient Greeks and their funeral blaze of glory.

She dragged the old man's body toward the house. The porch had not yet been consumed in flame. She wrapped his body in her quilt, and pulled it onto the porch, jumping down before her skirts caught on fire. She stood praying for his soul as the funeral pyre did its work.

Ella collapsed on the ground, hating herself for being grateful for the inferno's warmth. She decided to allow herself the luxury of tears. But none came. It was too late for that. In a minute, she'd have to start walking. All she could think of now was how to make it to the Mississippi River.

Eight hundred miles south, another woman was wondering exactly the same thing.

CHAPTER 8
DECEMBER, 1864

The house on Gallatin Street was just a few short blocks from the Mississippi River. For the sailors who arrived en masse, Madame's was convenient to the docks. However, for one person, those few short blocks would be the most dangerous. Still, there was no time for careful planning of an escape route.

It had to be now. For Charity Boudry, time was a luxury she no longer had. Ever since she'd been old enough to understand her situation, she knew the problems inherent in leaving and knew she'd have to rise above them. She'd seen other girls leave the house, but with no money whatsoever, they didn't get far. Usually their road out – and their lives – ended permanently before they even left Gallatin Street.

There was an endless supply of poor girls and young immigrant women to take their place. Sometimes Charity heard about girls who had tried to return to the house after running away, finding life on the street to be more of a nightmare than what they'd left behind. Madame made sure everyone knew the prodigals had been refused admittance. It was a lesson meant to discourage ingratitude. The door would never be open to them again. Girls in Madame's house would leave only when she wanted them to.

Madame kept all of the money the customers paid in return for what the girls "owed" on their "room and board." Sometimes a client left a small gratuity for one of the girls, but rooms were searched regularly. Anything other than a worthless trinket was confiscated, accompanied by a beating. No one was meant to leave with anything other than the shabby dress on her back.

That was one of the reasons Charity kept her shawl well hidden. Especially now, when it held the laudanum vials that were her ticket out.

As Madame instructed, Charity had increased her workload to pay for the brandy and laudanum. She was determined to turn it to her advantage. She learned to identify newcomers rather than regulars. She could tell visitors to New Orleans apart from locals. She trained her ear to detect accents from far away, preferably the Northeast. She could detect a businessman or merely a *poseur.* She recognized wealth, though much more important was whether the client carried a great part of that wealth with him in his wallet. Charity felt that anyone insane enough to do that in a place like this deserved whatever he got.

From Charity's viewpoint, the ideal candidate was a young visitor from the North who carried money but wouldn't want to be bothered coming back for a trial if a thief was caught. It was important to spot someone arriving alone rather than with a friend. He must never have been to a house like Madame's before, otherwise he'd know what to look out for. He had to be uneasy, not knowing what to expect. He had to have his mind on the contents of his trousers rather than the wallet in his pocket. And he had to get there soon, before the brandy and laudanum were stolen.

She watched the front door, ready to cut one out of the herd as quickly as possible. It required the patience of hunting alligators. But she'd seen that up close. As a child, she'd been used as gator bait by her father.

Charity hoped Madame would attribute her keenness in expanding her workload to paying off her debt, now several days old. And then, like one of the Christmas gifts being opened all over New Orleans in places beyond Gallatin Street, the right one presented himself.

She made sure to catch the young man's eye as he studied the goods on offer. The other girls could be forward, vulgar, hard. Charity had always done well with an innocent look tinged with eagerness to try this exciting new carnal experience she'd heard so much about.

Shyly, she smiled. He smiled back. She had him!

He paid Madame and she watched him replace the wallet in his jacket. Charity took him by the hand, walking him up the stairs to her room.

Once inside, she kept her conversation simple, friendly. She forced her eyes to reflect a timid admiration for his masculine physique. She allowed herself to stammer bashfully, adding a touch of Cajun French flavoring to complete the effect.

"I am so sorry, *monsieur.* I am not quite sure how to begin. You may wish one of the other girls, one who knows more than I do."

Turning to the only chair, he removed his jacket, reassuring her that she was doing just fine. Reassuring her was the least he could do, he thought, a man of the world like himself. And she quite obviously was taken with *him.*

Charity kept her eye on the jacket.

He turned back to face her and did what they all did, told her how beautiful she was. She lowered her head demurely, as if it was the first time she'd heard such a fine compliment.

"Oh, *pardon, monsieur,* I must confess I am a bit nervous. And you are being so kind to me. May I return that kindness? Would you join me in a glass of brandy to warm us?"

Before he could respond, she hastened to the small table, turning her back to fill his glass. Would he feel it might be rude to refuse once she started pouring? Was he so *stupide* he'd actually drink anything in a house like this?

She saw in the cracked mirror that he was loosening his collar stays, turning away from her to place his shirt on the chair with his jacket. This was the moment. In went the laudanum. She swirled the glass, cupped it with her hands, and offered it to him before returning to get a glass of her own. Hers would contain only brandy, but she would not drink a drop. He would never notice.

How fast did the drug act? She'd had no way to test it. She might have asked Madame, as if to innocently gauge how soon sleep would come, but she feared arousing suspicion. Now the important part was getting him on the bed, relaxing him, biding her time.

The routine was second nature to her, the preliminary sighs as she stroked his chest. She just hoped for the blessed sound of him snoring. Soon.

He dropped off faster than she'd expected. Now, the question was how deep he was under – and how long it would last. She retrieved the wallet from his jacket. Not as much as she'd hoped, maybe thirty or forty dollars, but they were greenbacks. They'd do.

Charity slid her black shawl containing the remainder of the vials from under the bed, careful not to jostle anything. She shrugged into the only dress she had other than her dressing gown.

She had hoped her ideal candidate would be wearing a long frock coat. That could have doubled as a winter coat for a small woman like her. No matter, his shorter jacket would at least keep her warm. With the wallet safe in an inside pocket, she wadded the vial-laden shawl into another. She hated to leave the brandy behind; it might come in useful at some point. But it would be too cumbersome.

She thought about relieving him of his pants. Modesty might slow him down in sounding the alarm when he awoke. But honestly – the sight of a half-naked man in a place like this would be nothing unusual. Modesty would be the least of his concerns.

She didn't bother checking on him as she quietly closed the door to her room. It was done. Her mind was set. There was no going back even if he woke up at this very moment. Now she had to move as quickly and quietly as possible, and pray no one saw her.

As she had made her plans, she'd never even considered going through the parlor and out the front door. Too many people there. She wouldn't under any circumstances go through The Cellar. And she wouldn't jump from the balcony off her room. Even if she managed the fall from the second floor, she knew there was a burly doorman lurking below. He'd turn her in to Madame. Or worse.

The only way to do this was to go up. Down the hall, there was a door leading an attic. From her balcony, she had observed that it had a small window looking out on the alley. She had never run the risk of going through the door, but the one time she had dared to explore and try the handle, it had been unlocked. It was quarters for the slave girls who did the cleaning. While Madame constantly shrieked at them to lock it when they came down, maybe in a small act of defiance, they had not.

Holding her breath, she tried the handle. It turned. She was in, bounding up the stairs. If one of the slave girls was up here ... well, they shouldn't be and that's all.

She wasn't sure what to expect up here, but whatever it was, the place was worse than she thought. The girls had only floor pallets to sleep on, and the attic was filthy. Charity tried not to breathe the foul air. She made her way to the window and tried to raise it. *Merde.* It was sealed shut. Nothing subtle now. She was desperate.

There was a pile of wooden slats stacked against the wall. They looked about six feet long. She guessed they'd be used against hurricanes, to protect the casements downstairs in a storm. She took one and smashed the window. On Gallatin Street, the sound of breaking glass was not uncommon. She just had to hope no one in Madame's house recognized the sound as coming from here.

Clearing the glass shards as best she could using the sleeve of the man's jacket, Charity kept one jagged piece of glass that was about as large as her hand. She put it in one of the jacket pockets.

Cautiously, she looked outside, and that was when she saw just how wide the alley was. There was no way to jump from the window to the rooftop of the next building as she'd hoped. That had been essential to her plan. Now she would have to improvise.

The slats! She slid one across from the windowsill to the rooftop next door. It was barely long enough, but it held. She grabbed another and did the same. Still too narrow. What was that sound? Someone coming down the hall?

One more slat and that would have to do. Three wide. She would walk across. She refused to submit to crawling on them, and anyway it would take too long. She climbed out onto the boards, forcing herself not to look down.

Taking a deep breath, Charity Boudry held her head high and looked straight ahead. Step by step, step by step, step by step. After what seemed like an eternity, she was on the other side! She started to scurry away across the rooftop, but quickly went back to pull the slats toward her so no one could follow. She doubted anyone else would be desperate enough to venture out on them if they came after her, but it was a symbolic act to her. Burning bridges. She'd never go back alive.

This building, the one next to Madame's house, stood on the corner. It had a filigreed *gallerie* that extended around to the other side, away from the prying eyes of Madame's doorman. Better yet, unlike the small iron balcony off Charity's room, it was supported by ornate posts that went all the way to the ground.

That was how she'd make it to the street. And whoever was down there had better not get in her way.

The great river that Charity sought was America's watery highway. After Union forces took control of the river in 1863, shipping ran fairly freely both up- and downriver. Steamboats carried cotton, goods, livestock, civilians, and military personnel.

During the desperate campaign for control of the Mississippi in 1863, traveling by riverboat could be a dangerous proposition. John Deacon's newspaper had carried reports of the steamboat *Ruth* being burned in August of 1863 below Cairo, Illinois.

Since the critical port town of Vicksburg had been taken by the Union a month before, some suspected this assault on river traffic to be the result of Rebel guerilla activity. Along with civilian passengers and two hundred head of cattle, the *Ruth* was carrying military supplies and had more than two million dollars in federal greenbacks locked in her safe. The money, supplies, about thirty people and all of the cattle were lost.

More reports came in about riverboats being burned after Vicksburg fell to the Union in 1863. An explosion was heard on the *City of Madison* at Vicksburg in August 1863 before about a hundred and fifty souls were lost in the fire. Over a hundred were reported dead on the *Robert Campbell* off Milliken's Bend, Louisiana, in September of 1863. October of 1863 brought news of the *Catahoula* burning with fatalities, followed by similar reports that same month for the *Chancellor* and *Forest Queen.*

As the war dragged on, more riverboats were sunk with loss of life. Usually they carried a contingent of Union troops. After each incident, some witnesses swore they heard the sound of an explosion before the steamers caught fire.

Steamboats were never the safest of vessels. Roaring fires in the boilers had to be kept stoked to generate the boat's steam power. With the wooden construction of the superstructure, fires from the boilers were known to turn the vessel into an inferno in a matter of minutes. But, people whispered, not like this. Not nearly like this.

People along the river were now speculating about "boatburners." Stories circulated about a Confederate secret service whose charge was disrupting the flow of shipping on the Mississippi. If the Union wanted to hold the river, people said, the Confederates would do everything they could make it harder. Some said they were the last desperate acts to save the Confederacy.

In December of 1864, the same month when Charity Boudry was making her escape from Gallatin Street, the boilers on the steamer *Maria,* carrying Union cavalry, exploded near St. Louis. Twenty five people were killed. When interviewed, crew members suspected the loss of the ship was due to a "coal torpedo" concealed by boatburners.

But people along the river felt that surely the war would soon be over. When that happened, certainly the attacks would end. Life along the great river could then get back to normal.

CHAPTER 9
WINTER, 1865

Moran was feeling lucky. They had been on the march, probably somewhere in Tennessee he thought, but they were stopped now. Perfect time to supplement the remains of his stake from Mr. Slick.

These were guys he didn't know well but he'd played cards with them once before and they seemed all right. Moran had won a little in the previous game, so when they asked him for another game tonight, as they'd put it, "to recoup their losses," he could hardly refuse. When they suggested upping the ante, he'd gone along. Moran had invited Deacon to join the group, but the man had bowed out with a friendly, "Too rich for my blood," before retiring to his blanket.

Card-playing wasn't exactly encouraged in their unit, so they had to be careful. Moran figured someone up the line apparently felt gambling could cause problems. Moran didn't agree with that. What could be more pleasant than a bunch of guys playing a friendly game of cards in front of a warm fire on a winter night?

At first, he did fine. But suddenly the tide turned against him. He was losing. The trick was never to let them think you'd run out of confidence.

"Deal another hand!" he said jovially. "Just waitin' for my luck to rally!"

The big man who was shuffling the cards scratched his chin thoughtfully. He had hair so blond it was almost white. Moran had heard him called 'Big Swede.' As he shuffled the cards, Big Swede said, "Gee, I don't know if we need to deal you in, buddy. Ain't you just about lost all of your month's pay?"

Moran didn't want to be dealt out. His luck was bound to change. He just needed to stay in the game. "No, no. I got plenty. Deal me in."

"Well, I don't know," said Big Swede. "If you already lost your pay, you ain't got nothin' left."

"Well, maybe I don't and maybe I do," said Moran without noticing the looks that the other players were giving each other.

"Then ante up."

Moran looked at his cards. He thought they showed some real possibility. "I'm in."

"Listen," said Swede. "It ain't me, you understand, but it might be best for everyone if you'd show us your money."

Moran felt it was time to show some indignation. "You accusin' me of bein' a welsher?"

"No one's accusin' anyone of anything," said Big Swede. "Just show us your money."

"Well, I ain't no welsher." With that pronouncement, Moran turned his back to the group and withdrew a gold coin from Slick's money pouch hanging around his neck. He tossed the coin into the pot and asked for three cards.

"Kind of a high stake, there, Moran, for someone wantin' three cards."

"Then maybe you're the one who shouldn't oughta play if it's too rich for your blood," Moran said with a smile to show he meant no offense. Just a friendly game.

Moran held two sevens. He tried to contain his delight when the draw brought forth three Jacks. A fine hand, well worth his trust.

The other players continued the bet, seeing and raising each other until a substantial pot was in front of them.

When it came time to call, Moran didn't mean to gloat, really he didn't mean to. But he did. "Read 'em and weep, my friends. Read 'em and weep!

As he started to pull the winnings toward him, one of the other players exclaimed, "Hold it! He's cheatin' I saw him!'

Genuinely aghast, Moran said, "What the hell you talkin' about?!"

His accuser kept on. "He pulled a Jack from his sleeve! Cheat! Cheat!"

Big Swede joined in the fray. "Yeah, I think I saw it too!"

"Wait! I never ...!"

Soon all the other players were eyeing him maliciously. This was really the first that Moran noticed the Swede acting as their leader.

"He palmed somethin'!" Big Swede said. "Search him."

They pulled Moran up, held his arms, and ripped open his shirt to reveal the money pouch.

"What's this?!"

"No!" yelled Moran. "Leave that alone! It's mine!"

Swede kept on. "He's cheatin,' I tell you!" Then to Moran, "You know the penalty for cheatin'! Ought to mark you with a hot branding iron! You're lucky you'll just have to pay a fine."

They tore the pouch from Moran's neck as he tried to wriggle free, all the while protesting, "No! I never! Stop!"

He tore one arm free and swung it wildly, hitting one of the men in the face. The others began punching him.

"No! Stop! No! Leave me alone!"

The commotion woke Deacon from a sound sleep. He jumped into the fray without really thinking, pulling the men away from Moran.

"Come on fellas," he said, "Save it for the Rebels! Let's not do this to each other. We're better than that! We got enough to worry about."

Moran's assailants drew back, but Swede held on to the money pouch. "This will satisfy our honor."

"Good," said Deacon. "Now what will it take for a man to get some sleep around here?"

"Guess we could make do with an apology from the cheater."

"You'll get no apology from me! You're a thief!" Moran looked around desperately, trying to get support from the other players or at least Deacon. "He's got my gold!"

"Shut up, you idiot," hissed Deacon. "You've been played. They'd kill you for a lot less."

"Yeah, and we'd have a right to do it. Don't hold with cheating," said Big Swede over his shoulder as he and the other players walked away laughing. "Quiet your friend down, Deacon, or we'll give him some more." Then they were gone.

Moran, in a frenzy, said, "Look what you did! You let them get away with it!"

"They'd a killed you," said Deacon. "You can thank me some other time for saving your skin."

"They took my gold!"

"You came away with your life. What do you want to do, complain to the sergeant? He don't like gambling. Anyway, you get them boys mad, they'll blow your head off next time we're in a skirmish. And then they'd take the gold off your dead body. As I figure, you got off easy."

"You called me an idiot," said Moran in his own defense.

Deacon laughed, "Well, it was in the heat of the fray. One more minute, they'd'a turned on *me*. Now, I'm tired. Can I please get some sleep without you gettin' into trouble?"

"Ain't gonna get into no more trouble. For now."

"Moran, as a friend, please listen. You're gonna have to settle into Army life."

"It's not for me."

"Look, I'm going back to sleep. Get some rest, Moran. We could engage the Rebs any day now. Gonna need your wits about you." Deacon went back to his blanket, turned over, and closed his eyes.

Toward sunrise, Moran looked down on Deacon's sleeping form. "Well, good luck against them Rebels, Deacon. You been a friend. But this life sure ain't for me."

As dawn approached, he observed the slumbering camp, and saw no one looking his way. Grabbing his rifle, Moran stealthily made his way to the woods. He ducked the sentries and began to run.

"Fight your own damn war," he said to no one in particular. "To hell with you all!"

As the skies became lighter, he noticed the horizon awash in gray. Fog? That would be good. It could provide him with cover if they came looking for him.

That was when he realized it was neither fog nor a good thing at all. It was the gray jackets of the Confederate Army stealthily making their way toward the sleeping camp, and what was worse, toward him.

Moran looked around desperately, trying to find a way to escape or even a place to hide. There was nothing. He flailed around like a dervish, wild-eyed. Then he knew what he had to do. He hated it, but he had no other choice.

He turned on his heel and stumbled back through the woods toward camp. As he ran, he heard someone shout from the Confederate line, "Look there! Yankee!"

"Hold your fire!" someone responded. "We can surprise them! Hold your fire!"

Moran crashed back into the federals' camp, shouting, "They're coming! Rebels coming! Everyone up! We're under attack! They're coming! Rebels coming!"

CHAPTER 10

WINTER, 1865

Ella was freezing, that was the fact of it. She was long past hunger; that was simply a constant and not worth thinking about. Right now the threat of freezing to death was keeping her mind occupied. She'd been on foot ever since the bushwhackers took the horse and wagon.

Every day she walked further westward, hoping each step was bringing her closer to the great river and that she hadn't lost her bearings. But the short, gray days made it hard to follow the sun.

She was surprised to find very few towns along the way. There was one, however, and when she came across it, she allowed herself the luxury of spending a little of the money Deacon had left her. It was heavenly! A warm room at the town's inn, a hot bath, a good meal, and a heavy blanket she bought at the general store. When she set back out on the road, she wrapped it around her like a shroud.

She would have loved to stay another night, but dared not. Winter was hanging on with a fearsome grip, and there was just no way to know what the days ahead might bring. Already, one of her worst fears was coming true.

The wind-blown blizzard never seemed to stop. As a child she had loved the snowfall. Now she saw no beauty, just hidden danger as the snow piled up almost to her knees. If she stepped in a hole and sprained an ankle, broke a leg … No, best not be thinking like that.

When she saw the entrance to what looked like a cave, she thought it almost as welcome as the gilded gates of a palace. The cave's entrance was on a ledge about two feet up from ground level, so maybe that would keep the snow out as well as most roving animals. She hoped. Unless there was already one inside.

When she peered in, she saw there was not very much of it. Really, it was more of an outcropping in the rock than an actual cave, but it still looked inviting. About four feet high and probably four or five feet of depth before it hit the back wall. A good enough place to curl up until the snow stopped, and plenty of snowmelt to drink. And no bears hibernating inside.

Perhaps she could light a small fire. Just being sheltered from the wind was glorious. She wrapped the blanket tighter, lay down on the bed of stone, and slept. Later, when she opened her eyes again, she was looking into the double barrel of a shotgun.

Well, at least it wasn't a wild animal. Perhaps she could reason with him before he ravaged and killed her. Perhaps he was a kind man, a good man like Deacon, a gentleman who would help her.

With what she hoped was more courage in her voice than she felt, she said the first thing that came to mind: "Hello."

The shotgun jerked upward as if ordering her to sit up. She did so.

Ella continued trying to sound reasonable, calm, friendly. "You have no need of frightening me with that gun, sir. You will not need to use it. I am not armed and there's nobody here but me. I have no food if that's what you want. Mine was stolen. I haven't eaten in several days. If you have any to share, I'd be most obliged."

For her next statement in the one-sided exchange of information, she decided honesty would *not* be the best policy: "I have no money, sir."

Ella could see nothing beyond the gun barrel. She had to know who or what she was dealing with. "Please put the gun down, sir. It frightens me."

Slowly, the gun was lowered. She could now see the soldier who held it. He was young with a very light beard. Small in stature, but bulky around the middle. He wore his forage cap low over his eyes, but some scraggly pale yellow hair poked from underneath. Ella didn't really care about the color of the uniform at this point, but she took note that it was Union blue.

"Looks like we're on the same side, sir. Are you an advance scout? Did you lose your way in the snow? Is your unit nearby?"

Instead of answering, the boy shrieked in pain and collapsed.

Ella knew she was not a worldly person. She had seen very little of the world beyond her father's farm and their own small town. But this was beyond anything she could have imagined.

She had pulled the soldier inside the little cave and wrapped him in her heavy blanket for warmth. He was breathing. He did not appear to be shot or bleeding. She found his canteen and dabbed a little water on his lips. She considered searching in his haversack for food but decided he might wake up and think she was stealing.

Perhaps he had simply succumbed to weariness. She spoke softly to him, urging him to wake up as she stroked his face. The boy's beard came off on her hand.

It was a layer of dirt covering cheeks as soft as her own. Perhaps he was one of the young boys she'd heard about who lied about their age to join the Army. Though the minimum age to enlist was eighteen, many recruiters looked the other way if the young man was halfway convincing. She'd heard of boys as young as fifteen – or even twelve if they were big, sturdy farm boys – joining up.

Perhaps this one was a drummer boy, a bugler, or a messenger. In any event, this one had seen battle. On his chest was a medal hanging from a red, white and blue ribbon. It had an eagle and a star-shaped emblem showing an ancient warrior with sword and shield. She knew from newspaper stories Johnny had written that it was for valor. Surely such a young man would not harm her.

The boy seemed to stir. He grasped his stomach in pain. Maybe he was shot after all. Ella decided to check. Keeping him warm in the blanket, Ella unbuttoned his Union blue jacket. That was when she had her first surprise: beneath the blue uniform jacket was one in Confederate gray.

Then came the next surprise. Beneath that was a woman. A very pregnant woman.

Ella had no idea how long she just sat and stared. Her first thought was that she'd endured so much, she'd become delirious. Perhaps she'd fallen in the snow and succumbed to a fever. But everything seemed so real.

She stopped staring when her new companion began stirring. Ella offered the canteen, then asked as if it were the most normal thing in the world, "How are you feeling?"

With the two uniform jackets hanging open, her companion seemed to recognize there was no further need for pretense. She looked down at her swollen midsection, then looked up at Ella. They both smiled.

"Well, I'll bet you were a bit surprised," the companion said.

"I was indeed," said Ella. "But it was sure a relief, all things considered. You scared me, pointing that shotgun in my face. Didn't know who was behind it."

"Most folks, if they're smart, sleep with their hand on their gun and finger on the trigger. Some'll fire right through the blanket before askin' any questions. I didn't know who *you* was or what you might do if taken by surprise."

Ella laughed. "Guess I'm not very smart then, because I don't have a gun at all. My husband took all the weapons when he went off to the war."

"He didn't leave you nothin' to protect yourself?"

Ella had actually never thought about that. *He hadn't.*

"Well, I'm just glad neither one of us did any shooting," said Ella. "Might as well get acquainted. We may have to be here for a while."

She held out her hand. "My name is Ella McAdams – my goodness, I mean Ella Ardent." *What had brought about that slip of the tongue?*

"You'd have to be careful to remember your name if you was in my position," the companion said. "My name in the before-life was Patsy Morrissey. The Army knows me as Patrick."

"Which would you like me to call you?"

"Pat does nicely either way, girl or boy. That's what the fellas in the outfit call me and it's easy for me to remember."

"Are you really in the Army?" Ella was at a loss for words. "In the Army? The real Army?"

Her new friend nodded.

"But you're a … I'm sorry, I don't know where to start. Well, yes I do. Pat, do you have any food?"

Patsy Morrissey laughed. "First things first, eh? Good for you. I remember you said you hadn't eaten in a while. Look in my haversack. There's salt pork and hardtack and a few other items I stashed away for when … for when my time came." Patsy looked down again at her swollen middle.

Ella dug through the pack. She found the salt pork and what looked like crackers. That, she assumed, was the hardtack. The she found a container of ground coffee, several potatoes, and some strange-looking cubes.

"What on earth are these?" she asked. "Are they food?"

"The Army decided that living for months on salt pork and hard-tack tended to be a drawback to fighting a war. We had men dropping from scurvy and dysentery. So they gave us these cubes, said we was to add them to water. Army calls them 'desiccated compressed mixed vegetables.' Once you taste it you'll call it just what soldiers do – '*desecrated* vegetables.'"

"What kind of vegetables do you think they are, Pat?"

"Probably turnips and carrots, maybe some assorted greens. Keep looking. There's some pickles and some sauerkraut wrapped up on the bottom. The real treasure is on top of them."

Ella unwrapped the crown jewel of the collection – cake!

"How would you feel if we have dinner backward, Pat? We could start with the cake, then I'll go find some kindling to build a fire."

"There are some Lucifers there in the pack."

Ella found the carefully-waterproofed package of friction matches, and felt hopeful for the first time in a long time.

They ate together, and while it wasn't the best meal Ella had ever had, she loved it. They shared Patsy's tin cup full of coffee, and it warmed and revived them both.

"Pat, do you mind me asking … about … your situation?"

Patsy laughed. "Which one?"

"Whichever one you want to tell me about. Being a soldier and being …"

Patsy finished the thought. " … in the family way."

"If you wish. There's just so much I want to know about you, I don't even know where to start asking. Or if you mind me asking. Might be too personal."

Patsy smiled. "Oh, it's personal, all right!"

"May I ask where you were headed? How you came to be here?"

Patsy seemed happy to tell her story. Ella was really the first person she could ever tell it to, and Ella was an appreciative audience.

"I was on my way to a little town over yonder way." Patsy gestured in a general direction, somewhere outside the cave. "Saw it over the rise when we marched through a few days ago. I knew my time was coming soon. Thought I smelled snow in the air. Thought I'd better make plans."

"Wasn't there a doctor in your ... your outfit?" Ella was still too astonished to be able to know how she could ask the questions she wanted to know without sounding rude. Then she thought she had it figured out! "Were you a nurse?"

"No, ma'am. T'weren't no doctor with us, and I wasn't no nurse. I was a soldier just like everyone else in out outfit."

"But ... all men? I'm sorry, Pat. I just don't know what to say!"

"Well, settle in. I can tell you all about it."

Patsy Morrissey and her bother Jamie had been orphaned as children. Only two years apart in age, they loved each other and pledged never to be separated. Sometimes other families offered to take one or the other in, either the girl or the boy, never both. The children clung together, wailing so piteously that the offer was soon withdrawn.

They located a distant cousin who invited them to work on his farm. In the all-male household, Patsy became used to wearing men's clothes to do her chores. She grew strong from the manual labor and healthy in the sunshine. On Sundays, she donned a simple dress and went with her brother to church.

There, she enjoyed the attentions of the local boys, and came to know some of the girls. But she was troubled by what she learned of women's lives. She already knew how restricted she felt in a dress on

Sundays, how hard it sometimes was just to breathe, even without a horrible corset. She hated women's shoes, how tiny and flimsy they were, how hard it was to walk in them, much less to run from danger.

Patsy knew girls were expected to find a husband to cook and clean for, then to raise children as fast as they came along – if the women were lucky enough not to die in childbirth. Patsy had heard of plenty who had, her own mother at the top of the list. She knew girls were not permitted to ride astride a horse, couldn't feel the wind in their hair while galloping across the countryside on a fine spring day.

Patsy wanted her own farm someday, maybe with her brother. But it had to be one where no one could decide to toss her off. That had happened to her father, just before he died.

"Then I found out women can't own property!" Patsy exclaimed to as if this was something Ella didn't know. "Not even if they inherit it from their own family!" Ella was well aware of this, too.

"And not only can women not *own* property, women *are* property! Property of some man! If he beats you, if he harms you or your children, if he does anything he wants, there is nothing a woman can do about it!"

Ella wondered what strange foreign land Patsy might be from, that this would come as news to her. Every woman knew it from the time she was born. William Ardent had reinforced the message.

"Well, to continue if I'm not taking too long." Ella could quite truthfully assure Patsy that the girl was anything but tiresome.

"One fine day disaster struck. One after t'other. Turns out our cousin did not own the land we worked, and the owner had decided to sell. He wanted us off. We tried to buy it but didn't have near enough money. The owner said there was a war coming, and a smart man like him could profit if the timing was right."

Soon after, war did indeed come. Patsy's cousin enlisted and encouraged Jamie to do the same. Regular salary of thirteen dollars a month, a fine adventure away from the drudgery of farm work, and serve their country at the same time. Maybe it could lead to a regular job. The cousin had made it all sound very attractive.

Later, Patsy's brother asked to speak with her privately, "more serious than we ever talked, Pats." She knew exactly what was coming. He felt honor-bound to enlist. There was nothing for them here. But the thought of leaving Patsy behind was unendurable. "What on God's earth would you do, girl?" he had asked.

Patsy never knew if it was her idea or his, or if maybe both at the same time. At first she laughingly tossed it into the conversation, as if it was the most outlandish thing she could think of. Well, she'd just go with him, off to war. Ha!

But soon neither of them was laughing. They only had each other in the world. It would take more than a war to separate them.

Jamie cut his sister's hair as short as his. Since he wasn't old enough to have a beard yet on his fair skin, they both experimented with rubbing dirt on their cheeks until it looked like a reasonable facsimile. If they had to prove their skills with a rifle, neither would have a problem. They'd been shooting their own food since they could lift a gun.

It was the physical examination that might prove troublesome. Jamie went into town to reconnoiter at the recruitment office. He was shocked at what was required.

After asking his age, which Jamie fudged a little, the recruiter asked the boy to walk a straight line. That was to see if a man could march long distances without being too lame.

Then the recruiter told Jamie to open his mouth. "Got to have at least three teeth, son, to tear into cartridge envelopes. You've got plenty. You'll do."

Jamie asked if the recruiter would be back tomorrow. He wanted the same one. Reassured that the man would return the next day,

Jamie asked if he could bring another would-be soldier, a cousin in as fine a shape as Jamie himself. Another good fighter to shoulder a rifle for the Union. The recruiter, who seemed more uninterested than enthusiastic, said he'd take a look.

The next day, Patsy bound her chest tightly with cotton strips made from a cast-off petticoat. She put on a shirt and trousers, then added another set from her brother to put over her own. Sure enough, it added bulk. She wore his heavy boots and walked with the heavy strides she'd seen the local men do. She pulled a cap low over her now-short hair, but had no fear of meeting the recruiter's eyes if it was required. That was what men did. They had no fear of looking boldly in each other's eyes. It was women who kept their eyes downcast.

Patsy's entrance examination was no more rigorous than her brother's had been. She walked a straight line and produced the required number of teeth. And soon Private Patrick Morrissey and Private James Morrissey were Union soldiers in good standing.

Ella was enthralled by the tale. "But how did you keep them from finding you out? And what would have happened if they had?" she asked.

"Never thought about them finding me out. Just told myself I was no different from the rest of the men in the outfit, and acted the same way as them. It helped that Jamie and me were supposed to be cousins, so it didn't arouse any curiosity that we spent time together and bunked near to each other."

"But Patsy … oh, I know this is indelicate … I shouldn't ask … but …" Ella faltered as she tried to pose the question.

"I should pretend not to know so'd you'd have to ask it out loud," laughed Patsy. "But you'd get all red and flustered, and 'twould be an unkind thing for me to do."

"Well, thank you. But I still want to know."

"Kept wearing two sets of clothes under my uniform for bulk. Helped to hide my chest, too. Everyone in our unit, probably the whole Army, slept in our uniforms, so no worry of being seen while changing. When we came to a creek or what have you, we all bathed in our clothes too. Ever'one held to modesty whilst we were in the water. And now you be wonderin' about Nature's needs."

Ella could only nod.

"Goin' to the woods was a man's private matter. No one showed any concern, and granted each other as much time alone as they needed. I just made sure to go further into the woods than most. They just thought I was a modest young boy, I guess. I could march as far as anyone and could shoot better than most. If I kep' my voice low and stayed to myself, no one seemed to mind a whit. They just figured I was shy. Or scared."

Patsy stopped and took a sip from the canteen. She looked down at her midsection and signed. "Guess you'll be wantin' to know about this."

"Only if you want to tell me."

"I'm going to need your help, probably more sooner than later. Not going to be able to make it to town, not in this blizzard. And not even sure I could make it on a nice spring day. I think it's going to come down to you and me."

Then Patsy looked worried for the first time and stared pointedly at Ella. "Do you know how?"

Ella wanted so much to lie, to give poor Patsy a confidence that Ella actually didn't share. But she couldn't. "No Pat, I don't. But they say women have been doing it for thousands of years, so it must come mostly natural. Do you want me to try to make it into town? You'll have to point out the way for me to go. What's the name of the town? Where are we, anyway?"

"We're prob'ly in west Tennessee somewhere by my calculations. Don't know the name of the town, looked like just a few shacks anyway.

We're a while from the big towns along the river. That's a kind offer, tryin' to get me some help, but I think we both better stay put."

Ella was secretly relieved. She didn't want to leave her new friend, not at a time like this. She wondered how Patsy's condition had come about, and after a few minutes of silence, Patsy seemed to want to tell it.

"It was whilst I was in the woods, of course. Had my britches down. Didn't see him or hear him coming. He must have been there a while, just gawking. Probably thought he'd lost his mind!" Patsy laughed, then sighed.

Ella was determined to remain silent until Patsy wanted to tell it. After a moment, she did.

"So there we both were, just staring at each other as if wonderin' what to do next. He came closer and I could see he was just a boy, probably not much older than me. I wasn't afraid. I just stayed put. All I could think to say was to ask him not to tell, which is what I did. He came closer, until he was right alongside me, and put his hand on my shoulder so's I couldn't rise. Remember, my britches was still down. He said he'd keep my secret on one condition. And then he lowered his own britches."

"So he ravished you. I'm so sorry, Patsy."

"You know, it wasn't really like that. He was young as me, scared as me. I got the sense he'd never been with a girl before. He cried afterward. Told me he was sorry. But he said he just had to know, in case he didn't make it back from the war. Had to know what it was all about."

"Did he? Keep your secret, I mean."

"He did fine. If we happened to pass each other in camp, he kept on going. He never asked for anything else."

"Did you tell your brother?

"How could I? First, I was scared Jamie might do something about it, call him out or something. Jamie might have been killed or I'd'a been found out because of all the ruckus. Weren't anything that Jamie could do about it, or undo what had been done, so I just kept things to myself."

Ella lowered her head, thinking she'd have probably done the exact same thing.

"We went back on the march. About a week later, maybe two, that was when we caught up with the Rebs. No idea where it was, just recall the smoke and noise. It was worse than you can imagine, worse than I can tell, so I best not even try."

"Were you terrified? I would have been."

"No, you wouldn't. When the time came, all you'd'a been thinkin' about was just like me, just like everyone else. You recall all that drilling, drilling, drilling. Form lines and dress lines and close up lines. Fire and hope you hit someone, reload, aim, and do it again before someone on the other side hits you. Try to stay down, try to stay out of the line of your own troop's fire. I was nicked in the arm, but not too bad. I took cover behind a big old tree and tried to catch sight of Jamie in all the smoke."

"Could you see him with all that going on?"

Patsy's eyes took on a strange new look, and her smile was grim. "Wasn't hard to spot him. Jamie was carrying the flag. I saw him go down. Ran to him. Never thought about the gunfire. Just had to get to him. Turned him over so's I could look in his eyes, let him know I was there, that I'd help. He couldn't see me. Eyes were blank. Bullet through his head, took off part of his skull."

Patsy's eyes welled up, and Ella could feel her own doing the same. All she could say was, "I'm so sorry."

In a few moments, Patsy continued. "I made a sound like I'd never done before, like an animal might. They said it sounded like the Rebel Yell. Only louder. Fiercer. Must'a taken the Rebs by surprise. I pulled the flag from Jamie's hand. He still held onto it, even after he was gone, bless him. I started running towards the Rebs with the flag in one hand and my rifle in the other. Never got off a shot. Before I knew it, their side had signaled retreat and was gone. I didn't have a thing to do with it. When our unit reassembled, I was still carrying the flag. Someone patted me on the back. Said I'd be up for a medal. For bravery. For taking up our flag. For charging the Rebels. Sure enough, that's the one I'm wearing, this medal here. Weren't even a big battle. Just a dust-up. Probably no one ever heard of it, or ever will."

There was a long silence as both women just looked at the fire. "Oh, forgot to mention," Patsy said. "Among our casualties was that boy from the woods. Saw him when they brought his body back to camp for burial. Didn't think nothin' of it, not one way or t'other."

Patsy looked down at her midsection. "Wasn't long after that when *this* started to grow." She laughed. "Thought about just stayin' in camp. Imagine their looks when a soldier – a soldier just been decorated for valor – gave birth to a baby."

Ella didn't know if that was supposed to be a joke, or what her response should be. She merely nodded.

"But I thought it best to try for town," Patsy said. "I'd pulled this gray jacket off one of the enemy dead after we fought 'em. Not much blood on it. Put it on under my own. Thought no matter, either way. If I came to a Rebel-held town, I'd have one less problem if I had Confederate gray to change into before they spotted me if need be. Plus twice the warmth."

She paused for a drink from the canteen. "So I snuck away and tried for town," Patsy continued. "Now I know I won't make it. That's why I fell out when we first met. Pain's coming sooner now, pretty bad. It's going to happen quick from the feel of it. And you've got to help. I'll do what I can from my side of things, Ella, but you've got to help."

On the other side of Tennessee, after yet another of the interminable skirmishes in the war, the sky had gone red. There was the smell of gunpowder in the air. A blue jacket with a man inside it began to move. The man realized he was on his back, and the red was warm, sticky blood in his eyes. He was having a hard time recalling where he was or even who he was. Lots of shooting, he remembered that. Lots of confusion. Not really being afraid. Just aim, shoot, reload. Aim, shoot, reload. Aim, shoot, reload. Now he was in pain, great pain, but mostly felt confused.

His ears were ringing. Who was he? And why was he lying down in the middle of the day, looking up at a sky turned red? Right, that was blood, he'd forgotten. Well, all right, one question asked and answered. So who was he and what was he doing here? Maybe a little rest would help.

The ringing in his ears was getting better but now some varmint was slapping his face, hollering at him when all he wanted to do was sleep.

"Deacon? Hey, Deacon?" a voice said. "It's me, Moran. You been shot up pretty bad. If you're alive, we'll try to get you some help. You alive?"

This was no time to be asked difficult questions.

CHAPTER 11
WINTER, 1865

It had been yet another nameless fight in a nameless place, a skirmish between two small units, one dressed in blue and one in gray.

The Rebs had shot their way into camp, but thanks to Moran's warning, the federals were awake and grabbing their rifles when the enemy swarmed.

There'd been about a dozen dead and an equal number wounded on both sides. Even with Moran's limited military background, he knew this scuffle would be of no importance to anyone. Not to anyone except the boys without use of an arm or a leg for life. Not to anyone but those with buckshot in their gut. Not to anyone except the families of the boys who died far from home, in nameless fight in a nameless place.

Moran had gotten nicked up near his shoulder, but nothing too bad. Lots of blood, good for appearances. Some of the Rebs were firing shotguns filled with buckshot instead of shooting rifles. Rifles were better for distance. But this set-to with the gray jackets hadn't involved any distance whatsoever. No one even formed the fancy lines that had been drilled into them. He wondered who he could take his complaint to, how to file a grievance for all that meaningless drill practice.

When it was all over, Moran thought he pretty much figured out the reason for the battle, if you could call it that. The Rebs had grabbed as many of the federals' horses and as much food as they could carry off, then disappeared back into the woods. Men had died because other men were hungry. He had a crazy thought that they should have just invited the Rebs for breakfast to avoid the shooting. He'd'a been happy to share his hardtack. Worms were optional, their choice. Sure would have saved a lot of trouble, and some sweet lady's tears back home.

Moran was sorry to see Deacon one of those on the ground, not moving. Deacon was the closest thing he had for a friend. Not that having friends was all that important, but still it wasn't too bad to have one.

Now there was a practical problem. Winter kept holding on, so the ground was hard. Sure would be a problem to bury him and the others. But Deacon had been a friend. It had to be done.

That's when Moran thought he saw some movement around the eyes. It was like he himself had felt at times after a hard night of drinking – waking up suddenly and trying to figure out where he was. There was blood all over the fallen man's eyes. He wiped some away. Was there more movement?

"Deacon? Hey, Deacon?" he asked, shaking the man, slapping his friend's face. "It's me, Moran. You been shot up pretty bad. If you're alive, we'll try to get you some help. You alive?"

Moran could see that getting his friend up was going to be a problem. The head wound didn't appear fatal, but Deacon's right leg was pretty well shattered. Probably took a direct hit from a shotgun at close range.

Moran looked around for help. This was one time he'd be glad to see that sergeant or corporal, someone to tell him what to do. He never saw the sergeant again after that day, but the corporal came around and knelt down next to them.

He spoke kindly to Moran. "Most of the unit is moving out. But the map shows a little town up ahead where the wounded can be cared for. Those who can walk are bringing along those who can't. I see you been shot in the arm. But can you help this man?"

"Sure can, Corporal, I'll do it if you can help me get him up. But he's bleeding pretty bad. His right leg is all busted up. We got to do something about that soon."

Moran and the corporal did what they could for Deacon's ruined leg, wrapped it as best they were able. The corporal helped Moran take hold of Deacon, and they hobbled over to where they grouped up with the others.

Those who could walk indeed helped those who could not. A couple of the federal boys even helped some of the wounded Rebels. At first, Moran had mixed thoughts about that, but ended up feeling kindly. It was almost like they were buddies who'd gone hunting in the woods, drank too much 'shine, and somehow things got out of hand. Just old friends who'd accidentally banged each other up whilst showing off with their guns.

Deacon wasn't much for conversation on this trip, but he was alive. Moran felt an obligation to keep his friend talking, or at least conscious. He was half-carrying, half-dragging the man, and was worried that if he let Deacon fall, he'd never be able to get him up again. So Moran offered a lengthy commentary, mostly made-up, about the scuffle they'd had with the Rebs.

He felt obliged to add for his friend's benefit, "Hey, you got off some good shots, Deacon. I saw a few of them Rebels fall."

Deacon just stared, as if that wasn't entirely good news.

Wrong thing to say? "Well, maybe it wasn't your shots that killed them. Lot of smoke in the air. Could'a been someone else, I s'pose."

Deacon didn't seem to care. But he kept upright, dragging the injured leg, and they plodded onward. No one in the rest of the group was saying much.

Moran thought he heard someone, back behind them in the pack, weeping. Poor fella, he thought. Must be busted up pretty bad. Must be 'shamed to cry but can't help it. Then he thought of one of the songs the men had sang in camp, back when Moran thought it was a pretty useless way to spend time. He wasn't much of a singer, but maybe others would join in. That way, maybe no one could hear the sounds of anguish. He wasn't sure he knew all the words. But the song would be as good as any.

"*My eyes have seen the glory of the coming of the Lord,*" he began. Was that the way it went?

"*He has trampled out the vintage where the grapes of wrath are stored.*" What did that even mean? No matter. Moran kept singing.

Then more voices joined in. "*He has loosed the fateful lightning ...*"

Louder now. "*Of His Terrible Swift Sword ...*"

Even louder! "*His Truth goes marching on!*"

And so did Moran and the rest of that sad little group.

With the others, Moran made it all the way to a little wooden courthouse in a tiny town smack in the middle of nowhere. He guessed they were still in Tennessee. But this part of Tennessee, no one knew if it was Union-controlled or Rebel.

Their rag-tag little group of soldiers didn't see many people around. No one was shooting at them anyway. So they entered the empty courthouse and settled in.

Moran had seen the insides of a courthouse or two, knew pretty much what to expect. Sure enough, there was a large room. That's where the judge and jury would sit while some poor fella like him waited to hear what they'd say about him. Then there was a room in the back where the judges usually came out of.

Moran gently lowered Deacon to the floor in the big room as the others around him did the same. Some of the men mumbled words of encouragement to the badly wounded like, "It'll be all right now" or "You're gonna be just fine, Doc is here."

Their unit had a man who'd acted as their doctor. Everyone called him Doc, so Moran just assumed he knew what he was doing. The man had traveled with them, along with an assistant who they called the "orderly."

Moran helped Doc and the orderly get set up in the smaller of the rooms. There was a table with papers on it, and another that looked like it acted as a desk for the judge. They moved both tables toward the middle of the room, and Doc pulled out the supplies he carried with him in his kit.

He quickly saw to Moran's arm, which wasn't hurt badly at all. A bandage did the trick. "Now, start bringing in the wounded," the doctor unexpectedly said to Moran. "We'll take two at a time. Put one on each table. I'll see to one while you're bringing in the next. We've got to be quick. Worst cases first."

Moran knew he wouldn't want to be anywhere near the room for what came next. There had been plenty of talk around the campfire. Everybody seemed to know someone who had first-hand information. In the field, Army surgeons would perform their operations outdoors where they had light and fresh air. Out in the open like that, all the soldiers in camp, sometimes hundreds, saw it all with their own eyes. And it was the stuff of nightmares.

Right from the beginning, Army surgeons were called "Sawbones." There was a reason. Medical science of the day grasped that infections were fatal. So the best way to save a man's life was to deal with the wound before infection could set in. However, that same medical science had not progressed past the point of amputation. Conventional wisdom held that to prevent infection, cut off the limb before the infection could spread.

Some campfire critics of the process had a theory. They proclaimed that eager doctors amputated just to get practice, to perfect their surgical technique for after the war so's then they could make real money cuttin' on patients, being experienced and all.

Others wondered if it wasn't because they simply didn't know what else to do. Maybe a man losing a limb was not as bad as losing his life. Maybe.

Everyone knew a story they'd heard about doctors sawing off arms and legs out in the open, then tossing them onto piles that grew higher and higher. One of the more literate men in Moran's unit – was it Deacon? – recalled reading something about the poet Walt Whitman witnessing such a scene. Whitman had gone to search for his wounded brother after the Battle of Fredericksburg in 1862. After that battle, it was reported that Union surgeons performed about five hundred amputations. Whitman had written that one of the first things he saw in camp was a big heap of arms, legs, hands, and feet under a tree.

Moran felt that was the kind of image that stayed with a man, poet or not.

The men had also heard Army doctors say that amputations were more merciful for the wounded because it was less painful to transport an amputee than for a soldier whose injuries made the slightest movement feel like torture.

Around the campfire, someone would inevitably add that he'd heard it on good authority, that about three out of four soldiers survived amputations. That orator was usually the optimist in the group. However, no one seemed to feel comforted by this information. They'd all heard what the procedure was like, and they were all terrified of it.

Anesthesia was available, but after four years of war and especially out in the field, supplies were limited at best. If it was available, ether or chloroform was poured on a cloth cone placed over the patient's mouth and nose.

Soon, the patient became unconscious, but you could never tell how long that state would last. The surgeon had to act quickly. The experts around the campfire had heard that the average amputation took about six minutes. But they'd all heard the stories of patients regaining consciousness before it was over. Those who'd heard the screams said the sound never left you.

Even if Deacon had not been his friend – even if he'd been a complete stranger – even someone as lacking in medical knowledge as Moran could tell that Deacon was one of the most badly injured. There was blood all over him, and Moran could see the insides of Deacon's shattered leg. The orderly was able to bring the first of the wounded into the operation room by himself, but Moran needed help with Deacon, so he was the second to go. Deacon was looking pretty bad.

Much as he wanted out of that room, Moran felt some obligation to help. The orderly said sadly he suspected there wasn't much that could be done for a leg that badly torn up. "And look here," he said to Moran after separating the cloth of Deacon's uniform pants from the wound. "There's already infection in this man's leg."

They cut away the remains of Deacon's trousers from hip to foot on that leg. "Look here," the orderly repeated, though it was the last thing Moran wanted to do. The orderly sliced into the makeshift bandages Deacon had made from the cloth napkin Moran gave him, back when they were walking guard together.

"Look at the blisters on this man's feet. They're all infected, and it's spreading. I can't imagine the doctor will be able to do anything other than take the leg. Blood poisoning will kill this man."

"Yeah, well, that's your opinion. No offense meant, but you ain't a doctor," Moran said, more for himself than to propose a debate with the man.

The orderly spoke kindly. "It gives me no pleasure to say that. I can't hardly stand to be around amputations. I was a medical student in Philadelphia before I got into the Army. If I'd gotten out a year or two sooner, they'd'a made me an Army surgeon and it would have to be me cutting off a man's leg like this. It gives me no pleasure to see."

Meanwhile, Deacon laid on the table without moving, just staring blankly into space. As the doctor worked on the other patient, Moran told the orderly he'd go get the anesthesia cloth ready to put over Deacon's face if the leg really did have to go.

The orderly looked truly sorrowful. He said they only had a little of the anesthetic left in their supply kit. And moreover, he and the doctor were under orders to use it only for officers.

Much as Moran wanted to raise a ruckus over this piece of news, he could not afford to alert the doctor. He was determined to appear reasonable.

Quietly – and rationally enough, he thought – Moran said, "You mean to tell me that the enlisted men, the ones out there doing the fighting, can't even be put under while their bodies are being cut up?"

"I am truly sorry, friend, truly I am. But the doctor and me, we're soldiers too. And we're under orders. I wish I could."

"Then, please ..." Moran was not used to begging but it seemed right in this case. "Please knock him out. Look, it won't be you. I'll do it myself. You can tell 'em ... tell 'em I threatened to shoot you." Which was not a bad idea, Moran thought. He'd already tried being reasonable and rational, and look how far it got him.

"I'm sorry, Private. I just can't do it. It's orders. We'll need you to help hold him down while the doctor cuts."

"But if this man was an officer, it'd be all right to knock him out?" Moran asked pointedly.

"Yes, I'm sorry. That's just the way it is," said the orderly, who expected the conversation to now be at an end. Or that Moran would take a punch at him.

The orderly therefore could not have been more shocked when Moran started taking off his clothes.

Moran strongly believed he was not as stupid as people seemed to think. Yes, he had worn the bulk of the gold pieces Mr. Slick had given him in the pouch around his neck. He'd used them for purchases at the sutler's as well as on the ill-fated night when he was gambling with the Big Swede. A lot of people most likely knew it was there.

So the Swede probably thought he lifted all the loot when he tore the pouch from Moran's neck. Which was exactly what Moran had hoped.

That night on guard duty when he gave Deacon the linen napkin to make bandages for those blistered feet – which had maybe turned out to be ill-fated, he reflected – Moran had torn off a strip that he kept for himself. Later, he cut the material into squares and sewed little pockets inside his drawers. He reasoned that no man would search him there.

Now, he dug into one of the little pockets in his underclothes and pulled out five gold pieces. He handed them to the astonished orderly. "How much would it take to make this man an officer?" asked Moran.

With the doctor's back still turned away, the orderly quickly pocketed the money as he said, "Well, guess there is such a thing as a field promotion."

If the doctor suspected anything out of the ordinary when it came time to see to Deacon, he never let on. He looked at the leg and saw the existing infection along with the appalling wound. He told the orderly to bring his amputation saw.

Without a word, the orderly administered the anesthesia. Deacon went under and mercifully, didn't wake up while it was all going on.

Moran held Deacon's shoulders down, just in case, and tried to keep his own eyes closed.

Within minutes, the doctor had separated Deacon from his right leg. "Next patient," was all the doctor said.

In Baton Rouge, someone else was pondering the effects of anesthesia. The drug in question was laudanum. Charity Boudry still wondered how to administer it correctly.

When she had emerged onto the sidewalk around the corner from Gallatin Street in New Orleans, she stopped for a moment just to breathe the air of freedom. Unfortunately, it smelled just like that on Gallatin, full of rotting garbage, human waste, and despair.

She longed to see the better part of New Orleans. She'd heard bits and pieces from the men in the parlor at Madame's. Just the sound of the street names could make your mouth water. Iberville, Bienville, Bourbon, Burgundy, Chartres, Royale, Toulouse, Ursulines.

It was when she thought of that last street name that she realized she had no clear idea of where she was in the city or where she would go to escape from it.

That boy in her room at Madame's would wake up sooner or later, and the charge against Charity would be robbery and assault. If he didn't wake up, the charge would be murder. This was no time to ponder the high life on Rue Royale. This was the time to see the last of New Orleans.

That was when the thought of the Ursuline Convent crossed her mind. She had a feeling it was near Gallatin Street. Perhaps she could go there for shelter. But if it was so near Gallatin, that pit of depravity, why didn't more girls seek sanctuary among the Ursuline Sisters? Because, she told herself, the nuns would be overrun in no time. Perhaps they simply turned the desperate girls away from their locked door. Perhaps they called the police. This was no time to find out.

So, as she'd always suspected, she'd make her escape from New Orleans on the river. She knew from the sailors that the wharves were near Madame's, and she was confident she could find the way. At first, she considered asking directions from passersby, but anyone walking these streets at this hour would not be kindly gentlefolk on their way to church. So, once again, she knew she could depend only on herself.

Within a few blocks, she did manage to find the Mississippi River. It ran right through town. She had gone a few blocks out of her way, but soon thought she'd gotten her bearings.

When she got to the river, she knew that it flowed south into the Gulf of Mexico. She'd go due north as far as she could. So it would be easy. Just follow the river north, upstream.

But New Orleans tried to trip her up, as if the city itself had no intention of letting her leave. When she found the river, it was flowing northward. Charity was completely disoriented. The river ran south, didn't it? Where was she? How could it be flowing north from where she was?

Huge bales of cotton were stacked at the dock waiting to be loaded onto riverboats. She knew, if she followed those bales, she'd be heading where they were going – northbound. On the one hand, she was terrified that the law was on her trail. Taking a boat out of the city was a tremendous risk. They could already be watching passengers who boarded, searching for her. But it was simply one she'd have to take. She was only a few blocks from Madame's and she'd already gotten lost. If she spotted the law – or worse – coming after her, she'd simply run to the water's edge, jump in and drown. If it was going to happen, let it be now. She was not going back to Gallatin Street. Whether or not the river was running northward, she was not going back.

It was still before dawn, but the docks were coming to life. Lanterns were being lit aboard the riverboats that were lined up against the pier like some sort of festive parade just waiting for the signal to commence. Steam started to drift from their stacks. For a moment, Charity simply stood and enjoyed the spectacle.

Her reading skills were not all that good, but her *Maman* had taught her some. She could read the postings of departures, and two boats looked promising. They were leaving that morning at dawn. The sooner the better.

The first was called the *Wild Wagoner.* What a strange name for a boat, she thought. She knew nothing of the vessels that plied the great river, but she could see it was a side-wheeler with a wooden hull. It looked fairly new, and was what she considered to be about medium size – not too big and not too small. Perfect. As she approached the gangway, she had a strange feeling of foreboding. A small voice in her head told her not to board that boat. And if she was reading correctly, the ship's owner and captain was named Henry H. Drown. That did it. Charity Boudry had spent enough time in the bayous to know about bad jingo.

The next boat leaving that morning was a side-wheeler called the *Silver Moon.* She didn't see a sign with the master's name. But unless it turned out to be Captain Watery Grave, the *Silver Moon* would be her magic carpet.

The first rays of dawn were breaking in what she assumed to be the east. Still, the river was running northward. She could not come to terms with that. Just then, she saw a man in an official-looking jacket and cap coming down the gangplank. Now or never, she told herself. Now or never.

With her head high and flashing her most alluring smile, she approached him. "Good morning, sir! How might one book passage on the *Silver Moon*? Heading north, of course." She didn't want to end up in the Gulf.

"That's where we're going, ma'am. All the way to the Ohio River. I can have the honor of assisting if you care to board now. How far you headed?"

Charity had no idea what the passage would cost and if she even remotely had the funds to cover it. She just knew she had to get off the wharf before she was spotted. In an instant, she reasoned that if she named a short distance, she could always book passage further down the line when the time came.

"Baton Rouge, please."

"And of course that will be cabin class?"

"Yes, of course." She did not want to arouse suspicion by quizzing him on the different categories. She had to look as though she belonged in the world at large. If he noted her attire, well, perhaps being on the river all the time, he'd just assume the man's jacket she wore over her dress was the newest fashion.

The fare he named was well within the funds she had taken from the man in her room at Madame's, but those resources would not last forever. She'd worry about it in Baton Rouge. She also had the thought that perhaps he had quoted her a higher figure for the fare and was going to pocket the difference. No matter. That was the price of doing business outside the law.

Their transaction completed, the boatman offered his arm and took her aboard. He showed her to a pleasant cabin with a window. When he left, she locked the door behind him but did not allow herself to feel any brief moment of relief. That would not happen until the big paddlewheels carried them out of New Orleans.

Then came a knock at her door. Instinctively, she looked to the window to see if she could escape that way. No. She could not. She grasped the jagged piece of glass in her pocket. Boldly, she called out, "Who is it?"

"Cabin boy, ma'am. Come wit' your coffee and to see about your breakfast."

Charity's first thought was "How wonderful!" but her second thought was, "How much will it cost?" It must be wonderful to go through life without ever having to ask that question.

Cautiously, she opened the door. Sure enough, he was what he said he was. He brought in a tray with the most intoxicating pot of coffee she had ever smelled. She could almost taste it already. He told her there would be breakfast in the main dining room, and the hours when it would be served.

"Oh, I'm not sure I can really afford that."

"It's included in your fare, ma'am."

Hungry as she was, she really didn't want to be out among fellow passengers. She told the cabin boy she was felling rather ill, and wondered if anything could be brought to her cabin. He was happy to oblige after mentioning a small fee for that service. No matter, it would be worth it.

Once again, she flashed her smile. "I'll bet you have lots of experience here on the river," she said. The boy probably didn't but said he did.

"Then perhaps you could answer a question for me," said Charity. She gave him her most unworldly, poor-silly-little-me look. "From the position of where the sun is rising," – it would not do to have him think she was a complete fool – "it looks like the river is running northward. Can that be correct?"

"Yes, ma'am! The river flows north in downtown New Orleans! Everyone knows the Mississippi River runs south, but here in this part of New Orleans, it's running north. The river runs mostly west to east from Baton Rouge to New Orleans. Here in town, it takes big meanderin' loops north and south. Like being in a funhouse, ain't it? That's N'awlins for you. Almost like the city is determined not to be like any other place on Earth."

So this was Charity's first clue that the larger universe was far different from what she had known. New Orleans might simply be its own little world apart.

Now she was ready to eat. The sooner the better.

The cabin boy was as good as his word. He quickly brought a fine breakfast, and she paid him a handsome fee hoping it would be enough. Apparently it was. He took a look and beamed, "Yes, ma'am. Anything you want, ma'am. Anything at all, you just call."

She devoured the breakfast in short order. It was the finest meal she'd ever had in her life. She set the tray outside her room where the cabin boy had told her to, and lay down on the cloud-like bed where she drifted off to sleep almost immediately.

Sleeping on and off, she lost track of time, except when the cabin boy brought meals according to their pre-established arrangement. She'd be happy to stay here in the cabin forever, just plying the river with its exotic-sounding river towns: Destrehan, Vacherie, St. Gabriel, Plaquemine. Uplifting parish names like Ascension, St. Charles, St. James, St. John the Baptist. Good food and a cozy bed beyond anything she had ever known.

Perhaps she had fallen from the slats as she made her escape over the alley at Madame's. Perhaps she was dead. Perhaps this was Heaven. Well, so far, it was fine with her.

CHAPTER 12
WINTER, 1865

Ella had never seen so much blood, didn't know there could be so much blood in one small human body. And worse, she had no idea how to stop it.

As they had both suspected, Patsy's time was very near. Ella had the thought that since the snow stopped, maybe they could get to a town after all. But the snowfall was too deep, roads were covered, and they had no idea where they were going. So they stayed in the little cave.

At least they were able to keep the fire going. For water, Ella melted snow. It was certainly in great supply, might as well use it. They could heat water for coffee, and even add it to the cubes of "desecrated vegetables" to make a meal. They had each other for comfort, enjoyed each other's company, and were reasonably content – as much as they could be in what they both knew was only a temporary respite.

Ella blamed herself. She had actually allowed herself to feel happy and hopeful. That's when it all started going wrong. Deacon had always said crazy things about not letting the gods know you were too happy or they'd be jealous and take it away from you. She didn't believe that. She thought God, the real one, wanted His children to be happy. But at times like this, it made her wonder if maybe she'd been feeling a little too good. Tempting fate, as Deacon had called it.

The pains started coming faster. Patsy sometimes seemed in agony. Other times, she smiled a brave little smile and said it wasn't all that bad. Then she'd share a story about being kicked by a mule, or dropping a log on her foot, or some such tale of calamity that had hurt much worse, to take both of their minds off the events at hand.

Finally it could be put off no longer. Ella made sure Patsy kept her jackets on, but removed what she could of her other clothing before wrapping the girl in a blanket. As Private Patrick Morrissey, U. S. Army, Patsy's field pack contained a sleeping mat that served as a barrier between her and the chill of the cave floor. Ella helped make the girl as comfortable as she could, and absolutely dreaded what would come next.

Suddenly, Patsy was lying in a pool of water. Ella wondered if somehow a spring had broken through the cave wall from melting snow. That was all they needed.

But Patsy kept saying she was sorry. Ella assured her there was nothing to be sorry about. She gathered it had something to do with the birthing process. She dried things up as best she could. Patsy went from lying on her back to sitting with her back against the cave wall. It did not leave a lot of room, but seemed to ease her pain.

Ella was a farm girl, and the McAdams farm had its share of livestock. She'd seen calves being born, and had a basic idea of the process. Once, her father said the calf was in a bad position, that he'd have to "take it" from the cow himself. Ella couldn't believe what she'd seen him do – just reached in and pulled. Both the cow and newborn had survived, but Ella now prayed she'd not have to do that.

Patsy's labor went on for most of the day. It was almost as agonizing for Ella to watch as for Patsy to endure it. Nightfall came, and the little cave grew darker. Ella had to remember to keep the fire going, not to lose sight of that. She kept water warming for whatever was about to happen. Though it was freezing, Patsy's brow had to be wiped as she grew flushed and heated. It was just a terrible ordeal for the girl, and Ella did not know what to do to help.

Sometime during the night, things began happening in a rush. Maybe, thought Ella, the darkness would be better than seeing it all in bright sunlight. Ella held Patsy's hand. What looked like a baby's head emerged, which Ella knew was a good thing. Coming out backwards would be a disaster.

In the semi-darkness, with only the small fire for light, the baby's head looked blue to Ella. It was very still. Patsy kept pushing, though she was becoming noticeably weaker.

Abruptly, the baby stopped coming, like a horse that had been suddenly reined in. It was so hard to see without much light. Soon Ella thought she could determine the reason: some kind of cord was wrapped around the baby's neck. It was like a noose. The baby couldn't breathe.

Patsy was still suffering. "Please!" she kept begging. "Please! Please!" Ella had no idea what the girl meant, what she was supposed to do. But she knew she had to do something, and do it fast. She searched through her bag for the little knife she carried. She tried not to think about using that same knife to cut another noose, the one around the old man's neck, the one that had strangled the life out of him by the light of the burning farmhouse.

So here she was again, by firelight, cutting another noose. Patsy was screaming, crying, writhing. Ella tried to be as careful as she could, just to cut away the cord from the baby's neck and injure neither mother nor baby. She hoped the cord wasn't something important that had to be left in place.

She made the cut into the cord and pulled the baby free. Patsy's labored breathing slowed down and the girl seemed to settle into a deep sleep. The baby never moved.

Ella tried everything she could think of to revive it. Once she'd heard of a neighbor boy who'd gone under while swimming with his brothers. When they brought him out, they thought he was dead. But one of the others had breathed life back into the boy. That was what Ella tried now, just put her mouth over the baby's and breathed into its tiny body.

The baby never moved.

Ella held it close to her, thinking maybe the cold had stunned it. She moved closer to the fire. She rubbed its arms and legs, trying to bring it some warmth.

The baby never moved.

She kept on, breathing into its mouth and warming it until long after she knew nothing was working. Still holding it, not knowing what to do, she went back to Patsy's side. She was glad the girl seemed to be sleeping peacefully after her ordeal, though Ella felt a pang of guilt for not checking on her while she had been trying to revive the baby.

Patsy appeared to still be in a deep sleep. Ella pulled the blanket tighter around the girl. That was when she noticed the pool of blood.

"Patsy! Patsy! Wake up!" Ella cried. "You have to tell me what to do! There's blood! Patsy, please wake up!"

It took the better part of the day. Patsy never did wake up. Ella sobbed as she watched the life literally drain out of the girl. Ella placed the dead baby in the arms of its dead mother, and said all the prayers she could think of. Then she begged God's forgiveness for what she was about to do. Ella needed the forgiveness of God because she knew she never would forgive *herself.*

Ella took everything of Patsy's that she could, everything that was not covered in blood. Patsy's blue jacket and the gray one underneath and the shirt beneath that. The blue trousers of a federal soldier which they had removed when Patsy went into labor. Patsy's army boots which they had also taken off. The other blanket, the one that was not covered in blood. The sleeping mat which Ella cleaned with water from melted snow. The haversack. And of course Ella's bag with the remains of the money Deacon had provided.

Ella thought she was beyond shame, but she had to do one more thing. She went through all of Patsy's pockets, those in the jackets and in the trousers. She found what she had hoped for. Somehow they had never discussed it, never thought they'd need to. But Patsy carried cash, probably from her pay packets. And Ella desperately needed it.

She would find people. She would beg for help. She would buy a horse, a mule, a donkey, anything to get her to the river. She would head downstream and she would make it to Vicksburg. Unknowingly, Patsy had seen to that.

And now, Ella felt, she was repaying Patsy's help in an unspeakable way. She knew she could not bury the girl and her dead baby. The frozen ground under the snow would be too hard, and there was nothing to dig with. But, as with the old man, Ella was determined they'd not be violated by predators.

She wrapped Patsy in the bloody blanket as tightly as she could. She searched around the cave and then dug under the snow for all the rocks she could find. She piled them over the dead bodies. She left her sweet, brave young friend entombed in the cave that had briefly been their salvation.

She tucked the bottom of her dress into the trousers, buttoned both jackets, and wrapped up in the blanket. She shouldered the pack and began walking through the snow. She would keep going. She thought of nothing but putting one foot in front of the other, one foot in front of the other. She would not stop. One foot in front of the other. One foot in front of the other. Left. Right. Left. Right. Left. Right.

Across the state, John Deacon was also determined not to think. He was lying on the floor of the little courthouse which had been conscripted into duty as a hospital. He had a blanket around him, and someone had gotten a fire going in the stove. It felt wonderful.

His buddy Moran was sitting next to him, chattering about how everything was going to turn out fine, how Moran had scouted the town, found a few people who weren't entirely unfriendly, and had even managed to secure a little food.

So, he kept telling Deacon, everything was going to be fine. Sooner or later, Union troops would find them, Moran said, would make them nice and comfortable in wagons, and take them home. Moran was proud that he'd been hit, though he quietly confessed to Deacon that it wasn't bad at all. As long as it got him out of this war, he'd moan and groan with the best of them

Deacon was still feeling confused. He recalled having his leg torn up in the skirmish, but right now it didn't hurt at all. In fact, it felt light and free. He'd been in some pain earlier, when they had him on a table in a smaller room, but for now, he felt no pain at all. Doc must be good at his profession.

He also felt groggy, wondering if his friend Moran had acquired some 'shine in which they'd indulged. Or maybe it had been something better, a bottle of brandy someone had left behind in this place, wherever he was. Deacon was having a hard time remembering a lot of things.

There were some fellas all around him, some lying still, some moaning and groaning. Deacon decided to be one of the quiet ones until he figured things out. Moran was keeping up enough conversation for both of them. And remarkably, as if they were out on the front porch on a warm summer day with nothing better to do, Moran was whittling. And bragging on it.

"Yep, Deacon, I figure this will do just fine. See, it's already got the dog-leg at the top. I can make it nice and smooth. But it's strong enough, just wait and see. Might be better to have another one too,

I'll go see about it in just a minute here. But I must admit, it looks right good and I think 'twill do just fine. Some of the other boys are mighty jealous."

Deacon tried to speak but his mouth was so dry. "Wa…ter?" was all that came out.

The new, ever-helpful Moran, obliged from his canteen. "Good, this is a real good sign if you're ready to take water. Mind my askin' how you're feelin' otherwise?"

The water helped Deacon to form sentences. "Feelin' fine, I reckon …Thanks for asking ... A little hungry … A little drowsy … We been drinkin'?"

Moran laughed as if that was the funniest thought in the world – imagine the thought, *him* drinking!

"Not hardly, but I wished I'd had some in there" – he motioned with his head to the smaller room. "After this war is all over, gonna need a mighty lot to help drown out some of what I saw. And heard. But you did just fine, Deacon. Just fine."

Deacon could only stare at his friend's face. He appreciated the compliment. But if he had done just fine, what was the alternative?

Moran was inquisitive again. "How's it feel? The leg, I mean. Mind my askin'? I took care of it myself, just in case you're wonderin' about it. Borrowed a shovel from one of the local householders. Ground was pretty hard. Couldn't do 'em all. But I took care of yours. It's safe out back. I heard some fellas say there's folks that want to come visit 'em after the war!"

Deacon was so groggy. "The man who loaned you his shovel?"

"What about him?" Now Moran looked as confused as Deacon felt.

"Come visit the man who loaned the shovel? After the war?"

Just then the doctor came around and knelt next to Deacon. The man looked plain exhausted, and Moran felt sorry for him. Grateful too. He did what he had to do, that was clear. That must make a man feel good, to know how to save lives. But Moran wouldn't want his job.

The part about saving people was all right, but only if that meant not ruining them for life.

"So, son," the doctor was saying to Deacon, "how are you doing?"

Deacon wondered why everyone was being so curious about how he was feeling. But no sense not to be polite. "Fine, sir," he said.

"Do not be surprised or worried or think you're going crazy if you start feeling pain or a tingling sensation from that leg. It's a fairly normal response. Some say they don't feel a thing, but others say they still feel something. No one knows why." The doctor laughed. "At least *I* sure don't know why. But you'll be glad to know, I think we got all the infection. It'd have killed you for sure. That leg was just eaten up with it, even before you got shot."

This was starting to sound like good news, thought Deacon. It was about time. "So you're sayin'.... Deacon took another sip of water. "You're sayin' you fixed up my leg, from where it was blistered and then from the shot? It was buckshot, wasn't it?"

"Yes, I think so. Chewed that leg up pretty bad. Surprised you didn't bleed to death."

"Well, then I thank you, sir."

The doctor smiled. "Sure glad to hear you say that. A lot of the boys hate me for what I'd done. Guess you're smart enough to know in your case, I had to. There was just no other choice."

The doctor then nodded toward Moran without looking directly at him. "And just in case your friend here thinks he pulled a fast one on me, I know all about the anesthesia. Orderly told me after. 'Course I knew it right then at the time. But it was an act of kindness. Orderly says we'll use the gold pieces to buy more supplies. It'll help other boys like you."

Deacon had no idea what any of this was all about. But no matter, the doctor was standing up, ready to move on to the next man.

"So, Doctor, you're saying I won't have any more trouble with that leg?"

"Trouble?" The man knelt back down, looking at Deacon very strangely. "Son, don't you know?"

"Know what?" asked Deacon.

The doctor looked at Moran. "Maybe you'd better tell him. I'm sorry, but it might be better coming from you. I'll be nearby if you need me." The doctor rose and walked toward the next patient without looking back.

Moran came closer to his friend and took a deep breath.

And that was when Deacon found out that his right leg was what Moran took such pride in burying out back.

The piteous animal howl that came from Deacon would echo in Moran's head for a long time. It was one of those sounds like Moran had heard the small room when the doctor had been cutting. The ones Moran knew he'd need a lot of whiskey to ever forget.

Moran would have been perfectly happy to stay in the little wooden courthouse for the duration of the war. Except for the lack of food, it was as good a place as any. But the doctor had said a Union scouting party would find them in a day or two, and the Army would decide what to do. Moran hoped the nick he'd received in his arm would be enough to disqualify him for further service. That was his only worry, that they'd send him back to the lines.

Sure enough, about two days later they heard the clatter of horses outside the courthouse. The door burst open, and Moran heard the words he had been longing to hear: "Boys, your war is over!"

The words were backed up by a few dozen men with guns. Unfortunately the words came out of a man wearing a jacket in Confederate gray instead of Union blue.

The first thought that went through Moran's mind was one of more curiosity than alarm. The man speaking was apparently an officer.

His uniform was gray, but his was one of the few in his unit that wasn't more of a butternut color. By this stage of the war, information in the North had it that the South was almost done, that its soldiers were a shabby bunch of skeletons in rags.

It looked to Moran that most of the men's jackets weren't a sharp, bright gray, but they surely were not a mismatched bunch of ragamuffins. The jackets looked like they'd started off gray but had faded into a tan color as the war dragged on. The past year or so, some Northerners started referring to Southern troops at this point as "Butternuts."

But as hungry as the Southern troops guarding them looked, they weren't done for, not just yet. They were still men in uniform, whatever the color of that uniform, and they were still fighting for their cause. Moran didn't plan to give them any trouble.

"Who is the ranking officer?" the official-looking man in gray asked.

"Guess I am," said the doctor with no great enthusiasm.

"It is my duty, sir, to inform you that you and your men are prisoners of war to be held by the Confederate States of America. Prepare your men for travel."

At that point, one of the Confederates began whispering at the officer who had spoken. The man nodded, then offered a small, wistful smile.

"Sir," he said to the doctor, but loud enough for all the men to hear, "it has come to my attention that your unit carried wounded from the Confederate Army to this place along with your own. And that you provided medical treatment to them no different from your own. Sir, I salute you and I thank you."

The doctor said nothing, just nodded almost imperceptibly.

The Confederate officer came closer to him, and spoke in a lower voice. Moran strained to hear the words.

"Sir, I am under orders to take prisoners wherever they might be encountered. Since your General Grant ended the exchange of prisoners, it is the official policy and I will follow orders."

He lowered his voice even more. "I regret I cannot offer much in the way of provisions or transport. Your men will travel exactly as mine will, on foot and with marching rations, neither more nor less. But sir, on my word as a gentleman, you and your men will be treated humanely. It is no less than you have earned for your humane treatment of the Confederated wounded."

"Thank you," the doctor said. There didn't seem to be much more he could add.

"But I must warn you, sir," the officer continued, stepping back and speaking in a louder voice, "I am also under orders to shoot stragglers. Those who cannot keep up. Or will not. My resources are limited, as are the number of men in my command. They cannot be utilized to go after escapees. If your men do not stay together in a group where they can be guarded, if they attempt to lag behind, I am sorry, sir. They will be shot without preamble."

"I will make sure the men understand," said the doctor. "But some of them are simply in no condition to be moved, let alone to march to God-knows-where."

"As I said, sir, I am under orders. Please prepare your men for travel."

Working with the orderly, the doctor got the men on their feet as best they could. Even as they did it, the two men exchanged glances that could be read no other way – that it would be more merciful just to shoot the wounded where they lay, right here at the courthouse. But they did as they were told.

Moran knew this would be the moment of truth for Deacon. He was glad he'd whittled what he preferred to think of as a "staff" rather than a "crutch." He helped Deacon to his feet and offered his own words of advice.

"The way I figure it, Deacon, is that the first little bit will be the most trying. You'll have to get used to the cr … to the *staff.* I'll stay with you as long as they'll let me. You can lean on me." Moran grinned. "No extra charge."

For a moment, Deacon just stared at him. Then he nodded, took the wooden staff from Moran and fitted it under his arm. Then-By-God, Moran watched Deacon lift his head and snap to attention. If he was to have a friend, Moran thought, this fella Deacon would do just fine.

Winter was still holding on, so it was cold, but the wounded men bunched together in a little group, and that provide some warmth. They all looked straight ahead as they marched. The Rebs had searched their haversacks for weapons, but didn't take anything else. They didn't taunt their prisoners, didn't treat them unkindly in any way. Moran recalled having mixed thoughts when they'd brought the Confederate wounded with them to be treated by their doctor. Now he gave a silent prayer of thanks that they did.

Most of the wounded prisoners held up remarkably for the first day or so. Most had lost blood and their strength was almost gone, even while they were back at the courthouse. Like Deacon and Moran, most walked with canes or what-have-you, and leaned on their comrades who sometimes half-dragged them along.

Deacon and Moran were toward the front of the group of wounded. No particular reason, that was just where they'd ended up. Soon, they started hearing moans from fellow prisoners back behind them. Once in a while, they'd hear one of their men say, "Cain't do it no more" and then the sound of a man falling to the ground.

That would soon be followed by the crack of a gunshot. Neither Deacon nor Moran looked back.

The first time it happened, Moran said, "Shooting stragglers, I reckon."

"They might be the lucky ones," said Deacon.

It was the last time Deacon spoke for the rest of their journey.

CHAPTER 13
MARCH, 1865

Charity Boudry never wanted to leave the *Silver Moon*. The cabin boy apologized that the trip was taking longer than usual, but she wished it would last forever.

"Storms dumped a lot of debris, tree limbs and the like, into the river," he told her. "All river traffic is taking it slow. Don't no one want to have the bottom of their hull ripped out by snagging a big old tree trunk. And of course, there's still the submerged hulls of boats that went down. Sure hope river traffic's about to get back to normal. Enough hazards on this river without boats blowing up too."

The cabin boy had been kind to her. Charity wanted desperately to lengthen her city of final destination and decided to chance it. "What if a person was to change their plans?" she asked the boy, as if on a sudden whim. "Maybe stay on the *Silver Moon* a while longer up the river, say Natchez or Vicksburg or all the way to St Louis? It's such a pleasant vessel. Sure am enjoying the rest, and hate to leave in Baton Rouge."

Perhaps he'd think she was a bored heiress from that new Garden District in New Orleans. All those tea parties could probably be mighty vexing.

"Ma'am, I'm as sorry as I can be. Enjoyed having you on board." *Enjoyed all the payoffs to bring food to my cabin, thought Charity.* "But soon as we hit Baton Rouge and on into Natchez and Vicksburg and Memphis, all the way to St. Louis, your cabin – all these cabins – are booked. Lots of Army officers going back North. Word in the stewards' quarters is that the war is goin' to end soon! Lots of things be different when that happens. Goin' back to the way things was. Riverboat traffic on the Mississippi as thick as her mosquitoes, just as far as you can see. Won't have to worry about no boatburners then."

Charity had stopped listening as soon as he'd said the cabins were booked. So she'd get off in Baton Rouge and make it worth her while. Supplement her depleted funds. She asked "just out of curiosity" what the fares were in cabin class out of Baton Rouge to points north. The boy didn't seem to suspect that she was anything other than a sheltered girl who couldn't be bothered memorizing all those tiresome financial details. At least, that was what she hoped.

Cabin class was of course the most expensive, but it was her safest mode of travel. Oh, the good food, the cozy bed, the blessed solitude! Perhaps the New Orleans authorities wouldn't think to look for her in such a splendid hiding place.

But she'd have to leave the *Silver Moon.* Already, the boat was starting to pull in at Baton Rouge. She'd have to keep her wits about her in town. Not enough money left to hide away in a nice private little world like this cabin. The word might be out on her with the local sheriff. Might be a reward offered. A girl of her description wanted for robbery in New Orleans – or if the man in her room hadn't awakened, the charge would be worse.

After leaving the *Silver Moon,* Charity tried to get away from the wharf as quickly as possible. It seemed to her that if New Orleans alerted Baton Rouge authorities to be on the lookout, they'd be smart enough to know she'd head for the river to make an escape.

But she also knew she couldn't go far. With the remainder of her money, she rented a room near the dockland. It was a disreputable-looking place that was none too clean and probably housed girls like those at Madame's. But Charity also felt she could leave whenever she wanted as long as there was no trouble. The man at the counter asked how long she'd be staying – she recognized the smirking look in his eyes. She told him it would probably be just one night as she had a boat to catch in the morning.

Still smirking, the man at the counter told her there were several payment plans available to a lovely lady like herself. She knew exactly what at least one of them would involve.

Somewhere on the *Silver Moon,* she had promised herself that whatever happened, however desperate she became, she would never go back to doing what she did at Madame's. Back there, she might have found herself in that circumstance, but now she had her own free will. She would never, ever sell herself again.

Pleasantly, Charity told the man she'd pay cash, right now, for the room. It would be so early when she'd be leaving, she said. She tried to make it sound as though there were any choice in the matter. At a place like this, payment in advance would be the rule.

He took the money – she had no idea if he'd inflated the cost to her, a woman alone – but she kept her sweetest smile focused on him as she said, "Might go out for a bit. Can you recommend a good eating establishment nearby?"

They both knew there would be no fine dining near this place. He mentioned the names of a few places and tossed in some directions. That might be helpful in getting her bearings when she left town. Charity just hoped it would be in the immediate future. She wanted out of Baton Rouge as quickly as possible.

She did not have the luxury of time to choose the perfect man who would be her way out, the one with all the right qualifications as she had done in New Orleans. She thought if she could just get out of Baton Rouge with a little money and with her life, she'd consider it a success. He had to be young, though. That was the key. No one with enough experience to know what to look out for.

So as dusk fell, she left her room and moved stealthily back to the docks. The man at the counter never looked up. Good. Her hope was that a boat would be putting in for the night, preferably with young, recently-paid deck hands. The best boat would be heading south, the opposite way from Charity's destination in the north.

She took up a secluded post next to one of the huge cotton bales that were piled on the wharf. From her cabin window, she'd seen the same sight on every dock that fronted the river all the way from New Orleans north. From her station here in Baton Rouge, she saw other girls sidling in next to other cotton bales, obviously with the same sort of commerce in mind. Charity would have to act quickly, to bag her prey fast but avoid getting knifed by another girl who saw her as a competitor.

She felt in her pocket and was reassured to find the piece of jagged glass she'd taken with her from Madame's attic window. She hoped not to have to use it, but it was hard to tell how things would go.

Finally she saw him. He was striding down the gangplank with one of the older deck hands. She'd have much preferred the boy to be alone, but this would have to do. From the corner of her eye, she saw one of other girls starting to make a move in their direction. As she'd said to herself before on this journey, *now or never.*

While she knew she could be identified for what she was about to do, she figured they couldn't arrest a girl just for being friendly. If confronted, she'd say she had made a mistake. Thought he was someone else. So hard to see on these dark wharves after sundown. A simple matter of mistaken identity, so anxious to see her sweetheart. She started running, throwing her arms open wide, aiming straight for the boy coming off the gangplank.

"Oh *mon cher,* it has been so long. I thought you were never coming back!" she kissed him in a way that best concealed her face from his companion. "Oh, *chérie,* I am so happy to see you! You must tell me everything of your trip!"

Charity took the boy's arm and steered him determinedly away from the older man who was laughing but who also had a look of admiration on his face. "Willie boy, you are a man of many secrets!" he shouted.

So now Charity knew the boy's name. She'd have to be careful using it, though. She might still have to use the mistaken identity ruse.

A moment later, the other girl on the pier had completed her approach to the older man. Now his mind was on other matters, not the sweet young thing who had so warmly embraced his young friend Willie boy. *See,* Charity wanted to say to the other girl, *there's plenty for everyone.*

Charity kept up the patter, how she had missed the boy, how she had been thinking only of him, how she knew now how much she loved him, how it had seemed so long since she had last seen him, how handsome he looked in his seaman's clothes! If he challenged her at any point, she knew she could evade his suspicions, claim she'd made a mistake, even resort to tears if need be. She managed to inquire with great curiosity about his work, about where his travels would take him next. The boy happily responded to this sudden interest in his career. South. Downriver. *Perfect.*

"*Chérie,* I have taken a room for us. We can be alone together. But I am so sorry, I was in such a hurry to see you, I neglected to buy food or refreshment. Could you stop in one of these taverns?"

She was careful not to use the word 'saloon,' which is what they were. She had to keep up the pretense that she was a simple girl, unfamiliar with the ways of the city. "Perhaps some sandwiches and a bottle of brandy to celebrate your return, *chérie?* I will of course wait for you outside." She made sure the last part was as demure as she could manage.

This was risky. He could get inside the place and then start to think things through. Still, once again, it was a risk she'd have to take. She needed the brandy for the dose of laudanum, and she needed the food because she didn't know when her next meal would be.

She watched as best she could from the open door. He was good at following instructions. He approached the bar, placed his request, paid his money, and came away with the needed supplies. She carefully noted he had money left over. He kept it in the left-hand pocket of his pants.

The plan went as well as it had in New Orleans, more or less. Willie, or whatever his name was, accompanied her to the room where the laudanum was handy, accepted his tainted drink, laid down on the bed, and was unconscious in less time than it took the one at Madame's. Or, Charity thought, perhaps she was just getting better at this.

She was, however, dismayed when she retrieved the money from his pants pocket. There was far less than she'd hoped. Well, nothing to be done. She'd take his jacket to wear under her own, and make a thorough search of it later. Perhaps he had more concealed somewhere in the jacket, to be kept away from girls like her.

This time when she left the room, she took the opened bottle of brandy along with the sandwiches. She scurried to the stairs, waiting at the top in hopes of a patron coming in to engage the counter man's attention. She wanted his memory of her to be vague when he found the boy knocked out upstairs. The counter man had probably seen it all before and would not be too shocked. But she wanted to avoid having the counter man be just one more person to identify her in the hunt. No new patron came in. She had to go.

The man behind the counter was reading something – she hoped it wasn't a New Orleans paper carrying her description – and hardly looked up as she passed. She'd paid for the room. For now, that was all he needed.

On the street, Charity moved as quickly as she could without attracting attention. This time, she knew she had to move away from the docklands. There, she could be identified.

She would look for railroad tracks. In this part of town, there should be some nearby. The counter man had said something about a restaurant near the tracks, so they were probably fairly close by. The railway men would have to eat somewhere. Though most trains in the South were private lines that only went a short distance before the rails were torn up, a train would at least get her out of town. She only hoped to make it to her next stop, Natchez, Mississippi. She'd created a pattern. She had to get out of Louisiana.

Just as Charity was trying to head north out of Baton Rouge, Alpha decided it was time for a little northward travel himself. He'd been in Vicksburg a little too long to suit his tastes. The key in his line of work was not to become too comfortable, too complacent in any one place. He didn't necessarily distrust his contact here, the one who had gotten him settled in at the siege caves. But he had no reason to bet his fate – and that of the Confederacy – on a stranger.

Alpha had assembled a few of the coal torpedoes and concealed them in yet other siege caves. He silently blessed the ladies of Vicksburg who had so bravely withstood the siege of their city by the hated Yankees. He liked to think it was a show of defiance that had led them to move so many household furnishing to the siege caves, and to leave so many there in case they had to return. Alpha made good use of them.

His existence in the caves was not unpleasant. He had plenty of money to take a room in town, but why bother? It only increased his chances of being out in public, accosted by Union troops, asked his business, subjected to their rude questions whether or not they had any idea who he might be. He was actually quite comfortable in the caves, had decent-enough bedding for sleep and even had some canned food to enjoy. Living in the siege caves had a great advantage in that it gave him the chance to familiarize himself with the network in some of them – how one led to another to another to another. He used some caves to hide his coal bombs, some his supplies, and some as bolt holes where he could scurry if the federals got too close.

But even so, he knew staying too long in any one place could mean his downfall. The coal barges at Vicksburg were extremely well guarded, but he'd still managed to conceal a few coal bombs among them. Once he thought someone spotted him as he swam away, but no one was foolish enough to dive into the waters of the Mississippi at flood stage. That took the skill of a powerful swimmer and the courage of the desperate. And Alpha was absolutely desperate to save the Confederacy.

As February of 1865 rolled into March, Alpha felt the Confederate States were in a bit of a slump. Perhaps, if there was cheerful news from the western theatre of war on the Mississippi, it could re-ignite the spark which the South needed to recover. And he dearly loved the thought that he could provide that spark, both literally and figuratively.

Nowadays, every time there was an explosion or fire aboard a Mississippi riverboat, people were attributing it to sabotage, whether he'd been anywhere near it or not. What a wonderful development! It was like having his own phantom army of nonexistent operatives. How delightful to instill fear and terror into those Northerners who'd never had their farms destroyed, their livestock stolen, their food confiscated. Let them see what war is all about. Let them feel the heartache of the South.

Though he would never say so out loud, Alpha did admit to feeling a bit downcast at times. He'd asked his Vicksburg contact to bring him all the newspapers he could find each day, and to leave them in a pre-arranged spot. Alpha would watch for hours to make sure he was not being observed, then swoop down to carry the papers to his latest siege cave home.

He absolutely had to remain current on the latest information, but it was starting to become discouraging. In mid-February of 1865, Charleston surrendered, followed almost immediately by that monster William Tecumseh Sherman capturing Wilmington, North Carolina.

Later that same month, General Lee had appointed Joe Johnston as commander of the only other effective Confederate fighting unit. Well, that was in the east. The Confederacy still had its secret weapon, Alpha himself, in the west.

According to the newspaper, the month of March didn't begin much better. On March 2, that Yankee upstart George Armstrong Custer defeated Jubal Early's Confederate troops in Virginia. The very next day, Alpha was shocked when the newspapers reported that Robert E. Lee had sent a message to Ulysses Grant asking for a conference to "iron out differences" between the North and the South. Though he was at first taken aback, Alpha realized that Lee, the master strategist, must have employed it as a stalling tactic to divert Grant's attention while old Bobby Lee merely re-grouped.

The papers from later that same week infuriated Alpha. On March 3, something called the Freedman's Bureau was established. Alpha did not like the sound of that. No good could come of it.

The news from March 4, 1865, enraged Alpha. Those idiots in the North had re-elected Abraham Lincoln to a second term as their president. On March 4, Inauguration Day, Lincoln made his inaugural speech – Why, the man talked as if the war was already over and the South had lost!

Alpha read and re-read every word of the repugnant oration that was printed in the paper.

Lincoln had first talked about how, four years earlier, "*all thoughts were anxiously directed to an impending civil war. All dreaded it, all sought to avert it.*" Well, Alpha thought, that was true, at least. The South had hoped to withdraw from the Union peacefully.

"*Both parties deprecated war, but one of them would make war rather than let the nation survive, and the other would accept war rather than let it perish, and the war came.*" So was Lincoln saying the South had caused the war?

"... *slaves constituted a peculiar and powerful interest,*" Lincoln had gone on. "*All knew that this interest was somehow the cause of the war.*" No! We went to war for States' Rights!

"*To strengthen, perpetuate, and extend this interest was the object for which the insurgents would rend the Union even by war, while the Government claimed no right to do more than to restrict the territorial enlargement of it.*" Hypocrites, damnable hypocrites!

"*Neither party expected for the war the magnitude or the duration which it has already attained.*" Well, Lincoln was right about that, anyway. Who would have thought the Yankees could hold off the cavaliers of the South as long as they had?

"*Both read the same Bible and pray to the same God, and each invokes His aid against the other.... It may seem strange that any men should dare to ask a just God's assistance in wringing their bread from the sweat of other men's faces, but let us judge not, that we be not judged.*" This was mightily close to blasphemy! Does Lincoln call himself a Christian?

"*Fondly do we hope, fervently do we pray, that this mighty scourge of war may speedily pass away....With malice toward none, with charity for all, with firmness in the right as God gives us to see the right, let us strive on to finish the work we are in, to bind up the nation's wounds, to care for him who shall have borne the battle and for his widow and his orphan, to do all which may achieve and cherish a just and lasting peace among ourselves and with all nations.*"

And that was the part that was an insult to Alpha's ears. It sounded to him as if Lincoln thought it was all over, that the South was beaten and humbly awaiting mercy. He'd show Lincoln and anyone else who thought the South was dead how very wrong they were. Before Alpha was through with his part of the war, it would be others begging for mercy.

So once again, Alpha was on the move

Wrapped in a blanket and trudging through the snow, Ella thought of nothing except forcing one foot in front of the other. At times, she even counted a cadence for herself: "Left. Right. Left. Right. Left. Right."

She did not worry about finding a place to rest when the sun went down, because there wasn't one. Everything was covered in snow. The odds of finding another little overhang to act as a cave were too remote to consider. She would just keep going until she found people or she fell. Whichever came first.

She felt somewhat heartened because Patsy had said there was a town around here someplace. It was where the poor girl had been going herself when she met up with Ella. Realizing it might be blasphemous but doing it nonetheless, Ella did not pray to God for salvation. She appealed to Patsy's spirit to guide her.

Ella did not see signs of a town as the sun started to set, but came across something almost as good. Wagon tracks in the snow. Either they were heading into a nearby town, or coming back home from someplace else. At the end of the wagon tracks, there would be something. Maybe just the end of the line. But something.

Was that a light? Ella strained her eyes to see in the approaching darkness. Smoke drifting lazily from a chimney – could it be? Ella followed the wagon tracks. They led to a small farmhouse. There was light from inside. The smoke could well be from a fire in a stove or fireplace. Warmth. Ella could hardly remember what that felt like. She could no longer feel her feet, but drove them forward to the farmhouse door. Left. Right. Left. Right. Left. Right.

Neither could she feel her arms. They would not move, frozen in the position where they held the blanket against her. No matter if her arms were useless. She simply kept up the cadence, then kicking at the door with her feet. Left. Right. Left. Right. Left. Right.

Suddenly the door opened. A woman screamed. "Clement! Clement! It's the Angel of Death!"

Ella was warm. So this was what it felt like. She had almost forgotten. It had been a long time, and she liked it. She was in front of a crackling fire. Someone was stroking her face, very kindly, and speaking to her in an equally kind voice. "Do you think you can take some soup now, girl?"

A spoon came up to her mouth and Ella gladly took a sip. Some heavenly nectar, hot and tasty. Ella thought of Heaven and wondered if that's where she was. She recalled something about the Angel of Death, so perhaps her time had come. As long as she could stay warm and have an endless supply of this soup, Ella was fine with all that.

She did not think the person feeding her was St. Peter, and looked questioningly into the eyes. A smile, warm as the soup, burst forth.

"Land, child – me and Clement thought you was a goner. Clement is my husband. He's that mean old cuss sitting over yonder."

Ella's eyes strayed to the general direction indicated. A man's voice responded.

"Don't you believe nothin' this old woman tells you. Let her talk, it'll help pass the time while you hurry up and get better."

Ella's eyes went back to the woman who kept feeding her the soup.

"Well, the old cuss is right about that," the woman said. "We both want you to get better. Oh, I'm Sarajane. That's who we are – Clement and Sarajane Ivey. Sorry if I skeered you with the Angel of Death business. It's just that – well, that's just exactly what you looked like there at the door. Wrapped up in a shroud, covered in ice, skin all blue, eyes that looked just plain dead."

"Didn't have no sickle, did she, woman?" contributed the man called Clement.

"Well, it just startled me is all," said the woman called Sarajane. "And I don't think it's the Angel of Death that comes with no sickle. That's the Grim Reaper. I swan, Clement, you just think you know it all."

So what Ella was starting to surmise was that she'd made it to a farmhouse, that they'd taken her in, kept her warm and were feeding her. And that they had been married for a long time and probably enjoyed the good-natured teasing. Affectionate, it sounded. Loving. Not like the cruel barbs William used to heap on her.

And William was what had gotten her into this in the first place. That was when fear kicked her like a mule. If these were sympathizers of one kind or another who'd ask her to leave, she might as well get it over with. Because she could very soon grow used to this.

Haltingly, between spoonfuls of the soup, Ella began. "Thank you for helping me," she said. "I was trying to get to the river. I would have frozen to death."

"Almost did," Clement interjected.

"Clement, hush!" the woman said. "Let her tell it. Meanwhile, make yourself useful, old man. Go get some more blankets and a pillow and the down mattress from in the loft."

"All in good time, woman. I want to hear this too."

So Ella told her story, leaving out parts that tore at her heart such as the death of Patsy and the old man who the outlaws had hanged, and how she'd not had the decency to give them a proper burial. She merely gave her name, told how her husband was wounded in the war, how she was going to Vicksburg to bring him home, how her horse and wagon and supplies had been stolen by the bushwhackers, how she'd walked westward toward the river, how the snow came, how she'd been walking and walking, and how she followed the wagon tracks here.

"That was Clement in the wagon," said the woman. "He can't stay away from Reelfoot even in weather like this, even in the middle of a war. Just got to trot over to that lake."

The man chimed in. "Brought you that fish, didn't I? What do you think you'd'a made that soup out of otherwise?"

Ella thought it best not to interrupt. She did not wish to offend at a time like this. But she also knew their routine had probably been perfected over decades of married life, and could go on most of the night. She had to know a few things now.

"Mrs. Ivey, can you tell me where we are?"

"None of that 'Mrs. Ivey,' dear – we're Sarajane and Clement, and we'll call you Ella, is that all right?"

Ella could only nod. There was almost no soup left in the bowl. Was there more on the stove?

Clement chimed in. "To answer your question, girl, which this old woman probably won't get around to, is that we're in the far northwest corner of Tennessee. This farm lays between Reelfoot Lake to the east and Tiptonville to the west. Tiptonville is on the river. Our daughter lives there with her husband and children. Our son is off at the war. We couldn't help but notice those jackets you's wearing, a blue one and the gray, one from each side." Was there suspicion in his eyes?

"Leave off, Clement," said Sarajane. "There'll be no talk of the war or what side is which or who's right or wrong or any of that. This girl is no fool. She probably needed whatever she could find to keep warm. No matter if it's blue or gray or apple green or mauveine." It seemed as though Sarajane wanted to keep the conversation away from the war whose duration still hung on like the winter snow. The old woman seemed to enjoy having a new face in the house, someone to talk to who wasn't Clement. Ella could certainly understand.

"Just brought it up, is all," the old man pouted.

To Clement, Sarajane said, "Is this about the time you think you can bring that bedding like I asked an hour ago? This girl needs some rest." To Ella, she said, "We thought we'd bring the down mattress from the sleeping loft so's you could stay in front of the fire. You need some warmth, that's for sure. You're still shivering. That's to be expected. We'll check later for frostbite. For now, you just get your temperature back to normal. You're still half froze."

Clement went grumbling up the ladder to the sleeping loft.

"That's where our son slept," said Sarajane. "Haven't heard from him in a while but sure hoping he's soon to be on his way home."

"I do too," said Ella, meaning every word of it. "Thank you for your hospitality. If you'd like, I'll keep the fire stoked until morning."

"That'd be right fine. Clement has a whole pile of firewood right over there." She motioned with her head. Ella knew she could handle that task. Happily.

"We could fix you up a bed pan, unless you think you can make it out to the privy before you bed down. We have a path cleared."

Ella said she could make it, so Sarajane helped her walk out back. On the way, the old woman said, "Don't pay Clement no mind if he starts talking about the war or wants to know what side you're on. You just change the subject or look faint. Bein' half dead-looking, you can manage that easy. As for me, I don't care what side you're on. Far as I'm concerned, you're on my side. You're a woman. You know all about what it takes to go through having children and then see them blowed apart because some stupid old fool men couldn't settle their differences any other way. Sorry if I offend, but that's the way I see it.'

"Mrs. Ivey, I wouldn't have it any other way. Thank you – both of you – for all you've done. You're right, you and I are on the same side."

"Snow should melt away soon. Clement will drive you in the wagon to our daughter's place in Tiptonville. Oh, he'll grumble all the way, but he'll do it. Now he'll head over to Reelfoot for fishin'at the drop of a hat, I don't care if it's earthquakes or tornadoes or ..."

The old woman kept up her chatter until they both returned to the house. Clement had made the bed beautifully atop the down mattress. It was close enough to the fire for Ella to keep warm, but far enough away so she was in no danger of setting herself and the house on fire. After their good-nights, Ella woke only sporadically during the night to keep the fire stocked.

Next thing she knew, there was the intoxicating aroma of something baking. Suddenly, Clement was kneeling at her side with warm biscuits on a plate. "You just keep restin,' young lady. I bake the biscuits around here. Don't let that old woman tell you otherwise. I'll leave 'em here for when you're ready. When you finish off one batch, I'll bring more. You just eat as many as you want, rest when you can, and get well."

Ella thought all three ideas had merit, and proceeded to do just that.

CHAPTER 14
MARCH, 1865

Ella lost track of the days and nights she spent in front of the fire at Clement and Sarajane's farm, but she thought it could not be more than two or three. The frostbite she had feared in her toes seemed to have subsided. She could feel with her fingers again. Sarajane's hearty soups and Clement's ambrosial biscuits had restored her strength. Time to leave this paradise. It came much too soon for her taste, but she still had a job to do.

Ella of course offered money to repay their hospitality. They of course refused it amidst great protestations. She of course left it under Clement's biscuit pan. They of course never said a word.

These lovely, generous people had been the targets of two armies. They now had to fear the ever-present bushwhackers whose boldness only grew as it appeared the war would end soon. When proper law was restored, the villains' free hand to rob and kill would be more restrained.

For now, people like the Iveys just struggled to survive. They saw their livestock taken, fields and orchards in ruin. But they still kept going, much as Ella had, one foot in front of the other. Left. Right.

Left. Right. They so enjoyed the simple pleasures in life. At least Clement still had his fishing at Reelfoot Lake to help keep body and soul together.

The plan was for Clement to hitch up the wagon and drive Ella to Tiptonville where they would stay overnight with his daughter. Then Clement would return home and Ella would figure the best way to Vicksburg.

As Sarajane had predicted, Clement grumbled but came around the front of the house with the horse hitched to the same wagon whose tracks Ella had followed to this house. Sarajane had washed Ella's clothes, provided a lovely hot bath, and helped fix her hair so Ella would arrive in Tiptonville looking slightly less like a specter of doom. Both Sarajane and Clement assured her they could reach Tiptonville before sundown.

At first, Sarajane had declined to come along, something about there not being enough room in the wagon, having to mind the farm, having to take care of chores even if Clement didn't bother doing his. She hugged Ella tightly and made her promise to keep in touch, to write in care of the local general store, to let them know she'd made it to Vicksburg safely and then back home again.

But after Ella had climbed into the buckboard next to Clement, he said, "Sarajane, stop this foolishness. You're coming along. Put on your cloak and put out the fire. Your daughter will want to see you."

Sarajane went back into the house to do as she was told, looking elated.

Clement looked straight ahead. "Now she'll take all day getting ready. Don't she know we're burning daylight? That woman is a thorn in my side. And if anything happened to her, I don't know what I'd do. I pray the Lord takes me first, or takes us both together. Because I wouldn't last a day without her."

Clement kept looking straight ahead. Astonished at his words, Ella burst into tears, crying great sobs, all the emotions of the past weeks bursting forth like a storm when the sky splits apart.

Clement and Sarajane. Patsy. The old man who was hanged. The tens of thousands of others fighting for an ideal, but who now were dead. John Deacon. He had to be alive. If America produced magnificent people like this, Ella knew even a bloodbath of a war wouldn't keep the country down. She tried to dry her eyes.

Clement kept looking straight ahead.

The happy little group made it to Tiptonville well before sundown. The sunshine was melting the snow as the weather suddenly became unseasonably warm. Trees glistened under the dripping, melting ice, making the whole journey seem like a trip across a sparkling fairy kingdom.

At first they chatted amiably. When the topic started flowing into hardship or the war, either the Union or Southern cause, the subject was quickly, gently changed. No one asked too many questions or wanted to know too much about the others. No one had even asked which army Ella's husband was in. No one wanted to anything that would break the spell of friendship. They were simply average Americans enjoying each other's company on a glittering sunny day.

At one point, they started to sing. Each one offered up a well-known tune. Ella noticed how Clement and Sarajane were able to sustain a lovely harmony. She guessed they had spent many a night together in song. How she envied them.

As if continuing their unspoken agreement, no one sang the opening notes to either *Dixie* or the *Battle Hymn of the Republic.*

Though it would have been a rousing song to sing as they jolted along in the wagon, no one suggested 1861's *Bonnie Blue Flag,* even though there was both a Union and Confederate version. It had been considered so incendiary that after Union General Benjamin Butler captured New Orleans, he had all copies of the sheet music destroyed and ordered that anyone caught singing – or even whistling – *The Bonnie Blue Flag* would be fined.

So they stuck to popular tunes of the day like *Shenandoah, Camptown Races, Oh! Susanna, Jeanie with the Light Brown Hair,* and *Beautiful Dreamer.* They included hymns they all knew like *Shall We Gather at the River,* popular songs like the bittersweet *Listen to the Mockingbird,* and even *The Yellow Rose of Texas,* which people said had a scandalous story behind it. Clement of course made sure to point that out, though he did not elaborate.

By the time they reached Tiptonville, they were as happy as it was possible to be in the wintry landscape of a devastated land. The Iveys' daughter, Margaret Ann Warren, came rushing out to meet them. She made all the loving protestations Ella would have expected – why they didn't let her know they were coming, the house was a mess, the kids looked like ragamuffins, there was nothing in the house fit for dinner.

Clement and Sarajane introduced Ella and briefly told her tale. Margaret Ann then bustled around the kitchen until her husband Thomas came home. After more introductions, she dispatched him into town to find better provisions for dinner.

Thomas Warren was a carpenter and was finding ample opportunities to rebuild things that had been destroyed by war. He was able to return home that evening with a goodly amount of beef. Margaret Ann started cooking it up with potatoes and some dried vegetables from her root cellar. Earlier that day, she had already put together an apple pie.

As they all sat down and asked Clement to offer a prayer, Ella felt her eyes welling up with tears again. She had almost forgotten what a miracle everyday life could be.

After dinner, the children clamored to play with their grandparents, who beamed with pride. Margaret Ann tidied up the kitchen after firmly turning down Ella's offer to help. Thomas Warren invited Ella to sit in front of the fire while he smoked his pipe.

After a few moments of companionable silence, Warren asked, "So ma'am, what might be your plan to get to Vicksburg? If you don't mind my askin'."

Ella didn't mind. She just wished she had an answer for him. Then she wondered if there was any more apple pie left over.

As they half marched, half-dragged themselves along a desolate road on the other side of the state, Moran told Deacon he figured they'd gone about thirty miles since they'd been captured. Wherever they were going, they'd have to be there, soon, wouldn't they? Deacon kept up his unnerving silence and blank stare, the demeanor he'd maintained since the goings-on at the courthouse.

Moran felt bad. He sure knew how he'd feel in the same situation. But he could use someone to talk to. Truth was, though he'd never admit it any time, any place or to anyone at all, he was scared to death. Deacon was leaning on Moran, using the crutch in place of his missing leg. Moran held his friend in place with his free arm, the one that had not been injured. He joked that it was like a Three-Legged Race at the county fair. Truth be told, Moran was pretty glad to have another human being to hold on to. He had a feeling they were dragging themselves into hell, and he was glad of an escort.

They'd all heard stories of the prison camps. Around the campfire, when the topic was not piles of amputated limbs at army hospitals, their horror stories centered around the prison camps. Some of the men said they'd shoot themselves before being sent to one.

It hadn't always been this way. In the early years of the conflict, prisoners of war from both the North and the South were exchanged. They could simply return to their regiments. But soon the flaw in this system became painfully obvious.

After General Grant captured Vicksburg in 1863, he took almost forty thousand Confederate prisoners of war. He found that when they had previously been exchanged according to the established system, they had simply returned to their regiments to continue the fighting. In a well-known quote that all the men around the campfire had heard, Grant said that the prisoner exchange was just sending enemy soldiers back to their regiments, and the fighting would continue until the entire South was, as Grant put it, exterminated.

Under the prisoner exchange, Grant saw the war continuing interminably, with the same men fighting each other over and over until they were all killed. From his desk in Washington, U. S. Secretary of War Stanton agreed. The edict came down. There would be no more prisoner-of-war exchanges.

Some of the men around the campfire saw the painful wisdom. The reason was humane in the long run – ending the death and suffering of the war more quickly. In the short run, the unfortunate men taken prisoner would suffer unspeakably. Grant and Stanton's policy condemned tens of thousands of captured soldiers on both sides to unimaginable horrors.

That was exactly what Deacon and Moran were hobbling into.

Ella was thinking of John Deacon right that very minute. Not entirely unusual. She thought of him so often, wondered how he was doing, prayed for this safety, despaired of ever seeing him again, despaired of what would happen if she did. But today her thoughts of Deacon were entirely happy ones.

How he would have loved this!

Her trip down through the river towns after she left Tiptonville was sporadic at best. After tearful goodbyes with Clement and Sarajane, Ella was presented with some sandwiches packed by Margaret Ann. Ella thought the kindness of Clement and Sarajane extended to their daughter, and wondered about the fate of their son. Ella would bet he was as nice as the rest of them. Anticipating protests from the entire extended Ivey clan, Ella quickly left some money for Margaret Ann under the apple pie plate. Ella just wished she had more money with her. The pie alone had been well worth a king's ransom.

Margaret Ann's husband, Thomas, decided to postpone a carpentry job that was scheduled for that morning. He could help Ella get started back on her journey. As he put it, he would "carry her" to the next town.

He asked to borrow the Iveys' wagon, meaning Clement and Sarajane could not get an early start home that day. They would simply have to spend another night. Clement grumbled about the children driving him near to distraction with their noise. As soon as he said it, he was grinning from ear to ear.

As Ella and Thomas left Tiptonville and followed the river road, Thomas offered as much help as he could. He apologized that he could not provide transportation all the way. Ella quickly interrupted with protestations of her own. She told him what she truly felt, that she had not expected even as much help as he'd already given.

That seemed to mollify the man. She hoped he had not been resenting her for the unspoken possibility of wanting more than he could give. Relieved, now he became a wellspring of information.

He said that normally a trip downriver to Vicksburg would not be difficult, even with the war. Though riverboat traffic was diminished – he blamed both the Army and the boatburners – there were usually a few steamers every day. Even if there weren't, there were usually plenty of boatmen along the river with small craft who would be glad of a fare. But the Army – *them* again – had issued an order that all small boats along the river were to be confiscated. The Army's theory was that the boatburners used them to smuggle bombs onto the coal barges. Well, how was a man supposed to make a living? … And another thing …

This was when Thomas interjected his first-hand knowledge of Army ways and the spurious orders they imposed on honest men like himself. He knew just how they acted. He'd served his hitch, returned home unscathed, and wanted no more of the military in any form. He began informing her of the greed, corruption, cronyism of the officers, poor treatment of the enlisted men … Ella feared he'd go on forever with an inexhaustible supply of his complaints about the

Army. She never asked him which army he'd served in, nor which color uniform he'd worn, blue or gray.

Instead, she steered him gently back to the subject most critical to her – getting from Tiptonville to Vicksburg. It seemed he knew a lot of the men along the river. Ella wondered if he'd had his own small boat, one that was confiscated. If so, now *she* had a complaint against the Army. A small boat and willing oarsman would have been perfect.

But he was able to provide her with names and places along the river where he knew "some ol' boy" might have been smart enough to conceal his boat. Just mention his name, he'd told her. After leaving him around noon with a firm handshake, she proceeded to do just that.

She could not remember all the names of the river towns she passed through, but recalled the overwhelming experience of crossing the great Mississippi into Missouri at Caruthersville. She had never seen and could never have imagined a body of water that big. And it was running fast and muddy. The snowmelt must be making its way into the river, she thought. She couldn't imagine what would happen if a small boat capsized into waters like that. And now she was traveling south in exactly that kind of craft.

Thomas Warren had been correct. A few of the rivermen had indeed protected their boats from confiscation. They were able to take her short distances by stealth. That was how she ended up in Missouri. One boatman ferried her across the great river to Caruthersville where he felt her chances of finding another ride would be better.

That was how she travelled. Back and forth across the Mississippi, downstream as far as each riverman could take her. She offered money to them all. After some degree of protest, most took it, for which she was glad. They would still have to make a perilous journey home in a contraband boat, and do it against the ever-swelling current of the river. If she'd had hundreds – thousands – to give them, it still would not have been enough.

All of them offered the hospitality of their home for Ella to rest, have a good meal, and spend the night. The wives and families seemed to enjoy having a new person to talk to, and seemed enthralled by Ella's highly-edited version of her travels. The subject of everyone's various affiliations never came up. Everyone, it seemed, was ready for the war to be over and for life to get back to normal.

The river meandered so badly through Tennessee, Missouri, Arkansas, and Mississippi that it seemed to take an eternity. It wound like a huge coiled snake, back and forth, back and forth. Suddenly the river would swivel wildly in one direction or another, then back again. Taking bearings by the sun was worthless. The boatmen seemed to know exactly where they were going. They knew the hazards, the depths, the shoals, the submerged wrecks. She thanked the Lord for these wise rivermen. She prayed for their safety and that of their families. They would scoff at the suggestion, but they were extraordinary people.

That was what Deacon would have loved if he could be on this journey. He adored writing about the unknowns of America. Men and women who would never have a statue in their honor, who would leave no glowing epitaph, who would die unmourned outside their little family group.

But these were the people who built America, he'd said. Not the puffed-up stuffed shirts – Deacon's exact words. He said America's story – its strength – its glory – lay in the unknown people who put in an honest day's work to provide for their own, who helped others when they could, and who carried a wealth of knowledge about their particular little world that outsiders would never know.

Everyone has a great story to tell, Deacon had said over and over. He said it was a blessing for him to be able to help tell it. Ella hoped that after the war, he could do just that. How she wished that somehow, she could be part of helping him do it.

The final leg of Ella's journey was a revelation. At Memphis, she was able to board a magnificent steamboat called the *Darling* heading downriver to Vicksburg. It took most of her remaining funds and there was no cabin available. Army officers had booked them all. She thought of Thomas Warren's many complaints about them and had to smile. But she took deck space which, she felt, was quite luxurious compared to most of what she'd been through so far. There were places to sit and enjoy the view, even to nap though she hated to miss a thing.

She was enraptured by the journey on the splendid steamboat and told herself that this – *this* – would be the only way to travel back home. Her husband was one of those well-paid Army officers Thomas Warren had groused about. Surely her husband would have the money to book a cabin.

As the *Darling* pulled into Vicksburg, Ella allowed herself to feel optimistic. She neglected to recall Deacon's caution about jealous gods.

Charity Boudry had never had any particular tendency to feel optimistic. But neither did she particularly tend to feel fear. A child used as alligator bait might grow up to be timid. Another could grow up to have a backbone of steel. She was of the latter variety.

Now, she told herself, what she felt was not exactly fear – that was against her nature – but an abundance of caution. The train out of Baton Rouge had served her well as long as it had lasted. It got her out of Louisiana. Maybe these days the law enforcement network didn't travel as far as the state of Mississippi.

But the track ran out right about at the state line, and she was now on foot heading north along the river. She aimed for Natchez, though it would probably not be a lengthy stay. That town was still too close to the grasp of Louisiana law. And now, she reminded herself, there was one more of her offenses, a man who was drugged and robbed in Baton Rouge like the one in New Orleans. They knew what she looked like in New Orleans and she'd been seen in Baton Rouge. Easy enough to circulate a description. Now her crimes were her calling card.

She kept having to scuttle off the Natchez road every time she heard the clatter of riders approaching. With every step she took, her eyes scanned the immediate vicinity for a place to conceal herself on a moment's notice. She asked herself if there was anyone she was *not* hiding from.

The law was bad enough. And she didn't know the relationship between local sheriffs and the soldiers in uniform who were everywhere. She knew they weren't exactly the same bunch but they might still be too close for comfort if a known fugitive crossed their path. Especially one still carrying vials of the drug she used in her work.

But the law and the Army had certain rules, so she didn't fear them nearly as much as the others. Villains came by all sorts of names nowadays, she thought. Bushwhackers, jayhawkers, scallywags – all just fancy names for lowdown murderous outlaws.

Charity did not consider herself to be an outlaw. She did what she had to do to survive, never hurt anyone for sport, never took anything but the money the men were already spreading around, never hurt innocent women or children, never killed. At least, she assumed the last part of be true, assumed the men in New Orleans and in Baton Rouge had eventually woken up. Women took laudanum all the time. That she knew. If women could handle it, so could the big strong men who had wanted to use her.

Well, best not dwell on any of that. Now was the time for survival, nothing more. Look forward, not back. Maybe *that* was what they called optimism, she guessed. She just needed a safe haven off the road, and Natchez would have to be it. She needed more money, and Natchez would have to provide it. So she walked on, sleeping under bushes when she needed to, diving for a hiding place whenever hoof beats approached. She just hoped to reach her immediate destination of Natchez, then to plan things out from there.

Her immediate destination was just about the worst she could have imagined.

Charity's vision of a place with the name "Natchez" included fine homes with scenic river views high up on the bluffs over the Mississippi. She didn't really think she'd be any more welcome in that part of town than she had been in similar districts of New Orleans or Baton Rouge. Nor did she have the money to finance being in those parts of town. But she hadn't bargained on the only part of Natchez where she thought she could seek refuge.

Natchez-Under-the-Hill was the most deadly river landing on the entire Mississippi.

She could see it from the road as she approached. It looked like about three long streets resembling terraces parallel to the river. A few lanes zigzagged off them as cross streets. Water Street, the lowest of the big ones, was bounded on the west by the river and on the east by a huge bluff. Buildings, warehouses, and wharves on Water Street stood on what looked like stilts. Parts of the buildings jutted out on their pilings over the Mississippi. She assumed they were built that way due to the rising and falling of the river, and could be used for dumping trash conveniently through trap doors underneath. Soon she would learn that the trap doors also served other purposes.

At first, it looked like every other disreputable part of town she'd been in. As she cautiously made her way down Water Street, a saloon door exploded open. Two men with knives careened out into the street, almost knocking her down. She shrunk back into a side alley, trapped. Before long, both were bleeding but one had the upper hand. He drove a lethal-looking knife almost a foot long into his adversary's heart. Charity thought the man was probably dead before he went facedown into the dust.

She worried she'd be trapped in the alley when the law came. She needn't have worried. No police came at all. Most people just stepped over the dead man as they continued on their way.

She was not as shocked as she might have been. She'd heard about Natchez-Under-the-Hill even on Gallatin Street, a place second to none in terms of crime and depravity. It was known that any New Orleans man in trouble with the law could head upriver to Natchez-Under-the-Hill. Police didn't patrol that area. It was just too dangerous in Under-the-Hill. There, a careful man could hide from the law until such time as he wanted to return to New Orleans. No one ever mentioned if it was also applicable to a woman.

Charity saw a few steamboats plying the river and wanted to be aboard one, fast. There was nothing to do but employ her usual method of financing. She saw a sign on the worst part of Water Street advertising rooms for rent, and followed the same procedure for booking one that she had done in Baton Rouge. The man at the counter smirked just like the one she'd encountered in Baton Rouge, but Charity had seen the type before. She paid the money he asked for, about the same amount as Baton Rouge. He announced that he was giving her his best room.

There was a stained rug on the floor, but the room had a small window with a view of the river, which she liked. She sat on the bed, disgusting as it was, to rest and to plan. There was a door inside the room which she assumed led to a small closet, but she had no intention of using it. After a few moments, there was a knock at the door of the room. Charity sat stock still, willing herself not to open the door even if the place was to catch fire. She heard departing footsteps and breathed a sigh of relief.

At first, she couldn't quite grasp what happened next. The closet door flew open, and the counter man from downstairs burst through, followed by another man. Her mind flashed that the closet must have a false panel as a back wall. Anyone who knew how to do it, like the counter man, could burst through, gaining access to the room.

That was really all she had time to follow. The counter man grabbed both of her arms behind her. The other one groped her body making grunting sounds. "Well, what we got here?' he leered to his friend.

In her pocket, the man found the shawl holding the laudanum. He knew what it was and tossed it aside, already speculating how it might be of use. With a sinister gleam, he knew exactly where to look for her money. Encouraged by the counter man twisting her arms, her assailant tore the front of her dress and pulled out the little horde of money she still carried there. Their grunting became more pronounced.

Charity remained as calm as she could. She was determined not to scream. That would just incite them to shut her up by any means. She willed herself to slow her breathing and just *think* while the two men grew more frenzied. Their topic of conversation amid the grunts was which one would take her first. *Of course.* She almost laughed.

Though the front of her dress was in shreds, she still wore the open jacket from that first man in New Orleans. In it was the jagged piece of glass from Madame's attic window. She was experienced in play-acting around men. She thought she could do this. She had to.

"Boys, boys, take it easy," she purred. "There's plenty enough for everyone. Why not show me the goods. Best man wins. And you know what I mean by 'best.' C'mon, boys, let's see what you got."

This threw them into utter confusion. First, they hated, absolutely hated, that she was not writhing to get loose, not screaming in terror. That always made it so much more fun. Now, the thought that *she'd* get to choose who goes first? Not likely. Not how it was supposed to work. But suppose the other feller here wasn't afraid to open up and show his goods? Suppose the other feller thought *he* was ashamed of what he got?

In that moment, with his attention diverted as he struggled to think it through, the counter man loosened his grip on her arms a bit. She broke free, grabbed the jagged glass out of her pocket and just started slashing wildly. Could she make it to the door?

She drew blood, she could see that. But nothing fatal. She'd never make it past them. In the struggle, her feet lost their purchase and got tangled up in the rug. That's when she saw it. A trapdoor! How many wretches had never made it out of this room, how many robbed, ravished, slain, and dumped into the river?

And now she knew she would join them in the river's depths. Except she would be alive.

She was able to grasp the rope handle and pull. Now the men were bellowing, variations of "Grab her!" and "Git her!" If they had been smart, one would be standing on the trap door so she couldn't raise it. But they were too stunned, too frenzied. It only took her a moment to slither through the trap door.

Tumbling down, she didn't have time to wonder how far below the river was. It met her sooner than she'd expected, but that was good. At least the fall hadn't killed her.

CHAPTER 15
MARCH, 1865

On the march, Deacon kept up his unbroken silence. Moran uncharacteristically stepped into the role of providing a cheerful monologue. He felt it was the least he could do. Losing a leg like Deacon had done ... that must be pretty bad for a man. The pain, the ... well, just everything.

And now when Moran saw what they were hobbling into, he knew Deacon would never survive. They'd been marched toward the prison camp for so long, he had no idea how far they'd come. He could not believe how well Deacon and the other wounded men tried to hold up. Each one of them in pain, each one hungry, each one weak from loss of blood, each one cold and in despair and utterly worn. Moran wondered how a person's body could survive such abuse. He wondered if it was that "human spirit" people like Deacon were always going on about.

Well, they'd sure need it now.

Moran abandoned the chatter as soon as he saw the prison camp. He decided that from this minute on, he'd need all his thoughts focused solely on how to survive.

As they entered the gates, guards searched the prisoners' haversacks for weapons again, even though it had already been done. This time, however, food items were confiscated. Then the prisoners were just sort of herded into the compound. The gates shut behind them.

Moran had seen a lot in his life. He'd seen enough just since he'd been in this war to last a lifetime. But nothing prepared him for what he saw now.

These weren't men, these were skeletons. Not even walking skeletons. Not many were on their feet. He helped Deacon just to sit down on the ground after their journey. There was one large building, a couple of smaller ones, and dozens of one-man tents. The new arrivals, like their pathetic little group, sat on the cold ground and were grateful of it. If many more prisoners were admitted, there would be no place left even to sit in the dirt.

Deacon removed his haversack, used it as a pillow, wrapped up in his blanket, and almost immediately fell asleep. Moran used this time to observe what they had gotten themselves into.

A man near where they were sitting offered Moran a weak salute, not in the Army way like when an officer crossed your path, but in a human-being way. Just to acknowledge that you were a fellow human in the same place and about to suffer the same fate. Moran thought this man might be a good place to start.

Moran left Deacon to rest, and slid a little closer to the other man. Neither offered their names. Probably because it wasn't a good idea to get too close to someone who might be dead by morning. Moran asked if the man would mind telling him something about the place, being as they were new arrivals and all.

Moran took it easy when he asked the question. It could be that any man here might be on the verge of breaking. Having to put this particular part of hell into words might push him over the edge. But this man didn't seem to mind talking. He said it sort of helped pass the time.

The man had been there for months now, since back in the fall. He named his unit, maybe Ohio, maybe Indiana, maybe Illinois, Moran didn't care. The man named the place of the battle where he'd been captured, but the location meant nothing to Moran. Naming the individual bloodbaths would have to be the make-work task of men at desks who had never fought in them, thought Moran. But he just nodded and kept quiet to let the other man speak.

The other man had no idea how many were in the camp, just that it was hideously overcrowded. Well, Moran could probably see that, the man said, having to sit on the ground and all. But, the man added, don't envy the men in tents or in the building. There was a gang who came around in the night, stole food and belongings, and even smothered some of the men just to get a spot inside.

With their bare hands, some of the prisoners dug trenches about three feet deep where they could sit or lie down out of the wind. He said the men had requested the use of logs or tree limbs or some other kind of covering to act as a roof over their part of the trench, but the commandant had refused.

"Guess you'll be wanting to know about food," the man said. "Ain't any. Or at least not any that you'd be safe eating. Sometimes we get tiny little portions of raw corn. Most who eat it fall ill. Ever heard of 'dysentery?' Well, you're about to hear about it, see it, smell it and probably get it yourself while you're here. Oh, and be real careful about drinking the water. That's the easiest way to come down with dysentery, bloody flux, whatever you want to call it. See where they diverted that river over there? It's a channel that comes into camp. Supposed to be for our drinking water. But that's also where all the human waste goes to. Like an open sewer through camp. Some fellas try to fish in it, but nothing can live in that muck. Some fellas sort through the waste for undigested scraps of food. Mostly, all anyone gets out of it is dysentery."

Moran acted like this was no more nor less than he'd expected, but he swallowed hard. The other man took a long look at Moran and asked if he'd been wounded. Moran told him he'd been nicked in the arm, but it wasn't bad.

"Don't bathe in that river water," the man advised. "Any wound or open sore will get infected right away from what's in it. Once the gangrene sets in, they have no choice but to cut off the arm or leg with a common saw. Nothing for the pain. Lot of fellas go through that ordeal wide awake, then die from loss of blood or what they call 'shock.' Make sure you tell your buddy that, the one over there you came in with, the one missing the leg."

Moran wished he could close his ears the way a person can close their eyes. Without emotion, the other man kept reeling off the diseases here in camp that were killing men in droves. Matter-of-fact, he ran down the list: pneumonia from living outside; smallpox that spread like wildfire through the jammed-together men; dengue, or "break-bone fever," which was carried by the lice that infested every inch of camp – "and every inch of a man," he added ominously.

"Be careful of frostbite," the man continued. "Maybe snow's over for a while if we're lucky, but we've had snow in March before and it still gets cold at night. Once you get frostbite, gangrene will probably set in. When that happens, they've got to cut, or else ... well, I've seen men whose fingers, toes, even arms and legs, just plain rotted off their bodies."

Moran was trying not to comment on any of this litany of horror, but he drew a quick, involuntary gasp.

"Not much you can do about the scurvy," the other man went on with continued nonchalance. "No fresh food here, surely no fruit whatsoever, no real vegetables, no protein. You'll start getting ulcerated from the scurvy. Again, keep the ulcers away from the river water or they'll get infected. But of course, none of that is the worst of it."

Moran couldn't fathom what could possibly be coming next. About halfway through, he had wondered if the man was exaggerating, trying to scare a newcomer. But a quick look around proved otherwise. It all looked to be true.

Well, Moran had enough. His first thought was to politely move away, begging off from further conversation in order to sleep. But, thinking it through, Moran knew he had to come to terms with it, to know it all, to understand what he was up against. That was the only way he could fight it.

So Moran stayed put and kept quiet as the man continued. "I've heard it said that those who came into camp as bad men – well, they stayed bad. Sad part is that a lot of men who came in as good men went bad just to survive another day, just to give themselves some hope. There's a few gangs here. They're mean. One's even proud of what they do, call themselves the Devil's Den Boys. DDBs. If I ever got my hands on a weapon, wouldn't use it on the guards. I'd use it on them."

The man said that after dark, the gangs attacked fellow prisoners, particularly the new ones. "Sometimes the rest of us go after the gang for an especially evil deed, beat one or two of them to death in reprisal. But don't that make us as bad as them?"

Moran assumed no response was required to this philosophical question. In any case, he was unprepared to offer one. He just flat didn't know.

"And the saddest thing …," the man went on. Moran was flabbergasted. *You mean he still hasn't come to the saddest thing*? "The saddest part is those who might just make it through without falling to any of those other things. They've got a chance, maybe one in a thousand, but still a chance. But I've seen 'em. They die from sheer … despondency, I guess you'd call it. Turn their face away and just let themselves die of despair. Hope I don't go that way, but you never know from day to day."

The man described the dead-house, where bodies were collected for burial. Their clothes and belongings were stripped off by their comrades and the guards alike. The men went naked to their graves. Each day, a wagonload of about eight each was hauled out. Bodies were thrown into open pits, then buried anonymously in mass unmarked graves.

"Worst thing I ever saw," the man said, "was when two men were still alive when dirt was bein' shoveled over their faces. Feeble as they were, they tried to climb out of the pit but no one did nothin' They were covered up with the rest. Now I ask you, that ain't right, is it?"

Rather than agree it sure *didn't* sound right to him, Moran started a conversational theme of his own. He lowered his voice to a whisper. "Well, is there any way out? You know what I mean?"

"I know exactly what you're talkin' about and I seen a few tries myself. Any given time, some bunch is digging an escape tunnel. 'Course, they hold their secrets close. They know others would betray their secret for one day of rations. So the rest of us only find out about it when the gunfire starts. Some try for a break over the wall whilst the guards are sleeping or not paying attention. Some find something to bribe the guards to let them out, but the guards turn 'em in. I never seen one succeed myself, but of course I wouldn't, now would I?"

Moran just kept listening. The man recalled one time when a large group of prisoners overpowered a handful of guards, took their weapons, and pushed their way out the gate. But after being alerted, other guards turned artillery on the escapees: three cannons at point-blank range. It was also the bad luck of the escapees that a Confederate troop train was stopped at a nearby depot. Those troops acted as reinforcements, pouring on a massive barrage of gunfire.

"Even after the escapees tried to surrender, the Rebs was so frenzied that they kept up the firing. About a hundred of our boys was killed in a matter of minutes. So that's it, that's the story about escaping."

Moran thanked the man for his wealth of information. He returned to his spot next to Deacon. He planned to reveal this new-found intelligence to Deacon only in bits and pieces, as much his friend needed to know or could handle at any one time. It was just too much awfulness all at once.

He didn't mind for himself. Moran guessed he would use the information to figure out a plan. But Deacon, now that was another story. Moran figured Deacon would be one of those who'd be dead before long. Disease, despair, freezing weather, loss of blood, lack of food, all on top of knowing he'd be maimed for life. He'd never take a normal step nor even stand on his feet. How would a man survive all that?

So as soon as Deacon awoke, Moran planned to return to his cheerful pose. Deacon slept most of the day while Moran considered all he'd heard. When Deacon opened his eyes, he looked directly at Moran. It was almost like Deacon was asking a silent question about what they'd gotten themselves into.

Moran knew he had to start in small, hopeful pieces. Which was why he was surprised when out of his mouth came every single heart-wrenching detail he'd heard from the other man. It was just a torrent of bad news rushing out of him. Moran's eyes even misted over at one point, though he figured any fool could see it was just the wind in his eyes.

Moran was sorry. Somehow it had just all poured out. He hadn't meant to. He guessed all the bad news had gotten to him worse than he imagined. So now he had done it. Deacon couldn't possibly take it. Moran figured he had probably killed his friend. He figured Deacon would just turn his head away and die.

Therefore, Moran was stunned at his friend's response. Deacon just started laughing and laughing and laughing and didn't stop for quite a while.

⁂

To: Mr. A. E. "Andy" Andrews

Dear Andy,

Well, I have no idea the day or the month or where I am or anything like that, so I can't give this letter a proper heading. I know I told you when we worked together at the newspaper, to always include the W's of who and what and when and where. And now here I am starting just exactly the wrong way. But I hope that in your twelve-year-old wisdom, you will understand.

I am being held as a prisoner of war. It's somewhere in the South, don't know exactly where. They searched our haversacks for weapons but they left the pen and paper and ink you gave me when I left Ohio. Guess the Rebs never heard that the pen is mightier than the sword – ha-ha.

I can tell you some other time how we got captured and all that. First I want to see if they will even mail this to you. Might take a long time to get to you in Ohio, but you know me. Never one to give up hope.

When my friend here at camp started telling me how bad conditions are, at first I was sad. And afraid too. Then he kept on and on, going from bad to worse, and all of a sudden it just started sounding funny to me. Funny that men – Americans – anyone, really – would do these devilish things to each other, to the creations The Lord made in His image.

Please don't think I hate the Rebs, and I hope you won't either. We are starving and sick, but they don't have any more than we do.

I apologize for not writing before now, but when our unit started out, they kept us busy with drilling and marching and guard duty. Now I have lots of time – ha-ha. So I hope you will bear with me if my letters become tedious. I already feel I am writing too much. Don't even know if the guards will mail it. But if they don't, even if it never gets to you, I am sending my thoughts your way. I pray you will become a doctor like you said. If I can do anything to help, I will.

It is getting dark now and the light is going. I hope this gets to you and most of all, I hope so much that your life is a good one.

Your friend,

John Deacon USA (that stands for U. S. Army, not United States of America – ha-ha)

PS – Do you know if Mrs. Ardent has made it back home from collecting her husband? If you see her in town (maybe on her own might be best), please let her know that her friend John Deacon sends his respects.

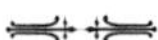

In fact, Ella Ardent was then in the process of collecting her husband. Once she made it into Vicksburg, she went directly to the hospital where he was supposed to be. She had expected the process to be fairly straight-forward. It was not. She had also expected some kind of order. She found none.

First, she simply walked right in. There didn't seem to be anyone on duty to challenge her or offer to be of assistance. She had the thought that a saboteur could walk through the door and wreak all sorts of havoc. Then she discovered saboteurs wouldn't have to bother. It was being done very well without them.

She was left to wander through a huge room filled with injured men. The place was squalid. Bloody bandages were being taken off dead men and given to others of the wounded. There was so much coughing. Some men were lying on the floor begging for food or water or something for the pain.

She walked through the place several times, going through the grueling task of looking at each man to see if she recognized her husband. Finally, she found him. He was at least in a bed. She stood looking at him. He appeared to be asleep. He seemed to be feverish. He had grown a full beard. Then she saw why shaving might be difficult for him. He had lost his right arm.

She leaned closer to him, stroked his forehead. Formally, but not without affection, she said, "William, it's Ella. Your wife. I've come to take you home."

His eyes opened and he turned his head to face her.

"Took you long enough," was all he said.

A soldier, possibly an orderly, walked by. He was tall, with a bushy red beard.

Ella said, "Sir, could you help me? Get me a stretcher or something? I am Captain Ardent's wife. I have come to take my husband home. My wagon was stolen, but if I can get him as far as the river ..."

The man cut in. "Ma'am, no disrespect, but I'm not an officer. Just a plain soldier. And no further disrespect meant, but you can't just come in and take him out. Need to get permission."

"Well, that's fine. I can understand that. Who do I talk to? And who would I talk to about the appalling conditions here?"

"Ma'am, that would be the same person for both. Major Fitch. He's the man in charge. That's him, over there," the soldier said, pointing to a smug-looking man who emerged from an office to sign some papers on the other side of the ward. Ella stopped herself short. She had no idea why, out of the blue, without knowing him, she had thought of him as smug-looking. She thought she was probably just upset at the conditions here, and was unfairly blaming him.

She circled her arm in a sweeping motion, taking in the ghastly sights in the ward "He knows about all this?"

"Ma'am, we don't have much in the way of supplies. We's lucky to have what we have."

"I understand, but honestly – food for the patients? Water? Is that so much to ask?"

"Ma'am, I promise most of us is doin' the best we can. Most of us give 'em our own rations."

After thanking the orderly, Ella started to move in the direction of that Major Fitch. But something in what he had said caught her attention. "Most?"

"Ma'am?"

"You said 'most' of you are doing the best you can. What does that mean?"

The soldier continued to be respectful, but he was quite obviously becoming nervous.

"Ma'am, you seem like a nice lady. Purty too, if you don't mind my sayin.' Your husband's a lucky fella to have you. Don't believe my wife'd come lookin' fer me like you're doin.' But don't you worry yourself about it, about how things are here."

Ella smiled. She knew the man was trying his best to deal with an irrational woman. That's what her husband always called her. Irrational. In a moment, William might just join the conversation to tell her to control herself. She moved farther away from his bedside.

But she just couldn't keep quiet about the appalling conditions here. Ella had seen too much, knew too much about what the soldiers had been going through. Maybe she was speaking for poor Patsy who couldn't speak for herself, not anymore. Maybe she was speaking for Johnny Deacon if he was off in some strange place, sick or hurt. She hoped some woman would fight for him if no one else would.

"Soldier, it's not for me. It's for these boys. Don't you think they at least deserve that? Haven't they been through enough?"

"Ma'am, please." The soldier took a deep breath. "Ma'am, please don't think less of me, but I'm mighty glad to be here on this duty. I'm grateful to the Lord for bringing me here, off the front. If I was to make things rough on myself by going against the officer in charge, I have no doubt I'd get sent back to the front. Since the Lord brought me here and spared me, that'd be like goin' against the will of the Lord, wouldn't it?"

Ella pointed to the floor. "But would you want to be laying there like them?"

"Ma'am, as the Lord is my witness, I swear we do the best we can. Why, they's our fellow soldiers. We fought together with some of 'em. Of course we're gonna try to help 'em."

"Then, what is it you are not saying? Something doesn't make sense."

The soldier looked around to make sure he was not being heard or observed. "Ma'am, I don't know nothing fer sure. But some of us, we have an idea that some of the officers are somehow keeping money meant for supplies, for medicine, bandages, food and the like. Maybe they get paid for not sayin' anything when the supply order comes up half short. That way, they sign off on it. Then them and the supplier both get a little something out of the deal."

"Then this man in charge, this Major Fitch needs to know about it!"

The soldier came closer and suddenly seemed threatening for the first time. "Ma'am, don't you say a word to Fitch. Not a word. Not one damn word. Now, git out." And then, more kindly, "Please! Please just collect your husband and go."

"It's him, isn't it? This Major Fitch – he's the one keeping the money!"

The soldier turned to walk away. "Don't know nothin' about that."

Ella gently took his arm. "All right. But suppose ... what if word of his doings somehow reached someone's ear, higher up?"

"Ma'am, leave it."

Ella tried to look as if she was considering that. "Well, you may be right. I'd be glad to. Glad to leave this place. No one has to know. See, that Major Fitch has gone back to his office. Now, I'll need a stretcher and a blanket and any medicine you can get that'll help my husband. We'll need to get him over to the nearest hotel where I can nurse him strong enough to travel."

The orderly looked at her a long time, then nodded his head. "Your husband, he's a lucky man to have you."

"I'm sure your lady wife would do the same for you."

"Then I'd hope she'd be as persuasive as you in gittin' someone to help her. Knowin' her, she'd just hit him with a frying pan."

Ella smiled. "I'm sure it won't come to that."

Ella returned to her husband's bedside.

"William, we're going to be leaving here."

"Oh, you done flirting with your soldier boy?"

"William, I was simply arranging to get you out of this place."

"Make sure I get something for the pain."

"Yes, William, I will."

"Where we going?"

"I'm going to have you taken to a hotel where you can get your strength back before we travel north. Do you have any money for a room?"

"That's all you think about, isn't it, Ella? Money."

⸻

Dear Andy,

A strange thing has happened here. Almost Biblical in nature. Reminds me of old Noah. The adjacent river overflowed its banks and flooded the camp. Must be the snowmelt from the north of us. It was quite a sight – can you imagine – all of the prisoners as well as the guards standing knee-deep in dirty cold water. Everyone had to raise their blankets and belongings up from the ground lest they be washed away. No one knows how long we will be on our feet. As you see, I saved your wonderful gift of pen and ink. I am using the back of my friend Moran (no first name that I know of) who agreed to act as a desk. But I must not outstay my welcome nor his good nature. Wish you could come paddling by in a rowboat and give me a ride – ha-ha.

Your friend,

John Deacon USA

PS – have you by chance happened to encounter Mrs. Ardent in town? I send my compliments to the lady.

⁂

It was horrific. The prisoners had to stand knee-deep for days in cold, filthy water. Many who were too weak to rise simply drowned where they lay. The sight of dead bodies floating by was not uncommon.

After several days, the water began to recede. Moran could not believe that Deacon stood on his one good leg the entire time. He kept his arm around his friend to offer some relief, but Deacon asked for no special treatment from Moran or anyone. Nor would he have received any from the guards. The bodies of the dead floating by was a clear reminder of the alternative.

When the water retreated, it left a sea of mud which sucked the shoes from those who still had them on their feet. Food was in even shorter supply as much of the storehouse had been flooded. Moran wondered why it was that Fate seemed out to destroy what little comfort they had. And he was nearly out of his mind with hunger. Something had to be done.

Deacon needed to sit down. He spread the sleeping mat and hoped it would not sink in the muck. Perhaps a letter to his young friend Andy might take his mind off matters. That always helped. It was almost dark, and soon he'd lose the light. At some point, he dozed off where he sat.

He was awaked by shouting. Some prisoners were attacking another. They were yelling about some man being a thief, about him stealing food. This was not uncommon.

What was unusual in this case was that Deacon could not cast a knowing eye at Moran. That was because Moran was on the ground in the center of the attack, fending off blows.

Deacon asked a nearby man to help him stand. The mud made it almost impossible to walk with his crutch, but he painfully made his way toward the uproar.

"Thief!" the crowd was yelling. "Rotten sumbitch!" "Stealing from the rest of us!" All the anger and frustration of the men was pouring out, heaped on the flailing Moran.

"Brothers!" yelled Deacon. "Brothers! Please stop! Save your energy! Leave him alone!"

Voices from the crowd. "He deserves to die! "He was stealing!" "Let's finish him off!"

"Brothers, we cannot become animals. What he did was wrong. Let us not become worse. Please! Let us not fight each other."

Moran used the opportunity to extricate himself from the mud and duck the remaining blows from the mob. "Thanks all the same," he announced to Deacon so the crowd could hear, "but I can handle this myself!"

Deacon transferred his crutch from his right arm to his left. He painfully made his way toward Moran. With his right arm, Deacon took a roundhouse punch at Moran, decking him flat on his back again. The angry crowd expressed its approval. Some even laughed.

Moran was on his feet again. "What the hell did you do that for? You was the one telling them we shouldn't fight each other. And then you sucker-punched me! Why the hell did you do that?"

Deacon returned his crutch to his right arm and approached Moran, looking him in the eye. "Because you're an idiot. And a thief."

The crowd seemed satisfied and started dispersing, still mumbling among themselves but in a less lethal way. "Damn right." "Told you he was a thief." "Glad he got what's coming to him." "He deserves worse." "Knocked on his ass by a cripple!"

Deacon took Moran roughly by the arm and dragged him away. "Let's get out of here before they change their mind."

Moran was indignant. "You called me an idiot."

"And a thief. Don't forget that part."

"Let me tell you, my righteous friend, it's going to take a thief and worse to get out of this alive."

"No!" said Deacon. "Especially as bad as things are now, we need our own – our *morality* – to survive!"

"Maybe, maybe not, but I know a little more than you about some situations. I truly appreciate you saving my skin back there, I truly do. They'd'a killed me, sure. And you're right about me bein' a thief. But not the other. People always callin' me stupid. Well, only the ones who are smart enough to break the rules are gonna survive. Those who follow the rules, gonna die. Me, I mean to survive. So don't you call me an idiot."

"Then don't be stupid enough to get caught." Deacon kept hobbling along as Moran looked at him in amazement.

CHAPTER 16
APRIL, 1865

The sign outside the room said "Court Martial in Progress. No Admittance." When the doors swung open, several officers emerged, talking among themselves in low, serious tones. One turned when he heard someone calling his name.

"Colonel Wakefield, a moment please, sir?"

The man named Wakefield looked annoyed and said, "One moment, Fitch. I am speaking with these gentlemen."

Scowling, Wakefield motioned in a quick, irritated gesture for the man called Fitch to wait in an alcove. Wakefield continued his conversation with the other officers. Finally, they all gave various versions of salutes toward each other, up and down the ranks, and then departed. Wakefield looked around to make sure he was not observed before joining Fitch in the alcove.

"Fitch, are you even more obtuse than I think you are?" hissed Wakefield. "What the hell do you mean, addressing me when I'm with those men? Right after your own court martial!"

Completely unperturbed, Fitch said, "I was brought up by Mama that it was good manners to say 'thank you.'"

"Don't you dare bring my sweet sister into this! She didn't bring you up to be a liar and a thief."

"If you feel that way, uncle, you should have found me guilty as charged."

"I happen to love my sister," said Wakefield, "and a charge like that that would have killed her. She did nothing to deserve a corrupt, vulgar cur like you for a son. I told her not to marry beneath her. And if you ever breathe a word that you and I are related, to anyone, at any time, I'll have you off to the front so fast ..."

"No need for that kind of talk, uncle. I mean 'sir.' There's no reason for anyone to know."

"Then I bid you good day, Fitch."

"No, honestly sir, I wanted to thank you. I'm sure you persuaded them I was innocent."

"Being found 'not guilty' is not the same thing as being innocent. The verdict was due to lack of evidence. In other words, no one actually had Matthew Brady take a photograph of you putting the money in your pocket."

Wakefield began walking away. He stopped and turned. "If you sincerely wish to thank me – and your mother – you may work at not being a lying thief. If you can't overcome your low nature, at least try not to be found out. Just keep your mouth shut. And stay away from me."

"But wait," said Fitch, taking Wakefield's arm. "There's some unfinished business to attend to."

"In what way?" asked Wakefield, looking at the younger man's arm on his as if it were a slimy leech.

"Well, my reputation at the hospital now is nothing to speak of," said Fitch. "Whoever made that report, whoever sic'ced the inspectors on me ... well, I can't go back there."

"Fine," said Wakefield. "There is still a need for men on the front lines. I can make the arrangements. Noble of you to request transfer to the front."

"No, I don't think so," said Fitch. "War's almost over. The South is done for. Way I see it, there will be a need for officers in charge of putting everything to rights again."

"I am sure you will find something. Preferably, far away from me."

"The sooner I get home, uncle ... I mean, sir, the sooner I can be of help to my dear Mama. And that would of course take me away from you. Which is the perfect solution for everyone."

Wakefield thought a moment. "I suppose we could have you attached to Transport, getting our men back home. There will be a great need for that."

"As long as I go with them. And we're in the perfect place! Vicksburg! I love travelling the river by steamboat. The sooner to hurry home. To help Mama, of course."

Wakefield, sounding resigned, said, "I'll see what I can do. Perhaps you won't get into mischief in the meantime."

Fitch saluted in what Wakefield thought was a mocking manner, but the older man decided just to walk away. He wanted nothing more to do with his dear sister's unpleasant son. Whelp took right after his good-for-nothing father.

Fitch, as usual, had to have the last word. He called after Wakefield, "I'll do my best," pointedly adding, "Sir."

When Charity hit the water, the strong currents started pulling her back downriver, the way she'd come. Back to New Orleans. She'd have to make it to the riverbank soon, or she'd be carried away. She had no intention of going anywhere but north, out of this miserable place. Natchez-Under-the-Hill should be called Natchez-Under-Hell.

There was a small outcropping of land before the town ended. If she could just make it there, grab hold of something, she had a chance. She told herself that anyone who'd been used as gator bait had no call to fear this river. She swam for her life, and was elated that she had the strength left to do it. She aimed for the remains of a burned-out building at water's edge. She grabbed a piling that had supported it. It was probably the same sort of building with the same sort of trap door from which she had just escaped. Fine. Now it could work *for* her.

The piling and charred remains of the building concealed her fairly well from anyone coming down Water Street who might be stalking her. The men she'd eluded certainly had no fear that she'd run to the police. There weren't any who dared patrol Under-the-Hill.

So there was a good chance they'd wait for her to make her way back down Water Street, right into their clutches. Though she was soaked from head to toe, though she was freezing in the brisk wind, though she had no clear idea where she was going, she headed uphill.

She remembered seeing the top-most street. It had looked slightly better than its counterparts closer to the riverbank. Shivering from the cold, trying to keep her torn dress together, she made her way up a crossroad named Middle Street. First it intersected another long street in the middle but she kept going until she reached the uppermost. A sign said, "Silver Street." That would have to do.

There were businesses and stores on Silver Street that looked somewhat better than their Water Street counterparts, but even so, what could she do? Her money was gone, all of it in the clutches of those two brutes she'd eluded. They could still come after her here. She had no reason to believe that stumbling into a store and asking for help would gain her a thing. Up to now, the sight of a half-drowned, half-dressed woman running down the street had captured the attention of absolutely no one. Probably some version of it happened here all the time.

Shivering harder now, she ran down Silver Street as fast as she could to get out of Under-the-Hill. Soon, Silver Street became a wagon road leading out of town, and she was determined to make it as far down that thoroughfare and as far out Natchez as she could.

But, still soaking wet, she continued to shiver in the cold wind despite running at full tilt. The shivering turned into shudders as her body seemed to convulse with its mistreatment. She took her mind off it by counting in her mind all the people she was escaping from. Added to her previous nemesis of the law and its military counterpart, plus assorted bushwhackers and highwaymen, were the men back at the room in Under-the-Hill. If one of them had a horse, they'd catch her in no time to finish what they'd begun. She figured they'd have an extra dose of brutality in store for her as repayment for her defiant act.

There was no real place to hide from men who knew the land and who knew exactly how far she might have gotten. And there was no real cover to act as an effective hiding place. Her body was convulsing from the cold. She stumbled and fell. She could not stop her body from its violent shaking.

If this was where she would die – and death was something she felt strongly would happen any time now – at least she had made it this far. She knew she was dying because she heard bells, like church bells. But instead of the sonorous tolling she'd heard from her balcony on a Sunday morning in New Orleans, these bells jangled.

As her body shook more violently, the jingle-jangle was becoming louder. She was on her way to Heaven. In a moment the bells stopped. She must be at the Heavenly Gates. She felt herself being lifted skyward in the strong arms of St. Peter. This was good news. She had often wondered if she would be admitted into Heaven or sent to some other place where bad women like her were doomed to more of the same that they had known on Earth.

But St. Peter lifted her, wrapped her in something long and dark and comforting. This was her shroud, no doubt. She was gently placed in his chariot. She relaxed, knowing that soon she would meet her Maker. And at least she'd be draped respectably when she did. It seemed like only a short time passed before the chariot stopped, and she was lifted again by St. Peter. She expected the sound of trumpets in the presence of The Supreme Being.

What she heard instead was, "Minnie! Draw a bath of hot water for this poor girl. And hot food! She's dying!"

Except for the last part, there were worse things Charity Boudry could have heard.

When her eyes opened, Charity was in a tub full of wonderfully hot water. Her jackets were gone, but her dress was still on. She watched its shabby folds float jauntily in the warm tides of the bath.

A sweet-faced woman dressed in black was looking at her with a concerned expression. Charity had no idea which Saint the woman might be. Mary herself?

"You're safe now, dear," the Saint declared. "We were very worried about you. Once we get you warmed up a little more, we'll dress you in dry clothes and put you in front of the fire. I didn't want to take the chance of removing your dress before you had the chance to warm up in the hot water a bit. The shock of the cold air might have killed you. But it should be all right to take it off now. Don't worry, it's just us ladies here."

The Saint – or perhaps she was simply a kind celestial handmaiden – then helped Charity off with her shabby dress. It was the threadbare garment that had seen so much, the one she had worn as she walked the plank over the alleyway at Madame's, the one that had concealed her money, the one that was now torn to shreds after the assault by those men. It had served her well. Still, as soon as she could, Charity would burn it.

It was starting to appear that this was not Heaven, that Charity was still on Earth. But if so, this was an especially nice part of the world, populated by kind people. This was probably not an actual Saint, but a sweet-faced, gentle woman. After laying out a warm-looking nightgown, heavy robe, and even slippers, the kind lady covered Charity with a thick towel and helped her from the tub.

"When you've finished drying off," the kind lady said, "there's some lovely talcum powder there on the little table. I think your coming back to life is a special occasion, so let's use it! I'll come check on you, or better yet, just come into the parlor when you're ready."

There was only a small amount of the powder left and Charity felt bad using it, but use it she did. It was glorious. Someday she would buy this dear woman a barrel of the stuff. Because Charity was now certain of her conclusion that she was neither dead nor in Heaven. She was still on Earth with some very saintly people. Her life experience had not been such as to expect such miraculous beings.

Warm, dry, clean, and powdered, Charity fixed her hair as best she could and moved to the next room. There, a pleasant fire was burning. There were kitchen sounds coming from the back of the house, and something that smelled wonderful on the stove. Charity hoped she would be asked to stay for dinner.

The kind lady poked her head out of the kitchen. "Good, you're here. Won't be long now, dear. I had some soup already warming for Abram. Oh – sounds like he's back now. He just went to unhitch the horse. We'll all have dinner in a minute."

Charity smiled in a way she hoped would convey the depths of her gratitude. Whoever these people were, they were truly Saints.

Entering the house just then was a bearded, stooped-over old man in a long black frock coat. He kissed his fingertips and gently touched the side of the doorframe as he entered. If Charity had ever had much access to the Bible, she might have said he looked like something out of the Old Testament.

"Well, that's better," he said with a smile as he waved an arm in her direction.

"Are you the kind man who rescued me, back on the road? I am obliged to you, sir."

"Who could look upon you there and not be moved to help? I wrapped you up as best I could in my coat and brought you here. Just hoped it was not too late."

"With respect, sir, where is 'here'?"

The old man made sure the warmth of the fireplace was reaching her, then settled in on a chair opposite.

"You are at the home of a dear friend of mine. Well, I suppose we are also relatives. She is the cousin of my late wife. I was on my way here for my usual visit when I saw you on the road. Her name is Minnie Silverman. I am Abram Stieglitz."

Even among the Cajuns, Charity had never heard such strange names.

"Is this still in Natchez, sir?"

The man named Stieglitz laughed. "It is indeed Natchez, but not the part you were in. This house is on the bluffs. Mrs. Silverman may look frightening, but I assure you even she is not half as appalling as the dwellers of Under-the-Hill."

The last was said for the benefit of the woman called Mrs. Silverman who was just coming into the room carrying a tray.

"Keep that up, Abram Stieglitz, and there will be no dinner for you," the woman said affectionately. "Our guest and I will manage nicely on our own."

"My name is Charity Boudry," their guest said without thinking. She quickly regretted it. In her effort to be polite, Charity had neglected to remember *not* to use her real name. If this man had access to WANTED posters, he might have noticed a reward being offered for a girl of that name. Well, too late now.

Mrs. Silverman set the tray next to Charity, on which she had placed a large bowl of soup and a small plate with warm bread on it. On a larger table across the room, she set out the same portions for herself and the man called Stieglitz. The soup smelled divine, and Charity did not hesitate one moment before tasting it. She thought it might be polite to wait for the other two to start eating, but who knows? The law might have been alerted by Stieglitz and come crashing through the door any minute, brandishing the reward money for his efforts. Charity ate without restraint.

She heard Stieglitz and Mrs. Silverman mumbling something in low voices in some kind of language she had never heard. Only then did they begin eating.

"I'm sorry I started without you," Charity felt obligated to say. "It's just that I am so hungry and this soup is delicious."

"Even Minnie cannot spoil chicken soup," said the man called Stieglitz. Mrs. Silverman reached for his bowl in a mocking gesture. "Then give it back," she said.

"Now Minnie, I said even *you* could *not* ruin it. Mind your manners in front of our guest. So you like your soup, do you, Miss?"

"Oh yes," said Charity, hoping there was more in the kitchen. She had immediately recognized it as chicken soup, though thicker and richer and more delicious than any she had ever eaten. It had big pieces of chicken and a few carrot slices. Also some green leaves she found later were called 'celery.' But it also had big round balls made of some kind of meal. They looked like snowballs but tasted wonderful.

Then Charity remembered to say 'thank you' to her hosts for the meal. They ate in companionable silence. The bread was equally delicious. It was a kind of braided, golden loaf that was so light and soft and fluffy Charity thought it might float away. She made sure to consume it before such a thing happened. She complemented Mrs. Silverman and asked if she had made it herself. Yes, she had and was so glad Charity liked it. Charity thought the woman said it was called "collie" but that, she knew, was a dog. She just wished she had more of the bread, more of everything.

As if reading her mind, the woman asked if Charity would like another bowl of soup. "Oh-yes-please," said Charity before anyone changed their mind. She did not know when her next meal would be. She wondered if this man and woman, kind as they were, would put her out into the street after dinner. For all Charity knew, they might be suspicious of Charity herself, fearful she would knife them in their sleep. Really, they were probably smart to think that way. You just never could tell. Best prolong this meal as much as possible.

"Minnie, could we have some wine for dessert?" said the man. "We can visit with our guest over a nice glass of Concord."

The woman brought back a tray with another bowl of soup for Charity and three glasses of a deep ruby red wine. The man and woman said something bowing toward the wine, again in some language foreign to Charity's ears. Then the man raised his glass and said something in more words Charity did not understand. They sounded like "La Kime." She knew of no verbiage in Cajun French that sounded like that.

"That means 'To Life,'" the man said for her benefit. Mrs. Silverman obviously knew what it meant already, and agreed with the sentiment.

"So," said the man called Stieglitz. Charity knew he was getting ready to ask the question she dreaded. He did. "Tell us a little about yourself, young Miss."

So she told them the story of her life. The one where she came from the Garden District in New Orleans, such a lovely place, did they know it? No? *Good. That reduced the chances of them asking if she knew so-and-so, or the such-and-such family.*

She had two older sisters who both married well, one to a banker and one to a cotton merchant like Charity's father. Now her mother's attention was on finding a suitable mate for Charity herself. There were so many to choose from, so many young men from good families. It was an important decision and so hard to decide.

Her father had allowed her to take a riverboat up to St. Louis where she could visit her cousin. She was unchaperoned for the first time in her life but they understood the *Silver Moon* was a very safe vessel for a young lady to travel on. When the boat landed at Natchez, she thought she'd do a bit of sightseeing while it was docked. Being unfamiliar with the area, she had wandered into an unsavory part of town where she was attacked and robbed.

Stieglitz and Mrs. Silverman made clucking sounds, bemoaning the violent state of the world today, war or no war. They tried to look as if they'd believed every word she had told them. The last part, however, they knew must certainly be true. The girl had found some trouble in Under-the-Hill. On that, they silently concurred. While Charity had been in the warm bath, Mrs. Silverman had quietly asked if she needed a doctor, "one who knows about ladies," the woman had added. Charity had declined.

Charity ended her story with the details – entirely accurate – of how Mr. Stieglitz had come to find her half-dead on Silver Street.

"My, that is quite an adventure," said the woman. "Abram was on his way here when he found you. Natchez is part of his route, his circuit I suppose you'd say. He is here – oh about every few weeks – would you say so, Abram? He delivers goods to the stores on Silver Street, you know."

Charity didn't, but nodded accordingly. Thank Heaven for Silver Street.

"You have no doubt missed your boat, yes?" the woman asked. Charity hadn't factored in that element while telling her story, but nodded in agreement.

"And you are going to St. Louis?"

Again, Charity nodded.

"Stieglitz, can you take our guest with you part of the way?"

"Of course, Minnie," he said, "if she doesn't mind riding in the peddler's wagon."

To Charity he added, "Minnie here thinks it makes a frightful racket, that wagon, with all the pots and pans clanging together. But it is good advertisement. The ladies know when I am coming and run for the money in the cookie jar! I am a purveyor of household goods," said Stieglitz proudly. "A fancy way of saying 'peddler.'"

"You should have known him before," said Mrs. Silverman. "He was a fine businessman." Were those tears Charity saw in the woman's eyes?

"Now, Minnie, we have this happy evening with our young guest here. And the blessing of being together. And a good, sweet Concord wine. Don't mind Minnie, young Miss, she comes from my wife's side of the family. Except for my lovely Rachel, that side of the family is a bunch of sourpusses, one and all!"

Charity missed most of that because she was starting to doze off. She did not think the wine was drugged. It was very sweet and rich and delicious. The drowsiness it brought on was of a very pleasant kind. After the events of the day, she was simply exhausted. Her head drooped.

Minnie came to her, stretched her out on the sofa, and tucked the blanket tighter.

"I shall sleep in the wagon," Stieglitz said.

"Nonsense," said Minnie. "I will make a pallet on the floor here with our guest. You take the bed in my room."

Even in her drowsy state, Charity could hear Stieglitz start to protest. Suddenly the clatter of hoofbeats startled them all. Charity's first thought was instinctive – was the law here to take her away? The rider was galloping up the street, shouting madly. At first they could not understand a word he said.

Stieglitz and Mrs. Silverman went to the door, cautiously opening it.

"It's over!" the man on horseback shouted. "It's over! The war is over! It's over! Lee surrendered! The war is over!"

Charity fell right back to sleep.

In her dreams, she thought she heard the Angel Gabriel with his trumpets proclaiming an end to war. That would be just fine with her. As she fell into a deeper sleep, there were three images, all linked together, that crept into Charity's mind. Silver Moon, Silver Street, Mrs. Silverman. There was a common theme there, but it was too difficult to comprehend right now. Charity would figure it out in the morning. And if morning never came, she would at least die happy.

On the other side of the river, riders were also proclaiming that the war was over. In Helena, Arkansas, one man was not as thrilled at the news as he knew he should be.

This man was the cousin of the shadowy figure known as Alpha. A few days ago, Alpha had turned up at the cousin's home on the river in Helena, requiring room and board for a while.

The cousin was a Confederate, of course, but still had no clear idea of what Alpha did as his part of the war effort. He never asked, and Alpha never revealed a thing. Once the cousin had dared to ask, just to be friendly, where Alpha had been lately. He was rewarded with a steely gaze that warned the cousin he had said too much.

Truth is, the cousin was never really much of a Confederate. He did what he had to do to get along in his town, in his state that had gone with the South. The men who made their living on the river were a kind of breed apart, he told himself, and political decisions had nothing to do with how they made their living. The river was a world of its own.

When orders came from the military that all small boats would be confiscated because of the boatburners, the cousin had hidden his. Sure enough, soldiers turned up looking for it. Whichever army it was at his door, he swore up and down that the other army had taken it. Now his biggest fear was that Alpha would want it.

Another fear was of Alpha himself. Sure, he was family and all. But he had no doubt that Alpha would cut his throat if the occasion warranted. And the cousin had feeling that sharing this news might be one of those times.

The Confederacy was Alpha's Cause. The few times they had discussed it, Alpha's eyes took on a fiery glare that looked like a man possessed by fever. And now the cousin had to pass along the news he'd just heard in town. He simply didn't know how Alpha would react.

So the cousin casually walked in the door, all's-right-with-the-world, friendly-like. He took a drink of water to calm his breathing. He commented on the weather. Shared his observation that the river was rising. Then he brought up the subject as if oh-by-the-way, just-now-remembered, as if to show that's how unimportant it was to him.

As calmly as possible, he said he didn't know if it was true or not, but there was word in town that the war was over. He made sure to keep it neutral, not saying Lee had surrendered or that the South had lost. Just that folks were saying the war was over.

Alpha just stared for a moment, and then that blaze came back into his eyes. "No, it isn't over," he said. "I'll need your boat."

Word of the war being over had not reached the prisoners in Deacon and Moran's camp. With no food, no untainted water to drink, no medicine against infection and disease, the men still hanging on to life were walking – or hobbling – skeletons.

Deacon sometimes thought the only thing keep him going were the letters to young Andy back home. He had no idea if they were being mailed, but he preferred to think they were. He kept the letters cheery, trying to make light of their ordeals. He did not want to boy visualizing the horrors of their existence. He also made sure to note in each letter that the Confederates were not being cruel, that the guards' food was in short supply too. They didn't give the prisoners any more to eat because they didn't have it to give. He did not want the boy growing up to hate people he'd never met.

Deacon thought that was the cause of all this mess in the first place, hate and revenge. One side does something, then the other side wants vengeance, then the first side wants revenge for that, then the other side has to come back at them again after that. And on and on. On and on. On and on. This was what some called "defending their honor."

Deacon wanted it to stop somewhere. He wasn't going to be part of filling a young boy's head with something he'd feel he had to avenge to be a man.

There were other things Deacon never mentioned in his letters. Never, ever. He once told Andy how one of the men had kindly shared his food. But that incident tore at his mind. Deacon had overheard Moran making a deal with a dying soldier for his remaining ration. In return for the tiny portion of bread, Moran promised to make sure the man's body was returned home to his family for burial. In his heart, Deacon knew Moran had no intention of honoring the deal. There was really no way for Moran to do it. Maybe the dying man knew it too. But maybe not.

When Moran brought the sliver of bread back to where they were sitting, he offered some to Deacon. At first Deacon declined, saying something not entirely pleasant: "You eat it. You made the deal."

Moran reminded him of his personal theory that only those who break the rules will survive.

"It's not rules, it's ... morality!" said Deacon.

"Fine," said Moran, starting to pop the entire piece of bread into his mouth.

Deacon put his hand out. Moran tore the bread in half and dropped a portion into Deacon's outstretched hand. Deacon devoured it greedily.

John Deacon then prayed for forgiveness, but had to wonder if anyone was listening.

Dear Andy!

It's Over! Oh, my dear sweet Lord, It's Over! Can you tell I am rather excited by this news? Back at the newspaper, I always told you not to use exclamation marks, and here I am using them to beat the band!

There was no word, no big celebration, no handshakes between soldiers of the two sides. When we woke up by the light of dawn, the gates were open! Just like that! No one told us a thing!

At first, some of the men here thought it was a trick, that the guards would open fire as soon as we approached the gates. Then they would say we'd tried to escape. It would be a way of getting more food for themselves, some of our men said. A couple of our fellas, maybe as a joke, said that really wasn't a bad idea, depending on who was doing the shooting and who was getting shot at.

But there was a medic in the big building who was packing up his things. He flat told us the war was over. General Lee surrendered the Army of Northern Virginia and that means the war is over! Sorry, there I go again with those exclamation marks.

The medic told us to follow the road into town, that a train would come for us. That's where I am now, waiting for a train. My friend Moran says I am writing too much. I am using his back as a desk again, so I better heed what he says. He loves to grumble but Moran is a fine fellow. Funny, I still don't know his first name. I hope you get to meet him some day. Of course, I hope I see you too!

Your friend,

John Deacon USA – but maybe not for long, the U S Army part I mean!

At the rail siding, Deacon and the other men, now *Former* Prisoners of War, waited. And waited, and waited. The interminable wait gave them time to think, maybe to pray. Along the road into town, barely-living men like Deacon and Moran had to step over the bodies of those who couldn't make it any further. Their lives just went out of them on the march to the station. Deacon was angry that the dead, who had endured so much, lost their lives when they were so close to freedom. He was angry, he knew that, furiously angry, but did not know at whom.

Finally, someone heard something like a whistle. "Train coming!" someone shouted. "Train's a-coming!" A tremendous cheer went up from the bedraggled men who started rising to their feet, or trying to. Everybody helped everybody else. Somewhere in their group, Deacon thought, were scoundrels who had robbed and beaten and maybe even killed their fellow prisoners. He himself had eaten the purloined bread, bought with a profane promise. Maybe because of that, he could not judge the others too harshly.

He never wanted to think ill of anyone, ever again. He was going home!

It was only then that he realized he had no idea where home might be.

CHAPTER 17

APRIL, 1865

The subject of "home" had brought conversation to an abrupt halt between an odd little pair of travelers riding in a jingle-jangle wagon out of Natchez.

Charity Boudry knew that the finishing school she had attended focused more on decadence than decorum. But she assumed it might be polite to ask Mr. Stieglitz something about himself. After all, experience had taught her that men just loved to talk about themselves. Now she was mortified and more than a little frightened she had said something wrong. Experience had also taught her that the slightest misstep brought grim consequences. Oh, how she had hoped to stay in that wagon and not be put out on the road to fend for herself – again.

And things had started off so well. After being provided with a lavish breakfast by Mrs. Silverman, that morning Charity Boudry and Abram Stieglitz set out towards Vicksburg. Before their departure, Mr. Stieglitz had gone out to hitch up the horse and wagon. When he came back into the house, he carried the most beautiful dress Charity had ever seen. How she hoped it was for her.

As it turned out, the dress was indeed for her as well as an array of undergarments Mrs. Silverman had chosen from the wagon. Charity had assumed she would not be permitted to make off with Mrs. Silverman's nightgown, heavy robe and slippers. But her thinking remained disinclined to go beyond that. She expected to be presented with the tatty red dress she came in with, plus hopefully the addition of some sort of device for keeping the torn bodice from hanging open.

After breakfast, Mrs. Silverman beckoned Charity into the back room. She spread out the lavish display on the bed. "You'll need some clothes for travel, my dear. That nightgown simply won't do!" The woman laughed cheerfully, though Charity was worried Mrs. Silverman might have thought Charity had planned to pilfer it. They did, after all, belong to the woman. Probably her only ones. Charity noticed Mrs. Silverman had slept in her clothes.

"Now, I do not wish you to take offense, child," continued Mrs. Silverman, "but I believe your red dress is beyond repair. I suggest we make a trade with Stieglitz for something new."

Charity had no idea what Stieglitz would do with her miserable dress. She was too concerned about what the cost of all this abundance might be. She assumed that at some point, the suggestion would be made that Charity wire her wealthy father for funds. Hard as she thought about a response, she could come up with no plausible excuse not to. Vacationing in Europe? Nothing really sounded right. But at least for now, Mrs. Silverman was chattering merrily and not bringing up the topic.

The dress was blue, but not faded and washed-out like the only ones Charity had ever seen. This was a rich, opulent blue the likes of which Charity had never before gazed upon. "I hope you like the color," said Mrs. Silverman. "It has some of that new mauveine chemical dye in it. Nowadays, the ladies are just calling it 'mauve.' The material is thick enough for travel, especially when you add this little caped jacket that goes with it."

Then Mrs. Silverman started on the array of undergarments, apparently from the inside out. At Madame's, Charity had never really had any underclothes unless the client requested something special in the way of lingerie. But it always had to be returned immediately after use. It had been worn dozens – maybe hundreds – of times.

These looked to be new and not previously worn by anyone. The long underpants were made of silky cotton. What Mrs. Silverman called a "chemise" was a long linen undershirt. There were stockings with garters to hold them up. There were short lace-up boots. Then, a white petticoat. Mrs. Silverman said apologetically that she would have preferred Charity to have a dark crinoline for travel ("All that mud and dirt," she had said, as if Charity simply had no idea what was out there.) But the white was all Stieglitz carried.

Then came a cotton camisole. "This usually covers the corset," said Mrs. Silverman, obviously in her element as a fashion advisor, "but I don't think you really want one of the horrible things for your trip, do you? Your waistline is so tiny as it is. Many women would envy you!"

Charity did not offer the explanation for her slim figure: a lifetime of starvation and malnutrition. It would have been rude, and things were going far too pleasantly here to interrupt the flow.

"Now, I know what you are thinking," said Mrs. Silverman. *Ah, at last, now we come to the part about payment for all this,* thought Charity. She could not have been more surprised at what Mrs. Silverman said instead.

"You are wondering about hoops. Well, this I know. I used to sew a lot, my young friend, and I followed the ladies' magazines. I know how to develop an eye for trends. Let me tell you this. Hoops are on their way out! Besides, how would you travel in one?"

Mrs. Silverman said all this as if Charity had been arguing vehemently for a hoop skirt. Charity had never worn hoops in her life, never even seen any up close. She decided to defer to Mrs. Silverman's superior wisdom and go without a hoop, as if it were just for this one time.

The dress turned out to be in two pieces plus the small caped jacket. The separate top buttoned over the full skirt. The sleeves were full, gathering to close at the wrist. The top had small jet black buttons, and a tiny bit of white lace around the collar. Mrs. Silverman added a white ribbon for Charity's hair.

"I think there may be more items to come, gloves and the like, but Stieglitz will have to provide those," said Mrs. Silverman. *Ah,* thought Charity. *That's where payment for the transaction will be completed. In trade, no doubt.* No matter. She wanted these clothes – needed these clothes – and if need be, she could defend herself against a stooped-over old man. She would check the wagon for possible weapons.

Fully dressed, she felt like a queen. A warrior queen, undaunted.

Mrs. Silverman packed all sorts of treats for the road, including some more of the "collie" bread Charity had quickly grown to love. The woman did not seem to have a lot, but she happily shared what she had with Stieglitz. From her muddled brain the night before, Charity seemed to recall that the woman and Stieglitz were some sort of relatives. Maybe that's how families – real families – treated each other.

The kind woman had hugged Charity, something the girl was not used to but found it was not unpleasant. Then Mrs. Silverman helped Charity into the wagon amid entreaties to come back soon, any time.

By daylight, Charity could see the wagon was full of the most bizarre assortment of items. Apart from the pots and pans dangling from its sides, Charity could identify paintings, mirrors, picture frames, linens, bedding, watches, jewelry, and eye glasses. There were bolts of cloth and ready-made clothing as well as dress patterns and samples of clothes and shoes. There were packets of needles, thread, lace, and ribbons. Underneath it all lay sturdy items like sewing machines and even stoves.

Off to one side was a collection of what looked to be discarded tin, rags, paper, and ... were those bones? She hoped her shabby red dress was among the rags.

So off they went. Charity felt happy and hopeful. That's when she made the mistake of asking Stieglitz where his home was.

"Nowhere. I have none," was all he would say for a very long time.

It was more than just the fear of being put out on the road. Charity was crushed to think that in some unknown way, she had hurt this man who had been so kind to her, who had no doubt saved her life. What had she said wrong?

At first, she hoped that if she kept quiet, he might forget she was there, jostling next to him in the wagon with the pots and pans clanging. Finally she could stand it no more. Summoning all her courage, she said in a tiny voice, "I'm sorry."

"Oh, it is I who should be saying I am sorry, young Miss. I was just thinking about something that I usually try to put from my mind. It is wrong to carry hatred. But I do. I hate. And I am not sorry for carrying that hate. But I just said a prayer asking for that hatred to be released from my heart. At least for a while. If you wish, I will tell you."

"Only if you feel you can," said Charity, again in a small voice.

"What do you know of General Order 11?"

About two years prior, on December 17, 1862, one week before Christmas, U.S. Army General Ulysses Grant had issued General Order Number 11. It expelled Jewish people from his administrative jurisdiction of Tennessee, Kentucky, and Mississippi. It gave the people twenty-four hours to leave or risk imprisonment.

They were only to take with them what they could carry. Their horses and wagons were confiscated by the Army. Their homes and businesses were to be sold within a day for whatever was offered.

Usually it was pennies on the dollar, if that much. Property left behind was considered "abandoned," and was up for the taking. In the icy December chill, entire families were marched out of town.

"And we were of course among them," said Stieglitz. "We lived in Natchez and were so happy, my little family and I. My beautiful Rachel and our daughter Rebecca. All of us who lived in town. Like all of our people in all the towns in Mississippi, in Tennessee and Kentucky. Mrs. Silverman, who you met, her husband Isaac, and even their little dog. Minnie left her life's treasures behind to carry that little dog."

As the horse clip-clopped along, and the pots and pans jangled, Stieglitz broke down and cried. Charity thought she herself was beyond tears, and anyway, she knew that her breaking down would not help matters. She steeled herself, quite sure that his story would not end well.

When he was able to continue, he said matter-of-factly, "General Grant, you see, accused my people of profiteering. I am certain some probably did, just as some Gentiles did. But it was only the Jewish people who were expelled with just the clothes on their backs. As Mr. Grant called them, 'the Israelites.'"

Stieglitz wiped his eyes again and continued. "I spent most of my life as a peddler. I knew the costs involved of buying goods, having them shipped, hoping someone would buy them. They said that Order 11 had to do with cotton traders, but it affected all of us. Women. Children. Even little dogs. By the time Mr. Lincoln heard about the order and revoked it …" Stieglitz had to stop again. Charity kept stock-still.

"It was December, you see. My wife Rachel was already sick with influenza. I went to Army headquarters and tried to get a postponement until she was better. But the officer in charge said no individual requests would be honored. So we were marched out of town, several families, about twenty of us in all. We had no idea where we were going, just that it had to be out of Mississippi, Tennessee, and

Kentucky. We walked, we nursed Rachel as best we could, but she died. Her lungs filled with fluid and she died gasping for air, as if she was drowning. The ground was so hard we could hardly bury her. We were not carrying shovels, you see." He smiled the most tragic smile Charity had ever seen.

He took another moment and continued. "My sweet daughter Rebecca caught it, from nursing her mother. Minnie – Mrs. Silverman – and I carried Rebecca until she passed away too. Minnie's husband Isaac died, a heart attack they thought. And one night while we slept by the side of the road, some animal of the wild ... it came and carried off Minnie's little dog. We could hear the awful sounds as the brave little creature fought for its life ..."

The man sobbed unashamedly. Charity had a feeling it was not the little dog he cried for.

When Stieglitz became calm again, he said, "Perhaps I should start at the beginning. Minnie hates me to say it, but today I am a peddler, just as I was a half century ago. It was nothing to be ashamed of. It was one of the few professions open to my people. And we were so grateful to come to this country. There were many, many of us who left Europe. In some areas, you see, there was the system of the 'matrikel.' It limited by law the number of Jewish people who could get married."

Charity had never heard any of this. Nor was she entirely sure she had ever heard of "Jewish" people. They certainly seemed nice enough, based on the two she had met so far. What exactly was the problem? And to live in some country where you were not allowed – by law – to get married? The world was a worse place than she thought. And from her personal experience, the opinion she had of it was fairly low.

"So as you can imagine," he continued with a little smile, "a healthy young bachelor like me dreamed of America. Perhaps there, someday, a man like me might own a little business, settle down, get married, and start a family. That was our dream. For so many of us. Not wealth, not power. But the right to make a living and have our own little family."

He had been born with the century, in 1800. He came to this country twenty years later. Charity was not very good at mathematics, but with the year being 1865, she could calculate his current age. Somehow, he looked older.

Stieglitz and the others like him often found help from those who had come to America before. Family members, friends, or even simply other people from their town in Europe were required by their religion to offer assistance. They extended interest-free credit and provided goods for the young man to get started as a peddler.

Through this informal network, each peddler had his own territory. They were discouraged from competing with each other. So that meant each one was alone, walking the back roads of their new country, selling to Americans with a language different from his own. In the scorching heat of summer and frozen tundra of winter, in rain and dust and mud, they trod the road. On their backs they carried their goods in heavy bags that weighed between a hundred and a hundred fifty pounds.

They rarely carried weapons and thus became attractive targets for bandits who quite frequently took the peddlers' goods, their money, and their lives. In lonely places, in a lawless foreign land, their dream ended violently.

"But for those of us who survived, we could often save enough to purchase a wagon and perhaps rent or even buy a horse," said Stieglitz with pride. "We could pile even more into wagons. We could also collect scrap – rags and paper and tin and bones that we could trade for more goods."

So that explained the hodgepodge in back of the wagon, Charity thought.

"And people seemed to like us," Stieglitz said with pride. "They seemed to think we were providing a service. We went door-to-door, you see, saving housewives the ordeal of going into town for their purchases. We were respectful of the ladies and gained the trust of the husbands. And since we carried the goods on our backs or in a wagon, there was not any of what you call 'overhead' – no rent on a building. So we could sell our goods much more cheaply than the stores in town. People loved that buying from us peddlers was a great bargain."

He stopped to laugh wistfully. "And we were the ones accused of profiteering and expelled from our homes."

Stieglitz had been one of those who worked hard enough to save for a horse and wagon. He stayed on the road, traveling his circuit. He slept in the wagon or on the ground. Eventually, he earned enough to rent a store and then to buy his own business. Success!

He met his beloved Rachel in Natchez and they were married. Then their daughter Rebecca came along. His back was bent from all those years under the weight of those heavy packs, but for a while his dream of a home and family came true. It was all he had ever asked of the world.

Under Order 11, Stieglitz lost his home, his business, and his family. Now he was back where he started a half century before. Going from town to town, looking in on old customers, now old in age as well as seniority. He called on their children who remembered the strange man from their childhood. He sold to the grandchildren of long-time customers.

He looked in on Minnie Silverman when he came through Natchez, where he was certain of a hot meal and a place to sleep indoors. He was able sometimes to stay with other friends along the way.

Charity ventured to ask if he and Minnie couldn't get married, as if this was a brand-new idea worth considering.

"Minnie and I are good friends, young Miss. We watch out for each other. Before we were expelled, Minnie had a fine home. Now she lives in that tiny place. I think she shares that little house only with her memories. Just as I bring mine with me in this wagon. We are good friends, Minnie and I, and sometimes that is the most important thing."

Then Stieglitz and Charity rode for a while in silence. Like good friends might do.

Deacon and Moran were also struck dumb by silence. Though neither admitted it to each other, both had tended to expect the kind of troop rain that had brought them South, crowded but bearable. Now, the former prisoners were herded into cattle cars that had recently been used for exactly that purpose – hauling livestock. There was foul-smelling manure everywhere. All they could do was stand in it, sit in it, or lie down in it.

The outside of the rail cars were slats. At least they could get some fresh air and see out.

Through the slats, what they saw was the devastated South – homes burned to the ground, women and children roaming the roadsides scrounging for food. Most held their hands out beseechingly to the train. As if the men had food to give. It would have ironic if it weren't so tragic.

Well, Deacon thought, at least they were moving, at least they were on the first leg of their journey home and were actually riding, not walking. Even if not riding in style, at least they were riding. He was happy and forgot all about jealous gods. Which is why he blamed himself for what happened next.

Dear Andy,

A terrible thing has occurred. I do not wish to upset you with news that is tragic, but I must share with you what I have seen here today.

The last time I wrote (in case you have not received that letter before this one arrives), we were waiting for the train to take us homeward. We were so happy to walk through those open prison gates that I do not think many of us feared more insult from the war. It was over. Lee had surrendered. Some of the men said Lee only surrendered the Army of Northern Virginia, that there were elements of the Confederate army who did not yet know, or who chose to keep fighting on their own. But for most of us, the war was over. We had survived! I will not be the same for the rest of my life, for reasons I have yet to explain to you. I will not live the life I had hoped. But I will live.

I say all of that to affirm that we all thought the war was over and could harm us no more. For our rail journey through the South, going west to Vicksburg, we were given short rations of flour bread and salt pork. Having not seen such opulent fare in so long, we were overjoyed. Almost all were dehydrated – that means thirst due to having no untainted drinking water for so long. We had been able to fill our canteens from a small creek as we marched to the town, a spring unadulterated by the poisons of our camp. Our accommodations by rail were not luxurious but no one seemed to mind. The train had ten boxcars which had lately been used to transport cattle. I leave the beasts' indelicate credentials to your imagination.

My friend Moran and I rested some, but soon even the open slats on the sides of the cars offered no relief from the foul air. Moran suggested we adjourn to the platform between the cars. Some men were already there, but there was room for two more. From there, we could see the shadows of our comrades riding on the tops of the boxcars which seemed to us an idea to consider. I demurred, having some insult to my leg and being unable to climb, but invited Moran to do so. You see, the smoke from the green wood stoking the engine's fires for steam settled on us, colored our skins with soot, and kept our eyes running with water. So I proposed we return to our original accommodations in the boxcar. Others took our place. Had we stayed between cars, I would not be writing this letter.

I will not describe to you the catastrophe of what happened next, but to say the men who took our place on the platform between cars also took our place in Heaven. You see, the rails on which we traveled, being heavily damaged in the war and hastily repaired, gave way. The locomotive toppled over in a deadly blast of scalding steam. The cars immediately following were crushed like matchsticks. The men within them, between them, and atop them, died at once. A woman nearby said the riders atop were "shuck off like peaches from a tree." The dead and soon-to-die were piled up in one horrible heap, most mangled and crushed beyond recognition.

Those of us still alive pulled our comrades from the wreckage. Many nearby townsfolk also came to our assistance. They, who had so little themselves and had reason to resent our presence. For their compassion, I am deeply grateful. A rumor spread that the accident was Confederate sabotage, to keep on with distressing the Federals, but I think not. I believe it was the hand of Fate that without warning or reason, cuts with a terrible swift sword. I am sorry, but have come to believe that way.

Anyways, Andy, the townspeople brought shovels and helped us dig. It was one long pit grave, wide enough to lay the men with only blankets for their coffins. It was near a lovely grove of oak trees, as if to remind us that there is still beauty in the world. Someone asked me to speak over their resting place – me! – why, I cannot comprehend. But I owed them that, both the living and the dead. I cannot remember exactly what I said, but it had to do with a common soldier asking only that his life not be sacrificed in vain, nor that he be forgotten. We can ease no pain for the men or their grieving families, but over that shallow mass grave, I said that we <u>do</u> – we <u>must</u> – honor their memory. Please always try to do that, Andy.

I must stop now. I will give this letter to one of the kind townspeople to mail. We are about to start marching again, in the direction of Vicksburg. Perhaps after that, our trials will be over.

Your friend,
John Deacon

In Vicksburg, William and Ella Ardent had a pleasant hotel room, rented with the officers' pay her husband had accrued. The hotel was on a gentle rise not far from the great river. From there, they could see the steamboats nosed in at the pier, letting off passengers, loading freight, taking on more fares. The boats looked festive, like floating wedding cakes.

It was from there that they heard the tumult in the streets over the news of Lee's surrender. Some of the people they saw from their window looked dejected. Vicksburg had suffered so much. Many were later seen at their siege caves, just sitting and staring.

But others in town looked elated. They were ready for life to return to normal.

Ella tried giving her husband a commentary from the window. He was still bed-ridden, suffering from a fever.

He had been struck in the arm, and as so often happened, the bullet shattered the bone, wreaking havoc with the wound. It had been almost certain to become infected, which was why the surgeons felt the only way to save the patient's life was to amputate the limb. A new type of bullet was held to be responsible.

A French Army officer named Minié had invented a new form of ammunition. Differing from the traditional round musket ball, Minié's had a shape like a cone. Its bottom had a hollow base that would expand when the rifle was fired. Because this expansion allowed it to fit snugly into the rifled grooves, it could be fired with deadly accuracy.

The .58 caliber bullet was often called a Minie-Ball by the troops, who grew to fear its destructive power. Bone, muscles, ligaments and tendons were mutilated. Some said gangrene of the huge wound was inevitable. Cutting away the limb was therefore the only solution.

Once, Ella had tried talking sympathetically to her husband about it. "I can't even imagine what you must have gone through," she said.

"No Ella, you can't," he said coldly. "But since you have such an interest, we were in a barn. They put me on a wooden door that had been taken off its hinges. They brought out the knife and amputation saw they used on the patient before me and probably the one before that. They held a sponge soaked in chloroform over my face. Lucky I was an officer or might not have even got that. When I woke up, I was minus my right arm but raging with the fever. They brought me to the hospital at Vicksburg, and that was where you finally saw fit to come get me."

Ella smiled and reminded him of what she'd read in the newspaper. The great general, Stonewall Jackson, had also lost an arm to amputation.

"Yes," her husband said, "and he died a week later from pneumonia. See, Ella, you're not the only one who reads *news*papers." He said the word with a sneer.

"But wasn't it beautiful, William, what he said at the end. They said a sweet smile crossed his face and that he spoke softly as if in relief. 'Let us cross over the river, and rest under the shade of the trees' was what he said. Isn't that touching?"

"Ella, you are a truly stupid woman," her husband said before turning away.

CHAPTER 18
APRIL, 1865

The bedraggled remnants of the prisoners were walking toward Vicksburg. Someone said it was about thirty more miles, but no one knew for sure. They measured the miles in dead bodies.

After going so long without food or water, being cold and wet, suffering injuries before, during, or after their confinement, there were men falling by the wayside, sick, hungry, exhausted.

Deacon and Moran hobbled along as best they could. They were both hungry and bruised after the train wreck, but Deacon felt especially bad that his friend was burdened with someone like himself. A lot of the time, Moran had his arms around his friend, half-dragging him. Deacon believed that if he'd had enough of his leg left to him, he'd have been happy to crawl along the road rather than burden his friend. He knew Moran could do much better without him.

At one point, Deacon had said, "I don't mean to sound all dramatic-like, but I just don't think I can make it. Why don't you just leave me here? You can make it without me. I can't go any further."

Moran had replied, "Well, as I see it, we made it through worse than this. It's only a few more miles and I don't want it hanging on my conscience that I left you behind. Don't want you haunting my dreams or anything!"

So they limped on. Deacon still had the crutch Moran had made for him. Moran had made a point of finding it after the train wreck. Deacon made sure to follow his friend's instructions by calling it a "staff," but it was still a crutch and it was still slow going on one leg. The others were pulling ahead of them, and soon the two would be on their own. Deacon couldn't fault the other men. They had only one thing keeping them going: the thought of home. He himself would probably *run* to the river if he could.

After about two days on the road, a rider galloped by, stirring up clouds of dust. Moran thought that was the height of rudeness. The rider not only had a horse to get around on, but covered everyone else in his dust. And now the rider was hollering as he hurtled by.

"Lincoln's dead!" the rider shouted. "They shot Abe Lincoln! Lincoln's dead!"

After the rider had vanished, Deacon roused himself to ask, "Did that man just say Abe Lincoln died?"

"Yeah, Lincoln's dead," said Moran. "And I ain't feelin' too good myself."

This morning, even with Moran mostly dragging him, Deacon knew he was getting weaker. Finally, he fell to the ground.

"I just can't make it any more. Go on without me, Moran. I mean it. Please. I ain't much of one for begging, but I'm begging you now. You go on without me, maybe send someone back to help. Please. Go on. Right now, before I change my mind and make you carry me!"

Deacon tried to make light of it by managing a smile. But he fixed his friend with a determined gaze.

"Go on, Moran. Send someone back for me. I need for you to do that."

Moran was obviously thinking it through, but the man was no fool. Finally, he brightened and exclaimed as if it had been his idea, “I got it! I’ll go on ahead and bring back some help for you!”

“I’d be much obliged.”

“See you soon!” shouted Moran, knowing he was seeing the last of his friend. He walked away reluctantly, but he did walk away, and with determination. “Good bye, Deacon,” he said to himself. “You been a good friend. See you in the next life, if there is one.”

Deacon felt relieved as he saw his friend disappear over the next rise. He knew he couldn’t have made it up that hill, small as it was. He closed his eyes and was glad of having stopped. The last thing he saw was the morning mist starting to rise. He closed his eyes with a peaceful look of acceptance on his face.

Moran kept walking. With difficulty, he made the uphill climb on the rise in the road. He was ashamed to admit it would have been a struggle to make it up the incline, hanging on to Deacon. He couldn’t tell if the other boys were up ahead. He’d try to catch up. But the morning fog was covering the land, making it difficult to see very far.

Suddenly, there was break in the fog. Sunlight filtered through. Oh, that felt good! He squinted westward, directly away from the sun and then he stopped short.

He could not believe what he saw. A river that big *had* to be the Mississippi! There was a town, and nudging next to it were riverboats with steam pouring from their stacks. He couldn’t be sure at this distance, but wasn’t that a U.S. flag flying over the city? *Vicksburg?* Vicksburg! It had to be! He choked and struggled to keep his composure but he could not. He was glad no one could see him now, with great tears streaking down his face.

“Damn!” he barked, though there was no one to hear. “Ain’t I the biggest damn fool!”

He turned sharply, like the way that had been drilled into them to do way back in camp. He marched with his head high, like the soldier he had never felt himself to be. He went back down the road and found his friend, who appeared to be dead.

Oh, no, Moran told himself. *Not here and not now.* He shook the skeleton of a man and bellowed, "All right you sumbitch, you done rested long enough. Get up! Get up! You won't believe what's just up ahead! We made it! There's Vicksburg and the river and boats to take us home!"

Deacon just moaned, but Moran kept shaking him. "I said to get up, you lazy sumbitch!" Moran tried lifting his friend, but that didn't work too well. "I can't carry you! You're too damn heavy! Thought you's supposed to be starvin.' How come you so heavy?"

Moran thought he saw Deacon start to stir. Obviously his approach was successful, he thought, so he kept it up. "You're gonna get up! You're gonna have to at least make it to that rise in the road if it kills you. After that, I don't care. You want to lay around and die, that's up to you. But the last sight you'll see on earth is the American flag flyin' pretty as you please. That's what you been fighting for, goin' through hell for! You ain't gonna die here. Don't make me drag you, ain't got the strength for that. Git up and do it yourself! You gotta see it! The town, the river, the flag. Make *them* the last thing you see, not some scrubby old dirt road!"

Deacon tried. Moran could see the man really did try. But he was too spent, and Moran couldn't do it by himself.

"Come on, come on, you can do it," Moran kept saying, though he was fairly sure Deacon could not.

That's when Moran saw the Grim Reaper coming their way.

Moran wasn't sure exactly what to say by way of greeting to the Specter of Death, nor if the Destroyer was coming for both of them or just Deacon.

Fortunately, the Angel of Darkness spoke first.

"Ain't you boys in blue ever goin' to leave the South?" the Specter said, though not harshly. "Ain't you done enough damage here? War's over. Git the hell back where you came from."

Moran was relieved that the Destroyer spoke some language he could understand, nothing to do with "smiting" or a bunch of "th-ee's" and "thou's." That's when Moran noticed for the first time that the Angel of Darkness was leading a mule.

"So you ain't the Grim Reaper?" was all Moran could think of to say.

"I'm one of those Rebels you boys been shootin' at. Now I'd like to see you gone."

"We's trying, brother. But my friend here has gone through a lot. He thinks he's fixin' to die and I can't be much use to help him. Any food or water you got would be most appreciated."

The former Angel of Darkness and more recent former Confederate actually smiled. "Food? Water? What's that?"

"Sorry, brother. You're right. What we've seen on the way over to here, you folks ain't got any more than we do."

The stranger walked over to Deacon, saw what he believed to be a dying man, and shook his head. But when he spoke, it was not unkind.

"Tell you what," said the man. "I'll tell you a story about when I was a boy. Small cabin just acrost' the river, yonder in Arkansas. Maybe it's still there. Just need to get acrost' the river to find out."

Moran had had enough. "F'raid we got places to go as well." If the man wasn't going to help him, what good was he?

"Naw, just listen a minute, Billy Yank. It's a good story. Up North, you got such a thing as worms?"

"You mean, like you go fishin' with?"

"The same. Worms. Them what tills the earth."

"Then I believe I know what worms is." This was wasting time, but maybe the Reb was deranged and could still shoot straight. Moran felt that the safest course was to let him continue.

"Well, when I was a boy, over there acrost' the river like I said, I was real small for my age. Know you'd never think so to look at me now, being big and strapping and all."

Moran guessed that was a joke, since the man looked just like they all did, a walking bag of bones. But he didn't want to insult the man by laughing, just in case it wasn't.

"I was the baby of the family. Ever-one was bigger than me. And they sure let me know about it. Anyway, after it'd rain, then worms'd come up out of the ground. Guess their burrows'd get all flooded and they'd seek higher ground. Mostly then, after they'd claw their way up, or whatever you'd say about worms, after all that struggle, they'd get trapped in the mud puddles and drown. Or a wagon'd run over them, or a bird would carry 'em off for breakfast. But when I was a boy, not knowing any better, I'd go out and pick 'em up, many as I could find, one after the other, and toss' em in the woods where it was dry."

"You're right," Moran said, still thinking politeness was the best policy with a loony. "That was a real good story. Appreciate it. Well, we really got to go, mister."

"Not through yet. Like I's sayin,' what I'd do was I'd pick them up and toss them over to higher ground where they could maybe survive."

"Where was this? Over yonder in Arkansas? Sounds like you didn't have a lot to do with your time."

The man smiled. "No sir, we had plenty to do, long before sunrise to long after dark, even a little 'un like me. But rescuin' those worms was something I ... I *had* to do, just for me. You a church-goin' feller?"

"Depends," said Moran, thinking he'd fudge a bit in case this man was a Bible-thumper. No sense making him mad.

"Well, maybe you won't think I'm blasphemin' when I say that rescuin' those worms made me think how God must feel, decidin' who's to live and who dies. See, even then, small as I was, I'd be huge compared to them worms. I had the power of life and death over them. Life and death. Just like God. Understand?"

Once again, Moran said politely, "I appreciate you sharin' that story. Listen, brother, could you help me with him? He's not going to hang on much longer. Appreciate the story, though!"

"Naw, you don't appreciate nothin.' But you may be about to."

Moran had enough. "I hate to appear rude, brother, but my friend here is dyin.' So if it's all the same to you ..."

Moran turned and tried to help Deacon up. He failed, lost his balance, and ended up sitting down hard.

The other man just kept on and on, didn't even help. So much for politeness.

"See, way I figure it, least you boys in blue got a way home if you can make it to the river. You'll get mustered out of the Army, all official-like. Us Confed-ruts, they jus' told us to go on home. War's over. Jus' go on home, jus' like that."

"Least you ain't got too far to go."

"See, Billy Yank, you're right. Just gotta cross the river. That's where I used to make my living, in a boat on the river. Mule ain't no good to me there. Land's a swamp. But we sorta became friends, this mule and me. She sorta kept me goin.' I can build a raft to get acrost' the river if I need to, but no place for a mule. She ain't much. Yanks over there would probably shoot her. But she's too fine a spirit for that."

Moran thought he sensed a transaction in the making. "You lookin' to make some sort of deal?"

"If you'd get up off your ass, we could load your friend on this mule. I think she could make it far enough to the river. Hope you don't expect me to load him myself. Got to do everything for you damn Yankees?" That was an expression Moran had not heard before.

"You mean, you'd really give us this mule?" Moran was suspicious. If a thing sounded too good to be true, it probably was.

"Two conditions, Billy Yank."

"Figured there'd be a catch." Moran was angry and frustrated. "What?'

"Well, first, let no harm come to her if you can help it. Like I said, she been a good friend to me."

Was this grizzled old Rebel really going to just give up the mule? Better make quick work of this before he thought it through.

"Done. Give me a hand here, brother," said Moran. With the helped of his former enemy, they loaded Deacon onto the mule with as much ceremony as if he'd been a sack of potatoes. Which both of them wished they had.

"Ain't you forgettin' about Condition Number Two?" said the Rebel.

"All right, what's that?" asked Moran, thinking that they were about to unload Deacon again.

"Condition Number Two is that y'all promise to git back North and not come back. Ever."

"No offense meant to your homeland, brother, but that will be real easy," said Moran. "Hope to never get anywheres near this place ever again."

"Deal," said the Rebel, and they shook hands.

Then, though he was anxious to be on his way, Moran couldn't help but ask. "So ... us savin' your mule, is that like your fascinatin' worm story?"

The Confederate chuckled as he started heading overland into the woods. He gave Moran and Deacon a last look with his parting words, "Far as I can see, the worms is played by someone else this time. I'm lookin' at 'em. Now, git the hell back North and don't come back."

"Deal!" shouted Moran, as he started leading the mule toward Vicksburg with Deacon on its back. "Good luck, brother! And thank you!"

Their former enemy called over his shoulder as he faded from view. "I mean it! Git and don't come back! Don't come back!"

Charity was spending two happy weeks on the road with Stieglitz, probably the two happiest weeks of her life. That struck her as strange because at first, she had hated it. She kept looking over her shoulder for approaching riders coming to apprehend her. Stieglitz, in his jingle-jangle wagon, was moving so slowly.

One day, she did indeed hear galloping horses coming their way. Instinctively, she scanned the roadside for a place to run. She'd have to jump from the moving wagon. She didn't want Stieglitz implicated for harboring a fugitive. She had heard that expression back on Gallatin Street. From the fugitive's point of view, she liked the image. A safe harbor, a place to stop and rest and take shelter from the storm. But she didn't want Stieglitz involved in any way.

She had come to enjoy the man's company and respect his wisdom. She wanted him to think well of her, too. She was so glad she had told him and Minnie the fabricated story that she was from the Garden District, glad she had constructed that tissue of lies about her upstanding family. She had never known what it was like to be accepted, to be respected, and now she craved it. She wanted Stieglitz to feel about her the same way she felt about him.

When she heard the approaching riders, her mind raced. Would it be better to jump from the wagon and run, a clear indicator of guilt, or to be calm when they were stopped, profess ignorance, and hope for the best? In the past, she never would have even considered the latter option. But now she had Stieglitz to think of. So this is what it felt like, to have someone else to care about. She could see where it could end up being a problem, but for now, she was not unhappy with the sensation.

Charity tried not to let Stieglitz hear her sigh of relief as the riders not only didn't stop them, they didn't even slow down. All they did was shout as they raced past, "Lincoln is dead! Someone shot Abe Lincoln! Lincoln's dead!"

Having only a vague sense of who this Lincoln was, Charity was not overly concerned. But when she saw how Stieglitz took the news, she was troubled. Stieglitz stopped the wagon and bowed his head. She could hear him saying what she assumed was one of his prayers, the kind he did every day in that strange foreign tongue. This one appeared to be special. She assumed it was something for the dead, like this man Lincoln who died.

When he finished and coaxed the horse forward, the clip-clop emboldened her to ask, "Did you know him, Mr. Stieglitz?"

It was not beyond the realm of possibility. Stieglitz knew lots of people, and was greeted warmly wherever he went on his "rounds," as he called them. People seemed to value his opinion, and listened to what he had to say. Everyone seemed to know him, and he knew everybody. Perhaps Lincoln was a friend of his.

Later, when she had a much clearer idea of who Abraham Lincoln was, she gave thanks that Stieglitz, that kind man, did not laugh at her for asking such a question. In fact, he made her feel better about it.

"That is a good question, young Miss, and one I must answer with a riddle." He did that a lot, Charity had noticed.

"Mr. Lincoln, President Lincoln if you will, was a kind of friend, I suppose. Not just to me but to so many. If you will look in my carrying case, just behind you in the wagon, you will see an envelope with newspaper clippings. These are things I have saved because they were important to me."

As Charity rummaged around, he asked if she remembered what General Order 11 was. She said she did. She was glad she was swiveled around in her seat, and didn't have to face him. It made her sad to think about all he had lost because of that accursed edict.

"Well, young Miss, you heard what it was and what it did. We do not have need to go into that again. But Mr. Lincoln, when he heard about it, he had the order revoked. As you will read in one of those clippings ..." Charity hoped he wouldn't want her to read it out loud – reading was not a required subject at Madame's – "as you see, when a delegation of my people met with Mr. Lincoln to express gratitude that he revoked it, he said he was surprised such an order had been issued in the first place. I always remember what he told them: 'To condemn a class is, to say the least, to wrong the good with the bad.' Mr. Lincoln said he drew no distinction between Jew and Gentile, and that he would allow no American to be wronged because of his religious affiliation. So you see why his death is a tragedy, to me and to the nation. Would you not call that a friend?"

The world of Stieglitz was still an unfamiliar one to Charity, something about religion and nationality, things that were all rather vague. And there was that word "Gentile" again; she had to find out what it meant. But she knew she'd fight down to her final breath for people like Stieglitz and Mrs. Silverman who had lost so much for no apparent reason other than for being who they were. And in Charity's opinion, they were mighty good people.

Insofar as who Charity herself was, she was so glad she had told them the story of being from a fine family in the Garden District. She wanted this good, kind man to respect her as much as she respected him. She did not want to be put out on the road if he found out the truth about what a low person she was. She did not want to be alone again. She was determined to keep her past a secret.

That was why she was so shocked when words started pouring out of her mouth.

The cabin out in the swamps, the starvation, the beatings, the disappearance of her mother. Her father's drinking, using her as gator bait, the things he did to her sisters, selling Charity at age twelve. Being auctioned off to the highest bidder at Madame's, her introduction to that cesspit of misery and sin. The beatings, the punishments, degradation, disease, medical procedures too ghastly to describe.

And then how she'd escaped by drugging and robbing that man. Walking the plank over the alley. Finding the river. The pure ecstasy of the *Silver Moon.* Drugging and robbing the man in Baton Rouge. Trying to do the same in Natchez until it was reversed back onto her. She was a criminal, and Stieglitz now knew he had inadvertently aided her.

She said she was sorry for lying to him and Mrs. Silverman, and started to say how grateful she was to them both, but broke down in huge tears. She knew this was where he would put her out. It was for his own safety, really, as well as the disgust he must be feeling, sitting there next to such a filthy creature.

"Young Miss," he said, "please reach again under the seat. There you will find a package wrapped in oilcloth. That is to protect it. You see, it contains things of great value to me." *Ah, he could say she tried to steal it and then turn her in for a reward.* Still, she did as she was told.

Inside were only trinkets. She'd expected money, pearls, jewels. The trinkets were wrapped in a white lace shawl.

"Please remove the shawl and wrap the other things back up again in the oilcloth."

Again, she did as she was told.

"That shawl was my dear wife Rachel's. We gave it to our daughter Rebecca on her thirteenth birthday. Rebecca always treasured it, as I do now. It is all I have left of them."

Charity could see why it was precious to him. Apart from the memories, it was a magnificent garment. The lacework was fit for a queen, and it was as soft a silk. *So this is what he'd accuse her of stealing when he turned her in. Clearly it was valuable.*

"It is yours," he said. "I do not know this Charity Boudry who is running from the law. Neither does Mrs. Silverman. Minnie will be glad you shared the story of that other girl, the one called Charity, the one who suffered so much in New Orleans. We both knew you would tell us when you were ready. Now, you are Rebecca, daughter of Stieglitz. That name, 'Stieglitz,' means 'goldfinch.' A pretty thought, no? A charming, gentle creature glowing like sunlight, flying free."

Charity Boudry almost never cried. But the new creation called Rebecca did. She could not stop sobbing, and did so without restraint. However, she made sure none of her tears fell on the white lace shawl.

So, like the great river whose banks they followed in the jingle-jangle wagon, the pair meandered back and forth, back and forth.

Sometimes she took the reins and tried her hand at driving the horse so Stieglitz could rest. It was certainly better than walking with a hundred-pound bag on your back, but it was tiring nonetheless and required skill. She felt happy when he dozed off while she was driving. That meant he was comfortable trusting her.

On these isolated back roads, he went from door to door. Sometimes those doors were miles apart. But people seemed glad to see him. From where she sat in the wagon, she could not hear if he was asked who she was. She wondered if he ever said she was his daughter, or granddaughter perhaps. She had never known any grandparents, but heard some of the other girls at Madame's bemoan being lonely for theirs. The new Rebecca thought she'd like having some of her own.

She was having a wonderful time, and learning a whole new world. It was gratifying that people thought as highly of Stieglitz as she did. When the sales presentation was over, they often welcomed both travelers into their homes. She watched with curiosity the first time Stieglitz politely declined anything at the dinner table other than eggs in their shells, or fruit and vegetables. She wondered if she should have done the same, but rarely declined anything that was offered.

Once she asked him about it, if she should only eat the things he did. He laughed and told her to eat whatever she wanted. He added things she didn't really understand, but it seemed to be about "his people" only eating special foods. Sometimes the two cooked their evening meal on the road, and often those foods were different from anything she had ever tasted, but were good. Quite good.

After eating, they would fall asleep under the stars, with her wrapped up in the wagon and Stieglitz on the ground. The first few nights, she wondered if this was when he'd ultimately become just like every other man she had ever known. But no one stirred, and after the first few nights she slept soundly, not worried about a thing.

But she felt an anger rising in her. She was becoming so fond of the old man. She hated, really *hated* that he had to spend his life this way. He had earned to right to be inside at night, to have a roof over his head, to have four walls to protect him, to sleep in a real bed. She didn't mind for herself, being outside. But he was an old man. She could see him sometimes struggle to get up off the ground in the morning, or to dismount stiffly from the wagon and limp to the customer's door. He should be inside, relaxed and warm, drinking that good, sweet, rich wine he called Concord. Not out on some hazardous road where he was an easy target. Not having to go from door to door, asking people to buy his goods.

Her anger reached its boiling point the night the sky split apart in a tempest of lightning, thunder, gusting wind, and a torrential downpour. At first, she retrieved the shawl and the package of his treasures from under the seat and scrambled under the wagon to huddle next to him. But then the rain flooded the ground, so they both clambered into the wagon where they sat up all night, taking shelter as best they could under a sheet of oilcloth.

Her mind was seething with angry thoughts. This dear old man should be inside! But she had no idea how to make that come about.

Sometimes, however, they *were* able to take shelter indoors. She loved that. They would be offered space in the barn, or sometimes in a spare room which he directed Charity to take while he adjourned to the "manger"' as he called it. "That was good enough for One who came before, so it is certainly good enough for Stieglitz," he'd say, much to her utter confusion.

The thing that was most interesting to her was when customers invited them to participate with the family in Bible reading. The customers seemed to genuinely respect his contribution, asking questions and seeking his opinion on Biblical matters. Her own Bible studies were limited to those few times when her late mother brought out what she called the "Good Book" while her father was gone from the shack, or passed out cold.

So when the horse drew the wagon over a rise in the road and they saw Vicksburg before them, her feelings were very mixed. What would happen to her now? Would she continue being Rebecca, or go back to Charity's world?

An innocuous little man in Helena, Arkansas, was also having mixed emotions. On the one hand, he was mighty glad to have his boat back in one piece.

On the other, here was the cousin called Alpha darkening his door once again. Alpha could darken up *any* room. Swathed from head to toe in black, Alpha looked like some demonic apparition.

Really, there must be a limit to what a man owed distant relations he hardly knew. There was a recent widow in town, a lady he'd had his eye on for quite a while. Now she was free, the war was over, and a man like him with a boat might make a good prospect for courting. Having a half-mad cousin at home could make things awkward.

But for now, he acted pleased to see Alpha at his door. In truth, he was too terrified of the madman to do anything else.

CHAPTER 19
APRIL, 1865

Vicksburg was the most wonderful place Charity had ever been in her life. She fell in love with it immediately. For the first time, she was entering a city exactly like a respectable person would. Gallatin Street in New Orleans, the docklands of Baton Rouge, Natchez-Under-the-Hill – those were the only places she had ever known, not counting that hideous house of horrors out in the swamp where she grew up. At Baton Rouge and Natchez, she had to seek refuge in the worst parts of town. She was on the run back then, and it was all she could afford.

And now – this! *This* must be what it felt like to be the kind of person she had never thought she'd be – respectable. With Stieglitz, she rode through town with her head high. She wished his back wasn't so bent for all those years of carrying the heavy pack. She wanted him to ride into town straight and tall.

But they were here. It was all that mattered. She rode thorough town swiveling her head from side to side, taking it all in, reveling in the loveliness of its fine homes. Even the shelling it had suffered during the war could not erase what had been, what was, and what would be again.

Taking in the sights also kept her from thinking about what it meant to actually be here. She was of course elated to have made it this far. But after Vicksburg – what? Would Stieglitz let her stay with him, or would he put her out? If he put her out, what would she do? She had no money, no skills to make a living beyond what she'd done on Gallatin. No, starvation and death would be better than that. She'd never do it again. She wanted to make Stieglitz proud of her.

So she said nothing until she had more facts about the pending situation. There were a few things she had to learn. An idea was forming in her mind, and she had to present it well. It was her only chance.

Stieglitz guided the horse to a pleasant part of town with pretty, well-kept homes. He had provided a running commentary about some of the sights they had ridden by, about the battle, about the siege caves, the town itself, and what he called "the community."

He said there were about ninety families now. She thought Vicksburg looked like it had more than that number of people until she realized he was talking about just those in "the community," the one consisting of "his people." Some of the stores they had passed coming into town bore names that sounded a lot like his, names that sounded foreign and exotic to her. Dry goods, furniture, jewelry shops, hardware, food, and drug stores boasted signs with names that were hard for her to pronounce even in her mind, names like Bazinsky and Kiersky. If they were like Stieglitz, she already liked them all.

A little before sundown, they pulled up in front of a pleasant home. "You will now meet the Levy family, young Miss. If you will wait here for a moment, I will announce us."

Being "announced" was also a new experience for Charity. Lately, she'd been used to skulking.

Stieglitz knocked at the door, and was greeted even more warmly that he had been by the customers on his "route." The lady of the house threw her arms around him, kissed his cheek, and held him close for a moment. They talked in that strange language Charity had heard him use in his prayers. She knew they were talking about her. What would this Mrs. Levy think? More to the point, what would the woman do? She might not be as glad to have a stranger in her home as Mrs. Silverman in Natchez had been.

After what seemed like an eternity of babble, the woman ushered Stieglitz into the house before coming down the walk toward the wagon. *This would no doubt be when she asked Charity to leave, to avoid embarrassing Stieglitz by making him do it himself.* Charity wondered if she should keep the white lace shawl.

"Good evening!" said the woman. "I understand your name is Rebecca. That was the same name as the daughter of Stieglitz, you know. I am Mrs. Levy – Esther. Welcome!"

The woman named Mrs. Levy extended a hand as if to help Charity down. Charity thought the woman might be making her get out of the wagon before telling her to be on her way. Then Mrs. Levy asked if Charity had "things" in the wagon that she wished to bring into the house. This was a good sign. Charity said she did not. *Should she add a 'thank you' at this point?*

"In that case," said Mrs. Levy, "we will get someone to move the wagon to the barn and unhitch the horse. Now, you must come in and rest and have a bite to eat." This was the best news of all.

Inside the house, Charity looked for Stieglitz who was nowhere to be seen. Mrs. Levy was bustling around her pleasant kitchen, and answered the unasked question.

"While the men are off at prayers, if you don't mind, Miss, we will have a 'nashn' in the kitchen. Then we will find a place for you to rest before dinner."

If what sounded like "nosh" meant food, and then there would also be a dinner to follow, Charity thought she had never heard sweeter words.

The rest of the evening went just as well. Several new people came to the Levy home, friends or relatives or both. Everyone in "the community" seemed to be related, and Charity lost track of who was kin to whom. She just knew she liked them all.

The dinner conversation was pleasant and sounded to Charity like it was intelligent. The only men she had ever known usually just talked about gambling and getting drunk. One was proud of establishing a reputation for being an expert only on "fast horses and fast women." The women Charity knew hardly talked at all.

But everyone spoke at the Levy home, women as well as men. Everyone's opinion was listened to and weighed. They talked about events in the world, both in America and the place called Europe. And of course they talked of the war, of the death of Lincoln, of what would happen now to the defeated South. Though Charity tried to keep silent, she noted several things that caught her attention. This helped form the plan she would bring up to Stieglitz first thing in the morning.

With a full stomach and feeling pleasantly drowsy on more of the rich wine they called Concord, Charity allowed herself to be led to the guest room after the usual protests of not wanting to be a bother.

"Nonsense," said Mrs. Levy. "You are our guest. That is what a guest room is for."

Then, the words were out of Charity's mouth before she realized how ungracious they might sound: "Does Mr. Stieglitz have a place to stay?"

"He likes to stay with the horse. He will be fine," said Mrs. Levy, which seemed to put an end to it. Charity thanked the woman for her kindness, put out the lamp and fell asleep, knowing she wanted to be up at sunrise.

At dawn, she could see the barn from the window in her room. Quietly, she made her way out of the house and over to the structure. But then she paused at the door. Suppose he was still trying to sleep. Suppose she walked in on the old man at a time when she would not be welcome? At prayers, perhaps. So she tapped lightly at the barn door and was startled when it immediately opened.

"Well, good morning, young Miss!" Stieglitz said jovially. "Did you sleep well?"

"Oh, yes sir," she said. "I was afraid of sleeping too late to see you this morning. Are you going on your rounds? May I come with you?"

Stieglitz paused. There was trouble coming, Charity just knew it. So she hastily spoke up to spare him the embarrassment.

"Perhaps me coming with you on your rounds, here in town, might not be ... seemly," she said. "But I was hoping to have some time alone to speak with you. As soon as we can."

"Well, I have said my prayers and Mrs. Levy will soon be inviting us for breakfast. Perhaps right now? If, of course, you don't mind the discussion being in a barn," he said smiling.

Charity didn't really catch the last part. What she heard was his haste in wanting to talk *right now.* She told herself that almost certainly he would be wanting her to leave as soon as possible, now that they had arrived at their destination.

He offered his arm like a gentleman might and settled her on a bale of hay as he sat on one opposite. The horse was happily munching his own breakfast. *Now or never,* she told herself as she had done so many times before.

"Mr. Stieglitz, sir, I do not have the right words to thank you for all you have done. You saved my life. You have given me the best few weeks of my life. I have loved being with you on your rounds. I have done nothing to repay you."

He started to protest, as she knew he would, but she quickly kept going.

"So, you see, sir, I was thinking. I wondered if I could stay with you, keep making rounds with you. I could help. Like an assistant. I could take the reins of the horse so you could rest more. I could ..."

Stieglitz interrupted, as she feared he would. "No," was all he said.

"I understand, so I have a better idea!" This was the moment she was working up to. Taking a deep breath, she began.

"A store. Right here in town, or Natchez or in another town, wherever you think. It will be small to start, but we can save money. I will be the unpaid assistant in your new store. You won't have to be on the road all the time. We can stay in the back. You can stay indoors where it is safe and warm and dry. You can ..."

This time Stieglitz interrupted, as she hoped he would not. "No," was again all he said.

"But Mr. Stieglitz ..."

When he looked at her now, he had a hardness in his eyes she had never seen in the man. He had never displayed anger or even lost his temper around her. Now she saw for the first time the toughness that had carried him to a strange country from over the sea, toughness that had sustained him with a hundred-pound pack on his back, trudging those strange and dangerous back roads. Charity had seen hardness in other men. She knew when to keep quiet. This was one of those times.

Then the moment passed. He was kind old Mr. Stieglitz again. He spoke softly, with affection.

"You are a good girl, young Miss. You have a good heart. But the time for all that is over. You must understand. The time for that is gone." He laughed softly. "No more stores."

This was not the turn of events Charity had desired. Her face told the story, and his face told her he understood what she was feeling.

"Your life is ahead of you, young Miss."

"No!" In her panic, Charity blurted it out. "I have no life! I have no skills, no way to make a living. The only thing I know is what I was. What man will marry me? I have no protection, no money, nothing in the world. And I want to stay with you!" Charity knew how selfish she sounded, so she tried to quickly interject another approach.

"So, I thought, with a little shop, we might look out for each other. Mrs. Silverman too. We could open a dress shop, the three of us. You know how to sell things, she knows everything about fashion. I could learn to sew, I could be the shop girl, clean up, anything. I'd learn fast, I know I would. I could take care of you both."

More gently now, again he said, "No."

She lowered her head, but she knew she wouldn't cry. The pain was too deep for that. Then something she had heard at dinner last night flashed across her mind.

Raising her head again, she said, "I'm sorry I sounded selfish just now, Mr. Stieglitz. It's true I am afraid for myself. But last night, at dinner, your friends talked about the war. All the orphans that are left, especially here in the South. A lot of the little girls will have to face exactly what I did to survive. They will have to do the only thing most men want from them. Hundreds of girls just like me, and maybe they won't survive. Maybe they won't have a savior like you."

"Stieglitz is no knight in shining armor, young Miss."

Well, he was *not* going to interrupt her now. She knew her idea was a good one. And not just for herself this time.

"So I was thinking, sir, you know so many people, so many good people. Last evening the Levy's talked of wanting to help, with all there is to be done after the war. So I was thinking of a kind of ... home, a place where orphaned children are loved and cared for and treated well. Someone could each them to read and write, someone wise like you. And I could help, I could clean, I could do something, I know I could ..."

Now she was finally out of steam. His next words would decide her fate.

He was thoughtful for a moment, as he usually was before speaking. Then he said one of those little prayers in that strange language. Then he thought some more, for a much longer time. She held her breath when he began to speak.

"You have a good heart, young Miss. Of course you are afraid. You are still a child. But now you are thinking about other children too. That makes you different. You are smart and I think you are a hard worker. I think you are not the kind to complain, I think you will enjoy helping others, feeling useful. And you are right, there is much need after that terrible war."

That was when Charity noticed she was still holding her breath. She'd have to breathe at some point or she would pass out. But she didn't dare do anything until he spoke again.

"Sooner or later, I must go to St. Louis to buy more supplies, young Miss. Perhaps I shall give the horse a nice rest here at the Levy's. Mrs. Levy will spoil him with apples and sugar when she can find some. He is a good horse, he deserves to be spoiled. So do you, young Miss."

Stieglitz paused again, once more collecting his thoughts. It gave Charity the chance to take a quick breath. "Let us do this: let us take a fine riverboat to St. Louis, just like your *Silver Moon* that you loved so much. I will purchase more goods, and we will visit with the community there. They have more savings than people here in Vicksburg, here in the South. They will make an interest-free loan to send you to a place called Cincinnati, in Ohio. My people have several schools there, and several benevolent organizations. You can be trained to work at schools and orphanages. You may come back to the South when you are ready. You may wish to help the Southern people who have been so good to Stieglitz. Someday you may perhaps wish to repay the loan, but I suspect your benefactors will not wish that. I will say a prayer for you every day. In time, you may forget your friend, Old Stieglitz. But you will be making him proud."

Charity was stunned. It was too much to take in. If she had prayed for her heart's desire, this would have been more than she would ever have dared to ask. She said the only thing she could say to this miracle: "Yes! Please! Thank you!"

"Fine," said Stieglitz. "And now, one of Mrs. Levy's excellent breakfasts. Then we will choose a boat to sail on."

The bustling docks at Vicksburg played host to a magnificent array of riverboats. Charity was dazzled. She read the names emblazoned in huge letters on the side of the vessels, searching in vain for the one called *Silver Moon.*

Disappointed as she was not to find her water-borne magic carpet once more, she was still enthralled by the other boats. Even their names were thrilling. *Autocrat. Brilliant. Burlington. Darling. Magenta. Pauline Carroll. Zephyr.*

Most of them had smoke gushing from their stacks, as if impatient to be on their way. Mr. Stieglitz checked their respective departures, and announced that the *Pauline Carroll* would work perfectly for their needs. It was leaving Vicksburg later that day, but would soon be back. There were also other steamers expected in a day or two from New Orleans.

Charity asked why he especially liked the *Pauline Carroll.* It was a small sidewheel, wooden hull packet like most of the others. He responded that the steamer made the run to St. Louis-New Orleans fairly regularly, so he might easily be able to arrange passage back to Vicksburg with his purchases. He added jokingly that the owner/captain was named John W. Carroll, adding, "So maybe he will be extra careful with a boat named for a lady in his family."

Stieglitz still had some calls to make in Vicksburg that would take a day or two, so they decided to postpone booking passage until the

Pauline Carroll returned. That way, he hoped to have extra funds from his sales in Vicksburg to make their trip a comfortable one for them both. He said the Levy family already extended an invitation to stay as long as they liked.

Charity was disappointed that Stieglitz still would not permit her to make his rounds with him in Vicksburg, but she thought that perhaps she could get her bearings from the Levy home and set out on foot to see the town. That was what she did, and was elated at the feeling of walking free, in the daylight, in a good part of town. How she loved Vicksburg. She was determined to come back. Most of all, she was determined to make Stieglitz proud.

The *Pauline Carroll* did indeed return to Vicksburg, pulling in behind a much larger vessel called the *Sultana* which steamed in from New Orleans on April 24. At over two hundred fifty feet long, and weighing about three times the tonnage of the *Pauline Carroll,* the side-wheeled coal-burning steamer *Sultana* was reported by some dock workers to be one of the largest and best ever constructed, though others in the docks had the opinion that she was not all that fine.

With telegraph systems disrupted by the war, one of the dock workers said the news of Lincoln's death had been brought to Vicksburg by the *Sultana.* It had been built fairly recently in Cincinnati, which Charity took to be an auspicious sign. She had no idea how the nation's river systems ran, but wondered if they took the *Sultana,* then perhaps she could just stay aboard all the way to Cincinnati after Stieglitz disembarked in St. Louis. She would broach the subject. She would also remember to ask him what a "sultana" was.

The *Sultana* was rated to carry two hundred and ninety passengers plus a crew of about eighty. After discussion and some thought, Stieglitz felt that having almost four hundred people on a boat like the *Sultana* was too many. He still opted for the smaller *Pauline Carroll.*

Sultana had been laid up at Vicksburg longer than her captain planned. There was money to be made, and every day – every hour – he delayed was costing him some. Probably a lot, since the greenbacks were coming from the government.

On her way up the swollen river from New Orleans, the boat had suffered a boiler leak. At around the time *Sultana* docked at Vicksburg, a grizzled sailor was telling others in a dockside New Orleans tavern that he left the boat before she sailed north this trip. He was concerned about the steamer's massive boilers, and had disembarked before *Sultana* left New Orleans. He said the boilers already had to be repaired – just patched, really – at Natchez and at Vicksburg on the two previous trips. And now the boat would again have to fight its way against the mounting current. Well, he had too much respect for the Mississippi to test his luck.

His concerns proved justified, as he would later discover from fellow crewmen. Steam was escaping from a crack in one of her four boilers as the *Sultana* reached a point about ten miles south of Vicksburg. It forced her to fight the current up the Mississippi at a greatly reduced speed. The steamboat's chief engineer finally put his foot down, declaring that he would not proceed beyond Vicksburg until necessary repairs were made. Other crewman joined him in fearing that the crack was a threat to the boat's safety.

So at Vicksburg, the boat's captain, who was also her owner, knew that time was critical. If *Sultana* did not leave right away, he would miss out on some lucrative business. The leaking boiler that had slowed her trip upriver from New Orleans had to be dealt with in a hurry.

The crew could not make repairs themselves on a problem this critical. So the captain summoned a local boilermaker to examine the problem. The man reported that extensive repairs were needed. The captain would have none of it. It would cost him too much time and money. He cajoled, begged, demanded that the man patch the leaking boiler so the boat could leave Vicksburg as close to its scheduled departure as possible.

At first, the boilermaker had refused, but finally agreed to place a patch over the area leaking steam. When he had finished, the man gave the captain a warning in no uncertain terms. He stated outright that the repairs were only temporary and asked for assurance that the work would be done right when *Sultana* reached St. Louis. The captain easily assured the boilermaker that it would be. Most certainly.

While the work was being done, the captain used his down time in Vicksburg an extremely profitable way. He went into town on a quest for passengers. The U. S. Army was commissioning privately-owned steamboats to ferry Union Army soldiers, mostly former prisoners of war, back to the North. He was not about to miss out on the action. There was money to be made.

At Vicksburg, where the soldiers were being funneled, the Army was paying boat owners five dollars per enlisted man and ten dollars per officer. The captain struck a fine deal. He agreed to carry the men at just three dollars a head. With the officer in charge of transport, one Major Fitch, collecting at least five dollars apiece from the government, the captain/owner did the math. In volume, there was a handsome profit for them both. The more they loaded, the bigger the income. He was ready for a windfall.

One small drawback was that *Sultana* was already carrying about two hundred fifty passengers and crew when they left New Orleans. Most of the cabins were already occupied, though there were a few left. No matter, the captain thought. These were enlisted men who had been in a prison camp. Deck space was probably all they really required. And there was lots of deck space aboard his boat.

Ella had been dispatched to the dock by her husband to secure their transport. Of course he required a cabin. As a captain, he was after all, an officer.

She saw a man on the pier who looked awfully familiar. Surely it was not the horrible Army officer who had let conditions deteriorate at the hospital, she thought. But her suspicions were confirmed when she heard someone call out, "Major Fitch!"

No, it couldn't be. She had lodged a complaint and was assured his actions would be investigated. But had he been simply transferred to another post? Was he now loading up soldiers on their way home? She eased her conscience by telling herself that there probably wasn't too much harm he could do simply by loading soldiers on a boat. Other people would know if something was amiss, and they would put a stop to it.

But just in case her name had been mentioned in the hospital investigation, she waited until she could speak to another officer in charge. He was helpful. He checked his paperwork, gave her two tickets, and assured her that she and Captain Ardent could board at any time. Cabin class, of course.

She placed the tickets in her bag, securely on top where she could get to them easily.

Still uneasy at seeing Fitch, she returned to the hotel but kept up a cheerful patter as she helped William get ready for the journey. She tried to help him dress, to shave, to get cleaned up for the trip. He kept swatting her away, hissing at her to "quit making a fuss."

On the way out of the hotel, he told her to stop at the desk and complete the procedure to check out, which she did. After they arrived at the pier, he told her to give him the tickets. She reached into her bag where she had put them. They were not there.

"Well?" he demanded.

She looked all through her bag, finally removing all its contents. Nothing. She knew she had put them there. William was growing more and more angry.

"Everyone is looking, Ella. You are holding up the line. Where are the tickets? Can't I trust you with the simplest things?"

She looked around. He was right. Everyone *was* looking. She *was* holding up the line. She felt her face go red, burning with shame.

Her hands were shaking. Her head began to throb. Sweat trickled down the front of her dress.

"Well, go back and find them!" he bellowed.

She turned quickly, both to do as he said right away and so he could not see her eyes welling up. He always detested the sight of her tears, taunting her unmercifully. After she had taken a few steps, she heard his voice again.

"Ella! Get back here!"

As he approached the officer in charge, he calmly reached into his tunic and produced the tickets.

"You took them from my bag?" she cried. "You had them all the time?"

"Keep your voice down and get on the boat," he said. "What's the matter, Ella? Can't you take a little joke?"

Her head throbbing now, she scurried up the gangplank after him. Perhaps it was just being confined that made him this way, she thought. First the hospital, and then the hotel room. Maybe now things would get better. Ella Ardent couldn't wait to get on the boat.

Charity and Stieglitz were also ready to leave Vicksburg. They approached the captain of the *Pauline Carroll,* docked next to the *Sultana,* and asked for passage to St. Louis.

"Sorry, folks," the *Carroll's* captain said. "The last cabin has been taken. By that Army fella over there, name of Fitch. Since he's an officer, there's not much I can do. You might try the *Sultana* or the *Lady Gay*. They're both getting ready to sail."

They decided to try the *Lady Gay* since she looked like she indeed looked ready to leave. But before they could reach that boat, her lines had been cast, the gangplank was pulled, and she was underway, heading north. It looked to Charity like there was hardly anyone aboard the *Lady Gay*.

There wasn't. Fitch had failed to reach a satisfactory financial arrangement with the captain of the *Lady Gay*, and as punishment, he told the ship's captain that the *Lady Gay* could just sail empty. None of the profitable soldiers would be aboard. This would teach him a good lesson, thought Fitch. Maybe next time, that recalcitrant man would be more eager to deal.

The master of the *Pauline Carroll* was also about to be taught a valuable lesson. Fitch was directing all soldiers aboard the *Sultana*, whose captain was easier to do business with.

One Mr. Stieglitz and his daughter Rebecca were at that moment boarding *Sultana*, two late passengers who had secured the very last cabin. Fitch then redoubled his efforts to herd the hundreds of waiting soldiers onto that boat. Record-keeping, all that paperwork – it was so time-consuming. He ordered his junior officers to dispense with it as much as they could. Except for officers, of course. Make sure their names were noted. They fetched ten dollars a head.

Seeing *Sultana* already so overcrowded, some of the soldiers started asking if they could board the neighboring boat, the *Pauline Carroll*. No, Fitch said flatly. Regulations. Then he ordered his underlings to spread the rumor that the *Pauline Carroll* was suffering from a bout of smallpox. It was a lie, of course, but extremely effective in quieting his unruly charges.

He decided to leave the rest of the boarding procedure to his junior officers. He himself had no intention of boarding *Sultana*. It was already too crowded for his taste. Fitch valued his privacy.

Fitch boarded the *Pauline Carroll*. In a short while, from the balcony outside his cabin, he watched with a satisfied smile as the *Pauline Carroll* steamed away from Vicksburg with a total of seventeen passengers. The *Sultana* was still loading, an endless blue line of men snaking up her gangplank.

Fitch loved his privacy. He loved that he'd taught the *Carroll's* captain a lesson. Most of all, he loved money. At that moment, he especially loved the fact that he had all three.

CHAPTER 20
APRIL, 1865

The aforementioned late passengers Stieglitz and daughter Rebecca found their cabin on *Sultana*'s starboard side.

"Starboard means the right-hand side of the boat. So, young Miss," he said, "You will have a good view of Memphis, Tennessee, when we land there."

That was not nearly as important to her as some of the amenities aboard. When she rode on the *Silver Moon*, her attention was simply on keeping herself concealed. She had her meals in her room, courtesy of the cabin steward. She kept her door locked and did not dare to venture on deck. When she was not succumbing to an exhausted sleep, she had looked out the window of the *Silver Moon* rather than taking in the décor of her cabin.

Though the *Silver Moon* had a special place in her heart, this cabin on the *Sultana* also suited very well. Now, she was a respectable passenger. "Rebecca, daughter of Stieglitz." She had once heard the phrase, "Mary, Queen of Scots." She liked her title every bit as well.

The steward had referred to the cabin on this boat as a "stateroom." That made it sound so elegant. It had two beds, thus sparing any nocturnal debates as to which of them would curl up on the floor. The carpeting down the passageway was worn, but still attractive. It had eyelets at the sides where it was buttoned down and could be taken up for cleaning.

The cabin itself was decorated with images of diamonds and half diamonds, along with a landscape picture of some indeterminate locale. She assumed it was someplace, real or imagined, along the river.

There was a little card inviting them to summon a crew member for their every need. There were stewards, waiters, cooks, and deckhands along with those whose jobs were unclear. Firemen, engineers, mates, clerks, pilots. The card also said there was a "life belt in each cabin," whatever a life belt was.

That was when she remembered to ask Stieglitz what a "sultana" was. He knew just about everything. This time was no different. First, he asked if she knew what a "sultan" was. She claimed she did but it had just slipped her mind, which was of course a lie.

Stieglitz smiled. "Wait until you get older. That will happen a lot."

"Mr. Stieglitz, that was not true. I do not know what a sultan is. Never have known. I'm sorry for lying." *What on earth had come over her? Lying was her stock-in-trade!*

"Well, at least you have asked me something I know. Or think I know," he laughed. "A sultan is a king or ruler in places like Turkey." Charity was determined not to let him know she thought turkey was a kind of meat she never got to eat. "And a sultana is usually his wife, or perhaps is his mother or daughter or sister or another female member of the royal household."

Satisfied, she was on to more important matters. She wondered aloud if they could order meals in their cabin just like on the *Silver Moon.* Stieglitz said he didn't see why not, if that was what she wished. As crowded as the boat was becoming, that might be the best way.

"I understand from the steward that there are about forty other ladies on board," he said. "With all these soldiers everywhere, the ladies' cabins might well be the only safe place. Perhaps, though, it might be nice for you to meet some. Perhaps find a friend among the ladies."

This was something Charity had not considered. In her new home, in Cincinnati, she could well have female friends. At Madame's, other women were competition. They stole from each other, informed on each other, sometimes got drunk and knifed each other. Charity thought the ladies she would meet in Cincinnati would be more like Mrs. Silverman and Mrs. Levy. That suited her just fine.

This reverie was interrupted by the sounds of hammering and banging just below their cabin. By this time, Stieglitz was trying to rest. How could he sleep with such commotion? Since she was a respectable paying passenger like all the rest, she could find out what the noise was all about and make it stop. What she saw when she stepped outside the cabin appalled her.

It was immediately apparent what the hammering was for. Wooden beams were being positioned under the cabin deck to prop it up. The decking had begun to groan and sag under the tremendous weight it was now required to support. It was a wonder the deck didn't fall through. She could not imagine what kept it from collapsing.

There were men in blue uniforms everywhere. Everywhere. *Everywhere.* Hundreds, maybe a thousand, maybe more. And still they kept coming aboard. And they all looked like skeletons.

Stieglitz had come outside the cabin to see what the noise was about. Charity could see the look of shock on his face as he watched the skeletal men pouring aboard up the gangplank, many helping their comrades to walk.

She heard him say one of his prayers in the strange language. When he was finished, he said, "Those poor boys. Looking at them I can only think of a certain Bible verse."

She wondered if it was one of those they had read when his customers invited them in for family Bible readings. "Which one, Mr. Stieglitz?" she asked.

"'*And the sea shall give up her dead*,'" was his reply. He shook his head sadly as he went back into the cabin.

Two of those men, nearer to death than to life, were making their way painfully up the gangplank. Moran hoped he could keep hold of Deacon, and not end up with both of them in the churning water. He thought he could swim if he had to, but this was not the time to test his theory.

There was a rumor that there would be some food aboard the boat, and he was feeling as happy as he could under the circumstances. They had made it to Vicksburg with the help of the Rebel's mule. Moran had sold the animal to someone who promised to treat her well, and he'd gotten paid in greenbacks.

The mule money would be his stake. The last few pieces of gold that he had stored in the little pockets of his drawers ... well, they were long gone. They had needed it to survive in the prison camp. There were guards to be bribed, a little medicine to be had for poor old Deacon, a few extra bits of food, even such niceties as mailing his friend's crazy letters. Moran felt it was worth it, felt the letters had helped his friend survive, though he wished the money had lasted longer. It was only when the gold ran out that he had resorted to stealing food. And almost got himself killed in the process. Every time Deacon saved his skin, Moran felt that his friend had been a good investment. If he'd only had some money left, he would not have had to steal. Well, that was all in the past. He'd use his newfound mule money to multiply his assets.

He spotted the obvious flaw in that plan as soon as they boarded. None of these walking skeletons were going to have any money. Why, he was probably the richest of them all, having had a mule to sell. But maybe there were others on the boat, folks in the cabin class, folks who had not been recent graduates of a prison camp. Moran would just wander around on a scouting mission soon as he got ol' Deacon settled. Deacon wasn't looking too good.

Two other passengers were settling in. When Ella and William Ardent arrived at their cabin, she thought it was quite pleasant, but he found fault with everything. Neither bed was comfortable, for one thing. She was privately delighted that there were two beds in the room, not just one. He tried both, found the one that was slightly more to his liking, and gave her the other.

She asked if he thought there would be dinner served in the main dining room. He made a cutting remark about the quality of the food they could expect. Her mind went back to the little cave, when the salt pork and "desecrated vegetables" in Patsy's haversack constituted a banquet.

"William, mightn't it be nicer – for *you* – if you looked for the good in a situation rather than the bad. Perhaps it would make you happier."

"Well, isn't that easy for you to say, Ella. You with your two good arms and me with my right arm gone. Can't imagine trying to get the farm work done with only the likes of you around."

As she recalled, before the war, there had been hired hands to do the hard work which her husband had avoided at all costs. But perhaps he was right, perhaps with the war, hired help would be harder to come by.

"You may be correct. It may be a struggle at first. But things are bound to get back to normal, don't you think? And William, may we not be thankful to God that you still have one good arm?"

He raised his left hand toward his face, turning it over, studying it with great interest. Then, without warning, he lashed out, slapping her in the face so hard she careened backwards into the wall.

"For once, you're right, Ella," he said. "I *do* still have one good arm."

After a nap and a light supper, Stieglitz joined Charity on the deck outside their cabin. He had felt the boat lurch away from the Vicksburg pier in its effort to get underway. He hoped to watch the shoreline receding in the dark, always interesting to see. Now, he had to fight his way simply to get from the cabin door to the rail where she stood.

He looked down at the dark, churning water and frowned.

"I do not believe I have ever seen the river this swollen, and running so fast," he said. "Snowmelt from up north, I would imagine. Why, I would venture it will be a mile, maybe two miles wide in spots. Feel how the boat strains against the current."

Charity didn't much care about such technicalities. She realized she had been missing the old man, just while he was only a few feet away inside the cabin. That was why she was feeling wistful and that was why she said what she did.

"I wish we could go together to that Cincinnati place," she told him. "I wish we could open an orphanage together. You could be a teacher. They will need that, and you are so wise." She lowered her voice almost to a whisper. "And I will miss you so much."

"We have had this discussion, young Miss. You have a good life ahead wherever it takes you. I will live out what is left of mine, here on my route, here along the river."

"But I can't bear to think of you out in the cold and rain, all alone on those lonely roads. That can't be a good life for you"

"Perhaps it is not the life I would have chosen," he said, "but it is life, nonetheless."

They were being jostled on all sides by ragged-looking soldiers all around them. Still, as pleasant as their cabin was, and as crowded as the deck was, Charity and Stieglitz enjoyed being out in the air for a while longer, watching the riverbank as the boat strained to glide by.

At first Charity thought they'd be able to see tomorrow's sunrise out their cabin door, being on the "star board" side of the boat. But then she remembered all the twisting and turning the river was capable of, how it had been running north in New Orleans when everyone knew it should be heading south. So she relaxed just to watch the darkening countryside before they headed in for the night. Whatever direction sunrise came from would be just fine.

But having been Charity Boudry for so long and having lived Charity Boudry's life, she never completely relaxed. And now she was glad of it.

A ratty-looking soldier was making his way through the crowd on the cabin deck. As he approached the two of them, he appeared to stumble, colliding with Stieglitz and almost toppling the old man over.

"Excuse me! I do beg pardon, sir!" the ratty soldier said. He bowed to Charity, acknowledging her politely by saying "Ma'am," as he sauntered off, touching his fingers to his brow as if he still wore a cap.

When the man had passed, Charity said, "Mr. Stieglitz, do you carry your wallet with you?" They had never really discussed the financial element of his business.

"Of course," he said. "I am never without it. I would never leave it behind where I could not see it, in the cabin for example." He patted his pocket and found it empty. The old man looked stricken, "Oh no!" he cried.

"Please don't worry," Charity said. "Please stay calm. Don't worry," she repeated. "Please go inside the cabin and stay there."

The old man eyed her suspiciously, asking, "What are you going to do?"

"Please, sir. Just go inside the cabin and stay there. I'll be back soon. Just be sure to let me back in!"

He looked at her warily, but did as she asked. As he reached the cabin door, he stopped. "Out here with all these men," he said. "Please, please be careful, young Miss."

He went inside as she had asked. She reveled in the sensation of someone caring about her.

Charity had asked him to go to the cabin because she was not entirely sure what her plan would be. If it involved doing something unsavory, she did not want him to see. She was so angry at the cur who had stolen from the old man that she wished she still had the jagged glass she'd lost in Natchez.

Although there were hundreds of soldiers on the deck, all looking just alike, all skeletons in blue uniforms, she recognized the thief right away. He was looking for more victims among the cabin class passengers who were on deck, and he was being none too subtle, in her opinion.

When Charity grew nearer, she watched him use the same stumbling routine, palming a watch from a portly gentleman in the process.

Though she knew a lot about the shady part of life, she was not adept at picking pockets. How delightful it would be to nab the watch and Stieglitz's wallet before this cur knew they were missing. She had not forgotten that she'd drugged and robbed men in New Orleans and Baton Rouge, but perhaps that was beginner's luck. Her experience at Natchez-Under-the-Hill taught her that maybe she was not as skilled a villain as she thought. And in any case, this man was upright and was not unconscious.

The thief was moving faster now. Soon he'd take the flight of steps to the next deck, packed with more hundreds of men, and she might lose him. She might not get another chance. She had to use one of the few gifts she knew she had.

Hoping to display a show of confidence she did not feel, she sidled up to the thief. Softly, gently, she took his arm. He looked shocked and possibly as scared as she was.

"Oh, Cousin Albert, I thought it was you!" she exclaimed, hoping to discourage anyone from thinking she was practicing the profession she perfected at Madame's. "Mother will be so pleased to know I saw you. How are your dear Mama and Papa?"

She easily turned him away from the flight of steps, and walked him back toward her cabin. If she had a problem with this one, at least Stieglitz was there to come to her rescue.

"Beg pardon, ma'am," said the thief. "I am not who you think I am, that Albert fella. Sure wish I was."

In her most sugary voice, she said, "You are exactly who I think you are, and exactly *what* I think you are."

She had been almost certain the thief would bolt, but he kept walking with her hand on his arm, as if taking a pleasant stroll.

"You," he said. "I saw you with the old man.'

"I am so glad you recall us," she said pleasantly. "Because I never want you near that man – or me – ever again. You stay away from us."

"You gonna turn me in?"

"You gonna give me back his wallet?"

She was shocked that the thief did just that.

She checked Stieglitz's wallet to make sure it wasn't empty. It bulged with greenbacks.

"I didn't take any of it," the thief said. "Didn't have enough time."

"Fine," she said. "Now, you to head to some other deck and leave us alone."

"What makes you think I'm not on this deck, that I don't have a cabin?"

Charity almost laughed. "Find a mirror and take a look at yourself," she said. "And by the way, you might wish to stay away from a life of crime until you're better at it. I've seen men who'd have already knifed you for trying to pick their pocket, and tossed your sorry self into the river without a soul seeing it done."

Her hand was still on his arm. Strangely, it was not unpleasant, even with a filthy cur like this one.

"So, you won't turn me in, ma'am?"

"Next little lady just might. From the looks of your splendid attire, I'm guessing you're still in the Army. That'd mean the stockade."

"I'm done with the Army and done with being treated like dirt by the high-falutin' likes of you."

That was the very first time Charity Boudry had ever been accused of being high-falutin.' She had to smile. And her hand was still on his bony arm.

"You must admit you're terrible at being a thief," she said. "Your trip-and-fall act wouldn't fool a child. I could probably have lifted that wallet from you just now and you'd'a never felt a thing!"

"Well, what I been through, guess I'm not at my most ... aware of things," he said petulantly.

She thought of poor Stieglitz, all he had lost in the war. *How dare this man try to excuse himself!* "What have you been through that everyone else has not? Look at the rest of these men! And you don't know anything about that old man or me. How dare you steal what other people have worked so hard for?"

As long as she was going to be called high-falutin,' she might as well take the high road. But she could swear the thief genuinely looked like she'd hurt his feelings.

"Guess you gonna want me to give back that watch too," he said in a small voice.

Charity could still see the portly man whose watch had been lifted. "I don't care what you do. Though it looks like he hasn't missed too many meals during this war. He can probably get another, no trouble. My suggestion is, whatever you do, don't get caught."

As they neared the cabin, she removed her hand from his arm. She was tired of getting jostled in the crowd, and thought she'd go back inside.

"Well, goodbye," she said. He was so pathetic. Something in her made her add, "Good luck." He would probably be handsome under all that dirt, even in this skeletal form. But still so pathetic. And he so obviously wanted to keep her by his side a little longer.

"So that old man you was with ... is ... who?" he asked quickly. "Your husband? Father? Somethin' else? Why'd he send you to do the dirty work?"

She had to smile. "He didn't. But as you see, I am good at it."

The boat swerved sharply, and two soldiers tumbled into her.

"Watch out for the lady," the thief said to the men. Incredibly, he added, "Best check for your wallet, ma'am. I'm sorry the boat is so crowded. Can't be very pleasant for you."

Did the rogue have a heart, or was he just waiting to take advantage of her good nature?

"Well, it sure is crowded. Must be maybe a couple of thousand. And some of them look even raggedy-er than you," she said, though with a kind smile. "I feel bad for the soldiers, being done this way after fighting the war. Now they finally get to go home, and look at how they're treated. Like someone saying, 'We're done with you – you ain't no good to us anymore' and then loading them up like cargo. Those cotton bales on deck are treated better."

He looked like he wanted to speak, wanted to form sentences that wouldn't come.

"Well, goodbye," she repeated. She wondered what he'd look like all cleaned up. Not too bad, she thought. She'd seen a whole lot worse. But this was not the time to be thinking that way. She started to walk away.

The thief took her arm, but so gently she could have shaken him off easily. She did not. The man was trembling. Must be the chill of the night air. It was still cold for April.

She wrapped her beautiful white lace shawl around her more tightly. "Please leave us alone."

He removed his hand from her arm and she realized she was sorry he did.

"I'm sorry, ma'am. I guess I just wanted to ... I don't know, I guess talk with you some more."

"Now, what makes you think I'd want to socialize with a scoundrel like you?" she said, but she said it with a sweet smile.

He tried to look indignant. "Ma'am, you don't even know me. You don't know for sure I'm a scoundrel, not really. Oh, I'm not denyin' that you're right. But usually it takes a little more time for most folks to find out."

"Maybe most folks *you* meet aren't as smart as me. Really, I must go to my cabin."

He reached out for her arm, but then thought better of it and withdrew his hand. She was inexplicably sorry he did.

"Ma'am, just a couple more minutes? You don't know what it'd mean to me, just to stand here with you. It's just been so long since I've had anything good in my life."

"I'm sorry," she said. "I'm not in your life. I'm trying to get you to stay out of mine."

"So you'd deny a soldier a few minutes of your time?" He pointed at the lower deck covered with soldiers. "Me and those fellas been through a mighty rough time. Some so sick they might not make it home, even after they get off this boat. They weren't like them professional soldiers, nor officers. They were farmers, just simple men who went to fight for their country. Some could'a stayed home, had an easier time of it. My buddy down there – see the fella with one leg, sittin' propped up against the railing?"

She saw dozens like that. But where his man was pointing, there was one who looked worse than most. "Yes," she said, fairly sure it was the right one.

"His name is Deacon, John Deacon. He owned his own newspaper back in Ohio. He's been to New York City. He's smart and he's brave and he could'a had a better life than what he's gonna have now. He don't even know where he's going when we land. Says all he had, all that was his home is gone. Now does that seem right to you?"

"No, of course not. But … I'm sorry. Please leave me alone." The friend's plight was one of the many things she preferred not to think about.

"All right," he said. "But before you leave, can you tell me your name?"

She wheeled around to face him. "What on earth for?"

"I don't know, so I could think about you, I guess. The one fine lady I ever knowed in my life."

"No," she said. "I'm sorry." One of the reasons she declined was that at this point, she herself didn't know if she was Charity or Rebecca. She was going to a place called Cincinnati. She was going to save children like herself from the life she had been sold into. She felt good about that. What was the point of starting up with this man? "I'm sorry," she repeated. She truly was.

He looked at her for a long time, as if memorizing every feature of her face.

"Yes, ma'am," he said, bowing his head and again touching his forehead as if he was wearing a hat. "My name's Moran, in case you care."

"It's not that I don't care …" she started, but then thought better of keeping this up. She sighed, and simply walked away.

The thief named Moran stood transfixed, looking at her sadly and so very longingly as she disappeared onto the throng "I care, ma'am," he said to himself. "I surely do care."

Someone was kicking John Deacon. He roused himself from whatever dream state he was in to investigate. It was one of the ship's young deckhands.

"Oh, I am sorry," said the boy. "This will sound maybe a bit cruel, for a man like you, I mean. But we were told to check for … for dead people, I guess you'd say."

"And you thought I looked the part?" asked Deacon. Well, he had a pretty good idea of the answer. If somebody thinks you're dead, you might be well on your way there.

"I'm sorry," the boy said again, starting off in search of his next potential corpse.

"Son, would you have a moment?" asked Deacon. "Could you tell me where we are, where we're bound? I never even asked before they loaded us aboard."

"Well, I shouldn't take the time, but …"

"I understand," said Deacon. "I'll bet there's a rule about you not sitting down on the job. But I sure would be obliged if you'd come a little closer to me down here than hovering over me up there."

"Well, I supposed in that case …" the boy said, happy to get off his feet. "If an officer comes …"

"… I'll tell them I threatened to toss you overboard."

The boy liked this poor damaged man, and felt sorry for him. Anyone could see he'd been through a lot, the boy thought, even apart from the leg being gone. So he answered every question he was asked, as well as he could.

They were bound for Cairo, Illinois. What happened to the soldiers there, the boy did not know, though he guessed the Army would divide them up according to their home state and send them on their way. Most of the men were from Ohio, Michigan, Indiana, places like that, the boy said as if Deacon had never heard of such mysterious points on the map.

The boy said they were claiming about two thousand passengers on the *Sultana*, but he had been watching and knew for a fact they hadn't counted a whole lot of the soldiers. They also didn't include the civilian passengers that were already aboard. Neither did they count the crew. So all told, by his calculations, there were almost twenty-four hundred people aboard. And the boat was rated for a total of about four hundred. Six times more than she was rated for!

But she could set a record with this voyage, the boy said. "Imagine! If we arrive safe at Cairo, it would be the greatest trip ever made on the western waters. There's more people on board than were ever carried on one boat on the Mississippi River! And we're doing it in the middle of the worst spring floods in the history of the river! She's three miles wide in places and running fast!"

"If?" asked Deacon.

"Sir? I don't understand," said the boy.

"You said *if* we arrive safe at Cairo. You think there's a chance of trouble?"Deacon expected to boy to quickly dismiss that far-fetched idea. But the boy was thoughtful.

"Well, I trust the captain," the boy said when he finally spoke. "He's also the owner of the *Sultana*, you know. So mostly I'd say if the captain made a decision, it would be a good one. All of us in the crew, we were told that if anyone asked, we were to say that the boat might be overcrowded but not *overloaded*. But between us, six times maximum capacity ... well, that seems like a lot, doesn't it?"

Deacon could only agree that it did. Of course, he told the boy, he was more of a civilian than a naval man.

"Well, that's something else," said the boy. "Like I said, I trust the captain. But sometimes we deckhands overhear things we ought not. I think the captain was having second thoughts about how many we were taking aboard. He went to talk to that Army officer on the dock. When he came back aboard, he was cussin' like I never heard before. Told his first mate that some Major Fitch wouldn't let him back out of the deal. That's what he called it, 'backing out of the deal.' Then I heard the captain say he would give all the interest he had in the boat if it was to safely land in Cairo."

"Well, how bad is it?" Deacon asked. "Are we in danger of sinking? Or capsizing?"By this time, the boy may have thought better about speaking too freely. These things had a bad way of coming back on a person.

"Oh, no sir. I believe we are fine if the captain says so. And we have life belts in the cabins and a lifeboat aboard."

"How may can fit in the lifeboat, son?"

"Oh, easily a dozen. Probably two," said the boy with more confidence than he felt. He was starting to do the math. "But we won't capsize, sir."

In fact, later the very same day, the *Sultana* came perilously close to doing just that.

At Helena, Arkansas, the word quickly spread among the passengers that a photographer was onshore setting up his camera to take a picture of the steamer and its human cargo. The photographer would be on the west bank of the river, the port side of the boat. This was exciting! The new medium of photography was really being refined during the Civil War. Many of the soldiers had their picture made in the early years of the war. And here was the chance to be photographed when it was over! When they were going home!

As the excitement swept through the massive crowds on deck, the passengers began running toward the port side rail, hoping to be in the picture. The top-heavy boat began to list.

On *Sultana's* starboard side, Deacon noticed the dangerous tilt to port. "What the hell?" he exclaimed for the second time in a few minutes. Deacon wasn't much given to cussing, but feeling the entire starboard side of the boat tilt upwards, having so recently had the unsettling conversation with the deckhand, drove him to it. Moran, however, did not seem to notice.

In fact, Moran appeared to be thrilled by the unexpected exodus of hundreds of passengers to the port side. He pulled Deacon up roughly without invitation and began half-dragging him to the starboard rail.

That was the first time Deacon had barked, "What the hell?"

Moran said they had to act quickly to take advantage of space suddenly opening up on the starboard side. He stated they could claim prime positions on the nearly empty right-hand side of the boat before order was restored.

When Moran dumped Deacon unceremoniously at the rail in front of the starboard staircase, Deacon had a feeling there was something he was not being told. He posed the question.

"Oh, all right," said Moran. "Why should you be the only one with a girl?"

"I don't have a girl," said Deacon. Moran hardly noticed the pained look on his friend's face.

"Yes, you do. You've called out her name on more than one occasion when you's delirious or something. Well, now I've got me one too. Oh, Deacon, she's the most beautiful girl you have ever seen! Rich dark hair that almost glows, hair that looks as soft as a meadow. Dark eyes that look almost like an oriental princess. Full lips that a man could lose hisself in …"

Deacon sat with his mouth open. He had certainly never heard Moran wax poetic before. Eventually, he grasped the notion that this dream woman had a cabin on the starboard side. Moran was going to lie in wait for her. His friend didn't exactly know her name, or anything about her, but by Heaven he was going to. And one way or another, she would be his!

At Helena, two men stood on a slope over the riverbank. One was concerned that the constantly-rising river would get all the way to his front door. All the commotion caused by a photographer taking a picture of some riverboat was not uppermost in his mind. He had other things to worry about. One was standing right next to him.

The problem that was standing next to him still went by the name Alpha, even though everybody knew by now the war was over. Worse, Alpha showed no inclination to leave Helena. Now Alpha was showing an uncharacteristic interest in the spectacle on the river. A boatload of blue uniforms so close he could almost reach out to them.

Alpha was silent for a long while. Soon his cousin thought he saw the ghost of a smile cross Alpha's usually dour face. Then he heard the words he had come to dread. In a grim drawl, Alpha said, "I'll need your boat."

CHAPTER 21
APRIL, 1865

Moran was off on a scouting expedition on the starboard cabin deck in search of his lady love. Deacon was just as glad for the silence. He was tired of hearing about someone else's great romance, even one whose name was a still a mystery to her admirer.

On the other hand, the absence of conversation gave him a lot more time to concentrate on the painful sounds of the overworked *Sultana* struggling against the current. He had been relatively hopeful before the chat with the deckhand. Now, even if the boat made it to Cairo, what awaited him?

A couple of fellow amputees – that was their organizational name, apparently – told Deacon he'd be in line for eight dollars a month in pension for his lost leg. While grateful and pleasantly surprised, he'd just as soon have his leg back.

But the real question was what happened after they offloaded the soldiers at Cairo. He had nothing to go back to in Ohio. Nothing. That was what drove him mad.

Deacon hated when he got into dark moods like this. That was one thing he'd say for Moran, the man always had some sort of brilliant idea for making a profit, for "setting them up," as he called it, after the war. So far, nothing sounded like it would pan out in the light of day, or when Deacon pointed out some glaring flaw in the plan, at which point Moran would sulk. Maybe it meant they were due for something good. Or maybe it just meant that his friend's ideas were simply bad.

Deacon stretched out on the deck, looking up at the stars. What if the Lord were to take him, right now, at this moment? He didn't think he'd much care.

"You ready to take me, Lord?" he asked the sky.

Then he discovered that might well be the case.

In his readings, he'd heard that men have visions right before they die, that someone from their life comes to meet them at Heaven's gate, sort of like a celestial usher into the wonders of the Great Beyond. Now he knew it was true.

As the smoke surged from *Sultana's* stacks, he saw through the mist the only thing he wanted to see. A vision of Ella above him, looking straight ahead into the night.

He kept staring. The apparition certainly looked real, though he guessed apparitions were supposed to.

"Lord, is that my last vision? Lord, please guide me."

At that moment, their eyes met. The apparition looked just as stunned as he was. He struggled to get up. *Where was Moran when he could make himself useful?* Deacon grabbed the starboard rail and pulled himself up. When he got his crutch under him, just as he feared, the apparition was gone.

Then, over the din of the boat struggling upriver, over the mayhem of hundreds of men around him, he heard the one sound that he would have given his life to hear one more time.

It could not be possible, not above the tumult of this boat. But then he remembered a story he'd read about an Iroquois chief who went with a Dutchman to some kind of event in New York City – his beloved New York again! As they walked up Broadway, the Iroquois said he heard a cricket. His friend said that was impossible, no one could hear a sound as small as that in the bustle of the jam-packed street. The chief then asked the man for the smallest coin he carried, which turned out to be an Indian head penny. The chief dropped it on the street, and a dozen people dove for it.

"You see," said the chief. "People hear what they want to hear."

Right now, Deacon was hearing his name called by the most unlikely person in the world, the one who he most wanted to hear.

"Johnny! John Deacon!"

"Ella!"

She flew down the staircase as he hobbled toward it. In her haste, she slipped on the last step just as he got there and crashed into him. They both collapsed in a heap. Some of the men around them just laughed, helped the pair up, and deposited Deacon on the nearest cotton bale. As they walked away, the men's comments were good natured: "He got him a good 'un," and "Wonder what kind of bait he used," and "If I could get me a woman like that, I might cut off my leg too."

The bale of cotton turned into a secluded arbor as they clutched at each other desperately. Ella openly wept.

"Oh my dear Lord, oh Johnny, is it really you?"

"Ella, oh Ella Rose, oh Ell …"

She ran her hands over his face, like a sightless person trying to record every facet of it. "Oh Johnny, you look near death. Oh my darling, what have you gone through?"

"I can't even remember. Why waste time on that when I've got you ... here ... now. Oh, Ell. I just cannot believe it."

They clung to each other.

"I just ... I don't know what I can say ... oh, Johnny. I've prayed for you every day."

"Guess it worked," Deacon said, "'cause here I am."

"Johnny, how are you? Truly?"

"Ella, I've always hated silly, overused expressions. Tried not to use them in my writing. But here and now, holding you, I am just fine. I can make this trip and I think I can face anything that's to come. Oh, Ella, you're safe and you're here."

He took her face in his hands and noticed her grimace in pain. It was the tiniest motion, but he noticed. Then he noticed the bruise on her cheek. An eye starting to turn black.

He touched her face gently. "Ella, you get this falling down the stairs just now?" Which he knew was impossible. It had been too short a time.

"Must have. I can be so clumsy, you know."

"No, I don't know that," he said. "I know you to be the most graceful woman in creation."

And then, as if just to change the subject, as if it were just out of curiosity, he asked, "Ella Rose, your husband on this boat? You find him? Wasn't he in the hospital at Vicksburg?"

"Yes, he is in the cabin up there," she said, pointing in the general direction of the port side. "I thought I'd come out for some fresh air."

Even in this moment of pure joy, Deacon took on a hard look. "Want to tell me about it?" he asked without emotion. That damnable husband of hers. Wonder if the brute would have the guts to try beating up on a man, even a one-legged, half-dead one. Deacon thought they might yet have the chance to find out.

"Johnny, while we have these few moments together, can't we talk about … something else … anything else?

Deacon swallowed his anger. She was right. They needed to make the most of this time. He held her close. He wanted this moment to never end. They embraced each other, yet both could sense *Sultana* painfully struggling against the current.

"This boat," she said. "It's so overcrowded. There are way too many people. You can almost feel the boilers straining. It'd be bad enough even if the river was calm. But the flooding is coming from the snowmelt up north. Look how high the river is – you can't hardly see the shore. And the current is running so fast. It feels like any second it could sweep us all the way out to sea! I can't imagine how those boilers can handle it."

"Well, the ship captain must know what he's doing. He's the owner too. Gonna protect his investment. They wouldn't'a loaded us all on here if they didn't think we could make it."

"Johnny, I ... saw someone. When we were boarding. I've had a kind of bad feeling ever since."

"Someone you know?"

"Saw him at the hospital in Vicksburg. He ... some of the men said he was stealing money the Army gave him to get supplies and food and medicines and who knows what all? They sent inspectors in, they found the conditions were a horror. I heard there would be a court martial."

"Was there?"

"I don't know, but what if it's the same man? What if he was reassigned? What if he's still doing the same kind of thing here?"

"And what if the world ends, right this minute? I've got you, that's all that counts."

"But look at all these men, John! A thousand – probably closer to two thousand. Don't you think this boat is carrying way too many? Suppose he did what he did before, what if there's a way for him to make a profit off how many men he could squeeze aboard? Wouldn't there be more percentage in a few thousand than a few hundred?"

"I don't know. I suppose so. If a fella was wantin' to."

"Perhaps if I'd left well enough alone at the hospital, he wouldn't have been here."

"But like I told you, the boat's captain is also the owner. Wouldn't he know best?"

"Wouldn't they all get more money the more men were aboard?"

"Well, maybe they're just bein' nice. I know how I'd'a felt if this boat left the pier without me. I am sick of war, sick of being hungry, sick and tired of feeling sick and tired. And I am by-God ready to go home! Even if I have no life with you, Ell, I know you're alive. And I'll always be somewhere close by, looking out for you."

He gently took her face in his hands and looked in her eyes meaningfully. "Now, I don't care who's on this boat with you or how many men are aboard or anything. Just you. Just me."

And they kissed for what seemed like a glorious eternity.

At one point, Ella had to take a breath. She was sure she'd faint dead away from the sheer rush of emotion. She took the opportunity to say, "Oh! I haven't yet thanked you!"

"For what?"

"For doing what I asked you *not* to do. The money ... from your newspaper... it was all I had. Bushwhackers – thieves, murderers – they took the horse, wagon, supplies, everything. Everything but what you gave me."

"Everything but that money, and my love. That was with you too. Listen to me. I'm a romantic! Me!" He held her close.

"It saved me, John," she said, safe within his arms.

"That was what it was supposed to do! You know, I'll declare I'm feeling some better now. So what if you saw some thievin' officer you think you recognized? We got each other now. We can look out for each other."

"It *was* him. He was the one checking in the soldiers, loading them aboard."

"Makes no difference to me how I got aboard. With respect, a little less talk now, Ella Rose."

He pulled her to him and thought there was nothing that could make him let her go. Husband be damned. Deacon wanted to strangle the man in his bed. Deacon thought about himself, the person he was now. He could do it. He wasn't a boy anymore. He was a man now. He had faced battle and gone through the pits of hell. And this was what it felt like to come back from the dead, to embrace life, to kiss the woman he adored. He sure wished they were alone instead of in the middle of a thousand men. And with her damnable husband somewhere on the boat, curse him. Finally, from deep within their embrace, she laughed.

"You find this funny?" he asked.

"I was just thinking I was wrong. You are nowhere near death."

Deacon smiled delightedly back at her. "Guess nursing is your specialty. Could use a bit more, though."

And, as in all good romances, they kissed as though they were the only ones who had ever been this much in love.

In the sheer joy of the moment, Deacon completely forgot his own caution about jealous gods.

CHAPTER 22

APRIL 26, 1865

The *Sultana's* overworked boilers needed more repairs when the boat reached Memphis around seven p.m. Many of the soldiers aboard were in good spirits because some of the ship's cargo, more than a hundred tons of sugar, was being offloaded. They felt it would make more room for human cargo.

Some were recruited to help with the unloading, which meant they could stretch their legs. The word spread that the boat would depart again around midnight. After stopping briefly just outside Memphis to pick up a new load of coal, it would then continue the journey upriver. The more enterprising of the men felt that even though they were ordered not to go into town, this was an ideal chance to slip away and see the sights of downtown Memphis.

Moran was one of those with wanderlust. He knew his precise destination: the first riverfront saloon he could find. Almost certainly he would find a poker game to join and augment his mule money. He decided this would be one venture from which it might be better to exclude Deacon. Moran planned to hit several games in the next few hours, and he had to confess his buddy would slow him down.

And at first, his plan was working like a charm. He won a few hands with unexpected ease and tried not to gloat. But after he bought a round of drinks for the other players, his luck inexplicably started to change. He lost, and lost, and lost again. He'd tried to give the impression that he had a lot more cash on him than he really had. Mule money would only go so far, and he wanted the other players to think he was what they called a "high roller." When he bluffed, he didn't want to be challenged.

But nothing was going right for him now. He excused himself from the group as politely as possible, though he doubted this bunch would notice good manners. They were sorely lacking in the social graces. He wouldn't want to meet any of them in a dark alley.

Off he went in search of another game, one where his luck would hold a little better. Never having been in Memphis, he had no idea where his next destination might be, but he knew he could not stray too far from the river. He had to make it back to the *Sultana.* His future was on that boat in the form of the most beautiful lady he had ever seen.

Perhaps because his mind was with that lovely lady, back on the cabin deck of the *Sultana*, he lost his bearings. He was suddenly in a part of the docklands that would have made him edgy even if he'd been carrying his infantry rifle, which he was not.

As he turned to backtrack, he found himself face-to-face with two of his recent fellow card players. They backed him into an alleyway and did not seem nearly as hospitable as when he'd first sat down at the table.

"You know what we want," one of them growled. He was the uglier and meaner-looking of the two, though it would have been a close contest. He carried a knife that looked about a foot long.

"This here's called an Arkansas Toothpick," the man said. "Ever seen one in action? It'll gut you like a pig in no time flat. Now put your money down on the ground. All of it."

"Now, listen fellas ..." Moran began, when suddenly the speaker toppled toward him. In that moment of confusion, Moran was able to blindside the other thug who was also puzzled by this turn of events. Moran pushed past them to the street.

It was only then that he saw the reason for the tumbling assailant. Directly behind the brute was a one-legged man, wielding his crutch … *staff* … like a club. Deacon! The man Moran had slugged was starting to get up. Deacon swung his weapon again. Moran was thankful he'd made it sturdy enough when he whittled it.

Without a word, he grabbed Deacon and they ran like the top entry in a three-legged race. Deacon, bless him, knew the way right back to the boat, and it was only on the *Sultana's* gangplank that they started to laugh.

"Well, much obliged," said Moran when they settled back down near the rail. "But you better not have been followin' me!"

"Moran, my brother," said Deacon, "I am much, *much* too tired to be playin' these kind of games. Why the hell did you have to get off the boat?"

"So you *did* follow me! Hell, I can take care of myself!"

Deacon looked in the direction of the gangplank. "Well, in that case, I think I see your friends from the alley looking for you." He rolled over as if to sleep. "I bid you a good night, sir."

Moran poked him with his foot. "Wait a minute, just wait a minute. I may have forgot to say 'thank you.'"

Deacon rolled over again and had the broadest smile Moran had ever seen on the man. His friend really did seem to be doing a lot better.

"I saw you leave the pier when the sugar was bein' unloaded. Thought that didn't mean nothin' good. First, of course, I checked all the local churches. When you weren't there, I tried the dives. Then, when I saw what was about to happen with those old boys, it looked like a parade – me followin' them followin' you! You shoulda' been in church giving thanks for getting through all we did. At least, no preacher gonna come after you with a knife."

"There's some that might."

"Only if they caught you with your paw in the collection plate."

Moran chose to ignore the insult.

"So you just had to go into town to *gamble*? Where'd you get your stake, Moran?"

"That was the whole point, to get some more."

"Moran, my brother, don't you know those riverfront dives just wait for boys like you to come stumbling off a boat into town? Right now, you'd be lying in that alley, life bleeding out of you, and when the boat sailed, no one would know."

Moran was glad Deacon did not add the unspoken phrase, 'Or care.'

He decided to deflect attention. "How'd you get off the boat, Deacon? Same way as me? Unload a few tons of sugar, did you?" Moran instantly regretted that last part. Sometimes he really did forget his friend had been cut up so bad. But Deacon seemed not to notice, or at least, didn't care.

"Pretty much," Deacon said. "When I saw you slip away, I volunteered to help guard the sugar shipment on the pier until we sailed. They didn't mind a one-legged man doing that. Then, I took off and like I said, checked the local churches ..." Deacon grinned. "And the rest, you know."

"You must be feelin' better to be actin' so ornery," said Moran. It was only then that Moran had noticed the strange glow in his friend's eyes, like the man was burning up with fever.

"Listen, Moran, you know I'm glad just to be alive. But have you given any thought to what's gonna happen when they dump us off this boat?"

"Sure. Army men's gonna be at the dock with a sack of gold for each of us."

Deacon ignored that. "I figure they'll have some sort of pension for us. Don't forget, we got thirteen dollars a month back pay from when we were on the march and in the prison camp. And lucky me, I hear I'll get an extra eight dollars a month for donating my leg to the cause."

"That's not much to live on. You plannin' on starting up your newspaper again?"

"Not right away, but hear me out for once, Moran. I've got an idea that's better than all your get-rich-quick schemes put together."

Moran's feelings were hurt, to be accused of not listening to his friend as well as the disparagement of his well-thought-out concepts.

"Such as?" he asked, none too enthusiastically.

"Moran, you ever hear of a place called New York City?"

"Of course." If it was the place Moran was thinking of, he thought he had, anyway. *Isn't that where the president and Congress live, the ones who sent us off to war?* Or maybe he was thinking of someplace else.

"Ever been?" asked Deacon, still with the feverish glow in his eyes.

"Not in a while," Moran said, assuming "not in a while" meant "never."

"Well, it's the most amazing place in the world! There's wonderment around every corner! It's so big, a man could get lost there. Start a new life! There are all kinds of opportunities if a man was willing to work hard."

Before Moran could interject, Deacon answered for him. "Well, hard work – that lets you out, I know. But still, my brother, there is a lot of mischief someone like you could get into!"

What on Earth? thought Moran.

"So this is what I's thinking," Deacon continued. "We take whatever pay the Army is willing to give us and we head for New York. I get me a job at a newspaper – they got about a dozen! And you do something, whatever you want to do, get a job at one of those theatres – they got about a dozen of them too! – help the actresses into their costumes or something ..."

His friend really was feverish, thought Moran sadly.

"Like you said, remember I owned a newspaper back in Ohio, back before the war?"

Moran had. He had used the fact quite recently, hoping to impress a lady.

"You know what it was called?"

Moran did not.

"It was called *The Phoenix*! You know what that is?" Deacon didn't even slow down. "A phoenix is a mythical creature who rose from the fire to be even greater than he was before! I'll work at some newspaper in New York until I can start my own – *our* own, Moran! You can be the janitor or something. And we'll call it *The Phoenix*, just like us rising from the ashes of despair like when we were in prison. What do you say?"

"Well, I'll sure think about it," Moran lied.

"There's one other thing you need to be thinking about."

"What's that?" Moran could hardly wait to hear what came next.

"We got to kidnap a lady away from her husband when we get off this boat."

Now Moran actually *was* interested. Maybe they could make it *two* ladies.

Around midnight, *Sultana* pulled out of Memphis. A clock somewhere in town chimed twelve.

"Listen to that," said Deacon. "It's tomorrow. It's a new day."

"You're right. Time's getting by us. Why don't you get some sleep. I'm feeling a bit restless. Think I'll stretch my legs." Damn, he'd done it again, used the word 'legs.' Deacon didn't seem to mind at all.

Moran tried to cover. "Guess I just can't get used to bein' out here free. No one shooting at us, starving us, marching us ..."

"You almost got someone knifing us."

Moran looked quizzical.

"Those old boys in Memphis?"

"You ever gonna let me forget that?" asked Moran.

"Not if I can help it." Deacon smiled such a genuinely sunny smile that Moran couldn't help but feel hopeful himself.

The steamer headed into the channel where she stopped to take on a thousand bushels of coal. Then *Sultana* resumed making her painful way northward, straining against the surging river.

CHAPTER 23

APRIL 27, 1865

It was after midnight. The damnable mosquitoes were swarming. Moran had never seen anything like them, not the way they devoured you here on the river. How could people stand to live here?

Moran was roaming the starboard side cabin deck. He had to step over sleeping men, had to take it slow and careful to avoid treading on one. Some of them looked so bad, he truly wondered how they'd made it this far. Poor, poor fellas.

He knew she was in one of these cabins. Certainly the door would be locked and there was no way to look inside, to see who was who. He only knew he had to do something, and do it now. Since Deacon was planning a kidnapping, Moran at least had to know where to stalk his own prey.

He pressed his ear against a cabin door. He could hear nothing.

He tried the next. Again, nothing.

Next. And then someone poked him in the back with a gun!

"Don't make a sound or you're a goner," said the disembodied voice. Then he heard a sweet laugh. It was a woman pretending her finger was a gun. No, not a woman. A lady. *His* lady.

"Oh my stars, ma'am – you scared me to death!"

"Well, catch your breath before I turn you over to the Captain. Imagine! Some awful night crawler! Breaking into cabins!"

But she was smiling as she said it. As breathtakingly lovely as she was in repose, her smile was enough to melt a man at the knees.

"Ma'am, I wasn't doin' nothin' like that!"

"I saw you. Trying to break into our cabin."

"Ma'am, I wasn't! Not ever! I was just trying to figure out who was inside."

"That supposed to make me feel better?" But she was still smiling.

"You don't understand. I was... well, I guess I was trying to find where folks was.""What folks exactly?"

"I don't know, just folks."

"You mean me?"

Moran hesitated, could think of no better story, and sighed. "I guess I do."

"You beat all, mister. First you rob us, now you're trying to break in to our cabin. Come away, we're going to find the Captain."

"No ma'am! Please! I didn't mean nothin.' Guess I just sort of wanted to see you folks – *you.* Just to talk."

"Why?"

"Because it's been a long, long time since I met anyone nice. And so beautiful. Like you."

"Think I'd fall for something like that? What do you take me for?"

"A fine lady."

She laughed softly. To him, it sounded like church bells.

"You sure beat all, mister. I don't know what you are playing at, but you sure are bad at it."

"What you doin' out on deck, ma'am?" Then he had to smile. "All these soldiers out here, no tellin' what kind of trouble a lady might get herself into."

He took a chance and moved closer. He felt like his soul was aching to touch her. His mind was muddled. *What was he thinking? 'Soul aching'?*

"Just needed air," she said. *She was actually talking to him!* "And wanted to watch the night. Didn't want to disturb anyone."

"So, that man you were with, is he your husband?"

She almost said Stieglitz was her friend, but opted for "father."

"Mind if I ask where you're from, ma'am?"

"Downriver."

"Mind if I ask where you going to?"

"Upriver."

Her replies were curt, but she was still smiling. And he could swear he saw a sparkle in her eyes.

"So, you goin' north to meet up with your husband? He a soldier?"

"If you're trying to ask if I'm married, why not just ask instead of all these questions?"

"You married, ma'am?"

"Why would a scoundrel like you want to know?"

"Because, if you ain't … I mean, if you're *not* …" Moran knew he was going to have to rise to her standards. "Because if you're not married, ma'am, or spoken for, then I'd like to put myself forward to ask for your hand."

He expected her to laugh, or at least to cut him dead with a mean remark. Instead she appeared to consider his proposal. He could feel the deck sagging and creaking beneath his feet from the weight of all these men. What she said next almost caused him to fall through it.

"All right."

"Beg pardon, ma'am?"

"'All right' is what I said."

"I don't think I'm hearing you correct, ma'am." Now he was really confused. He'd expected her to scream or slap him. *What on earth was happening here?*

"You asked for my hand in marriage. I said 'all right.' Now, let's go find the captain. I hear they can marry folks just like a preacher does." She was not entirely sure if that was true, but she was enjoying the game.

He really seemed to be a sweet man. She found she liked talking to him. Other than Stieglitz, no man had ever just wanted to *talk* to her before. And it was obvious to her that beneath the rough, dirty, starved-out, pathetic exterior was a handsome man. To her utter shock, she found herself wanting to know what it would feel like in his arms. She had thought such notions were dead to her.

She moved a bit closer, on the pretext of removing her white lace shawl.

"See, I've got my wedding veil right here," she said, draping it over her hair. Moran thought it made her look like the holiest of angels.

She saw the way he was looking at her, and felt something stir in herself she thought she would never have known after the life she'd led. She took the shawl off her head and tied it around her waist. She wanted her arms free.

"Well ma'am, I'm not sure I meant getting married right this minute." Then he thought it through, figured he'd hit on it. "Probably be a trick anyway, you'd get me to the cap'n and then turn me in for trying to rob you or assaulting you or somesuch."

"Well, you're right," she said mockingly. "That was exactly the plan. I guess you're too smart for me, mister."

"Name's Moran."

"Guess if we're to be married, I'd best start remembering that. Now, we'll need a best man."

Moran was enjoying this more than anything he'd ever done in his life. He knew she was play-acting, but it was sweet and fun and he could spend a lifetime hearing her voice.

"We got one! I told you about my buddy, name of Deacon, the one who owned a newspaper. He's gonna own another one soon's we get home. He's a real smart fella. He already offered me a job. In New York City!"

"Well, that's a good thing. Because you look too scraggly for farm work or toting heavy loads."

"Few home-cooked meals and I'd be good as new."

"Then we'll have to hire a cook."

"For you, ma'am, we'll have a cook and a maid and a butler to answer the door and lots of servants for all the elegant parties we'll give. We'll know all the best people in New York. And you'll be the belle of the ball, the most beautiful of all."

This was the silliest conversation Charity had ever had in her life. And she adored it. In the past, when men said she was beautiful, she knew exactly what was coming. But this one seemed so... different.

She wanted Stieglitz to meet him and see what he thought. Stieglitz would know. Oh, she was still determined to learn how to help the war orphans, but maybe there were some in New York City. Maybe this man could write about it in his friend's newspaper.

"Would you care to meet my ... father ... tomorrow morning?"

"It would be an honor, ma'am. And I will tell him just what I am telling you now. That I will work every day of my life to make something of myself, to make you happy and proud of me, to give you a life of comfort and joy. Because you would be the treasure of my life."

Charity actually felt her knees going weak. She moved closer.

When she did, Moran realized he still didn't know her name. But there were more pressing matters at hand. He took a deep breath, prayed a silent prayer, and took her in his arms, arms which he honestly believed had never felt so strong, so capable. He was becoming a man worthy of this lady.

As he brought her lips to his, the world crashed into the sun in a hideous, blazing roar.

CHAPTER 24

APRIL 27, 1865

The flames, the flares, the sparks, the explosions lit up the night. Charity's first thought was of Stieglitz. As she turned toward their cabin door behind her, she saw the deck give way where Moran stood – where she had stood just a heartbeat before. She screamed her heart out as she saw Moran disappear into the flaming pit below. There was no hope for him, that was clear. He was gone.

She had to get to Stieglitz before the entire cabin deck followed Moran into the fires of hell. Bodies, hundreds of them, were flying through the air, propelled by the force of the explosions or trying to jump, trying to save themselves from the inferno. Some were in flames themselves.

Stieglitz emerged at the cabin door just as she dove for it. He had a strange object in his hand.

"Put this on!" he ordered.

"What is it?"

"It is a life belt. Put it on now and jump. Swim toward shore! It is your only chance."

"Do you have one?"

"Yes! Now put it on! Now!"

"Well, go get yours and we'll stay together."

"There is not time!"

"I'll wait for you!"

"Put it on, damn you!"

In that moment of her stunned silence, she stopped resisting. As if it was exactly what he was expecting, he slipped the life belt over her, picked her up, and threw her over the rail into the swirling, black depths of the Mississippi.

When she hit the cold water, for a moment she couldn't tell which way was up, towards the air. But even with her eyes closed, she could see the inferno of what used to be a ship, now illuminating the darkness in its hideous, demonic glow. Distorted echoes in the water, men screaming, crying out for their God to save them. Wooden decks creaking and collapsing, sparks flying, towering smoke stacks collapsing in a dreadful groan. And always, always the screaming.

The lifebelt helped Charity get her head above the water, but the deadly current was dragging her away from the shoreline, drawing her toward the channel and dragging her in its downriver rush. She struggled to keep calm, just to keep breathing, to keep telling herself that a child used as gator bait could survive in this river, keep enduring whatever catastrophe had happened. She kept straining to see Stieglitz in the mayhem.

Suddenly, there he was. Right outside their cabin. But he was still on deck! Why didn't he jump? Did he lie to her when he said he had a life belt for himself?

Against the demonic flame, she could see him with his arms outstretched, looking to the sky. He was calling out. She would never be able to hear him over the bedlam but she tried, oh how she tried. Then suddenly there it was! She could hear his voice. She would know it anywhere, even above this hellish noise. It was a sing-song chant, sweet and sad and loud and strong. It was in his strange language again, but she clearly heard the word "Yis-roe-ALE."

She hoped he was talking directly to God.

She hoped he'd be taken to his wife Rachel and daughter Rebecca in Heaven.

She hoped she could come live with them there.

Charity Boudry didn't mind dying as much as knowing the current would carry her body all the way back to New Orleans, the place she had tried so hard to escape. She had almost made it.

"What the hell?" shouted William Ardent on his way to the cabin door as he shoved Ella out of his way.

"William!" she cried. "The boat ... it's on fire! We must jump! Here – it's a life belt!"

Instead, he ran to the railing and started to climb over.

She thought of his missing arm, knew she'd have to help him.

"William! Wait! I can help you!" She grabbed his arm, trying to put the life belt on him. She had two good arms, she thought. She could swim. When she looked down, she saw what he was aiming for. There was a piece of debris from the boat. Four or five passengers were holding on for dear life. They saw him too. And they were shouting at him. "No! Too many! No! You'll kill us all!"

Ella still had hold of his arm, but he shook her off. She came back toward him. "We should stay together!" she shouted.

As he climbed over the rail, he slashed cruelly with his arm, spinning her face-first into the plate glass window near their cabin. As she hit it in a shower of glass, the incoming rush of oxygen caused the flames to explode from the window. It threw her into the water, but she saw nothing. The last thing she heard was the people on the makeshift raft cursing her husband for capsizing them as he jumped on their only salvation, condemning them to certain death.

John Deacon's only thought was of Ella, but in the chaos, a one-legged man didn't stand much of a chance. The cabin deck was almost gone in a cataclysm of flame as the ship broke apart. He could not have made it on the stairs even if they were intact, which they weren't.

He had no idea where Moran might be, and said a quick prayer for his friend. Right now Deacon had to think about Ella, and he'd be no good to her if he was drowned or burned alive. A one-legged man was at a disadvantage.

Just then a large chunk of the staircase broke apart. It was wood! It would float! Some of it was smoldering, so he grabbed what he could. It was part of the metal handrail.

The metal had become super-heated in the flame. It was like grabbing on to the business end of a branding iron. He screamed in agony, but he held on. If he could get the debris into the water, it would cool the metal. He was still holding on when he hit the water, and held on as the current took him downriver. He called Ella's name until everything went silent.

CHAPTER 25
APRIL 27, 1865

Wilburn Cole hated the water.

He'd hated it as a child, hated it as a Confederate soldier, and he hated it now. He had come so close to being on dry land, he often thought.

His granddaddy had fought in the War of 1812. To entice soldiers into service, the U.S. government promised generous land grants in the Arkansas territory. Veterans and their families headed west to claim their land. When they arrived at their destination, they found a most unpleasant surprise.

Their land grant was underwater, habitable only by the rampant snakes and mosquitoes. At first they cursed the government, but they soon found out that this calamity was the result of a natural disaster rather than man-made mischief. While the full story calmed their threats of shooting every government man in Washington, it didn't really help in the short term.

When the New Madrid earthquakes began in December 1811, the region of today's northeast Arkansas was sparsely populated. Lack of communication made damage reports impossible for years. When reports did eventually come in, they told of the earth erupting, sending up huge plumes of water and sand, leaving chasms where the ground had burst open.

Giant lakes such as Tennessee's Reelfoot were created. In Arkansas, land sank as far as fifty feet. Huge fissures became stagnant pools. The once bountiful region of verdant forests, abundant game and fertile ground was now a swamp.

Some newcomers braved the snake- and mosquito-infested sunken lands out of tenacity – or desperation. Others moved closer to the Mississippi River where at least they could fish in waters that were not poisoned by stagnation.

Wilburn Cole's family was one of those who headed for the great river. He hated every minute of it. Everything was always humid or just plain wet. Every time the river overflowed its banks, which it often did, they had to head for higher ground. And the mosquitoes – good Lord, the mosquitoes. They never stopped. They ate you alive. How such a tiny creature could wreak such havoc was impossible to fathom for anyone who had never braved them. Just going to the privy meant dozens of bites every single damn time.

Certainly, people were saying that the nasty creatures spread disease. But on top of that, the bites were just plain awful. The itching would drive you crazy. Big red welts that never stopped making your skin crawl.

Apart from all that – and Wilburn Cole would never have admitted it to any human being – he was flat-out afraid of the water. That big river was evil. It was *too* big. When the snowmelt from every stream up north fed into it, the Mississippi became a monster – cold, fast, wide and voracious. It seemed to enjoy the thought of devouring a man in a little boat, a man just trying to make a living.

Wilburn Cole hated the water. But for this former Confederate soldier, the river was the only way he could make a living. Thank the

Lord his wife had the presence of mind to hide their small boat when the Army – both armies, really – came around to confiscate. And now here it was, daylight already and he had to head out on the river yet another day.

Wilburn Cole hated the water, and guessed he just slept late today to avoid it for a few hours. Looked like mid-day already. The night had seemed to fly by, and he'd missed the dawn. He stretched, put on his clothes, and went out the door of his cabin. Strange. The tremendous glow came from the east, all right, just like sunrise, but for some reason the light wasn't in the sky where it ought to be.

It was coming from the river. That demon river.

Wilburn Cole hated the water, but he rowed his little boat across miles of the swollen Mississippi dozens of times that night. As he fought the river's raging current, he was being eaten alive by mosquitoes, just like always, he thought grimly. The rotten creatures couldn't let up for a minute, he thought, not even in the face of an awful thing like this. They even chewed up his sad, wretched cargo.

From the waters around the flaming hulk that used to be a steamer, back and forth he went. From the Arkansas side to Tennessee, and back again. He rescued dozens of men in blue, the same men who'd been his enemy just a month before.

Wilburn Cole hated the water and now he also hated its cruelty. He would never forget the sight of what he witnessed that night, though he would try for the rest of his life.

CHAPTER 26
APRIL 27, 1865

The citizens of Memphis awoke to a logjam in the swollen river. The horrid spectacle consisted not of dead trees but dead people. Hundreds of them, a thousand, two thousand. More than populated many Tennessee towns.

The citizens of Memphis rushed from shore to save the very few left alive. They did their best in the utter chaos. Many could not fathom the enormity of the tragedy until the next day when they read the *Memphis Argus* newspaper of April 28, 1865:

Yesterday morning our city was startled with the news of one of the most appalling disasters which ever occurred on American waters. By this terrible catastrophe no less than twelve or fifteen hundred persons were hurried into eternity.

The steamer Sultana, one of the People's and Merchants' line of packets, Capt. Cass Mason commanding, bound from New Orleans to St. Louis, arrived up on the evening of the 25th at 6:30 o'clock, having on board, it is understood, 1,966 men and thirty commissioned officers. Besides this there was a considerable passenger list, including forty ladies and the boat's crew.

Having discharged the freight for this city, the Sultana proceeded on her way up the river, leaving our wharf at about 2 o'clock yesterday morning. When about seven miles above the city she exploded her boilers; the entire middle portion of the boat, including the texas and pilot house, was hurled high in the air and scattered over the water. Immediately after the explosion fire broke out; a vast volume of flame swept through the cabin from the front to the stern of the boat. Then ensured a scene which language cannot describe - the most terrible that can possibly be conceived.

The explosion occurred in a wide portion of the river, there being no land for a mile on either side. Many were scalded to death immediately; those who were not injured were jumping overboard. The river for a mile around was full of floating people; the light of the burning boat shone over a scene such as has never before been witnessed; such as language cannot paint or imagination conceive. The screams of women, the groans of those who were wounded and thrown from the boat by the force of the explosion, the cries for help when there were none to assist - all contributed to create a scene over which we are compelled to shudder with horror.

The steamer Bostona was on her way down and about a mile above the Sultana at the time the explosion occurred. Her officers, perceiving the light of the burning boat and hearing the cries and struggles of the drowning people, made all haste to the scene of the disaster. Her yawls were sent out, stage planks thrown overboard; everything that could float was thrown into the river for the sufferers. Every effort was made by the officers of the Bostona in this trying emergency to render aid to the drowning multitude.

A passenger from the Bostona, Mr. Deson, rendered noble service by his courage and daring. It is said that this gentleman took one of the foot planks from the Bostona and went out on it and succeeded in saving the lives of no less than eight persons. Such deeds should not go unnoted.

The flames burst in great fury in a very few minutes after the explosion on the Sultana. No time was allowed for the people to do anything. Ladies rushed forth from their berths in the night attire, and with a wild scream plunged into the angry flood and sank to rise no more. The pitiful cried of children as they, too, rushed to the side of the wreck and plunged into the water were mingled with the hoarser voices of manhood in the desperate struggle for life. More than 2,000 people were thus compelled to choose between a death by fire and a sleep beneath the wave. Hour after hour rolled away, and the struggle for the great multitude in the river continued. Manhood was powerless. Husbands threw their wives into the river and plunged into the water after them, only to see them sink in death. Some had secured doors and fragments of the wreck and were thus enabled to keep a longer time above the water. Those who were swimmers struck for the shore, where they could find trees and bushes to keep them above the water. Some were carried down by the current until opposite the city, where their cries attracted the attention of the people on the steamers lying at the wharf. Yawls, skiffs, and every available small boat was put into immediate requisition and sent out into the stream to pick up the survivors. A considerable number were thus rescued from a watery grave. One lady with an infant in her arms was forced by the current several miles, and was finally rescued by some of the small boats that were cruising around. She exhibited the most remarkable heroism -still clinging to her precious charge and supporting it above the water until rescued. The small boats from the United States gunboats did good service.

Messrs. John Fogleman, Thomas J. Lumbertson, George Malone and John Berry, citizens of Mound City, Arkansas are entitled to the eternal gratitude of every right-thinking mind. When they saw the burning, floating mass, and heard the cries of the struggling thousands, they made haste to construct rude rafts of logs and put into the stream. With these, they succeeded in saving the lives of nearly a hundred persons. They were unceasing and labored faithfully and courageously as long as there was any possibility of relieving a suffering fellow mortal. Mr. Fogleman's residence was converted into a temporary hospital for the sufferers, and every possible care and attention were bestowed on them by Mr. Fogleman and his family. The number who had been brought in - rescued from the river - at 12 o'clock yesterday were 110 enlisted men, ten officers, four ladies and fifteen citizens.

The Sultana had been in service three years. She belonged to Capt. Cass Mason, Sam DeBow, W. J. Lewis and Mr. Thornberg, and was valued at $80,000. She was insured to a large amount.

The officers and crew of the ironclad Essex deserve unstinted credit and praise for the part they took in picking up passengers of the ill-fated steamer Sultana. Lieut. James Berry, ensign of the Essex, was awakened yesterday morning about 4 o'clock and informed that the steamer Sultana had blown up and was now burning; that the passengers were floating down the river and crying for help. The lieutenant jumped up immediately and was startled and horrified by the agonizing cries of the people in the river. He said that never in his life did he hear anything so dreadful, and hopes it may never be his lot to hear such screams again.

He immediately ordered the boats to be manned, which was done in very quick time. The morning was very dark; it was impossible to see twenty feet ahead; they had nothing whatever to guide them but the shrieks and groans of the wounded and scalded men.

The first man picked up was chilled through and through. Lieut. Berry, seeing the condition the man was in, very generously divested himself of his own coat and put it on this man. The second man they took up died a few minutes after being taken aboard. The men who had Capt. Parker's gig picked up a woman out of some drift. She was at that time just making her last struggle for life. About the time this woman was picked up a steamboat yawl came there and helped pick up some more who were clinging about the drift. Lieut. Berry said it was impossible for him to give any description of the scene; he said it beggared all description; that there were no words adequate to convey to the mind the horror of that night. He continually heard persons cry out, "Oh, for God's sake, save us! We can not hold out any longer!"

The boats of the United States steamers Groesbeck and Tyler were on hand and displayed great vigilance and zeal in picking up drowning men. Lieut. Berry, with the help of the crew, picked up over sixty men. With commendable forethought Capt. Parker sent out ten boats to explore the shore from Memphis to the place of the disaster. Up to 3:30 yesterday afternoon only five of these boats had returned. They had found a few dead bodies, but could not find any survivors along the shore.

Had the disaster occurred an hour or two later Capt. Parker feels assured that the naval force could have saved several hundred lives instead of the sixty alluded to. Unfortunately the night was dark, and the boats were compelled to steer in the direction of the cries, being unable to see more than a few of those struggling in the water.

After the explosion of her boilers, and the rapid spread of the flames, the burning mass of what had been the fine steamer Sultana floated down with the current until within a few hundred yards of Mr. Fogleman's residence, where it grounded on the Arkansas shore. We visited the wreck about 10 o'clock. It was sunk in about twenty feet of water; the jackstaff was standing up before the black mast, as though mutely mourning over the terrible scene, a silent witness of which it had been. The boat was almost entirely consumed. The charred remains of several human bodies were found, crisped and blackened by the fiery element. The scene was sad to contemplate, and those who witnessed it can never forget it. The Rose Hambleton, Pocahontas, Jenny Lind and Bostona were cruising around the place, ever and anon picking up the breathless body of some unfortunate who slept the sleep of death; or some more fortunate who had escaped a watery grave, though exhausted by a fearful night of struggle for life.

The names and places of many of those who were hurried into eternity by this terrible catastrophe will never be known. Capt. Cass Mason, who was in command of the Sultana, was among the lost. Capt. Mason was well-known to many of our business men as the former commander of the Belle of Memphis. It is said that he did well his part. During the trying scenes ensuing the explosion he stood upon the deck of the fated vessel, throwing buoys into the water, or anything that would float, encouraging others by his example; and was last seen after everybody else had left the burning wreck. His body is probably beneath the mighty river's surging waves. The two clerks, W. J. Gamble and William Stratton, were among the lost. One of the engineers, lost. Harry Ingraham, one of the pilots, was lost. Mrs. Hardin of Chicago was among the lost. She was lately married, and was on a bridal tour.

DeWitt Clinton Spikes (whose father, mother, three sisters, two brothers and young lady cousin were all lost), a young Louisianian, with a noble courage that is beyond all praise, notwithstanding his exhausted condition, used every effort to assist his fellow sufferers and succeeded in saving no less than thirty lives... A soldier procured a log; several drowning men were seen; he directed his log toward them; they laid hold on the log, and were thus taken ashore. By this means he was instrumental in saving the lives of five men... Capt. Curtis, master of river transportation, sent out boats on the first intimation of disaster, and had the Jenny Lind fired up and dispatched her to the scene of distress. He and his assistants were very active, and performed many noble deeds.

Capt. George J. Clayton, pilot of the Sultana, was on duty at the time the explosion occurred. He says they were going on about as usual; that they had gotten about seven miles above the city, running at her usual rate of speed - if any difference, not as fast as usual. All of a sudden he saw a flash, and the next thing he knew he was falling into the water with a portion of the wreck of the pilothouse. He thinks that he must have been hurled at least forty feet into the air. When he reached the water he saw the flames bursting up from the furnace and soon enveloping the entire boat. The scene which ensued beggars all description. He says the river was full - a sea of heads for hundreds of yards around. Screams and cries arose, rendering the scene appalling. Mr. Clayton was slightly injured in his fall.

The following statement from Private Friend Albard, of the Second Michigan cavalry, is given: "I was awake when the explosion took place, lying on top of the wheelhouse. As soon as I discovered that the boat had exploded I caught hold of the fender and slid down to the water and let myself in, having nothing on me at the time. I judge I swam about two miles. The river was alive with people crying and calling for help in the greatest agony - it was heart-rending in the extreme. Just as I was coming down off the boat, I saw two ladies who had thrown themselves into the water. They had nothing to keep them up, and they sank, and I saw them no more. When the explosion took place it threw the cabin into the air, and it fell back on the boat in one mass of ruins, crushing many of the passengers who were thus caught, and were undoubtedly burned to death. Very many caught hold of horses by their manes and tails, but whether those escaped or not, it is impossible to tell. I never heard of them afterwards."

Another survivor was William Long, a civilian passenger. His statement is also given. Mr. Long said: "At the time of the explosion I was in room 10. I jumped up and saw that the partition separating my stateroom from the next room was knocked all to pieces. I ran out in the cabin and back to the stern, and saw that we were not near the shore. While standing there I saw fifty persons jump overboard every minute. I stood there for five minutes, but seeing the boat in flames, I ran back to my stateroom and got some clothing. I returned and jumped from the cabin floor down to the lower deck. I got up on the taffrail and stood there until I saw three or four hundred people go overboard. I stayed on board until the boat was burned clean to the stern and the whole upper deck had fallen in, when I jumped overboard, having a door to keep me up. I tried to make the Tennessee shore, but failed. I then tried to make the Arkansas shore, but failed again. I then let myself float. Pretty soon I saw lights. I then knew I was opposite Memphis. In floating I ran across a large saw-log. I got on this, because I was almost exhausted and ready to sink. I kept floating down, and pretty soon I picked up a soldier, and soon another, and then another, until I had picked up four. We would keep quiet for a moment and then hallo; and thus we went on until I was taken into a yawl with the rest."

The following week, on May 6, 1865, an editorial in the same newspaper added a succinct postscript to the fate of the souls aboard the *Sultana*. Truer words have rarely been spoken:

"We have, as a people, become so accustomed to supping of horrors during the past five years that they soon seem to lose their appalling features and are forgotten. Only a few days ago 1,500 lives were sacrificed to fire and water, almost within sight of the city; yet even now the disaster is scarcely mentioned--some new excitement has taken its place."

A few other newspapers carried brief summations of the story, each mentioning the fact that there were about forty women on board. Most were said to be female relatives of the soldiers. Only three of the women were saved. One was picked from a tangled mass of floating driftwood below Memphis, more than seven miles from the scene of the wreck. As one report put it, *"The rest found graves in the Mississippi River or were laid by reverent hands in resting places upon its banks."*

No newspaper story could do proper justice to the efforts of the people of Memphis. Still impoverished by the war, Memphians put aside both sectional views and the still-raw memories of their own Civil War dead. The men and women of Memphis gave unstintingly of themselves and all that was theirs to aid the survivors. They opened their homes, provided much-needed clothing, and sought out medical attention for the victims. One group even held a benefit concert to raise money for those still clinging tenuously to life. All this they did for the wretched boys in blue who had been their enemy just weeks before.

John Deacon, the former newsman, never saw the newspaper articles, nor did he have any idea how long he was in the Memphis hospital or who had brought him there. But he said prayer after prayer of thanks for whichever nameless person had done so. It could not have been easy.

Amidst the overcrowding in the hospital after the disaster, he was given a spot on the floor, for which he was grateful. Sometimes he would hear disembodied voices hovering above him, doctors or nurses probably, wondering if he would last another day. He had been almost dead from hypothermia, exhaustion, and burns on top of the amputated leg which was still prone to infection. Floating seven miles down the surging black river in the dark had landed him in Memphis, but had almost killed him in doing so.

One day, from the floor of the hospital, he opened his eyes to see an angel. The vision looked like a biblical Madonna, draped in white lace. If she were a real woman, he thought she'd be the second most beautiful creature he'd ever seen in his life. After his Ella Rose, of course.

But surely she must be an angel, he thought, an angel who was there to help him, to show him around Heaven. Instead, he was surprised when she asked him, "Can you help me?" He had assumed angels could take care of themselves, certainly without help from the likes of him.

"Can you hear me, sir?" the angel repeated. "I need your help if you have any to give."

Deacon tried to speak but realized his mouth was too dry. The angel brought him some water, helped him to prop up against the wall.

"I'm looking for a soldier named Moran, sir. Did you know him? Do you know if he is here?"

"Where is 'here'?" asked Deacon, quite sensibly, he thought. Perhaps this was some celestial ante-chamber to Heaven.

The angel explained he was in a Memphis hospital. She had no idea how he had gotten there. She had no clear idea how *she* had gotten there.

Deacon still had to ask the question: "Are you real?"

She did not laugh or even smile at the question. "I was aboard the steamboat *Sultana,*" she said. "I am looking for a ... friend. I do not know if he survived. You may know him. A soldier. His name is Moran."

So he'd been right the first time she'd said it. That was what he thought he'd heard! He felt his spirits rise, as much as possible under the circumstances.

"Yes, I know him, ma'am! We went through the war together!"

Things were becoming clearer to Deacon now. "I pray he made it. He was a fine fella. Ma'am, if you find him, would you let me know?"

"Of course," she said. "Can I do anything to help you?"

"Yes, please," he said. "I am looking for a lady who was on the boat. A lovely lady with blond hair. Her stateroom was on the cabin deck. Her name is Ella. I could look for her myself if they could fit me up with a cane or crutch ..."

When he tried to raise himself using his right hand, he noticed the claw at the end of his arm. It was only at that moment that he felt the pain.

"What ...?" was all he could manage.

"Many people were horribly burned," she said without emotion. "Looks like you got hit with something red-hot. I'm sorry. That hand looks pretty bad. I'm sorry," she repeated, adding, "Perhaps the doctors can help."

Deacon just stared at his hand. So now he was without his right leg and his right hand. It looked like a solid fused mass at the end of this arm. He felt no real anger, but was somewhat surprised when the only thought that went through his mind was whether he'd ever be able to use it to write with.

He *had* to write. It was the only way he knew to help others make sense of the past four years, to avoid something inconceivable like it ever happening again. They had to learn. He could make them see in word pictures. Writing was his only gift. Oh please, Lord, please don't take that away from me too!

No, the Lord wouldn't do that. Deacon would find Ella and get out of this place and they'd be together always and she'd help him write. If he couldn't make his own hand work, Ella Rose would take down what he said, compose it in her lovely script. All those thoughts went through his head in a single moment.

And the Lord had even sent this beautiful angel to help him find Ella.

"So ma'am, I'd be obliged if you could do me that service. Until the doctors help me figure out a way to use a crutch and walk, could you please look for a lovely blond lady named Ella? Tell her Johnny from back home is here and looking for her. And ma'am? I truly believe you'll find Moran here somewhere. If anyone could survive this, it'd be him. Please tell him John Deacon sends his compliments."

"So you're Deacon," she said. "The newspaperman?"

He nodded. It was all he could think to do.

"Moran said you'd offered him a job at your newspaper."

He nodded again.

"Well, that was mighty kind. It seemed to mean a lot to him"

"Offer's still good," said Deacon. "Just please ask the sorry rascal to get over here and help me up off my ass. Oh, beg pardon, ma'am. No offense intended."

"None taken. I will tell him that, Mr. Deacon. I surely will."

And then she was gone.

As he watched her departing figure, Deacon realized this must be the woman from the boat, the one Moran had lost his mind over. Well, Deacon could certainly understand that. Moran had made a good choice.

In Helena, Arkansas, the courtship of Alpha's cousin with the new widow was going along splendidly. He felt uncharacteristically confident. If she accepted his suit, he might be able to go live in town at her home. He could get away from the river. It was just getting too dangerous on the water. That terrible *Sultana* riverboat disaster up past Memphis had gotten his attention. Worst thing anyone had ever seen.

At first he wondered if the cousin known as Alpha had been involved. Then, he thought better of giving it any thought whatsoever.

It had been a few weeks since Alpha had commandeered his boat without even a word of thanks. Of course, if the cousin moved to the widow's house in town, he'd have no real need of it. Maybe Alpha took the boat downriver to try getting over to Texas where the fighting still was dragging on. That was probably it.

As soon as the widow accepted his marriage proposal, the cousin planned to leave his cabin on the river and not tell any of his neighbors where he was going. He'd done his share of tending to distant relatives. If Alpha came back, he had no doubt the madman could still find him, but would have to work at it. If losing his boat meant seeing the last of Alpha, he believed it was a bargain at any price.

Deacon chose not to feel the constant pain of his charred hand, but did not object when a doctor administered a dose of morphine. In his dream state, Deacon had a vision.

Two distinguished-looking men alight from a carriage. One looked a whole lot like Moran, only well-fed and well-dressed. Both men were laughing. As for the other man, Deacon figured that was himself.

In the dream state, he caught his reflection in a magnificent picture window, perhaps at a fancy hotel. They were in New York, there was no doubt about it! Everything sparkled!

He was appalled at his own vanity, but thought he and Moran cleaned up pretty good.

The two men turned to help a pair of elegantly-dressed ladies alight from the carriage. The one who took Moran's arm was dark-haired with full lips and eyes that looked like an oriental princess. She was magnificent.

Finally, the belle of the ball emerged from the carriage, his own Ella Rose. Ella's rich honey-blond hair was piled high on her head. The ladies had discussed it while on their way in the carriage. It was the latest fashion. The men made good-natured fun of them, detailing the cut of their own masculine coiffures. Everyone laughed. It was all in fun. The truth was, he and Moran were almost painfully proud of their ladies.

They went inside the sparkling hotel in the sparkling city. Ladies nodded and gentlemen doffed their top hats at the foursome. Everyone knew them, everyone smiled admiringly. Maybe Deacon was getting some sort of prize! For his newspaper! The *New York Phoenix*!

But as the vision faded while Deacon succumbed to a morphine-induced slumber, he saw in the dream that he and Moran already had their prizes. The loveliest ladies in the world.

What a happy ending.

CHAPTER 27

NOVEMBER, 1868 – THREE YEARS LATER

In 1868, America had a new president. The Civil War general, Ulysses Grant, took the Electoral College in a landslide. The country seemed almost giddy with prospects for the future.

For the past three years, since the official end of the Civil War in 1865, America was still in turmoil. Reconstruction was imposed on the defeated South, with varying effects. At the time of the 1868 presidential election, Mississippi, Texas, and Virginia were not yet restored to the Union.

For the three years following the war, the U. S. president had been Andrew Johnson, who many felt was the unluckiest man in American history. Johnson was forced to take up the bloody mantle of his now-sainted predecessor, Abraham Lincoln, who was awarded a mythic status. The sanctification of Lincoln came from those even including – *especially* including – his most vehement critics in life.

Reconstruction under Johnson was considered too harsh by some, not harsh enough by others. His own party failed to nominate Andrew Johnson for re-election.

But Grant signaled a fabulous new age. Even the name – "U. S. Grant" – well, it restored confidence in the country. Some people, Grant included, seemed anxious to forget the war as well as the November election, and move forward toward the Grant presidency. General Order 11 had reared its head during the campaign, and Grant wisely tried to distance himself. Some newspapers reported he claimed not to have read the edict, having relied on an underling to draft it.

Grant courted Jewish voters and financiers, promising to appoint Jewish people to his administration. Many Jewish voters considered the national interest, considered how good Grant would be for the country, considered whether to exchange the fate of a few for the future of the many.

Like the rest of America, they turned out for Grant in droves. He, in turn, was as good as his word, appointing more Jewish people to public office than any of his predecessors.

The country somberly honored its dead, but by 1868, people were also ready for amusement, for *life*. Within the past year, Americans turned out to hear famous British writer Charles Dickens on a reading tour in the United States. The author's first stop was New York City, where a new elevated railroad, the first-ever in the country, brought theatregoers from all over town.

That same year, the first Mardi Gras parade with floats livened up New Orleans. And that year, a man named Thomas Edison applied for his first patent. New forms of entertainment were mushrooming in a country hungry for diversion.

In 1868, one of the most popular diversions was the traveling "freak show," where those with oddities or deformities were touted as "freaks of nature." They included such attractions as tiny people, giants, tattooed ladies, fire-eaters, bearded women, and sword-swallowers.

Freak shows were popular bookings at taverns and fairgrounds where the "freaks" often demonstrated displays of talent.

After the war, the country had more than fifty thousand amputees without arms or legs, and probably at least an equal number disfigured by war-inflicted burns, scars, and other deformities. Therefore, it took something really special to be considered a "freak."

On a pleasant November evening soon after the election of 1868, one of those amputees was hobbling around a county fairground in Ohio. On his arm was a nicely-dressed lady who at one time must have been lovely. Now her delicate features were scarred, and her eyes were closed. Even without being open, her eyelids revealed the dead, vacant, unfocused stare of blindness. Her mouth seemed to droop at an odd angle. She did not appear to speak, but to those close by, she seemed to softly hum happy little tunes.

Still, the man on whose arm she walked looked at her as if he was honored to escort the most elegant duchess in creation. His right leg was gone, though he was able to hobble using a crutch. His right hand was a claw, not fit for clutching objects either large or small, but somehow he was able to grasp the crutch in a way that would allow him to move, if only slowly and painfully. He sported a pleasant smile on his face, exuding good cheer. When he passed other amputees – and there were plenty here tonight as there were everywhere after the war – he nodded politely. Both parties knew they shared a secret world that the able-bodied would never know.

He spoke almost without cease to the woman with him, describing everything they passed.

"It's called Rutland's Freak Show, darlin.' Now normally, I would not put much store in making sport of people with misfortunes, but it's so festive, like a carnival. Can you hear the calliope? There's a man selling snake oil over yonder. Claims to cure anything that ails. Shall we go listen to his show?"

On the way over, the man pointed out signs for the various attractions inside tents. A barker stood at the entrance of each, trying to entice the curious. The one-legged man with the woman on his arm kept walking, politely declining each solicitation to enter any of them. As they walked, he kept up his commentary.

"This one says 'World's Tallest Man.' And over there, on the other side of the midway, there's one for 'World's Smallest Woman.' Can you imagine? Dancing might be a problem for those two. Guess it'd be worse if it was the other way 'round, don't you think? Now this next one's called 'Beauty and the Beast.' Well, I don't mind telling you it's a bit naughty. On the sign, there's a half-naked 'Beauty' cowering in front of a black-caped figure. He must be the 'Beast.' We only see him from the back. But we can see Beauty's face real clear ..."

At that, the man stopped so short that the woman with him almost stumbled. "I'm sorry, darlin.' But it's just that I ... I think I know that face ..."

Just then there were blood-curdling screams from the audience inside the tent. People, mostly women, began rushing outside. From their excited chatter, the man guessed that the 'Beast' must have been unmasked, much to their horror. There was applause from inside the tent, and then the rest of the crowd poured out. The barker up took his perch and bellowed into his megaphone.

"Wasn't that somethin', ladies and gentlemen? Come back again! Tell your friends! Gents, remember tonight's midnight show! Males only! Sorry, ladies! It would just be too much for your delicate constitutions. Gents, buy your tickets now for the special midnight show! Beauty and the Beast! Special Midnight show! See the Beauty as she's never been seen before! Get your tickets now! They're going fast!"

For once, a carnival barker did not exaggerate. Tickets were indeed going fast. Men pushed and shoved to get in line, brandishing greenbacks. The one-legged man watching it all noticed that the ticket-buyers did not come away with much in the way of change. This attraction, especially its midnight show, was obviously the money-maker for the whole shebang.

Midnight was still a few hours away, and the man with one leg had no intention of waiting around. It was just too hard to stand, trying to hold his crutch in such an awkward manner. But he had to do something before he left.

The barker's attention was still consumed by the flourish of greenbacks being thrust at him. The one-legged man hobbled over to the opposite side of the tent with the woman still on his arm.

"Let's be real quiet now, darlin.' We might not be allowed to be back here." The woman kept quiet, as if there were other alternatives for her. She continued her humming, but it was so low no one else could hear.

There was no one to be seen in the back behind the tents, just horses grazing freely. They no doubt pulled the brightly-painted caravan wagons when the show went from town to town. The man saw one painted on the side, "Beauty and the Beast!" He smiled at the exclamation mark. While possibly not grammatically correct, it was certainly an attention-getter.

He tapped on the closed back door of the caravan. No response. He tapped louder.

"Hello?" he said loud enough to be heard from inside the wagon but not loud enough to alert the barker that there was an intruder in back.

"Hello?" he said again. "I was wondering if I could talk to you."

He was gratified to see the back door open slightly. He was not as pleased to be facing a double-barreled shotgun just inches from his face.

"I'm sorry. I mean no harm," the one-legged man said quickly. "I'd just like to talk for a moment. I live here in town and I was in the war, and coming home, I was on the *Sultana* when she burned, and I was hurt and I'd lost my leg, well, that was before, and then when I was in the hospital at Memphis…."

The man knew he was babbling. It would be sure to frighten whoever had the gun in his face. They might think he was a loony.

But he kept stammering, "I was in the hospital at Memphis and it was so bad and so horrible and so sad, and people were looking for survivors, and there weren't many, and I was looking for my friend, and a beautiful dark-haired woman was looking for him too …"

He was running out of steam, and therefore was quite surprised when the voice behind the gun said, "Hello, Mr. Deacon."

Out from the wagon stepped 'Beauty,' known to him as the dark angel from the Memphis hospital, and Moran's dream woman. Deacon knew the minute he saw her. It was the kind of face a man never forgot.

If anything, she had grown even more lovely in the past three years. The terrible hollows in her face had filled in. She was breathtaking when she allowed herself to smile, as she did now. Maybe now she had something to smile about.

There was the matter of introductions. "Ma'am, this lovely lady on my arm is my sweet Ella Rose. I'm happy to say I *was* able to find her at Memphis. As you can tell, her eyes were damaged so she can't see. And she has some trouble … with other things too … but looking at me, you can tell most of us do! Here she is, stuck with a man who has only one leg plus a useless hand. Ella, darlin', this is … I'm sorry, ma'am … I don't recall the name."

"My name is Rebecca. Rebecca Moran."

"Oh my dear God … he made it! He made it! I knew, if anyone could survive all that, it was Moran!" Deacon's wild response startled Ella. He patted her arm gently to let her know all was well.

And it was. It was so very well. He couldn't wait to see his friend! Why, he'd probably embarrass them both and hug the man's neck!

He'd be so glad to see him alive! And that scoundrel Moran had even managed to marry his dream woman!

He banged on the side of the wagon. "Come on out, you rascal! It's me, Deacon! We got us some catching up to do!"

Rebecca Moran shook her head. "Best not do that, Mr. Deacon."

"John! Call me John! None of that 'Mr. Deacon' stuff!"

"Might want to keep your voice down," she continued. "The show people, they are real protective of Moran and me. I'd like to think it's because they care about us, but I reckon it's really because we make the most money for the show. Keeps everyone employed."

Suddenly, she looked concerned. "You *didn't* see our act, did you, Mr. Deacon?"

"No, but I can't wait," he answered. "They said the midnight show is Men-Only, but I won't be going to that. I don't go anywhere without Miss Ella here." He patted her arm lovingly. "She's my girl."

"Don't come to our midnight show or any other," said Rebecca Moran flatly. "I don't care so much for myself, but I think *he'd* prefer you to think of him in the before-time." She nodded toward the wagon.

"Why won't he come out? Taking off all that awful make-up like on the sign?" Deacon tapped on the side of the wagon, spoke more softly. "Come on out and be sociable, Moran! I seen you a lot worse than covered in a bunch of makeup! Hell, I seen you on that prison train, covered in manure! Oh, beg pardon, ladies."

Rebecca Moran took his arm and walked them a little way from the wagon. When they stopped, she shook Ella's hand gently and said, "It's very nice to meet you, Mrs. Deacon."

"She don't mind you callin' her Ella. Fact is, ma'am, we're not exactly man and wife. I mean we are, but maybe not to the world. They say it'll be a while before her husband is declared dead. Officially, I mean. But you were there, you saw what it was like on the *Sultana*. I know he's dead. And good riddance."

Deacon told Mrs. Moran how Ella had been with her husband on the boat but he had jumped without her. To save *himself*, Deacon added silently, though he was not actually sure. Still, that was what he thought.

"The doctors at Memphis said it looked like she'd fallen through a glass window, or maybe one exploded in her face," he said. "That was how she came to be scarred and blinded, from the flying glass and the flame."

"A good man, a fine man brought her in," Deacon added. "Confederate. Month earlier, we'd'a been shooting at each other. He ferried his boat across that big river dozens of times that night. Dodging dead bodies, saving the ones he could. He saw what looked like a log, reached out with his oar to avoid it crashing into his boat, and he heard a kind of moan. It was Ella, face-down in the water. Only reason she stayed afloat was that she was clutching a life vest. Well, face-down like that, doctors said her brain was deprived of air, and that damages your mind. But I think she's doing just fine. She don't speak, but there's some men who'd say that's a good thing in a woman." He caressed her arm lovingly. "Just kidding, darlin.' You know I'm just kidding."

Deacon went on to say that while Ella never spoke, she hummed almost constantly. "It seems to make her happy. Maybe like a pleasant memory or something. Just simple songs like *Camptown Races,* and *Oh! Susanna* and *Beautiful Dreamer.* Even *The Yellow Rose of Texas,* though Lord knows where she heard that one!"

Rebecca Moran pulled over a circus barrel for Deacon to sit on. "Obliged, ma'am," he said, lowering himself awkwardly.

"I'm sorry," she said. "I should have thought of it before."

"You know, I'll admit this leg was a bother, but I had the crutch your Moran made for me. Oh, sorry! He never let me call it a 'crutch.' Had to be a *'staff'* like we's frontier explorers or something."

Deacon glanced expectantly at the wagon, did not see Moran approaching, so kept up the conversation with his friend's lovely wife.

"Lost that staff on the *Sultana,* guess it floated down to New Orleans," Deacon said, smiling. The woman now known as Rebecca Moran had learned not to flinch when she heard the name of the city Charity Boudry had escaped.

"Well, anyway, about what happened with the hand. I reached out to grab something to hold onto. Turned out to be a red-hot pipe. Lost the use of my right hand. It all sort of melted together. So now I can't hold my crutch real well and guess I walk kind of funny-like!"

He paused to smile before adding, "Ma'am, I don't mean to rush you, but Ella probably needs to be getting home. Think you can hurry up that rascal you're married to?"

Without emotion, Rebecca Moran said, "We're not really married either. No one would marry us. Said it'd be a sin against Nature or somesuch. So we married ourselves."

Deacon laughed. "Well, we're a matched set of four-in-hand!"

She ignored his attempt at humor. Her mind was elsewhere, in another time.

"Back in Memphis, at the hospital," she said, "well, you know what it was like. Dead and dying everywhere. Bedlam. I searched everywhere. Calling his name didn't help. Everybody was calling people's names, or screaming in pain. I had a beautiful white lace shawl. I had it over my head. They might have thought I was one of the attending Sisters. I just went wherever I wanted. No one stopped me. After I'd looked everywhere, I went where nobody was supposed to go without an escort. Someone said they wanted an attendant to be there to pick up anyone who fell out, man or woman. It was a room where they piled up the worst cases of the dead, too terrible to see, the ones hardly recognized as humans."

She stopped for a moment to take a deep breath before continuing. "I saw this one … the worst of the worst. Both arms and both legs burned away. Eyes singed shut. Ears burned off. Skin on most of the body scorched. Don't know exactly how I knew it was him, but I knew it was. I *knew* it. Something about the face, what was left of it. Something about the way it felt in my heart to be near him. I just *knew.* I held what was left of him as best I could, trying to say a prayer for the dead, when he moved."

She paused to smile gently. "We had been out on the cabin deck talking, you see. That night."

"So that's where he disappeared to," said Deacon. "He was mighty sweet on you ma'am, from the first day you met."

She ignored the compliment and continued, "Last thing I saw, the deck collapsed under him and Moran fell into a pit of fire below. No telling what happened next."

Sweeping her arm to take in the traveling show, she said, "So that brings us to this. He can't really talk, but can make sounds. He understands what I say if I speak real close to his head. He understood what we were going to do when we joined this show. And we are able to live just fine. We make good money, for Rutland's show and for ourselves. Now, that Men-Only show at midnight, I do that alone. 'Princess Silver Moon,' I call myself for that. I wear extra veils so it looks like I'm taking more of them off. The men in the audience throw money, on top of buying high-priced tickets. I can use what they throw to buy the medicines Moran needs for the pain and to fight off the infection. Special foods. I feed him, soups and whatnot … well, I do just about everything for him."

"I'm so sorry," was all Deacon could think of to say.

Rebecca Moran smiled sadly. "So you see, I'm not sure he'd want you to see him the way he is. He doesn't wear any makeup for the show. That's … him."

After a few moments of silence when they both studied the ground, Rebecca said, "Back on the boat, back when I first met Moran, he pointed you out to me. I remember he said you were a newspaperman.

I asked you about it in Memphis. Were you really, or was he trying to impress me with his high-flown friends?"

Deacon smiled. "Not sayin' the man was above that sort of thing, but no – that time he was telling the truth."

"You still do that? Have a newspaper, I mean."

Deacon's smile faded. "No, lost the paper when I went into the Army. Then when we got out, I knew Ella would need help. She still had the land, but it was in her husband's name. Even her father's land that she grew up on. Women can't own property, you see," he added.

Rebecca Moran just nodded. She had really never thought about it, but the former Charity Boudry believed it certainly sounded like the way of the world.

"So after I found Ella in Memphis, we both made our way back to Ohio, to this town. We live in her parents' old house."

"Well, you may know anyway," said Rebecca. "On the boat, Moran said you were smart, that you knew things and the like. All this time I been wonderin' ... can I ask? ... did you ever hear what caused the ... the trouble on the boat?"

Deacon collected his thoughts for a few moments. Just like Stieglitz always did, Rebecca thought. Finally, Deacon said, "There was a hearing. Everybody blamed someone else. When it was over, everyone just kind of shrugged and said it was tragic but no one would ever know what really happened. Some said it was Confederate sabotage, the boatburners who planted bombs in with the coal supply. Of course, they could have planted it long before the end of the war, so the bombs just sat there in the coal bins like time bombs. No telling how many were out there, just waiting."

Rebecca Moran shivered, though it was a warm night.

"Other folks blamed the boat being overcrowded. That was the doings of the ship's captain and a Major Fitch who just kept piling us on board. They said Fitch and the ship captain split a commission on our heads, so it was to their advantage to load as many on as possible. Five dollars each for enlisted men and ten for officers. So I guess that tells you, an officer is worth twice as much as us!" Deacon laughed, but not very convincingly.

"A few blamed the river itself. It was running high and fast from all that snowmelt. You remember how cold it was in that water. And the current was so bad. Boat had to fight it all the way. They said the boilers just couldn't take it and they burst apart. Some said they'd been patched in Vicksburg, but not very well. They said the patches just couldn't hold against the weight of all those passengers aboard, plus trying to run against the current. And some said every time the boat careened to one side under all that weight, it didn't do the boilers no good. Created what they called 'hot spots' that weakened the metal. And those weak places burst."

"What do *you* think?' she asked.

"Well, Mrs. Moran, I think I picked up a little too much in the way of suspicion from your husband." She appreciated that this man Deacon offered her the mantle of respectability, even after she had told him otherwise.

"I think it was greed, pure and simple," Deacon said. "Maybe it was the work of the boatburners as well, but there was some greed in that, too. Keeping the war going for their own reasons. Inflicting as much pain as they could. All to hang onto their way of life, which meant making a profit off the sweat of another man's brow. And all that slave-breeding … oh, I'm sorry, ma'am."

Rebecca almost laughed when she thought about her life as Charity Boudry. She knew more than Deacon ever would about women being used for financial gain. She merely nodded at his apology.

"I think it was the greed of the boat captain, the greed of the officer in charge, greed in making a cheap patchwork repair, greed in overloading the boat, just greed all down the line, one way or the other. Greed. The lust for money. All that death and suffering so a few men could profit."

"Does anyone know how many died and how may were saved?'

Deacon paused to recall the numbers. "I've seen everything from more than fifteen hundred to almost two thousand. They said about five hundred may have been saved, but at least two or three hundred of those died soon after. To tell the truth ma'am, probably no one will ever know. They stopped taking names. There was just too many piled on that boat. Every one of them was an extra dollar sign."

Deacon again thought a moment before he continued. It was exactly what Mr. Stieglitz used to do. "I don't set much store in those numbers, ma'am. Because the souls on that boat were more than just numbers, more than dollar signs or the number of ... of how many died. They weren't rich and they weren't famous and no one knew of them or ever would. But ma'am, every one of them had a story, had walked a long road to that boat. Just like we all did."

He swept his arm to encompass himself and Ella, Moran and Rebecca before adding, "Sure wish I could help tell it. I tried, but this hand won't let me write. And no one in the newspapers cared to tell the story at the time."

"I never met anyone who ever heard of the *Sultana*," said Rebecca Moran. "Never could understand why."

"Because people were sick of hearing about the war. It was out West, which to most people was just the frontier, not worth caring much about unless maybe if someone discovered gold. And there was bigger news to report, things that sold papers. Abe Lincoln being shot, John Wilkes Booth getting caught. And like I said, people were just sick of hearing about the war."

Neither one of them wanted to state the obvious, that the war was something everyone in their little foursome lived with every day. They didn't have the luxury of not wanting to hear about it.

They were quiet for a few minutes, until Deacon decided to lighten the moment.

"Well, at least we got our extravagant pension from the Army," he said. "Earned myself an extra eight dollars a month. Didn't have to do a darn thing to earn it, just give 'em a leg!"

"Moran never got a thing," said Rebecca. "His identity disc was too badly burned up in the fire, couldn't read it at all. I didn't even know his full name. The Army said they had no record of him. No record, no pension."

"Well, of course he served!" shouted Deacon. "He was right there with me, every step of the way! Who do I need to talk to?"

"No one," said Rebecca Moran. "That's a kind offer, but we're doing fine without begging. Maybe there's someone else who fought, or their family, someone that needs it more."

"I don't keep mine either," said Deacon. "Every month when it comes in, I give it to a neighbor boy. His name's Andy Andrews. Fifteen years old now. Fine young man. Helps out on the farm. Want him to be able to help other people, not hurt them. They can't never pay enough money for what me and Moran went through, so might as well use their eight dollars a month for the good. Trying to send Andy to medical school in Cincinnati."

The woman formerly known as Charity Boudry briefly looked shaken at the mention of Cincinnati. It had been part of a dream very long ago. She tried not to think of Stieglitz, though she did so quite often. Sometimes if she had to make a decision, she would silently ask him what to do. She kept wanting to learn some of his prayers in that strange language and offer them up to him in Heaven, but somehow the chance never came around. Perhaps one day the traveling show would make it to Cincinnati. Perhaps maybe then.

They stood again in silence, lost in their own thoughts. When they spoke again, Rebecca Moran asked, "What do you think happened to those men, the corrupt ones, the ones collecting the money for how many soldiers they piled aboard?"

"I heard the boat's captain had the decency not to survive the wreck," said Deacon. "Ashamed to admit I was glad when I heard that.

But that Major Fitch, I heard he never even got on board *Sultana.* Couldn't get a private cabin, so took another boat where he could have his own stateroom. His name came up at the hearing, but I heard he got out of it without too much trouble. Some newspaper a few months ago – and I sure hope they got it wrong – said Fitch was running for political office as a 'war hero.'"

"Prob'ly win," was all Rebecca Moran could add.

There were a few more moments when they were both quiet. They thought about the enormity of such a disaster caused by a few little men, a few greedy little men. The corrupt ones might still end up having a fine career in what they called 'public service.' Probably be in a position to help declare another war, now that they knew where the profit was and how to get it. Long ago, Moran had said something once about the necessity of breaking the rules to get by. It didn't bear thinking about.

Suddenly Deacon broke the silence.

"Come live with us!" he cried, overcome with emotion. "Both of you! We don't have much, just a little farm where we grow our own food. But between the two of us, me and Ella, plus young Andy who comes by to help, we make it work. You two come stay with us forever!"

"And leave show business?" Rebecca asked with a sad smile.

"That's a kind offer, Mr. Deacon," she continued. "It truly is. And maybe someday we will. But for now we do just fine on our own. We make our own money, don't have to depend on no one. And as you saw earlier, I can handle a shotgun if there's ever a problem with 'admirers.' Moran and me, we do just fine."

She paused again, but Deacon knew to be quiet. He suspected she had more to say. She did.

"And you know, Mr. Deacon, at night, in the dark, I see him just exactly as he was on that boat. I knew that even after what you'd all gone through, that scoundrel was a fine-looking man. All you boys, you just looked like the walking dead. Never saw such a bedraggled bunch."

Deacon and Rebecca both smiled at that. Time had made it possible.

"Mr. Deacon, in the dark, I see him as he was then. A handsome rogue. In the dark, to me, he still is. I'm lucky to have him."

"I'd say you're both lucky, Mrs. Moran. So I guess that's it then, if you feel like he won't see me. Not even to shake my hand?"

"He has nothing to shake with," she said without emotion. "But I'll ask."

They walked back to the wagon, and Rebecca entered. Deacon could hear her sweet voice, asking if Moran would let his old friend see him.

Then Deacon was startled to hear the most terrible howling sound he had ever heard in his life. An other-worldly demon, howling in fury, in pain, in fear, in sorrow. Nothing Deacon had ever heard prepared him for that horrible sound.

"Nooooooooooooooooooooooooooooooo!"

The next thing Deacon heard was the sound of running footsteps coming his way. When he looked up, what he saw all around him would have been funny if it weren't so pathetic.

There they were, surrounding him: tiny people with pistols, giants with shotguns, tattooed ladies with clubs, bearded women with knives, fire-eaters and sword-swallowers with the respective tools of their trade.

Their beloved 'Beauty' jumped out of the wagon. "It's all right, brothers and sisters! Just a slight misunderstanding! Sorry for the commotion! Thank you, my friends, thank you!"

The crowd lowered their weapons and dispersed. "As I mentioned, Mr. Deacon," she said, "our friends tend to be protective of us. Who could ask for a better family?"

"No one, I reckon," Deacon could honestly say. "Mrs. Moran, I always told myself if I ever saw my friend again, I'd squeeze the breath clean out of him for all the kindness he showed to me in the war. Guess he won't let me do that now. Would you mind if I held the closest thing to him?"

Rebecca said nothing, so he turned his attention to the silent, sightless woman on his arm. "Ella Rose, would you mind if I hold this lady very close for a moment? She's an old friend."

Hearing no objection, Deacon took Rebecca in his arms, tenderly, respectfully, but so tightly he thought he'd never let her go. Soon, she felt his body shudder and felt warm tears on her neck. She herself hadn't cried since that day on the road with Mr. Stieglitz, but she knew what it would cost Deacon for her to see his tears. She pretended not to notice.

When they parted and turned away from each other, Rebecca climbed back into the wagon. Then she stopped and faced him.

"You know, Mr. Deacon, it's not the life I'd have chosen, but it's life nonetheless."

She closed the door to the caravan, back to her life with the soul who Deacon used to know as Moran. Deacon despaired of seeing either of them ever again.

Ella's twilight world was not an unhappy place. In fact, there were parts of it that made her very happy indeed. She liked feeling happy. The guardian who took her … what was the word? … oh, yes … her *arm* … was very kind. He spoke gently, and though she couldn't understand most of the words, she could hear the kindness in his voice. She thought there had been someone once in the before-time who had been just plain mean when speaking to her, but she couldn't remember if that was real or just a bad dream.

Her world was only difficult sometimes. Like now. The guardian who had hold of her … her … *arm* … yes, that was the word, must remember … *arm* ... was gently propelling her forward, but she still had to remember how it went, how to do it correctly. Left. Right. Left. Right. Left. Right. It was exhausting to remember all that.

Sometimes he asked for her help, shelling peas and the like. But that was hard to remember too. He showed her every time, and mostly she could do it right after a few tries. It made her proud.

Mostly, though, he did things for her. Kept her warm and fed. And oh, sometimes there was something hot and filling and smelled wonderful! He called it "ap-pull-pye." She could barely remember the name from one time to the next, but it sure made her happy when it came her way.

For the most part, the place where she lived was a bright, cheerful, sparkling kingdom. Everything shined and glittered. She was riding in a wagon and therefore didn't have to remember that complicated business of Left, Right, Left, Right.

And the people she was riding with were nice to be around. They seemed to like her. She knew their names real well. One was called Clement. One was Sarajane. One was Patsy and one was … well, isn't that just the strangest thing? She never could remember the old man's name. She remembered a tree and a rope … but then it went away. That was all right, though. He still seemed to like her just fine.

So Ella and her friends all rode through the sparkling kingdom where everything shined and glittered. The best part was when they sang. She loved the songs. They made her happy. *Camptown Races. Oh! Susanna. Beautiful Dreamer.*

But right now she had to concentrate on the guardian's difficult task at hand. Left. Right. Left. Right. Left. Right.

The man Ella thought of as her guardian was named John Deacon, and now he was lost in his own thoughts. As he hobbled toward home with Ella on his arm, he tried not to think about his friend Moran or the beautiful Rebecca or … any of it. He hoped that some fine day, he'd look outside and there they'd be. They would come and stay. If he'd been a gambling man, though, he was not sure if he'd take that bet.

So it was better to think about just getting home tonight, caring for Ella, putting her to bed and hoping she'd favor him with a sweet smile. Sometimes she did, and it was all he lived for.

He thought Andy might stop by tomorrow. Andy turned out to be a fine, handsome young man. Deacon didn't know what they'd do without Andy coming by to help with the heavy work on the farm. He wouldn't always be there, so Deacon cherished the time they had.

Soon Andy would go away to medical school. Deacon wanted that for the boy more than anything. He wanted Andy to part of helping people, not hurting them. That was God's work, thought Deacon, helping the beings that were created in the Lord's own image rather than tearing them apart. Helping them in life, comforting them in death.

His plan had always been to write about the war, to make people understand what it was really like, what it meant when someone at a desk sent someone else to get blown up. What it meant for those left behind. What it meant even for God's green earth. It would take decades for the poor, proud, defeated South to recover from the scorched earth it had suffered.

He would have written about honor, about the simple soldiers who went to fight the war. And he would have written about greed, how one man's lust for money could create such torment for so many others. He'd have been sure to write about that.

But with the claw of a hand the *Sultana* had awarded him … well, that made it impossible. He'd tried writing with his left hand, but it didn't really work well. Took way too long, and you couldn't even read it afterward. And all that time, struggling to write, well, it just gave him too much time to think.

Deacon would grow sad, with visions of what he'd seen torturing his mind. That hideous, ugly, accursed war. Maybe he didn't need to go back there. Maybe instead he'd think of tomorrow. In the morning, he'd try to find some apples on the ground in the orchard, then he'd bake an apple pie. He'd gotten pretty good at that. And Ella always seemed to enjoy it.

He remembered what Rebecca Moran had said. No, it wasn't the life he'd have chosen, he told himself, but it was life nonetheless.

So Deacon and Ella kept on, hobbling toward home. Left. Right. Left. Right. Left. Right.

CHAPTER 28 – EPILOGUE

APRIL 14, 1912

William Howard Taft was the U. S. president in 1912, though some were saying Governor Woodrow Wilson of New Jersey was the man to watch in the election that November.

That year, New Mexico and Arizona were admitted as the forty-seventh and forty-eighth of the United States. Everyone said their admission marked the end of the American frontier.

Also that year, Thomas Edison introduced the Diamond Disc phonograph, and a new kind of cylinder recordings, and the Kinetoscope on which to view the new "moving pictures."

Moving pictures were all the rage in 1912. In hopes of evading Edison's patents on them, one Carl Laemmle started the Yankee Film Company in New York City. Laemmle also broke with Edison's refusal to identify performers in his films. Laemmle thought that by naming the performers and calling them 'stars,' they might attract a following among audiences. His instincts proved correct with the popularity that year of Mary Pickford, Lionel Barrymore, and Lillian Gish.

Mr. D. W. Griffith was directing a lot of the new "movies," some of which dealt with a historical Civil War theme, now a half-century in the past.

In March of 1912, a man was reported to have made the first parachute jump from one of the new flying aeroplanes. That same month, Japan sent three thousand cherry trees to Washington D.C., as a symbol of friendship between the two nations.

New York City was booming, soaring skyward. Buildings such as the Flat Iron building, *The New York Times* building, the Singer Tower, and Metropolitan Life Insurance building rose up to a dizzying fifty stories high.

The year 1912 would see the fifth games of the modern Olympics, which had begun in 1896. Sweden would host the games in 1912, following Athens, Paris, London, and even St. Louis in the booming United States of America. There were those who said that nations might settle their differences on the Olympic playing field, thus signaling an end to war. Despite some rumblings in Europe – and when *weren't* there rumblings in Europe? – things in 1912 looked quite promising for the world.

In 1912, at age seventy-two, John Deacon was still a handsome man. With steel-gray hair and a craggy face that surrounded piercing eyes, he still attracted admiring glances, though he rarely noticed. He did not notice now as the girls sitting across from him on the train were giggling softly.

He kept a lap robe over his legs, or *leg*. All the girls saw from the waist up was a fine-looking man. They would have been surprised to know he had fought in the Civil War almost fifty years before. They were two generations removed from that conflict. It was something they studied perfunctorily in their history books.

Like most young people their age, they had been impatient but polite at first when their grandfather would tell tales of battles with strange-sounding names. Antietam. Shiloh. Cemetery Ridge. At first it had been somewhat interesting, but after repeated tellings, over and over, it became tiresome.

And their grandmothers were no better. The women told how their homes had been burned, how everything was gone, about eating roots to survive, about all the beaus they had lost in those battles with the strange-sounding names.

Sometimes a grandmother told about her own mother, widowed by the war and alone with four children she could not feed. After farming them out to various relatives, the older woman had taken to bed, "turned her face to the wall," and willed herself to die. But that was too far removed from the young people who were compelled to sit there and listen. That would have been their *great*-grandmother, they figured. That was back in the age of those dinosaurs whose bones kept being discovered these days.

But the man on the train – now, *he* was of interest to them.

"He's not bad-looking, for an older man," whispered one.

"Bet he was fine-looking when he was young," said the other.

"I'd'a sparked with him in a minute back then," said the first.

"I'd spark with him *now*," sighed the other before they both dissolved into giggles.

John Deacon wouldn't have cared even if he'd known he was the object of their interest. He had other matters on his mind.

For the first time in over half a century, John Deacon was on his way to New York. And the damnable train was late!

There had been flooding along the tracks even before they got out of Ohio. Andy Andrews and his wife had been kind enough to take care of Ella while Deacon was gone, but he would not impose on their good nature for long. Andy was sixty years old now, starting to slow down, but he still kept his medical practice. Deacon was proud of calling him "Dr. Andrews" in public. Andy had tried various techniques to help with Deacon's missing leg and deformed hand, what with emerging advances in prosthetics and all, but nothing had really worked.

Although almost fifty years had passed, John Deacon still fought the Civil War. The nightmares were terrifying for him and what's worse, his thrashing scared Ella. The visions were so real, his comrades-in-arms horribly maimed, dying slowly or dying quickly but always dying. When they'd started out, most were as young as he was, or younger. Those boys had dreams for their own future, bright ones. For them, the future never came.

Now it was as if they were calling to him, demanding some sort of reparation for Deacon's having survived. Moran was the worst. His spectral image taunted Deacon, mocked him, goaded him: *"Get off your ass and do something!"* Even in dreams, Moran could be a roughneck.

Deacon just didn't know what he could do.

It seemed like for many years, no one wanted to remember the Civil War. Everyone just wanted to "get on with life." And those who did remember it, widows and orphans and just about everyone in the devastated South, remembered it with bitterness.

Right after the war, Deacon had struggled like many enlisted men. He had to find work to support himself and Ella. It wasn't easy. All the jobs he might have been able to do were already taken by those who stayed behind. He'd have worked as a sales clerk, a janitor, anything to make a living. But with his obvious limitations, none of those had panned out.

So he and Ella lived in her parents' old farmhouse, and with Andy's help, scratched out their subsistence as best they could from the land. Deacon could still read, so that was a plus.

As time passed, he noticed something interesting in his reading. After a few years, the Civil War became fashionable again. There were military reunions that started small and ended up being remarkable big affairs where sometimes men on both sides came together to recognize their shared hardships. Whether that hardship was borne while wearing the color blue or the color gray, well, it did not seem to matter so much anymore. Many ended up shaking hands, Americans all. Some could laugh. Some wept.

Deacon could never bring himself to go. He told himself it was because he couldn't leave Ella. But that was not the entire reason. He just didn't think he could bear it.

Last year, 1911, saw the biggest Civil War reunion so far, marking the fiftieth anniversary of the its start in 1861. With all the hoopla surrounding that milestone, the dreams started coming more often and got much worse. He'd wake up wild-eyed, screaming, shaking. He couldn't catch his breath. Ella didn't understand but he could tell it scared her. He couldn't abide that.

And always when he awoke in terror, the clock was chiming two in the morning. The time when the boat exploded in a raging river on a long-ago dark night.

John Deacon had never stopped thinking of himself as a newspaperman. Sure, he was a subsistence dirt farmer, but his instincts were always with the presses he had lost so long ago for pennies on the dollar. How would he have used them? What would have sold papers?

Now he was quite sure what would sell. Since 1911, all fifty-year anniversaries of Civil War-era occasions were in the news. Fifty years since this battle, fifty years since that event. The year 1915 would mark the fiftieth anniversary of the end of the Civil War. And of the tragedy known as *Sultana.*

Well, maybe people were sick of hearing any more about the war back in 1865, back when *Sultana* exploded, but they sure weren't sick of it now.

As a newspaperman, he knew. Anniversaries sell.

There were two reasons Deacon chose to go now, in 1912. First, he wasn't entirely sure he'd be around in 1915 for the fiftieth anniversary of the *Sultana.* No man ever really knew, but at age seventy two, Deacon figured he was closer to the last chapter than most. This might be the last year he *could* go.

The second reason was that he'd been reading about all those reunions that started small and grew into big, important events. If he could get the word out about *Sultana* right now, in 1912, maybe there would be some interest. Maybe there'd be some small affair this year that could become huge by 1915.

Surely *Sultana* would be something everyone would be interested in. It wasn't just the tragedy itself, he thought, though that was bad enough. But there were stories of bravery, of courage, of love, of miracles. There were cases like his, when things didn't turn out perfect, but people still managed to have a decent life. It was a story of greed and corruption, a cautionary tale. It was a story of rising from the flames phoenix-like, the emblem of his old newspaper. Damn it, *Sultana* was a story people needed to know!

So when Andy agreed to care for Ella, Deacon boarded a train for New York. As far as he was concerned, that city was the center of the universe. That was where he would go to tell his story. Every paper in the city would be interested. And if for some reason, the first one wasn't, he'd just go on to the next until he found one that was.

For the first time in an agonizingly long time, John Deacon felt like a newspaperman again.

Which is why he was so angry and frustrated at this moment.

His original plan had been a morning arrival. He'd get an early start at the newspaper offices. But now this. Rivers flooding, overflowing their banks onto the tracks because of all the snowmelt.

Instead of arriving early in the morning, it was now nine at night. He had to leave again as soon as possible to get back. There would probably be delays in the other direction as well. He couldn't ask Andy to wait forever.

Selfishly, he'd wanted to see a little of New York by daylight. He had thought about seeing if the cobbler shop was still there, though the boot maker today would no doubt be the grandson of the man who had made Deacon's New York Boots fifty years before. Maybe it was for the best, he thought. He might have been tempted to order just one boot. Just to see the man's reaction before noticing Deacon only had one leg. Deacon wondered if they'd even do that.

But no, the boots were a young man's conceit. They had no place in his life now. There was only one goal – getting the story told.

He'd collected as many New York newspapers as he could before he left. On their masthead, he could tell where their offices were. Most seemed to be located fairly close together. Just the names were intoxicating! *The New York City Evening World, the New York Herald, New York Tribune, New York City Sun,* and of course, *The New York Times.* Its office had been in Longacre Square, but in 1904 after the *Times* moved its headquarters to the newly-erected Times Building, it was now called Times Square.

Deacon hobbled from the train as soon as it screeched to a stop in the station. He'd get his bearings in the dark and move as fast as he could to the first newspaper office he could find. Maybe there'd be someone there.

He got lucky on his first try. It was nine at night, but there was a young reporter on duty. The young man seemed bored. It was sleepy news cycle and he seemed glad to have someone to talk to.

After Deacon established his credentials as "a fellow newsman," the two settled in over a companionable cup of coffee. Then Deacon began telling the tale.

The young reporter took pages and pages of notes. He seemed amazed by the story.

"Almost fifty years now!" the young man exclaimed. "Never heard a word about it, not anywhere."

"Not your fault," said Deacon. He went on to enumerate the reasons: end of the war, Lincoln's death, capture of John Wilkes Booth, people being sick of death and destruction. He almost added that part of the reason was that the boat carried simple enlisted men, not anybody famous. But he thought better of it. The young man might think he was being churlish.

"I still don't understand why no one has heard any of that! From what you say, Mr. Deacon, more than two thousand souls died – needlessly, in my opinion - after surviving so much. What a story!"

"I was hoping you'd be interested. If I were a young newsman today, I'd run it in banner headlines. Maybe there will be a reunion in the next year or two. Then, when the fiftieth anniversary comes up in 1915, there might be a huge one and you'll have an even better story to write. Interviews with the survivors, for example. Just a suggestion, of course."

Deacon didn't want to push too hard, didn't want to seem like he was telling the young reporter how to do his job.

So Deacon added, "Anyways, that's what I'd'a done with my newspaper."

"You are absolutely right, Mr. Deacon. You have good instincts. I cannot imagine that my editor won't want us to run with this."

"Then, you're the only one I'm going to with this," said Deacon. "You'll have your scoop."

"I swear to you I will write this story, sir! People will remember the name of the *Sultana*. They will remember those dead men."

"Well, that'd be fine," said Deacon. "I'd appreciate it. So would they. So would their families."

"I can get right on it. I've got good notes here. It's a story that needs to be told, and I think you are correct. Now is the right time. I am quite certain my editor will agree."

Deacon hoped so. He hoped the nightmares would end now. He hoped he was doing his duty, his duty to those dead men, his final duty of that cursed war.

"Well, don't want to wear out my welcome," Deacon said. "Been here more than three hours. It's past midnight now."

"Can't believe it's that late already. The time just flew by. Anyway, I was glad of the company. This is the perfect morning for it. Looks like a slow news day. I'm already writing the story, here in my head. Now, just need to get it down on paper!"

"Obliged," said Deacon, nodding in farewell. He extended his hand to the young reporter.

The reporter watched as Deacon struggled to rise. Deacon could almost see the debate in the young man's mind on whether or not to offer assistance. Might be a source of shame to the older man, the boy might have thought, that he'd need help just getting up.

Deacon smiled at him sympathetically. It was all right, he wanted to say.

Awkwardly, the young man spoke. "Sir, I'm sorry ... sorry for your ... your loss."

Deacon thought a moment as to what his response might be. Finally, he said, "Well, it's not the life I'd have chosen, but it's life nonetheless."

Deacon nodded his head in farewell as he turned to leave. In thirty minutes he was on a train headed back home. Therefore, he never saw what happened next in the newsroom.

The young reporter rose from his desk and stretched. "Well, guess it's tomorrow already," he said to himself as he walked over to flip the wall calendar to the next day. It was April 15, 1912.

Suddenly, the clatter of the teletype jarred the newsroom, clanging incessantly. It was spitting out the words: "WHITE STAR LINER TITANIC STRIKES ICEBERG IN ATLANTIC."

The other reporters and editors on the graveyard shift came to life. The newsroom burst into action. One editor was shouting at the young reporter.

"Grab your notebook and head to the Marconi station! See what ships were in the area! Then go the pier and wait there until rescue ships start pulling in! You can be the first to get stories from the survivors!"

The young reporter had to get there before any of the other papers. His career could be made this night. He tore the previous pages from his notebook, tossed them toward his desk, and flew out the door. In the commotion of the newsroom, as other reporters started pouring in, looking for a place to write, the young reporter's notes from Deacon were inadvertently swept aside in the rush. Amid other papers, they fluttered to the floor and were buried.

Most reporters were busy writing variations on the same theme: "WHITE STAR LINER TITANIC STRIKES ICEBERG, SINKS IN ATLANTIC. MORE THAN 1,500 LIVES LOST. WORST MARITIME DISASTER."

POSTSCRIPT

The young reporter's notes on Deacon's story were inadvertently swept away with the trash. The reporter later recalled his meeting with the old man, but then had to rush on to write other late-breaking items about the *Titanic*. In 1912, *Titanic* was the top story everywhere, and his newspaper was one of those scrambling to get the latest angle. The *Titanic* sold papers.

News about the *Titanic* was carried by almost all newspapers in the U. S., and many around the world. There have been numerous commemorations on the anniversary of its sinking. For those who measure human tragedy by numbers, the estimated loss of life on the *Titanic* is generally placed at 1,514.

The estimated loss of life on the *Sultana* is estimated at between a bare minimum of 1,547 to well over 1,800 and possibly 2,000. Several hundred more died in the days and weeks after they were pulled from the ice-cold waters of the Mississippi. The actual number will never be known because so many soldiers were herded on board at the last minute without their names being recorded.

When the fiftieth anniversary of the *Sultana* tragedy took place on April 27, 1915, the world was seeing war again. Though called the Great War at the time, it was later re-labeled as "World War I." Newspapers in 1915 were consumed with the news of Germany using poison gas, of the bloody Battle of Ypres, of Gallipoli. Within two years, U. S. troops would be engaged in that war.

By 1965, the hundredth anniversary of the *Sultana* catastrophe, another American president had recently been assassinated, with a successor also named Johnson. By that time, America's soldiers had fought World War II and the Korean War. In 1965, newspapers carried the story of the first U.S. combat troops arriving in an Asian country called Vietnam.

At the time of the 150th anniversary of the *Sultana* tragedy, in April of 2015, U. S. troops were dying in other Asian countries.

The story of the *Titanic* has been told in countless books, movies, documentaries, and television productions. The story of the *Sultana* seems as lost as the ruins of her burnt-out hull, covered in mud after the meandering river changed its course.

The men and women whose lives ended on the *Sultana* had traveled a long, hard road to get there. They were for the most part simple enlisted men and about forty women. Their names are not generally known. Since 1865, they have asked nothing, except possibly that their long road be remembered.

Please, let us remember.

AUTHOR'S NOTE: AFTERWORD

For more information on the events chronicled in this book, there are many fine works of nonfiction. This is by no means a comprehensive bibliography, but a suggestion for the reader who wishes to find more detailed factual information.

The Civil War

For more information about the American Civil War, the place to start is with Ken Burns, our national treasure. *The Civil War: A Film by Ken Burns* is available in a variety of formats. More information on the documentary and how to purchase it can be found at http://www.pbs.org/civilwar.

The *Sultana*

It is the most deadly nautical disaster in American history. Yet the grisly death of the steamboat *Sultana* and her passengers is little more than a footnote in history while the *Titanic* is a household word.

The dean of *Sultana* researchers is Jerry O. Potter of Memphis. His book, *The Sultana Tragedy: America's Greatest Maritime Disaster* (Pelican

Publishing, 1992) is required reading for anyone interested in a factual study of the tragedy.

The following nonfiction works are also highly recommended in providing information about America's worst maritime disaster:

Loss Of The Sultana And Reminiscences Of Survivors: History Of A Disaster Where Over One Thousand Five Hundred Human Beings Were Lost, Most Of Them Being Exchanged Prisoners of War On Their way Home from One to Twenty-Three Months In Cahaba And Andersonville Prisons by the Rev. Chester D. Berry (CreateSpace Independent Publishing Platform, 2012, reprinted from 1982 edition.)

Cahaba Prison and the Sultana Disaster by William O. Bryant (University of Alabama Press, 2001.)

Transport to Disaster by James W. Elliott (Holt, Rinehart and Winston, 1962.)

Sultana: Surviving the Civil War, Prison, and the Worst Maritime Disaster in American History by Alan Huffman (HarperCollins, 2009.)

The Sultana Saga: The Titanic of the Mississippi by Rex T. Jackson (Heritage Books, 2003.)

Sultana: A Case for Sabotage by D. H. Rule (Variations on a Theme LLC, 2013.)

Disaster on the Mississippi: The Sultana Explosion, April 27, 1865 by Gene E. Salecker (Naval Institute Press, 1996.)

One of the most remarkable tales focuses on passenger Ann Annis who was widowed three times – each husband drowned, including the "landlubber" who booked passage on the *Sultana*. There is an excellent recounting of her story called *Ann, aka Anna Vessey Laired Sims Annis and the Sinking of the Sultana* by Helen Chandler at http://www.rootsweb.ancestry.com/~nwa/aa.html

Charity's World

The bordellos of New Orleans have attained mythic status in our culture through such vehicles as the song, *House of the Rising Sun.* Tales of the "sin and misery" at Gallatin Street and its later counterpart, Storyville, hardly scratched the surface.

Little girls were indeed sold into prostitution just as they are today in what some call the "sex industry." A recent book takes a non-sensational look at this sexual exploitation of girls and women. It relies on court records and newspaper articles to track the beatings, brutality, addiction, violence, and murder that were the facts of life – and death – in Charity Boudry's world. This excellent source is Judith Kelleher Schafer's *Brothels, Depravity, and Abandoned Women: Illegal Sex in Antebellum New Orleans* (LSU Press, 2009.)

The Coal Torpedo

It was small enough to fit in one hand, and looked innocuously like a simple piece of coal. Gunpowder was poured inside, then it was sealed and coated with coal dust to disguise it. When mixed in with coal and shoveled into a ship's firebox, it would explode. At the very least, it damaged the boilers which the steamships depended on. At worst, it created a blazing inferno on the wooden boats, destroying people, livestock, and precious cargo such as food.

These books offer more information on the deadly "coal torpedo" and Confederate secret service agents such as "Alpha":

Confederate Operations in Canada and New York by John W. Headley (Time-Life Books, 1984.)

Confederate Coal Torpedo: Thomas Courtenay's Infernal Sabotage Weapon by Joseph M. and Thomas H. Thatcher (Keith Kennerly Press, 2011.)

Infernal Machines: The Story of Confederate Submarine and Mine Warfare by Milton F. Perry (Louisiana State University Press, 1985.)

General Order Number 11

On December 17, 1862, U. S. Army General Ulysses S. Grant, the future 18th president of the United States, issued General Order No. 11, expelling Jewish people from three states occupied by the Union Army for being suspected of war profiteering.

Grant's underlings were zealous as they immediately began enforcing the order. Entire families were marched out of town with only what they could carry. When Abraham Lincoln heard of the order, he directed Grant to revoke it. He promised not only to rid the country of slavery, but to protect Americans from religious discrimination.

An excellent source for further reading is Jonathan Sarna's *When General Grant Expelled the Jews* (Schocken Books, a division of Random House, 2012.)

Greek Fire and the Burning of New York

There was indeed a plot to burn New York during the period depicted in this book. At the time, it seemed to make perfect sense, just as later groups determined that attacking New York would advance their cause, or at least inflict the maximum amount of pain and gain the biggest spotlight. Some websites with more information about the nineteenth-century attack on New York include:

http://history1800s.about.com/od/civilwar/a/Confederate-Plot-To-Burn-New-York.htm

http://www.historynet.com/american-history-1864-attack-on-new-york.htm

http://www.bbcamerica.com/copper/blog/the-1864-plot-to-burn-down-new-york-city/

http://www.murfreesboropost.com/the-man-who-would-have-burned-new-york-city-cms-15166

One of the more bizarre footnotes to that plot was that it happened to take place on the night of the first and only occasion that the three Booth brothers performed together. At New York's Winter Garden Theatre on November 25, 1864, the three sons of America's great tragedian, Junius Brutus Booth, performed in an ensemble to raise funds for a statue of William Shakespeare in New York's new Central Park

Junius Brutus Booth Jr., Edwin Booth, and John Wilkes Booth took the spotlight in a one-night-only, toga-clad production of Shakespeare's *Julius Caesar.* Four months later, John Wilkes Booth would assassinate Abraham Lincoln in Washington as he cried out the historic words of Brutus in ancient Rome: "Sic semper tyrannis," the Latin phrase meaning "Thus always to tyrants."

Their mother watched from a box as the three Booth brothers reenacted the tragedy of Julius Caesar in a theatre that was by all accounts, "packed to the rafters." Edwin Booth did indeed calm the audience when firebells began to clang, but if the Greek Fire plot had been more successful, a great tragedy might have taken place that night.

The production of *Julius Caesar* raised $3,500 to build the statue of Shakespeare in Central Park which still stands today. Two fascinating books about the Booths which include this incident are:

American Gothic: The Story of America's Legendary Theatrical Family-Junius, Edwin, and John Wilkes Booth by Gene Smith (Simon & Schuster, 1992.)

My Thoughts Be Bloody: The Bitter Rivalry Between Edwin and John Wilkes Booth That Led to an American Tragedy by Nora Titone (Free Press, 2010.)

Women Soldiers in the Civil War

Unofficially, American women have fought for their country side by side with males since before the nation was born. They served for the same reasons men did, but did not receive the same benefits after victory. If discovered, their reward could be imprisonment. Still they went.

After the Battle of Gettysburg during the Civil War, a burial detail found the body of a dead woman in the uniform of a Confederate private. She was discovered near Cemetery Ridge, and was assumed to have died during Pickett's Charge.

Hundreds of women served undetected on the front lines of that war. Since they were forced to keep their gender secret, it is impossible to make an accurate count of the women who served, though most scholars place the number of women soldiers in the Civil War between 250 and 400, even up to a thousand.

They fought for many reasons, just like males. Some women went to be with their loved ones, some craved adventure, some sought regular wages, and some were simply patriots.

Since boys as young as twelve were said to have joined the ranks, a soldier with a high voice and no facial hair was not cause for alarm. Sometimes women soldiers cut their hair short and rubbed dirt on their faces to simulate the growth of a beard. With the soldiers sleeping and often bathing in their clothes, the women's guise could be carried out under layered bulky attire. For all soldiers, modesty prevailed when handling bodily functions.

The only known collection of letters by a woman soldier in the Civil War are those of Sarah Rosetta Wakeman. "Private Lyons Wakeman" died during the war and is buried in Louisiana. Only the family knew that the body was that of their female ancestor, Rosetta.

Like Wakeman, many women soldiers in the Civil War were lower-class girls who came from farms and factories. The Union Army provided regular wages of $13 a month, more than triple what they could earn elsewhere. Even with its hardships, army life had more to offer than their very restricted existence.

A few women soldiers in the Civil War have become known to us today. These include Sarah Edmonds Seelye who was known as "Franklin Flint Thompson" of the Michigan infantry.

Frances Clayton fought for the Union in the Missouri artillery and was wounded at Shiloh. She was still able to keep her gender undetected. Albert Cashier fought alongside the Illinois infantry. After the war, Cashier lived life as a man, working as a laborer and living in an Illinois soldiers' home. In 1913, a doctor discovered that Cashier was a woman. The aged Cashier, whose original name was Jennie Hodgers, was sent to an insane asylum, dying in 1915.

Maria Lewis of New York appeared in a diary written by a Quaker abolitionist who quoted a fellow soldier. If accurate, Lewis performed a remarkable double deception as an African American woman passing as a white male soldier.

Generally, women soldiers' gender was detected if they were wounded, got sick, or were taken prisoner. In one case, a "male" soldier in the Union army who had been promoted for bravery in battle was discovered a month later—giving birth to a baby.

Military officials denied the existence of women soldiers, dismissing diaries or letters as a hoax. Officials denied that the women could have gone undetected at induction. However, historians note that medical examinations were hardly thorough. The conscripts were asked to prove they were not too lame to march, and that they had at least three teeth.

In 1948, the Women's Armed Services Integration Act was signed by President Harry Truman. It officially allowed women to serve their country in the military. Most women soldiers who served unofficially in earlier times are virtually untraceable since they were often illiterate and not able to write of their experience. Another source of record-keeping would have been military records, but women generally did not request—or receive—government pensions for their service. These books are excellent sources of more information:

They Fought Like Demons: Women Soldiers in the Civil War by De Anne Blanton and Lauren Cook (Vintage, 2003.)

She Went to the Field: Women Soldiers of the Civil War by Bonnie Tsui (TwoDot, 2006.)

An Uncommon Soldier: The Civil War Letters of Sarah Rosetta Wakeman, alias Pvt. Lyons Wakeman, 153rd Regiment, New York State Volunteers, 1862-1864 by Sarah Rosetta Wakeman and Lauren Cook Burgess, editor (Oxford University Press, 1996.)

ABOUT THE AUTHOR

Dr. Nancy Hendricks is an award-winning author whose books include *Senator Hattie Caraway: An Arkansas Legacy,* published by The History Press, and *America's First Ladies: The Remarkable Women of the White House,* published by ABC-CLIO.

Her play, *Miz Caraway and the Kingfish,* portrays the colorful story of the first woman elected to the United States Senate, Hattie Caraway of Arkansas. Its New Orleans production was held over for an extended run and nominated by the American Critics Association for "Best Play Produced Outside New York."

In her signature role as Caraway, she can be seen in the documentary *Hattie Caraway: The Silent Woman.* Hendricks performs nationwide in her one-person program, *Hattie to Hillary: Women in Politics.*

Professional productions of her plays include *Second to None* and *Boy Hero: The Story of David O. Dodd.* She is also author of the children's books, *Hello Howl* and *Howl's Journey.*

She has been a newspaper and magazine columnist, and is a major contributing author for the *Encyclopedia of Arkansas.* Her writing can also been seen in *American Historic Sites and Landmarks; Women in American History; Disasters and Tragic Events: Catastrophes in American History,* and *Music Around the World,* all published by ABC-CLIO. *To Can the Kaiser: Arkansas and the Great War,* and *Too Much or Too Little: An Encyclopedia of Arkansas Women* are published by the Butler Center Press.

Hendricks is a founding member of the National Women's History Museum in Washington D. C. She also belongs to the Southern Association of Women Historians, and the Queen Elizabeth I Society. She is the recipient of a Pryor Award for Arkansas Women's History, Arkansas Governor's Arts Award, and White House Millennium Award for her writing.

Dr. Hendricks is available for programs, in costume and in character, about both the *Sultana* and Senator Hattie Caraway.

CPSIA information can be obtained at www.ICGtesting.com
Printed in the USA
LVOW07s1547091015

457651LV00012B/455/P

9 781507 764688